Praise for Anne Emery

Praise for *Death at Christy Burke's*

"Emery's sixth mystery (after 2010's *Children in the Morning*) makes excellent use of its early 1990s Dublin setting and the period's endemic violence between Protestants and Catholics."
— *Publishers Weekly,* starred review

"Halifax lawyer Anne Emery's terrific series featuring lawyer Monty Collins and priest Brennan Burke gets better with every book."
— *Globe and Mail*

Praise for *Children in the Morning*

"This [fifth] Monty Collins book by Halifax lawyer Emery is the best of the series. It has a solid plot, good characters, and a very strange child who has visions."
— *Globe and Mail*

"Not since Robert K. Tanenbaum's Lucy Karp, a young woman who talks with saints, have we seen a more poignant rendering of a female child with unusual powers."
— *Library Journal*

Praise for *Cecilian Vespers*

"Anne Emery has already won one Arthur Ellis Award for her first Monty Collins mystery, and this one should get her on the short list for another. *Cecilian Vespers* is slick, smart, and populated with lively characters."
— *Globe and Mail*

"This remarkable mystery is flawlessly composed, intricately plotted, and will have readers hooked to the very last page."
— *The Chronicle Herald*

D1105982

Death
at Christy Burke's

Published by ECW Press
2120 Queen Street East, Suite 200, Toronto, Ontario, Canada M4E 1E2
416-694-3348 / info@ecwpress.com

Library and Archives Canada Cataloguing in Publication

Emery, Anne
Death at Christy Burke's : a mystery / Anne Emery. (Collins-Burke mystery)
Originally published in 2011 (978-1-55022-988-2).

ISBN 978-1-77041-169-2 (PBK.)
Also issued as: 978-1-77090-091-2 (EPUB); 978-1-77090-092-9 (PDF)

I. Title.
PS8609.M47D43 2013   C813'.6   C2013-902494-8

Cover and text design: Tania Craan
Cover image © IIC/Masterfile.com
Typesetting: Mary Bowness
Production: Rachel Ironstone
Author photo: Precision Photo
Printing: United Graphics   1   2   3   4   5

The publication of *Death at Christy Burke's* has been generously supported by the Canada Council for the Arts which last year invested $20.1 million in writing and publishing throughout Canada. We acknowledge the support of the Ontario Arts Council (OAC), an agency of the Government of Ontario, which last year funded 1,681 individual artists and 1,125 organizations in 216 communities across Ontario for a total of $52.8 million. We also acknowledge the financial support of the Government of Canada through the Canada Book Fund for our publishing activities. The marketing of this book was made possible with the support of the Ontario Media Development Corporation.

Printed and bound in the United States

Death
at Christy Burke's

A MYSTERY

ANNE EMERY

ECW Press

Prologue

July 3, 1992

Kevin McDonough was early arriving at the pub. Eight-fifteen in the morning. The sooner he got the place scrubbed to a shine, the sooner he could get to rehearsal with his band. Tonight would be their third paid gig, and this time it was at the Tivoli. At this rate, they'd soon be opening for U2! These odd little jobs had been tiding him over till he could earn his living as a musician. He didn't mind cleaning the floors, washing the windows, and polishing the bar at Christy Burke's pub twice a week. It was no worse than his other jobs, and there were articles of interest to him inside the place.

Oh, would you look at that. Finn Burke was going to be wild. Finn had just repainted the front wall after the last incident of vandalism, and now some gobshite with a can of paint had hit the pub again. Kevin noticed a glass of whiskey on the ground, tipped against the wall. The fellow must have been lifting a jar while doing his handiwork. More than one maybe, by the looks of the paint job this time round. Or perhaps it was the heavy rain last night that threw him off. The message was "Come all ye to Christy's, killers own loc . . ."

1

Must have meant "local"; the words ended in a smear. If the message was meant to slag Finn Burke about his Republican activities, Kevin suspected Finn would be more vexed about the look of it than the meaning; no doubt he'd faced worse in his time. Well, Kevin wasn't about to call Finn at this hour of the morning. Finn would be seeing it with his own eyes soon enough.

Kevin picked up the glass, singing to himself, "There's whiskey in the jar-o." It was the rock version by Thin Lizzy that Kevin liked, and he tried to draw the words out the way Phil Lynott did, "I first produced my pistol and then produced my rapier." There was a bit of a mess in the garden beside the front door. "Garden" was too grand a word for it really. A few years back, the city had torn up the pavement to repair some water lines. And before they replaced the pavement, one of the patrons of Christy's had talked Finn into letting him plant some flowers. The man didn't keep it up, so now it was just a little square of patchy grass in the midst of all the city concrete. But still, Finn was none too pleased when the rubbish collectors drove their lorry right onto the grass and tore it up with the spinning of their tires. They'd obviously been at it again; a big clump of grass had been gouged out and overturned. Early, though, for refuse collection; they usually didn't get to Christy's till at least half-nine. Ah. Sure enough. Kevin checked the bins and they hadn't been emptied.

He went to work inside. Washed the glasses, polished the bar, filled a bucket with water and suds for the old stone floor. But his mind was on music, not mopping up the pub. He decided to take "Highway to Hell" off the set list and replace it with "Whiskey in the Jar." Maybe the band should dust off some other old standards. Could they work up a heavy-metal arrangement of "The Rose of Tralee," he wondered. Ha, wouldn't his old gran be turning in her grave over that! Just as he was heading to the loo for his last and least favourite chore, he heard a lorry roar up outside. He glanced out the window and saw the rubbish collectors, out in the roadway where they were supposed to be. No worries there.

When his work was done, Kevin grabbed an electric torch and treated himself to a trip downstairs. He loved the once secret tunnel that had been dug beneath Christy Burke's back in the day when the pub was a hideout for the old IRA. Somebody said Christy had dug the tunnel in 1919, and Michael Collins himself had hidden in it, when Ireland was fighting its War of Independence against the Brits. Nobody was supposed to go in there, but Kevin did. And he knew some of the regulars had made excursions down there as well, when Finn Burke was away. The fellows who drank at Christy's day after day knew everything there was to know about the pub, including where Finn kept the tunnel key, under one of the floorboards behind the bar. More than once Kevin had tried to prime Finn for information about the old days, hoping he would let his hair down and regale Kevin with some war stories from his time fighting for the Republican cause. Kevin's da was a bookkeeper and stayed away from politics and controversy; a great father, no question about that, but Kevin thought of him as a man without a history. Not like Finn. But Finn kept his gob shut about his service to the cause. So what could Kevin do but poke around on his own? He inserted the key in the padlock, opened the heavy trap door, and eased himself down into the tunnel. You could only get into the first part of it, which was around twenty feet in length; the rest of it was blocked off, and Kevin didn't know of any key that would get you in there.

But that was all right. There was lots to see right here. The place was a museum. There were old photos, hand-drawn maps, packets of faded letters, uniforms, caps, and, best of all, guns. Kevin had no desire to point a gun at anybody, let alone fire one, but he was fascinated by the weaponry stashed beneath the pub. A Thompson submachine gun, some rifles, and two big pistols. But there was one weapon Kevin particularly liked, a handgun, wrapped in rags and squirrelled away from everything else behind a couple of loose bricks. He had noticed the bricks out of alignment one morning, and took a peek. He'd handled it a few times since then. The gun was all black and had a star engraved on the butt of it — deadly! He thought it might create a sensation at a party some night. He knew it was loaded, but he'd take the bullets out first, if he ever got up the nerve to "borrow" it. Where was it? Not in its usual spot. Not anywhere. Kevin looked all over, but the gun was gone.

Maybe Finn took it himself. But Kevin doubted that. If Finn needed a weapon, he'd likely have one closer to home, and it would be something a little more up-to-date. Well, Kevin certainly wasn't going to mention it. He wasn't supposed to be here in the first place. He was supposed to do his job, cleaning up the pub. And, whatever had become of the gun, he knew this much: there were no dead bodies on the premises to clear away. So his job was done. He locked up and left the building. When he got outside, he kicked the overturned sod back into place. Didn't look too bad.

Chapter 1

July 11, 1992

Michael

Nobody loved Ireland like Michael O'Flaherty. Well, no, that wasn't quite the truth. How could he presume to make such a claim over the bodies of those who had been hanged or shot by firing squad in the struggle for Irish independence? Or those who had lived in the country all their lives, in good times and in bad, staving off the temptation to emigrate from their native soil? Nobody loved Ireland *more* than Michael did. He was on fairly safe ground there. He was a student of history, and his story led him straight back to Ireland. A four-cornered Irishman, he had four grandparents who emigrated from the old country to that most Irish of Canadian cities, Saint John, New Brunswick. His mother was fourteen when her parents brought her over on the boat in 1915, and Michael had inherited her soft lilting speech.

He was in the old country yet again. How many times had he been here? He had lost count. Monsignor Michael O'Flaherty cut quite a figure in the tourist industry. The Catholic tourist industry, to be more precise. Every year he shepherded a flock of Canadian pilgrims around the holy sites of Ireland: Knock, Croagh Patrick, Glendalough. And he showed them something of secular Ireland as well — all too secular it was now, in his view, but never mind. He conducted tours of Dublin, Cork, Galway; it varied from year to year. All this in addition to his duties as pastor of St. Bernadette's Church in Halifax, Nova Scotia. He had moved to Halifax as a young priest, after spending several years in the parishes of Saint John. Why not pack his few belongings in a suitcase and cross the ocean once and for all, making Ireland his home? Well, the truth was, he was attached to Nova Scotia, to his church, and to the people there. He had made friends, especially in the last couple of years. And two of those friends were in Dublin right now. He was on his way to meet them, having seen his latest group of tourists off at the airport for their journey home to Canada.

He looked at his watch. It was half-noon. Brennan Burke had given him elaborate directions but there was no need. Michael knew the map of Dublin as well as he knew the Roman Missal, and he was only five minutes away from his destination at the corner of Mountjoy Street and St. Mary's Place. His destination was Christy Burke's pub.

Michael, decked out as always in his black clerical suit and Roman collar, kept up a brisk pace along Dominick Street Upper until he reached Mountjoy and turned right. A short walk up the street and there it was. This was an inner-city area of Dublin and it had fallen on hard times. But the pub had a fresh coat of cream-coloured paint. There was a narrow horizontal band of black around the building above the door and windows. Set off against the black was the name "Christy Burke" in gold letters. Lovely! He pushed the door open and stepped inside. It took a moment for his eyes to adjust to the smoke and the darkness after the bright July sunshine.

"Michael!"

"Brennan, my lad! All settled in, I see. Good day to you, Monty!"

Michael joined his friends at their table, where a pint of Guinness sat waiting for him. Brennan Burke was a fellow priest, Michael's curate technically. But it was hard to think of Burke, with his doctorate in theology and his musical brilliance, as anybody's curate. He had lived here in Dublin as a child, then immigrated to New York before he joined Michael at St. Bernadette's in Halifax. It was a long story. Christy Burke was Brennan's grandfather, long deceased by now, of course. Brennan himself was fifty or a little over. Young enough to be Michael's son, if Michael had been tomcatting around in his seminary days, which he most certainly had not! In any case, they looked nothing alike. Brennan was tall with greying black hair and black eyes. Michael was short and slight, with white hair and eyes of blue. Monty Collins, though, could be mistaken for Michael's son. Same colour eyes and fair hair. A few years younger than Brennan and deceptively boyish in appearance, Monty was their lawyer and confidant.

Michael greatly enjoyed their company. So it was grand that they were able to arrange this time together in Dublin. Brennan had signed on to teach at the seminary in Maynooth for six weeks. Michael was on an extended vacation, with the blessings of his bishop. It was the first time he had been away for more than two weeks, ever. And why not? In any other job, he'd be retired by now! They had left the home parish in the capable hands of another priest they both knew. Monty, too, was on vacation. Told his office he was taking a month off. Made whatever arrangements he had to make for his law practice, and boarded the plane. So here they were.

Brennan

Brennan Burke was a man of firm opinions. He knew where he stood, and those who were acquainted with him were left in little doubt about who was standing and where. But that sense of certainty deserted him each and every time he came home to the land of his birth. He was glad to be in Ireland, to be sure, but he was afflicted with sorrow, anger, and frustration over the violence that was tearing apart the North of Ireland. Catholics and Protestants, Nationalists and Loyalists, Republicans and Unionists — however you labelled them — had been blasting one another to bits for the past two decades. This was the nation that had sent monks into continental Europe to evangelize and educate the barbarians after the fall of Rome, monks who had helped keep the light of European civilization glowing through the Dark Ages. St. Thomas Aquinas had been taught by an Irishman in thirteenth-century Naples, for the love of Christ. And look at us now.

Brennan's own family had been steeped in the events of Irish history, certainly in the first half of the century. History had stalked his father, Declan Burke, all the way to New York City. Declan had fled Ireland at the point of a gun when Brennan was ten years old; he remembered as if it were yesterday his loneliness and terror as the ship slipped out of Cobh Harbour in the dark of night and began the long, heaving voyage across the Atlantic. Brennan's father had not laid shoe leather on the soil of Ireland since that hasty departure in 1950. But that wasn't the end of it. History caught up with Declan as recently as a year ago in the form of a bullet in the chest, at a family wedding in New York. The wound was not fatal, but nearly so.

Well, his son was a frequent visitor to the old country even if Declan was not. And here he was again. The Burkes of Dublin were spoken of as a "well-known Republican family." Were they in the thick of things still?

But there was pleasure to be had today, so why not just bask in it for a while and banish dark thoughts to the outermost chambers of his mind? He picked up his glass of whiskey, inhaled the alcoholic fumes, and took a sip. Ah! Tingling on the lips, honey on the tongue. Cigarette? No, wait. As usual. Enjoy a pure hit of the Jameson first. The warmth spread through him as the whiskey went down. And there was more to come.

Michael

"When did you fellows arrive?"

"This morning," Brennan replied.

"And how long have you been planted in here?"

"Not long at all, Michael. We've barely got our throats wet."

Christy Burke's was a typical Dublin pub with a dark wood interior, old flagstone floor, long counter with its pumps and glimmering bottles of spirits, brass foot rail and stools, and tables along the walls, some of them separated by wooden partitions. Tacked to the wall beside the bar was a tattered copy of the 1916 Proclamation of the Irish Republic, one line of which had always resounded in Michael's mind: "We place the cause of the Irish Republic under the protection of the Most High God, Whose blessing we invoke upon our arms." The walls bore numerous old photographs, including one dated 1922, showing a group of men wearing trench coats or jackets and ties, tweed caps or fedoras — slouch hats, he guessed they were — all carrying rifles as they marched down Grafton Street on patrol. There was a faded sepia-toned picture of a man tending bar. Christy himself? A score of dedicated drinkers, most with cigarettes smouldering in ashtrays beside them, were scattered throughout the pub. To a man, they had turned slowly, pints in hand, when Michael came in.

Someone had left a newspaper draped over the arm of Michael's chair. The *Irish Independent*. Michael picked it up and turned the pages. Ah, there it was. The missing preacher. Michael had been following the story. An American evangelist who ran a television ministry based in South Carolina had vanished in the early hours of the eighth of July while on a visit to Belfast. He and his wife had been touring England, Scotland, and Northern Ireland with a group of fellow evangelicals. On his third day in Belfast, he left the Europa Hotel at six o'clock in the morning and had not been seen since. The photo showed a man in his early sixties, smiling around a big set of bright white teeth, grey or blond hair blow-dried and puffing out from a side part. The Reverend Merle Odom.

"Still no word. What a shame," Michael remarked. "Pray Mary he'll turn up unharmed. What do you think of my idea, Brennan?" He had mentioned the plan to Brennan over the phone.

"What idea is that?" Monty asked.

"I'm thinking we could gather a bunch of Catholic clergy and issue a statement calling for the man's release. Sort of an ecumenical show of support. The message would be: 'This hurts all of us. Let's put our differences aside and bring the man home.'"

"Do we even know he's been captured?" That was Monty, a man for the facts, but perhaps a little naïve if he thought Odom had just embarked on a long, solitary walk along Great Victoria Street in Belfast three days ago!

"No, we don't know that at all." The voice came from the bar. Michael looked over to see a handsome, white-haired man around his own age. He looked remarkably like the publican in the old photo on the wall, except for the fact that his eyes were obscured by dark glasses.

"Finn!" Brennan called to the man. "Come introduce yourself to my pastor."

The man left the bar and came over to the table. He held his hand out to Michael. "Finn Burke. I've heard nothing but good about you, Monsignor."

"Call me Michael. Or Mike if you prefer. So you're the new Christy Burke."

"Ah, I'll never be the man my father was. This place was a shambles when he bought it in 1919, and laboured night and day to get it restored. But when he started to get feeble near the end of his life, I came in to help and I've been here ever since. I'm still involved with the trucking business — Burke Transport — but behind this bar is where you'll find me most days."

"It's lovely."

"Where are you staying, Michael?"

"I'm in a bed and breakfast on Lower Gardiner Street. I've brought them so much business over the years, they've given me the room for free!"

"You've been lugging busloads of tourists all over the island, I understand, Michael. How long have you been at that now?"

"I've been at it such a long time, Finn, I'd have to puzzle out the answer for you. But I can tell you this: I've kissed the Blarney Stone so many times I feel I ought to do the right thing and marry it!"

"Well, nobody here has ever been intimate with the Blarney Stone, so you'll find no competition from these quarters."

"Don't I know it, Finn? It's only the tourists who want to see it, but they insist. So back I go every time. They always want to wear silly hats too, whether it's something that looks like a pint of stout on their heads, or a Viking helmet here in Dublin. What can you do?"

"Leo Killeen will show you a slice of Irish life you've never seen before."

"Oh, yes, I'm looking forward to it. When will we be seeing Leo?"

If there was anyone Michael was anxious to meet on this trip, it was Leo Killeen. Leo was a priest and friend of Brennan Burke's father. Michael had read Irish history; Leo had lived it.

"Well now, he's tied up today," Finn said.

"Is he in the city?"

"In the city, no. I believe he's in the North doing good works. But he'll be back in the parish before too long."

"What kind of good works is he performing in the North, Finn?" Brennan asked.

Finn turned his head in Michael's direction, then in Monty's, before returning his attention to Brennan. A slight nod from that quarter seemed to be the assurance he wanted that he could speak freely.

"You've heard about that, em, accident. In Dungannon."

"The bombing, you mean?"

"It was a bombing, Brennan, yes. But you know it was never meant — from what I hear — never meant to harm a human soul. It was only after —"

"The owner of the business, and his sister visiting from England, were blown to bits, Finn."

"It's a tragedy, to be sure. But they wouldn't have been scratched — they wouldn't even have been on the premises — if the Royal Ulster Constabulary hadn't decided, for reasons of their own, to ignore the warning. It's well known that a warning was given. It's all been in the papers. The warning wasn't acted upon. And the lads — the organization — issued an apology, as you know. It was meant to be a routine commercial bombing, the kind of thing . . ." Finn's voice faltered against his nephew's unyielding expression.

Another bombing in Northern Ireland. This clearly wasn't the time to probe further into that. And what, if anything, did it have to do with Leo Killeen? Well, Michael would find out soon enough. In the meantime he would keep his own counsel. Brennan had given Michael a friendly warning that his interest in this country's past and politics might not be shared by everyone he would meet on the trip. Most people would be more interested in getting on with their lives than reliving and rehashing their history. Others would be all too interested, and Michael could bring trouble on himself if he said the wrong thing in the wrong company. He understood that.

But he couldn't banish the poor American preacher from his thoughts. "Perhaps Finn could put his two cents in. What I have in mind, Finn, and you can tell me whether you think there's any value in it, is a press conference held by Brennan and myself, and other priests, perhaps bishops and sisters, all of us calling on the Reverend Merle Odom's captors to release him to his family, no questions asked. Maybe Father Killeen would have some advice for us."

The dark glasses turned to Brennan, who eventually spoke up. "I think we're a little out of our depth here, Michael. These things tend to be more complicated than they might appear."

"Sure, you're right, I imagine. It's just that I can't get it out of my mind. An event like that, it tends to take on a life of its own, causing repercussions farther down the line. What did they say on the news about him leaving the hotel? Was he carrying anything with him? Was he in the habit of being up so early? Who was the last person to see him?"

"You'll have to forgive Mike, Finn. He missed his calling as Sergeant O'Flaherty of the Garda Síochána."

"Ah, now, Brennan," Mike said.

But his fellow priest had a point. Mike was a bit of a crime buff — no, better rephrase that! Mike wasn't in favour of crime of any sort. He deplored and feared violence, and did not understand how a person could bring himself to cause pain to another human being. Or even to animals. He himself feared stinging insects of all kinds, broke into a cold sweat whenever they buzzed around him; yet he felt guilty every time he squashed the life out of one. But he was keenly interested in detective work and crime-solving, and spent the little free time he had reading detective stories. Brennan was right: Mike liked to think that if he hadn't been called to the priesthood, he might indeed have become a policeman. And Sergeant O'Flaherty had a ring to it, no question! There was something else, too: the Protestant minister was a man of a certain age, as Mike was himself, and even if the fellow was in error theologically, even if he "dug with the wrong foot," as was often said of the Protestants, still, the thought of the elderly man being snatched from the street . . .

"A man of his age, off for a little holiday, and he becomes the victim of a crime." Mike shook his head.

"We're on holiday too, Mike. And we too are on the premises of a crime scene," Monty said. "Isn't that right, Finn?"

"It is," Finn agreed.

"What do you mean? What happened?" Mike asked.

"Dastardly deeds were done right here," Monty replied.

"What was done? To whom?"

"To Christy's itself. Christy Burke's pub is the victim."

Finn explained: "Nothing too dreadful, Michael, but an annoyance all the same. Some louser has been vandalizing the pub. Spraying graffiti on the walls outside."

"Oh! I'm sorry to hear it, Finn. Such a fine building. I didn't notice anything."

"No, we've cleaned it up. Painted over it. Getting a little weary of it. But pubs on this island have come to more grievous harm than this, so I shouldn't whinge about it too much. Still, I'm not happy."

"Who could blame you for being aggrieved? When did it happen?"

"Happened three times. Just over a week ago, most recently. We got it painted yesterday."

"This is a foolish question, I suppose, but have you any idea who's doing it?"

"If I did, he'd not be doing it again, the fucker."

"I suppose you have to throw someone out of here occasionally . . ."

"I have to turf someone out from time to time, but either they come back promising to sin no more, or they come back to give me a bollocking. Either way, I get them sorted. There's also a handful of hard cases that have been excommunicated. Barred for life. But none of these fellows are going to tiptoe quietly about the place and write mysterious messages on my walls."

"Could the fellow be targeting you for . . . some other reason?"

"Michael, I won't deny I've made enemies from time to time. But they've always been more direct in their retaliation! Don't be worrying about me."

"What does it say, the graffiti, or is it just scribbling?"

"'Come all ye to the killers own loc . . .' Unfinished but obviously meant 'local.' That was the latest."

"Killers in the plural or killer's with an apostrophe or was it plural and . . . ?"

"No apostrophe. We've got it narrowed down to people who didn't take the cup for punctuation when they were in school!"

"And the other messages, the earlier ones?"

"Same class of thing. 'Guinness for the Guilty' or 'Guinness, Guns, and Guilt' or some such rubbish. Then something about 'A Pint for the Perpetrators of Crime,' with 'perpetrators' spelt as 'perpetaters.' What a tool!"

"Don't be a tool, stay in school! You can spray-paint that on his T-shirt if you locate him, Finn," Monty said.

"He'll be lucky if that's all he gets from me."

"Maybe he 'got it' from somebody else," Michael said. "The fact that your artist — or poet — didn't finish his message suggests he was interrupted in the middle of things."

"Well, we didn't find a corpse in the morning, Michael. Or any signs of violence. If the man received a thumping, there was no indication of it left behind. I'll tell you this much: if I'd caught him while he was at it, there'd have been blood spilt! But I didn't and there wasn't. Maybe somebody walked or drove by, and he scarpered so he wouldn't be identified. Most likely, though, the vandal is some head-the-ball who doesn't know what he's talking about!"

A middle-aged woman approached the bar, and Finn poured her a pint. When she returned to her table, Michael resumed his interrogation: "What time does the last person leave here at night?"

"I'm the last man out usually, after one. Closer to half-one, most nights."

"And you open in the morning at what time?"

Brennan interrupted at that point. "Mr. Burke is tired now, Sergeant. Perhaps he could answer your questions another time, if he thinks of anything that could assist in your inquiries. Do you have a card you could leave with him?"

Michael had to laugh. "Pardon me, Finn. I'm getting a little too deeply into my role!"

"The role you were born to play, Mike," said Monty. "I'll have to hire you as my investigator when we get home. I often require the services of a private eye in my law practice."

"I'd be pleased to be of service, Mr. Collins."

"You'll have to show me a good track record. Solve this crime against Christy's, and come see me."

"I may surprise you!"

Finn said to his nephew: "There's never a lull in the conversation with these two, Bren. Lets you save your voice for the pulpit on Sundays, I guess."

"Ah, they're a grand pair, Finn. Why don't you station them outside the pub in the wee hours? They'll catch your vandal, and the money you save on paint you can hand over as a reward for their efforts."

"I'll give it some thought. But in the meantime, I've pints to pour and thirsts to slake."

He went back to his work, and Monty and Brennan turned to another subject of conversation, namely the differences in flavour they seemed to recognize between Guinness and Murphy's stout. But Michael's thoughts were on the lines that had been spray-painted on the wall of the pub. "What do you think about those messages, Monty? You're a student of criminal behaviour."

"I'm out of my league here, Mike, though it strikes me that the accusations escalated over time, from 'guilt' or 'guilt and guns' in the beginning to 'killers' at the end. Or, as you pointed out, he may have meant 'killer' singular, in the possessive."

"Escalating, yes, you may be right. Which makes you wonder what he'll say next. Or do!"

Brennan said: "You've done enough on it for now, Sergeant. We've a session starting up. You can resume your investigation next time you're in."

Michael had a mouthful of questions but they would have to wait. At the far end of the room a group of musicians took their seats, and the session started up. Mandolin, tin whistle, fiddle, and bodhran. Fresh drinks materialized in front of Michael and his cronies; they sat back with their glasses and enjoyed the music. Still, Michael's mind was abuzz with other matters. The allegations of murder scrawled on the pub wall. The vanished preacher. And the upcoming introduction to Father Leo Killeen. Michael knew that Brennan's father, Declan Burke, had been involved in the "politics" of his day in Ireland, and that he had spirited his family out of the country in the dead of night as a direct result of that involvement. He knew something else too: Leo Killeen had been Declan Burke's commanding officer in the IRA before discovering his vocation to the priesthood. What was Killeen doing in the North? Michael felt a little frisson of excitement. He didn't intend to miss a thing.

And there was something else. The cream in the cocoa, really. Not only was Michael on holiday in Ireland with his two closest *male* friends, he was also going to be seeing . . . Kitty Curran. Sister Kitty Curran was a native of Dublin, and she had done missionary work in some of the poorest and most war-torn areas of the globe. She now worked in the heart of the Vatican, with one of the church's peace and development organizations. It was in Rome that she and Brennan had become friends. The nun had paid a short visit to Halifax earlier in the year, at Brennan's urging. She and Michael had hit it off right from the start. And why not? Two people in middle age — well, a little past that in Michael's case. Two people living consecrated lives. It was only natural for them to get along. He gave his watch a discreet glance.

"Don't be fretting now, Michael. She hasn't stood you up." That was Brennan. Wouldn't you know he'd catch Michael checking the time.

"We should have met her at the airport, Brennan. Helped her with her bags, a taxi, all that."

"Kitty has been carrying her own bags around the world since she left this country for Africa as a newly minted nun in the 1960s. Rumour has it she took over the controls of an old turboprop that had been hit by gunfire in the Belgian Congo. She's well able to look after herself."

"Ah, now, Brennan. That doesn't mean we can't be gentlemen."

Brennan leaned towards Michael and spoke with urgency. "Let's clear out now, while we still can. Give her the slip. She'll only break your heart, Michael."

"Have you ever thought that's why men go into the priesthood, Brennan? So they won't have their hearts broken?"

"Maybe that's it. I know it's worked for me."

"Has it now."

Brennan did not reply, but took a long sip of his John Jameson.

They listened to the band's final number before their break, a haunting piece on the tin whistle called "The Lonesome Boatman." When the music died out, Michael and his companions pondered their empty glasses. Time for another round?

"Here she is!" Monty exclaimed.

There in the doorway, peering into the dim interior, was Kitty Curran. Short, a little on the plump side, with reddish curls turning grey, the nun was dressed in civilian clothes: a navy skirt, a sky-blue sweater over a white shirt, and a discreet gold cross above her left breast.

Monsignor O'Flaherty sat rooted in his chair, beaming in the direction of the door.

"Monsignor?" Brennan prompted him with his left eyebrow raised.

"Good heavens, where are my manners?" Michael rose and made for the new arrival. "Kitty! Kitty! Over here. Isn't this grand! How are you?"

She held out her arms, and he stepped into her embrace. She planted a big kiss on his cheek and then tugged him to his table. "That lipstick on your cheek, Michael. Whatever will they say at the parochial house?" Michael's hand shot up to his left cheek, and she laughed. "I don't paint my face, *a chara*!"

"How've you been, darlin'?" Brennan asked. "Any big shakeups in the Vatican I should know about?" He stood and embraced her.

"They're talking about you for the red hat, but I told them the Reverend Doctor Brennan Xavier Burke is content to serve as a humble parish priest to the end of his days. Monty! Is all of Halifax over here?"

"Everyone who's anyone is here in this very room. Good to see you, Kitty."

"Now make yourself comfortable, Kitty," Michael said. "Here, would you like this seat? You'll be able to see the band. Or how about this one? Farther away from Brennan and his cigarettes, should he be so inconsiderate as to light one up again."

"I'm grand, Michael, thank you. I'll sit right here. If Brennan does anything to get on my nerves, I'll crack his knuckles with my ruler."

"What can I get you to drink, Kitty?"

"Considering the company I'm keeping, I'll have a parish priest."

Michael stared. He wasn't sure how to respond, until Brennan started to laugh, then called over to Finn: "Something tall and black with a white collar for the lady here, Finn."

"Coming up." He proceeded to pour her the customary pint of dark stout with white foam on top, and Michael caught on.

"Now. Kitty. Are you hungry at all? Should we be thinking of something to eat for you? Finn doesn't serve meals here, but . . ."

"No, Michael, I'm grand, I'm telling you. There are Dublin men who went to work for a day with nothing but Guinness to sustain them, and I'm in solidarity with them. Bring it on. Speaking of solidarity with the workers, Monty, where is your lovely wife? She's a bit of a commie, is she not? And don't waste my time telling me she's not your wife anymore, or whatever trouble you imagine you've brought upon yourself. Life is short. Is she here?"

"Not yet, but she's coming with Normie and the baby. She's very keen to see you." The two women had struck up a friendship in the short time Kitty had been in Halifax.

"Splendid! When can we expect her?"

"A week from tomorrow. I'm at the Jury's Inn, Christchurch, and all I could get is a single room; they're very booked up for the summer. I'll have to find another place."

"Tell her I have a convent with several rooms vacant, if she and the children would like to stay there. Much more economical than a hotel. I can't invite you, Monty, sorry to say. Mother Superior's ninety-two but, from what I hear, she doesn't miss a trick. So she'd notice if there was a man lurking about the premises . . ."

"No problem. I'm sure Maura would love to join you there."

"Perfect. Where are the rest of you staying?"

"I'm at a B and B in Gardiner Street," Michael replied, "and Brennan's not far from Monty's hotel, staying with some other priests in a house near the John's Lane church. One of the priests is his cousin, if I'm not mistaken."

"Another Father Burke," Monty remarked. "That's all we need, two of them tag-teaming us."

"Fear not. This is a Father Brennan, my mother's side of the family."

"You've got both flanks covered."

"Can't be too careful."

Kitty noticed the *Irish Independent* folded on the table and picked it up. "I'm going to be bringing death to the table now, I'm afraid. Is it safe to walk the streets of Ireland these days at all? You have to wonder. I hope somebody can tell me this is not the Rory Dignan I knew. It can't be him if it happened in the North, surely. They're a Dublin family. Northsiders like myself."

"It can't be who? What's this about Northsiders?" They looked up to see Finn Burke approaching the table.

"Kitty, this is my uncle, Finn Burke. Finn, Sister Kitty Curran."

They greeted each other, then Finn joined them at the table.

Kitty smoothed out the newspaper and read the article. "It says a funeral is to be held in Endastown tomorrow afternoon for Rory Dignan, one of three men shot by Loyalist paramilitaries last week. The shootings are widely believed to have been reprisal killings for the bombing of the factory in Dungannon two months ago." She looked up. "The Rory Dignan I knew would no more take part in a bombing than I would take part in a game of strip poker."

"There goes your game plan for tonight, Michael."

"Brennan!"

Monty chimed in, "I've seen Michael at poker, Kitty; you wouldn't lose so much as a headband. Michael might want to layer on the garments, though. Or not . . ."

"Monty!"

"Don't be blushing now, Michael," Brennan chided him. "We were only slaggin' yeh."

This was what Michael was going to have to endure, all because he had a friendship with someone who happened to be female! Just like two bratty younger brothers, when you thought about it, annoying and slagging him without mercy.

"Pay them no mind, Michael," Kitty urged. "If I had the power to hear confessions and dish out penance, Brennan Burke would not be up off his knees till the Second Coming of our Lord. And even then he'd have some explaining to do. Now, back to Rory Dignan. He wouldn't be one of the Drumcondra Dignans now, would he? The lad used to come by the school where I taught, to walk his little sisters home. An angel of a boy. It wouldn't be him."

"It would, unfortunately, Sister," Finn replied. "His father landed a job in the North, so they went up there when young Rory was, what? Eighteen or so."

"And did he involve himself in the Troubles?"

"Em, well, he made quite a name for himself up there. Well respected. In Republican circles, I suppose you'd say."

"Oh, Mary Mother of God. They're burying little Rory Dignan. I remember him stopping to tie the shoe of one of the little girls at school. Then another girl saw the attention her friend was getting from this dashing young boy, and wouldn't you know it, her shoe came untied too. In the end, Rory had a queue of little girls waiting for him. Didn't mind at all. He tied every shoe and had a little joke or a remark for each of the children. Now," she said, returning to the newspaper, "they're saying it was a reprisal hit. Well, I've been wrong before and I may be wrong today, but I'd say they got the wrong man. I just can't believe he'd have any part in a bombing."

"He didn't." Finn was no longer the smiling barman. His mouth was set in a hard line, his eyes invisible behind the dark shades. "It was murder, pure and simple. They wanted Dignan out of the way, and here was their chance."

"By 'they,' you're referring to the UDA."

"What's the UDA?" asked Monty.

"Ulster Defence Association, a Protestant paramilitary group. And if that wasn't enough, there are efforts afoot to stop the funeral."

"What do you mean?"

"The funeral was supposed to take place yesterday. Family flew in from as far away as Australia for it. They're not people of means; they can't afford to change their flights, buy new airline tickets. If the funeral doesn't go ahead tomorrow, those people will miss seeing him laid to rest."

"I don't understand. What's the holdup?"

"There were some matters to be negotiated. Things are tense in Endastown these days. Some of the boys were going to read a statement that accuses the security forces and the British Army of turning a blind eye — more like giving the wink of an eye — to assassinations carried out by the UDA and other paramilitary groups. Word went round about the planned speech, and they got a belt of the crozier."

"I take it that means the bishop disapproved," Monty interjected.

"The bishop indeed. The Cardinal Archbishop of Armagh, Primate of All Ireland."

"Some crozier, some belt."

"Exactly, Monty. Himself considers the statement too inflammatory. The Dignan people have gone out of their way to compromise. They brought in a negotiator from here. Somebody known to you and me, in fact, Brennan. Anyway they've agreed to modify the statement. Water it down. And they've even agreed that Dermot Cooney — one of the lads who's a little hotheaded — will not be reading it as planned. Somebody else will. So they rescheduled it for tomorrow. Now they've got the Orange Order to contend with."

"How's that?" Monty asked.

"Well, you know what day tomorrow is."

"July the twelfth. Ah yes, the Glorious Twelfth."

"Orangemen's Day. Wouldn't I like to be up there to peel a few of them myself. Fuckin' marching season. I'd have them marching. Right off the edge of this island!"

"Finn," Brennan cautioned.

"I don't get it," Monty said. "What's that got to do with a Catholic funeral?"

"Well, it's like this. They're expecting a huge crowd of mourners for the Dignan send-off. Buses full of people from here as well as people from all over the North. The time of the funeral procession will conflict directly with the Orange march."

"So why don't they change it?"

"Why doesn't *who* change *what?*" Finn snapped.

"Can't they schedule things so that both events can take place?"

"No, they cannot. Or will not, in the case of the Orangemen. We, that is, the Catholics, cannot change the time of Rory's funeral. There's another funeral Mass scheduled in the church in the morning. The only Catholic church in the town. And the Aussies have to fly out just after tea time. So it has to be in the afternoon. And that's when the Orange eejits march through the town beating their drums and crowing about the victory of King William of Orange over the Catholics at the Battle of the Boyne in July 1690. Now they're trying to get another victory over us, three hundred years later."

This was the kind of talk Michael had heard around the family table all the time he was growing up. He was well aware of the past three hundred years of Irish history. Eight hundred years, really, if you measured from the time the English first landed in Ireland. It was eight hundred years exactly between the Anglo-Norman Invasion of 1169 and the beginning of the modern-day Troubles in Northern Ireland in 1969. Things had always been bad for Catholics up there. The Loyalists, those who wanted to remain united with Britain instead of with the Catholic republic to the south, had gerrymandered the electoral boundaries to make sure they held on to political power; this enabled them to discriminate against the Catholics when it came to jobs and housing. Catholics began to demand their civil rights in the late 1960s, resulting in beatings from the police. It was in 1969 that the British Army was sent in to the northern counties. The army was still there. More than three thousand people — soldiers, Republican and Loyalist paramilitary forces, Catholic and Protestant civilians — had been killed in the Troubles since then. The casualty list said it all: there was aggression and there were victims on all sides of the conflict. No side was blameless. The death toll was still nearly a hundred people a year.

In spite of it all, Michael firmly believed that peace would soon be at hand. It had to be. He prayed every night for Ireland, offered Masses for peace. He followed the news of developments like the Anglo-Irish Agreement of 1985, which brought the British and Irish governments together to pursue a solution, and the new round-table talks involving several of the main political parties in the North. When Michael escorted his tourists around the island, he incorporated the latest news in his spiel. A turning point was near, he always said, and he believed it.

Brennan's voice brought Michael back to the present. He was speaking to his uncle Finn: "The negotiator you said is known to us, trying to broker the funeral across the border; that wouldn't be . . ."

"Leo Killeen."

Brennan

The whiskey might have had something to do with it, and the Guinness consumed by the rest of them, but mainly it was compassion for the young victim of a sectarian killing, and priestly solidarity with Leo Killeen; all those factors went into the late-night decision to travel from Dublin to Endastown in the North of Ireland for the funeral of Rory Dignan on the twelfth of July, 1992.

Finn was not amongst them. When they formulated the plan, Brennan had invited him along. But he shook his head. Not willing, or perhaps not allowed, to cross the border. Brennan didn't ask. Again. Every time Brennan came home to Dublin, there were questions he didn't ask.

So he had Monty, Kitty, and Michael with him as passengers in a little black sedan he had borrowed from his cousin at the John's Lane church. Brennan and Michael were in clerical dress. Kitty was not in a nun's habit, but her navy suit and gold cross were the next best thing. Monty wore a dark blue tweed sports jacket with a white shirt open at the neck. A thoroughly respectable contingent.

Traffic slowed ahead of them as they approached the border with Northern Ireland. British territory.

"Ah, the timeless architecture of County Armagh," Kitty remarked. A massive watchtower, surrounded by a metal cage to withstand a rocket attack, loomed ahead of them. "Did you know, Michael, they built this guard post because the police force, the Royal Ulster Constabulary, couldn't take the chance of using the roads to get to their station? Everyone and everything had to come in by helicopter. So here's the result."

"That's what they get for putting the border on the wrong side of a Nationalist area of Ireland," Brennan said.

This was known in some circles as "bandit country." The Provisional

Irish Republican Army was a dominant force here in South Armagh.

They stopped at the crossing, and a young, heavily armed British soldier emerged from a hut and signalled for Brennan to roll down his window. Brennan did so and warned himself to keep his thoughts to himself. The soldier peered around inside the car, taking note of all the occupants, and addressed them in a strong North British accent.

"Where are you headed?"

A few seconds went by before Brennan answered. "Endastown."

"For what purpose?"

Brennan pointed to his collar. "Religious purposes."

"How long will you be staying?"

"As long as it takes to carry out our religious duties."

"How long?"

Brennan glared at the fellow and considered many possible replies, several of them inconsistent with his religious duties. But Monty gave him a cautionary nudge with his knee, and Brennan finally answered, "A few hours is the plan."

"May I see your driving licence?"

There shouldn't even be a border here, with this young functionary demanding to see his papers, but Brennan told himself to focus on the funeral, and not to do anything that might jeopardize their arrival. He was a frequent traveller and he always carried an international licence. He leaned across Monty's legs and opened the glove box, drew out the licence, and handed it to the British soldier, who glanced at it, then back at Brennan.

"Passport?"

Without a word, Brennan leaned over again, opened the glove box, brought out his passport, and gave it to the soldier, who examined it, then held on to it.

Brennan put his hand out to get it back, but the soldier asked him, "Irish? Why does your licence say you live in Canada?"

"Because I live in Canada."

"How long have you lived there?"

"A couple of years. Like the couple of years I've spent at this border crossing today when I'm trying to get to Mass in what is, however improbably, your country."

"Did you live in the Republic of Ireland until a couple of years ago?"

"I lived in New York City until a couple of years ago."

"But you have an Irish passport."

"My family immigrated to the United States. I reclaimed my Irish citizenship. As so many others would like to do." Others on the northern side of this border, is what he meant.

The soldier made a signal of some kind to a couple of other soldiers on patrol. Brennan heard him say "a Burke," and the other two trained their gazes on him. They came towards the car while the first soldier disappeared inside the hut. Brennan crossed his arms over his chest and faced forward, ignoring the military men at his side.

A minute or so later, the first soldier returned and said to Brennan, "Open the boot, please, sir."

"And what exactly do you expect to find in there?"

"Open it."

Brennan took a deep breath. He received another nudge from Monty, and a softly spoken "Now, Brennan" from his pastor in the back seat. It was times like these that the ancient rage welled up in him, the rage that had fuelled his grandfather, his father, his uncles, in their revolt. But there was a practical side to his character, and it saved the day here as it had on countless other occasions. This was not the time for a showdown with the British Army; Brennan and his companions had to get to the funeral. So he kept his mouth shut, got out and opened the trunk, and did nothing more aggressive than give the Brits a damning look. Then he glanced at Kitty, sitting beside Michael in the back. Her lips were clamped tight, her eyes straight ahead. She, too, was exercising extraordinary control over her mind and her mouth. But the indignities were finished soon enough, and they were permitted to cross into British territory.

They travelled through the farmland of South Armagh for a short while, until the traffic slowed again. Brennan saw vehicles parked on the side of the road, people walking forward in groups. A sign informed them that they had reached Endastown. A young man with a black arm band signalled for them to pull over.

"Good afternoon, Fathers. Sister. Here for the funeral?"

"We are," Brennan replied.

"I think you'd be better to pull over and walk the rest of the way. Through traffic is being rerouted around the town, but anyone here for the funeral had best go on foot. There will be no place to stop your car up ahead."

"All right. How far are we from the church?"

"A mile or so. But there's trouble."

"Oh?"

"They're not letting us through."

"Who's not letting us through?"

"The RUC. The Orangemen are on the march. The funeral procession is going to be held up."

"What?"

"I can't tell you any more right now. Because that's all I know."

"Thank you. Appreciate your help. We'll head up there."

It was a brilliant sunny day, and the four new arrivals joined the throngs of people gathering for the funeral. The closer they got, the thicker the crowds. There must have been two thousand people on hand. The streets were lined with three-storey houses and shops in pastel colours, with chimney pots at each end of the buildings' roofs. A short distance away Brennan could see a tall spire topped with a cross. That would be St. Áine's, the only Catholic church in town. It was then that he heard a rhythmic pounding. The Lambeg drum, the traditional drum in the Orange parades. He thought they didn't carry it much anymore, it was so heavy. Well, they were wielding it here today. Loud and insistent, primitive and threatening, it seemed to alter the very beat of his heart. He sent a murderous look in the direction of the sound.

"Let's see if we can find the funeral cortège," Michael said. "Try to spot Father Killeen. Brennan, we'll follow you."

They all fell in behind him as he moved forward. He heard a cacophony of accented speech in the crowd, as people from the Irish Republic mixed with their separated Northern brethren. Nobody objected as the priestly contingent passed them in the queue. There, up ahead, was the hearse, and the rest of the vehicles halted behind it. Flanking the hearse on either side was a line of men dressed in camouflage jackets and dark berets; black balaclavas covered their faces. Directly ahead of the hearse, and stopping it in its tracks, was a barricade manned by armed members of the Royal Ulster Constabulary. And on the other side of the barricade were three armoured personnel carriers, each one a squat and menacing presence with its massive steel plates, its pipe-like gun pointed away to the side. A slightly built grey-haired man in vestments of white stood before it, in animated conversation with two enormous British soldiers who loomed over him.

"There's Leo!" Brennan announced, and charged ahead.

"Let's see what this is all about!" Michael exclaimed as he followed behind.

"Michael, the less said the better," Kitty warned him. "You don't know these people."

"She's right, Mike, keep that in mind," Monty echoed.

"Oh, I'll not be saying a word. No worries there."

They stopped and observed the vested priest at the barricades. Leo Killeen. Now there was a man with a past; Brennan wondered how long it took *him* to be cleared at the border. Before taking Holy Orders in the church, Leo had been issuing orders as a commander in the IRA, and one of those under his command in the 1940s was Brennan's father. Declan Burke was a formidable man by any reckoning and, ever since Brennan had met Leo the year before, he had marvelled at the notion of Leo being in command of Declan and keeping him in line. Did Leo even weigh a hundred and forty pounds? Well, he was certainly having his say now, in a strong Dublin accent.

"No, the Mass cannot be put off any longer. The man's family has to be at Belfast airport in two hours' time. It has to be now. Let us through. The man has a right to a decent Christian funeral in his church, and a decent burial outside it. Halt the march, and let us pass." The words were mild, but Brennan could hear the metal beneath them.

"I can't let you through, Father. I have my orders. You'll have to turn them back. Return to the table and come up with an alternative plan. I'm sorry."

"No, we won't be turning back. Get those bowler-hatted, drumbeating gobshites to turn back. This is a young lad's funeral. Take a look at his mother, why don't you. What sort of a man prevents a mother from burying her son?"

"There's nothing I can do."

Father Killeen turned then, and Brennan could see the cold white anger in his face.

"Leo!"

It took a couple of seconds for Leo to recognize him. "Brennan!"

He joined Leo at the barricades and the two men conferred, then

Brennan returned to the head of the crowd and caught the eye of one of the women.

"What can I do for you, Father?" she asked him.

"Could you get us a table and round up as many loaves of bread as you can find? And a bottle of wine and a cup?"

"Sure there's a bakery right in the square, and I'll duck into the off-licence for the wine. I'll be back in a jiffy."

"Bless you!"

She turned and ran down the street. People made way for her, and she returned a few minutes later with the wine and a silver goblet. In her wake was a man holding a small wooden table above his head. There were gasps from the crowd, and murmuring, as they realized what was happening: the Mass was going to take place right here, right now. Behind the man with the table came a little girl, pulling a clanking cart behind her. The cart was stacked with loaves, and people moved to help her with the load. Michael, Kitty, and Monty sprinted to the bread cart, and began helping people shred the loaves into tiny pieces. They put the hosts in a large basket. More baskets appeared, and the work went on at a frantic pace.

Brennan rejoined Leo to serve as an altar boy. Turning his back on the army of occupation, Father Killeen raised his right arm, made the sign of the cross, and the requiem Mass began, "*In ainm an Athar agus an Mhic agus an Spioraid Naoimh. Amen.*" In the name of the Father and of the Son and of the Holy Spirit. Amen.

Quiet descended on the congregation, almost in a wave. The only sounds were the voice of the priest, reciting the ancient prayers, and the Lambeg drum on the other side of the barricade, its pounding rhythm marking the enmity that had blighted this island for centuries. The orange sashes and bowler hats came in sight, and a loud rumbling started among the worshippers. Brennan looked into the congregation and saw Kitty leave Michael's side and climb up on the concrete base of a light pole. The base was wide enough to stand on if she leaned against the pole for support. From her perch Kitty faced the crowd, placed her hands together in prayer, then spread them out and lowered them. Keep the noise down, she was telling them. You're at Mass. Ignore the interruption. The crowd fell silent again.

The men in balaclavas and berets lifted the coffin from the hearse and draped it with the Irish tricolour. With quick, efficient movements, two of them assembled a folding stand and placed the coffin upon it, then they all arranged themselves around it.

By this time, a news van had pulled up. The film crew emerged and began to record the scene: Father Killeen dwarfed by the armoured cars behind him, the IRA honour guard, the grim-faced Orangemen marching on the other side, Sister Kitty standing on her concrete platform and urging the crowd to silence.

At the consecration, the great crowd fell to its knees. Priests and altar servers came forward from the crowd to distribute communion. The drumming never let up. Priest and acolyte did their best to ignore it, and the huge congregation followed the Mass as if it were their first. Or their last. When Father Killeen lifted a ragged piece of bread and spoke the words of consecration, suffusing the bread with the real presence of Christ, a feeling of unearthly peace came over Brennan, as it often did during the most sacred moment of the Mass. The strife, the hatred, the ugly backdrop of tanks and guns receded from his consciousness. It was as if a veil had opened between the seen and the unseen world, for an instant in time, and rays of brilliant light bathed the worshippers in front of him. The joy for Brennan at these moments was indescribable. This was what it was all for; this was why he had become a priest and, despite his many struggles, remained a priest.

When the Mass was nearly over, one man emerged from the honour guard and strode towards the light standard where Kitty stood. He swiftly discarded the balaclava and beret, revealing a hard-looking face incongruously topped by strawberry-blond curls. He drew a sheaf of papers from his pocket. Father Killeen gave a quick shake of his head. The man kept on. Killeen said, "No, Dermot." The British soldiers behind the barricade seemed to snap to a new level of alertness; they gripped their machine guns more tightly. Dermot hesitated, then turned and leapt up on the concrete base with Kitty. A soldier took aim, and the gun on one of the tanks rotated slowly to the front until it was levelled at Dermot and Kitty. Brennan's heart missed a beat. He saw Michael O'Flaherty's mouth form the word "No!" Dermot hesitated, then shoved his papers into Kitty's hand and hopped down. He and his cohorts moved off to the side and stood in formation with their hands behind their backs. The British soldier lowered his weapon, and the tank gun was turned aside.

Kitty, alone on the makeshift podium, shuffled the papers, obviously trying to absorb what they said. Brennan saw the Dignan family looking up at her. It seemed they were pleading with her to read what she had been given. As the television camera captured every word, she spoke of the short and intense life of Rory Dignan, from his days as an altar boy and student and loving brother to seven siblings to his calling as a Volunteer for the Irish Republican cause, from the kindness and humorous banter he always displayed to the depth of his commitment to a united Ireland.

"And it was in that struggle that Rory came to know at close hand the terrible sectarian slaughter perpetrated by Loyalist paramilitaries, aided and abetted by their masters in the British . . ." She stopped and scanned the text, flipped to the next page and resumed reading, "Then, Rory was the victim of scurrilous and baseless accusations that he was involved in the factory bombing in Dungannon in May of this year. Absolutely false. Rory was innocent, as anyone who knew him would realize. But his innocence did not save him from being targeted and hunted down by the very same forces that did the factory bombing, a put-up job, a Reichstag fire, so to speak, to make it look . . ." Her voice came to a halt again, then she turned the page and finished with, "Rory was a beloved son and brother, a faithful Catholic who never missed his Sunday Mass, who looked upon his life and work as service to God, and who now will be carried by the angels of heaven to his new home with God the Father, the Son, and the Holy Spirit, and with the Mother of God and of us all, the Blessed Virgin Mary. May she and the saints receive him, and may perpetual light shine upon him."

It was only after the Mass had ended, the marchers had drummed their way out of sight, and the procession had made its solemn way to the gravesite and seen Rory Dignan committed to the earth that Brennan and Michael were able to make their way through the throng to Kitty. Monty emerged from the crowd and joined them.

Brennan could see the effort Michael made not to fling his arms around her in relief.

"Kitty, *acushla*, you put the heart crossways in me!" Michael exclaimed. "I thought they were going to blow you away! When you got up there and that fellow leapt up with you, and the guns were turned on you —"

"Michael, my darling, I've survived the Congo, I've survived El Salvador. And do you know how I survived? By being the biggest, yellowest chicken God ever created." Brennan, behind her back, shook his head. Nothing yellow about this woman. But Kitty kept up the fiction. "They're not going to waste government property — bullets — on a harmless little oul nun in holy Ireland. If I thought they would, I'd have been hiding myself under a rock at the arse end of the congregation."

"But it wasn't the holy Irish who had their guns trained on you; it was the British Army."

"It wasn't me they had in their sights, Michael; it was that ruffian Dermot they were after. And they didn't even pop him. So stop your fussing. Ah, here comes Father Killeen. It's time we all introduced ourselves."

Michael spoke up. "It's almost like the days when our people had to sneak out in the fields to have Mass, Father. You're a courageous man, and it's an honour to meet you. I'm Michael O'Flaherty." He put out his hand, and Father Killeen shook it.

"Michael. I've heard your name from Brennan. We meet at last." Leo turned to Monty. "Mr. Collins, welcome to Ireland. Better late than never at all."

Leo and Monty had met in New York, when Leo flew over to straighten some matters out for Brennan's father after the shooting. Leo had taken Monty to task, him with the name of Collins and never having set foot in Ireland. The New York shooting, an eruption of Irish history on American soil, and now Mass at the barricades with tanks facing them; was any of this likely to engender in Monty an attachment to the land of his forefathers? *Let's hope things don't get any worse*, Brennan said to himself. He half expected a wisecrack from Monty about Leo and guns and trouble, but no. Even Monty, who had seen it all in the criminal courts for over twenty years, hadn't seen anything like this. He appeared to have been left speechless by the spectacle today.

Michael O'Flaherty said to Leo, "I have been attending Mass for seventy-one years, and saying Mass as a priest for forty-five years. Never, ever has the Mass moved me as profoundly as it did today."

Leo nodded. Obviously, there was a world of conversation O'Flaherty wanted to open up with Killeen, but this was not the time; Leo was a man with a lot on his mind.

Chapter 2

Brennan

When Brennan arrived at Christy's the day after the tank-and-barricade Mass, Finn had a set of keys in his hand and appeared to be on his way out. Standing in his place behind the bar was a young man in his twenties, with very short auburn hair and a close-cropped beard. His light brown eyes had a humorous look about them.

"Ah. Brennan. You caught me on the fly," Finn said. "Sean will be taking care of business while I'm out." He made the introductions. "Brennan Burke. Sean Nugent. Brennan is my nephew, Sean, but you don't have to take any guff off him. Feel free to toss him out if he gets scuttered and starts a row with somebody."

"I'm well able for him, Finn."

"Knew you would be. Brennan, come round the back with me for a minute."

Brennan followed his uncle into the darkness behind the bar. Finn turned to face him.

"This vandalism has me concerned, Brennan."

"As well it might."

"I'm afraid the fellow has targeted one of the faithful here. I don't know which one. But I'm afraid it might go beyond that. One of the lads could be in danger if this gouger thinks he's a killer. And obviously I don't want somebody coming in and shooting the place up, or setting fire to it."

"Have you called in —"

"I don't want the guards nosing about in here."

Why not? Brennan wondered. But he knew from long experience there was no point in asking.

"So, would you help me out here? Keep your ears open. If you hear anything, let me know. Don't get me wrong; if anyone has got himself into trouble, it's not my business and it won't go any farther than here." He pointed to himself. "I don't care what they've done; I won't be informing on them. My concern is what might be done *to* them, by this unknown quantity with the paint can. Who knows what kind of weapon he might use next?"

"I'll do what I can for you, Finn, certainly. I can hardly fault you for being concerned."

He fixed his eyes on his uncle's dark lenses as if he could penetrate their obscurity. But he could not, which, he had always assumed, was the point. If the eyes are the windows of the soul, Finn apparently preferred to keep his soul, pure or impure as it might be, hidden from public view. And, of course, the shades afforded him the opportunity to scrutinize the eyes of others while remaining inscrutable himself.

"But," Brennan asked him, "aren't you the most obvious target here?"

"It's not about me. We've covered that ground already. Look elsewhere."

"Very well. Who do you have by way of regulars that I should be observing?"

No reply.

"Finn. The messages refer to someone who is known for spending his time here, not a blow-in who stopped by for a pint and never darkened the doorway again. Now, who drinks here?"

"Well, I have four in particular who call the place home." Brennan waited. "Frank Fanning. I have to say I value his custom."

"All right. Fanning's a pisshead. Who else?"

"Tim Shanahan. Tim takes a drink, but he's a gentleman. An intellectual."

"So. He might have bested somebody in an argument. Judging by the quality of the graffiti, that wouldn't be hard to do. Go on."

"Jimmy O'Hearn. Lives on a boat out there in the harbour. And there's Eddie Madigan. He was with the guards. Now he isn't."

"Why not?"

"There's been talk of corruption. I don't believe it. Whatever it is, it's unknown to me."

"What can you tell me about the other three, or any of them, that might account for the slander spray-painted on your wall?"

"Nothing. If I knew, I'd know. And I wouldn't be bothering you about it. I'm hoping you'll hear something I've never heard."

"Well, they've got their faces hanging over your bar day in and day out. If your ears haven't picked up anything, my chances are slim."

"Maybe so. Give it a try."

"I will." He understood his uncle's concerns, and wanted to help him out. But it was not in Brennan's nature to go probing into other people's lives. He was a fiercely private individual himself, and was quite content to see others keep to themselves as well. Michael O'Flaherty, on the other hand, loved to gab with people and get their stories. He would be ideal for this assignment, unless and until it took a turn that might prove to be dangerous. Brennan would put O'Flaherty on the case. He tried not to think of it as fobbing the whole thing off on his friend and pastor. It wouldn't hurt to have Michael distracted from the case of the missing American preacher; no good would come of that, and no good would come of Michael associating himself with it in any way. Brennan returned to the subject at hand. "I'll have the others listen to the pub talk as well. Michael O'Flaherty is someone people open up to. The kind, sweet face on him."

"I know what you mean about him. Just as long as he doesn't . . ."

"I'll caution him to be discreet. He'll understand."

"Very well then."

✝

After they emerged from behind the bar, and Finn had taken his leave, Michael O'Flaherty arrived. Brennan introduced him to the young barman.

"Nice to meet you, Monsignor."

33

"Good to meet you, Sean. Please call me Michael."

"Okay. What can I get for you, Michael?"

"A pint of Guinness would go down nicely, I'm thinking."

"Two would go down even better," Brennan said.

"Coming up."

Brennan and Michael sat at the bar and took delivery of their drinks.

"Now, you don't sound like a local boy," Michael remarked to Sean. "Would you be from County Cork by any chance?"

"I would. The fellows here are forever slagging me about my Cork accent. Better dan soundin' like a Dub, I'm after tellin' dem all!"

Michael laughed at his imitation of the broad North Dub accent. "I know Nugents in my home town. I'm from Saint John, New Brunswick. That's an old port city, in fact the oldest city in Canada, and it —"

"Sure I know it well."

"You've been there?"

"No, but it's familiar to me even so. I had an uncle over there. He was my grand-uncle, really. And up until the week he died we were getting letters from him, telling us all about it."

"I may have crossed paths with him. You never know. I grew up on Waterloo Street, right across from the cathedral. The faces you'd see around that church, Sean, you'd swear you were in Ireland. And most of the Nugents, as far as I know, originated in Cork or thereabouts."

"You're right. They would have. And from what my uncle had to say, it sounded as if history followed the Irish people over there and wouldn't let them go."

"There's something in that, for sure. When I was a lad we — the Catholics — stayed well inside when the Orangemen were on the march. We were told to keep our doors and windows locked when the parades wound through the city. I remember it all too well."

"Ah, yes. You'd want to be far from all that, so."

"But the Catholics weren't angels either. A gentleman of my acquaintance was among those who painted one of the rooms in the Admiral Beatty Hotel green from floor to ceiling on St. Patrick's Day!"

"I suspect there was drink taken," Nugent replied with a smile.

Might as well get the investigation under way, Brennan decided. But O'Flaherty got there ahead of him. Which wasn't a bad thing at all; O'Flaherty needed no urging to relieve Brennan of the task.

"Do you work nights as well, Sean, or just the day shift?"

"I do both. Nighttime's a lot livelier."

"I can well imagine!" Michael said. "A busy place in the evenings, I'm sure. Better earnings behind the bar. But you'll want to watch yourself on the way out at night. You don't want someone getting in your face with a can of spray paint! Finn has told us about the vandalism. A nasty business, by the sound of things."

"Sure I'm not worried about being here at night. I'd be well able for him if I found him at it. But he must have come in the dead of night because nobody ever caught a glimpse of him."

"What time do you open in the morning?"

"Half-ten."

"And Finn leaves . . ."

"Last orders are at half-twelve, with thirty minutes' drink-up time. So he wouldn't get away before one in the morning."

"That leaves a span of around nine hours for the fellow to creep up and do his dirty work."

"On some days, not even that, Michael. Kevin, our cleaner, would be in well before opening time. But he didn't come in every day."

"Kevin? Who would that be now?"

"Kevin McDonough. Used to give the place a complete mop-up a couple of times a week. But he called in yesterday to say he's giving up the cleaning job. He's in line for bigger and better things, is Kevin. His band was brilliant at the Tivoli, and they're booked for two more gigs. Tonight and tomorrow. They'll hit the big time, no question about it."

"Good for him! What kind of band does he play in?"

"Rock band. Call themselves the Irish Problem."

"Maybe we'll buy a ticket, eh, Brennan?"

"Sure."

"Enjoy rock music, do you, Father?"

"I'm a fan," Michael claimed. "You, Brennan?"

"Me too." In his case it was the truth.

Michael

The investigation was on! Brennan told Michael that Finn had requested his assistance in the Christy Burke's graffiti case, had asked him to keep his eyes and ears open. And now Brennan had asked Michael and Monty to do the same. Of course he chided Michael for muscling in on the first interrogation. But Brennan was obviously just taking the mickey out of him; Michael's initiative had not hurt his chances of promotion. Brennan had a warning, though: "Now you know Finn wants this kept *sub rosa* . . ."

"Don't be worrying about that, now. I'll be discreet."

"Carry on then, lads."

"Does that mean you've deputized us, Brennan, me and Sergeant O'Flaherty?" Monty asked.

"Just don't tart yourselves up in police gear, all right? No little tin badges, gadgets hanging off your belts, none of that. Do I make myself clear?"

"We're undercover, you're saying."

"Well, plainclothes at least. And for tonight, that means no Roman collar."

They were standing in Brennan's digs in the working-class area of Dublin known as the Liberties. The area was a little rough, and the two-storey brick building where he was staying needed some major repairs, but none of that seemed to bother Brennan. They had just met his cousin Ciaran, who lived in the building with a couple of other Augustinian priests. Tall, dark, and bearded, he appeared to be in his early forties; he had a good sense of humour and a devotion to the poor. He was interested to hear about the graffiti investigation, and wished them well on the night shift.

That was how Monsignor O'Flaherty ended up with his eardrums nearly splitting open at the Tivoli Theatre in the Liberties, listening to the Irish Problem, surrounded by young people, some of whom appeared to be on drugs. Not that they were behaving badly. They seemed happy and good-natured. What was the word, mellow? Well, there were worse ways to be than mellow.

"Are they any good?" he shouted into Monty's ear. "I can't tell for the noise!"

"They're great!" Monty shouted in return.

Well, he would know. He played in a band himself. Not a hard rock band, or at least Michael didn't think so. But it was something else you didn't dress up for. Blues, that was it. Here, the guitars seemed to scream, and the drumbeat was loud and incessant. The vibration went right to the very heart of him. Kevin McDonough was the lead singer and when they did a "quiet" number, Michael could tell the lad was talented. He was tall and skinny with dark hair cropped in front and longer in back. They all had that haircut.

"And now for all you traditional music fans out there," Kevin announced. "There's whiskey in the jar!"

Grand! That was a song Michael knew and liked. The Knights of Columbus were known for a rousing version of it after lifting a few jars of their own. Wait a minute, what was this? That guitar was distinctly rockish, and the drums — was it the same song? Yes, apparently so. But it wasn't bad. And it wasn't long before Michael found himself singing along with the chorus. And joining in the wild applause at the end. Monty gave him the thumbs-up.

When the concert was over, Michael, Brennan, and Monty stood in the lobby with a couple of dozen teenagers, mostly girls, waiting for the band. A squeal issued from the mouth of one of the girls, and there was Kevin, followed by the other — what would one call them? The other Irish Problems?

"Oh, Matt!" a young girl called out. "Would you ever be givin' me a ride in the band bus? You don't even have to have the wheels goin'." This was met with loud shrieks of laughter from the girl's friends. Matt was the bass guitarist; Michael saw him lean over and whisper something in the girl's ear. She covered her mouth with her hand and giggled.

"Kev!" another girl shouted. "Will you sign my ticket? Make it out to Sheena, with love from Kevin? Or just your name would be good too."

He smiled at her and scribbled something on her ticket, signed a couple more autographs, then excused himself. Brennan took the opportunity to approach the singer and introduce himself as Finn's nephew. He introduced his companions as well.

"Finn is not letting on, but he's very concerned about the vandalism at the pub. Afraid it might escalate to something worse. More serious property damage, or even violence. He wants it looked into, but doesn't want the Garda Síochána involved."

"I can believe it," Kevin said.

"So we decided to take in your concert — brilliant by the way — and have a word with you if we could. You were the first on the scene after the last incident, I believe."

"I was."

"Would you mind if we asked you a few questions?"

"I don't mind. Best not here, though. I'm meeting somebody at the Brazen Head, so we could all go over there for a pint."

The four of them made small talk on the short walk to the Brazen Head, Ireland's oldest pub. There had been a pub on the site as long ago as 1198. The front part of the establishment had the look of a medieval stone castle with an arch leading to a courtyard. A larger white-walled building rose behind it, and that's where the party of four headed. It was jammed inside, no seats available, so they stood at the bar and ordered pints of Guinness all round. The Brazen Head was dark and low-ceilinged, the walls covered with memorabilia.

"This place was the scene of plotting and planning for every rising in our history, and it was duly raided after every one of them," Kevin said. "Robert Emmet drank here and so did the hangman who took his life. Emmet's speech from the dock is posted on the wall."

Michael was content to sip his pint and peer around in the smoky darkness, luxuriating in the history, while Monty and Kevin discussed the music scene in Dublin and Brennan listened with interest. The door opened, and Kevin waved to someone at the entrance. She was a very attractive and very pregnant young woman, with honey-blond hair tied up in the back and a fine, freckled complexion. It was plain that she had something on her mind as she stalked towards the bar.

"That poxy fecker, Matt, he should be checking himself in to a clinic, he should. If I ever caught you carrying on with those little tarts, you'd be shredded into so many pieces, they'd need an industrial-strength vacuum to suck enough of you up to give you a funeral, and don't expect any kind words to be said over your coffin because —"

"Brenda, we're not alone."

"Oh!" Brenda looked past Kevin and caught sight of his three new acquaintances. "I'm sorry to be giving out to him like that in front of you."

"More like giving sound advice, I'd say," Monty replied. "My name is Monty Collins and this is Michael O'Flaherty and Brennan Burke."

"I'm Brenda. But I guess you know that already."

Kevin put his arms around the woman then, and gave her a kiss. He turned to his companions and said, "Brenda is my wife. With her is our child-to-be."

"Your first?" Michael inquired.

"Our third!" Kevin replied, and laughed. "She keeps me busy at home and out of the . . . well, out of the clinic! Brenda, let's see if we can find a chair for you."

"No worries. I'm fine standing. I'd be finer with half a Harp in me."

Michael raised his eyebrows, and Brenda caught him at it. She laughed. "That's all I allow myself, is half a pint. Couple of times a week. It didn't do any harm to the first two, so . . ."

"It never hurt me," Kevin proclaimed, "and my mam took more than half a pint when she was looking forward to me! All right now, gentlemen . . . They're asking about Christy's, the vandalism," he explained to Brenda. "Brennan here is one of the Burkes."

"Right. We'd better get on with our questions so you can get on with your evening," Brennan said.

"Not at all. Ask away."

"I guess you could begin by telling us what you saw that morning, when the graffiti last appeared."

"It was green paint and it said, 'Come all ye to Christy's, killers own local.' Or it started to say local but the paint just dribbled down. Rain must have got at it. Though maybe not. When I think of it, there wasn't any water in the whiskey."

"Whiskey?" Monty asked.

"Yeah, there was a glass of whiskey sort of leaning against the wall at an angle. The bollocks that did the paint job must have been enjoying a jar while he worked. The drink wasn't watered down, so the rain must not have been hitting against the building. So maybe that's not what stopped him writing."

"What kind of a glass was it?"

"Usual kind."

"The kind you have in Christy's."

"Sure. In all the pubs."

"What else?" Brennan prompted.

Kevin shrugged. "Didn't notice anything."

"You came home with muck on your shoes," Brenda said. "Remember, Kev? What did you tell me about that? Some mess in the garden."

"Oh, right. The grass had been torn up by tires. So I kicked it back into place. Lot of muck after the rain. I thought it was the rubbish collectors that had driven up on the grass again, but turned out it wasn't. They came later."

"So, a vehicle on the premises that night or morning," Brennan said.

"And somebody having a drink outside," added Monty.

"Yeah. Nothing stood out."

Kevin looked down at his pint. Michael had the impression suddenly that he was avoiding something.

"Kev?" Brenda spoke up.

"Mm?"

His wife gave him what Michael thought of as a significant look.

"Tell them. It's not as if you did anything wrong."

The young man looked uncomfortable. "Come on, Brenda, you know I wasn't supposed to be down there."

"You did no harm."

"But Finn will have my bollocks. Especially if . . ."

"What is it, Kevin?" Brennan prompted him. "Finn wants to know what happened. I'll do my best to keep him in good humour."

"It's just that . . . there was a gun down there."

Michael looked at Brennan. The younger priest's face was without expression. All he said was "Where?"

"The tunnel they dug under the place. You know, during the Troubles — the *old* Troubles — when they were fighting the English. Finn has something of a collection stashed in there."

"Yes?"

"Didn't he tell you about it?"

"We're aware of it," Brennan answered. Suavely, Michael thought.

"Yeah, well, one of the guns was missing. The black pistol he kept in a little niche behind the bricks. But that doesn't have to mean anything. Finn might have taken it out to, em, clean it. Or put it in a safer place." Kevin shrugged and took a sip of his pint. "I don't know any more than that."

"What did you do?"

"Just what I always did. Cleaned around, washed the glasses, locked up, and went home."

"Including the glass you found outside?" Monty asked. Kevin nodded.

"What's your take on it, Kevin?" Brennan lit up a cigarette and drew the smoke into his lungs, then asked, "Any thoughts about what's behind it?"

"I figured it was about Finn himself." He glanced uncertainly at Brennan. "You know, some nutter who doesn't share his Republican views. But I really don't know. I saw it, but I have no idea what it meant. I imagine there are lots of dark theories making the rounds, and dark thoughts about the fellow that did it. Christy's is sacred ground to some."

"People are fond of the place," Brennan agreed.

"Fond indeed. There's some that practically live there."

"Right. Would you be acquainted with any of them? Do you spend time there in the evenings? Or just do your shift in the mornings?"

"Oh, I lift a jar there from time to time. After all, I know the place is good and clean!"

The others laughed and, when Brennan didn't ask, Michael stepped in: "So, who would they be, Kevin? The regular patrons of Christy Burke's pub."

"Well, you've got Frank Fanning. You'd need a grenade to get him out of Christy's. And Jimmy O'Hearn. He's a fixture as well. Eddie Madigan. He used to drink there when he was with the guards. Still there, as a civilian. And Tim Shanahan. Brainy sort of fellow, Tim. There was old Joe Burns, but he hasn't been in Christy's for months. He'll be breathing his last any day now in the Mater — the hospital. They've got him all hooked up to tubes. There were a couple more who used to spend time there, but they moved on."

"Who would they be?"

"The Buckle brothers."

"Buckley?"

"No, it's Buckle. Because they get so buckled by the end of the night the legs go on one or the other of them, and they have to prop each other up. They drink at Dec Gallagher's now. They were out of Christy's before any of this started, with the graffiti."

Michael continued the questioning: "Why did they leave Christy Burke's?"

"Dec Gallagher's is closer; they live two doors away from it. Every step counts for that pair. You'd never get a sensible word out of them."

"I see. Anybody else?"

"Well, there's Nurse McAvity."

"Oh, a woman?"

"No. Just drinks like one! Ha. No, can't say that, can I now? There are some women who can drink us men under the table. They call him Nurse McAvity, or My Cavity; bit of a joke on his name, which is really Bill McAvity. You could set your watch by Bill; he'd arrive at Christy's at a quarter to six on the dot. He runs an auto repair shop, and he'd close up at five, give himself a wash, and take his place at Christy's. But he's gone back to the Bleeding Horse. They put up with him there, same way Finn Burke did."

"Why 'put up'? Did he cause trouble?"

"No, nothing like that. It's just that he doesn't drink. He'll order half a pint and — here's the other part of his name — he'll just nurse it all night, take a sip or two every half hour or so. He'll finish it off right at closing time, then say, 'Lads, it's time,' and he'll head out sober as a Paisley Prod on a Sunday morning. Something wrong with the man, that was the thinking. And there are the oul ones who get table service because of their backs."

"Their backs?"

"They have all these health complaints. That's what they talk about the whole time, their sore backs, their arthritis, their pills. One's got a bad leg, another one's waiting for an operation. They rabbit on about this stuff all the time, but they look healthy enough to me. They manage to get to Christy's once a week. Drunk as owls, a couple of them, by the time they leave. The fellows at the bar have a name for them. Can't remember it right now. You probably won't get any useful information out of them, since they're not there every day, and they keep to themselves at the back. Anyway, Fanning and O'Hearn and Madigan and Shanahan, they'd be the regulars who would have an intimate knowledge of the pub and its goings-on."

"There you have it: the Christy Burke Four," Monty declared.

"I like it," Michael said, "though it has a bit of a political ring to it. Let's hope we're not looking at anything political in this."

"Political or otherwise, I suspect it won't be pretty," Brennan warned.

They spent a few more minutes with Kevin discussing his musical career. Then, after extending best wishes for the family present and future, Michael, Brennan, and Monty said goodbye to the McDonoughs and headed towards Monty's hotel, nearby in Christchurch Place. Brennan would walk home from there, and Michael would call a taxi.

"Now there's an oddity for you," Michael said, pointing at two churches side by side. "Two churches called St. Audoen's, one dating from the twelfth century and the other neoclassical. Strange to say, the medieval one is Protestant — that is, it *became* Protestant — and the newer one is Catholic."

"History around every corner here," Monty remarked.

"And you don't always see it coming."

Brennan

The next day Brennan went to work, so to speak, at Christy Burke's, and he had his sergeant with him. He had assigned Michael, with his mild, friendly manner, to chat up the regulars during the early rounds of questioning. Brennan would observe the proceedings from his bar stool. He was in civilian clothes, Michael in his collar. When they entered the pub at around five in the afternoon, they saw four men sitting on stools at the bar, pints in hand. Brennan realized he had seen them before, planted in the very same spot. Quintessential pub regulars. The Christy Burke Four. Was one of them the victim of the spray-painted slander on the wall? Was one of them a killer, right at home in the "killers own local"?

Brennan chose a place at the other end of the bar. Michael sat right beside the last man in the row of four and nodded at the group.

They all nodded back and said, "Father."

"Gentlemen, I'm on vacation. The collar's a habit I can't seem to shake, but call me Mike."

"Mike," they said in unison.

"And that's Brennan." They all acknowledged each other.

"Is Finn not in today?" Mike asked.

"He's got the young fellow on. Sean will be back in a jiffy." The man who spoke had a pleasant, roundish face, round eyes, and sandy hair going grey. "My name's O'Hearn. Jimmy."

The young barman came in then, greeted Mike and Brennan, and took their orders for pints of Guinness.

Jimmy made the introductions: "This is Mike, Sean. And Brennan. Gentlemen, Sean Nugent."

"We're acquainted already, as a matter of fact. Good day to you, Sean. You've given Finn the day off, have you?"

"Sure I told him to take all the time he needs."

"And he could use it. A finger in many pies, has Finn Burke." This came from a hard-looking man sitting next to Jimmy O'Hearn.

"Keeps the man sharp," a tweed-capped regular put in. "If we had half the business sense Finn has, we'd be . . . em, well . . ."

"We'd be swimming in money and in drink. Wouldn't be good for our health!" O'Hearn exclaimed. "Here's to us, the leisure class!"

Everyone lifted a pint and took a sip.

"Let me introduce everyone to you," O'Hearn said then. "The oul fellow in the cap is Frank Fanning."

Fanning wore a shirt and tie, a grey cardigan sweater and a tweed cap, even though it was a warm July day. He wore heavy-framed glasses and had the red nose and broken capillaries of a heavy drinker.

"Oul fella, is it?" Fanning groused. "We'll see who'll be the last man standing!" He spoke in a broad Dub accent.

"And this is Eddie Madigan."

The man with the hard-looking face had high cheekbones, and cropped, bristly grey hair. He raised his glass in greeting.

"And the quiet fellow with the specs is Tim Shanahan. Can't you tell from the look of him he's always got his face in a book?"

"When it's not in a pint of porter," Shanahan replied in a soft west-of-Ireland voice.

"He's the voice of wisdom, is Tim."

A few years younger than the other three, maybe his late forties, Shanahan was a handsome, ascetic-looking man with a thin face, black hair parted on the side and falling over his forehead, and small rimless glasses. He looked like a scholar. Or, Brennan thought, a priest.

There was a companionable silence then as the men returned to their drinks. Brennan had advised Mike not to cut to the chase but to warm them up first with a bit of friendly chatter.

"How long have you been coming here, Jimmy?" Mike asked.

"Oh, it must be twenty years now. Since I moved here from Donegal."

"Ah, there is indeed a trace of the North in your voice. Do you still have people there?"

"I have a sister there. Sarah. She works in a lovely spot called McKelvey's Bar, so it's a double treat whenever I go and pay her a visit."

"McKelvey. I was telling Sean here that I know Nugents back home in Saint John. McKelveys too. Is the bar in Donegal Town?"

"No, a few miles from there, a place called Ballybofey."

"What brought you to Dublin, then?"

"I came to seek my fortune."

"I hope you found it!"

O'Hearn laughed. "So does my wife! Then she's going to let me back into the house!"

"Oh, are you and your wife separated, Jim?"

"Well now, we are and we aren't. We don't live under the same roof, haven't for many years, but we get along better now than we ever did. That should tell you something, but I'm not sure what!"

"And you, Frank?" Mike inquired. "You sound like a Dublin man."

"Right you are. I'm a Dublin jackeen and right now I'm off to the jacks." He got up and headed for the men's room.

"Well now," Jimmy O'Hearn said, "there goes a brilliant pintman, brilliant!"

"He is," agreed Eddie Madigan.

"Legendary, you might say."

"He has a bar stool now, but for the longest time he stood, did he not, Eddie?"

"He did. But now he'll have a seat."

"He has all the time in the world for the pouring of the perfect pint. Frank never rushes you, does he, Sean?"

"A gentleman and a connoisseur. It's a pleasure to pour a pint for Frank Fanning."

"Not like some that come in the door. They want their pint and they want it now. Sure if you're that pressed, go to Temple Bar, grab your glass before it's even settled, and blather away to the rest of the . . . what is it you call them, Tim?"

"Poseurs," the younger man replied.

"Frank's one of the regulars here," Jimmy explained.

You'd have to wonder how much time the man spends in here, Brennan said to himself. They all seemed to be regulars as far as he could tell.

"How often does Frank come in?" Mike asked. Three pairs of eyes stared, uncomprehending. "I mean, on average, you know . . ."

"Well, he'll come in twice, Michael," Tim replied.

"But how many days of the week?"

Again the stares.

Sean spoke up. "He's in every day, so."

"Like the rest of us," said Madigan.

"Daily communicants, you might say," added Shanahan.

Mike took a sip of his pint and then got down to business. "Finn was telling me he's had to do some painting lately."

"That fecker with the spray can is fortunate Finn Burke never caught him at it. Finn'd spray him from here to Bantry Bay!" Frank Fanning had returned to his seat and punctuated his remarks by taking a big gulp of Guinness, then brought his glass down on the bar with a resounding crack.

"He won't fare much better if the four of us get hold of him," Eddie Madigan warned. "Defacing a public house like that. Little gurrier."

"It seems to be over now," Tim Shanahan stated.

"Let's hope so," declared Fanning. "Maybe he came crawling round and spotted us on the job, and ran away. Wise move on his part."

"What do you mean, on the job?" Mike asked. "Were you keeping watch on the place?"

"Sure we were," Jimmy O'Hearn said. "Thought we'd help Finn out a bit, stay around late at night, see if we could nab the fellow."

"But," Frank said, "he never showed up on the nights we were on patrol. Maybe, as I say, he saw us and backed off."

"What was he getting at, do you suppose?"

"I'd say what he was getting was off his meds!" Frank asserted. "Well, I hope we've seen the last of him. And of his sacrileges against this place!"

"I'll drink to that," Tim said with a smile and took a sip of his pint.

"Here's Mr. Burke now. Howiyeh, Finn," Frank said, as Finn arrived, saluted his patrons, and installed himself behind the bar. Sean said goodbye and left the pub.

Brennan listened to Mike and his new companions making small talk until their attention was caught by the television. It was six o'clock.

"Oh! I didn't even notice the TV over there," Mike remarked. The television sat on a shelf where the wall met the bar.

"Well, Sean enjoys it once in a while, but Finn's not keen on it," Jimmy O'Hearn explained. "He rarely turns the thing on except at news time or when they're showing a football or a hurling match. But here's the news."

"God love the RTÉ," Mike commented, as the Irish broadcaster duly played the Angelus bells before the news came on. The first story was from the United States, where a group of evangelical Protestants had issued a demand for the release of the Reverend Mr. Odom. There was still no word on his whereabouts. Then the news presenter announced that tourism was up this year. Particularly tourism from the Far East.

"A planeload of Japanese tourists touched down at Shannon Airport today. But these are tourists with a difference. They're actually landowners here in Ireland. Diane Brosnan explains."

The reporter's voice came on and said, "A hundred and forty-four people from Japan have arrived in the country today to stand for the first time on Irish soil. *Their* Irish soil. These are all people who have purchased lots of land in the Republic, and have chartered an aircraft to bring them here and make their dream come true. Soon they'll be standing on their very own little piece of —"

"Fuck!" Finn muttered, and thumped the TV off with a punch of his fist.

The regulars raised eyebrows and exchanged glances but made no comment.

Immigration might be a topic to avoid with Finn, Brennan reflected. But there was no lack of other subjects of conversation in the pub. Somebody piped up from a table in the rear, and described his luck the day before at the Leopardstown races. His horse was seconds from the finish line, promising big returns, when he, the horse, fell and broke his leg and had to be put down. Things had gone better at Croke Park, someone else noted; Dublin had trounced Kildare in hurling. This set off a round of sports talk, and Frank Fanning sought Finn's views on the hurling season so far. But Finn had the appearance of a troubled man as he stood behind his bar with the TV battered into silence at his side.

Chapter 3

Brennan

Brennan Burke enjoyed a drink, to be sure, but it wasn't every day you would find him in a guzzling den ten minutes after opening time. On Wednesday morning, though, after early Mass at the John's Lane church, he had headed out for a stroll and then decided to visit Christy's to have a look around the crime scene, without people eyeing his every move. When he got to the pub, he took a walk around outside the building, calling to mind Kevin McDonough's description of the scene the morning after the latest incident of vandalism: the unfinished message, dripping paint, whiskey glass propped against the wall, clumps of turf disturbed by the tires of a vehicle.

When Brennan entered the pub, there was just one lonely soul drinking at a back table. The man looked up, kept Brennan in his gaze for a few seconds, then returned to his pint. Brennan stood at the bar and peered into the shadows. Yes, Finn was back there, cutting up some boxes and doing other chores. It wasn't long before he sensed his nephew's presence and emerged to greet him.

"Morning, Brennan. You're here to add an element of respectability to the place, are you?" He gestured to the Roman collar.

"Things are going to change around here, Mr. Burke. You're looking at the reincarnation of Father Mathew."

"God help us and save us."

They shared a laugh at the idea of Ireland's early "Apostle of Temperance" coming to life again in the unlikely form of Brennan Burke.

"Actually, I was out for a walk and decided to survey the crime scene. But I didn't learn much, I have to say."

"I hear you. But sit down and rest from your labours. What will you have?"

"I feel Father Mathew asking for a ginger ale."

"Are you sure?"

"I am. It will do me for now."

Finn poured him the drink and waved away his currency. "Help yourself to the papers."

Brennan saw the *Irish Independent* and the *Irish Times* folded on the bar, so he thanked Finn and took them to a table by the window. He sat, had a sip of his drink, and spread the *Times* out before him. He looked over at the bar and saw Finn's face, partly obscured as always by the dark glasses, turned in the direction of the man at the back of the pub. The man paid no attention. Brennan directed his attention to his papers. There was a short piece on the Reverend Merle Odom, still missing a week after vanishing from the streets of Belfast; Brennan would have to make sure Michael O'Flaherty didn't try to involve himself in whatever was going on there. God love Michael for his tender heart and the loving eyes through which he regarded the land of his forebears. Michael would walk through a bombed-out store front in Derry and see a pot of gold at the end of the rainbow made by the sun blazing through the shards of glass. But he'd be all right as long as he didn't meddle in the Belfast crisis; there was no pot of gold waiting at the end of that.

Brennan was jolted by a sudden loud bang as the front door flew open and several men burst into the pub. Before he could take in what was happening, one of the men vaulted right over the bar and landed beside Finn.

The stranger from the back of the pub had bolted out of his seat and joined the invading party. He said, "Finn Burke, you're under arrest for forgery, using a false instrument . . ." The list of charges went on and on. He had Finn's arms pinned behind his back. Finn's face was expressionless. Brennan got to his feet and approached the bar.

One of the policemen shot his arm out to keep Brennan away. "Leave him be, sir."

Finn spoke up, "Let me have a moment with my priest, boys, would you?"

"No, Finn, we're not going to wait here so you can pass the secrets of the empire along to Leo Killeen."

"Not Leo, no. We have a priest in our midst right now: Father . . . Brennan."

The new arrivals looked over and saw Brennan's collar. Brennan made an effort to arrange his features into what he hoped was an expression of bland and benign goodwill. He suspected he looked like a simpleton. With obvious reluctance, the guards released their grip on Finn and let him go. Finn grasped Brennan's elbow and moved him a few feet away.

"Stop where you are, Finn! You'll be having your conflab right here."

Finn said, "*In ainm an Athar agus an Mhic agus an Spioraid Naoimh. Amen.*" Finn and Brennan both made the sign of the cross. Finn spoke softly in Brennan's ear. "Bless me Father, for I have sinned. It has been three months since my last confession. I confess to Almighty God and to you Father that I have items in the tunnel of this building and I would like you to go down there and remove them. Now put your right hand on my left shoulder."

Brennan put his hand out in a priestly gesture and placed it on Finn's shoulder. Not having reached the point where sins had been specified and absolution could be given, Brennan just mumbled the words, "Go my son and sin no more." Despite the dire circumstances, it was all he could do to keep a straight face while uttering the pious formula. When he was speaking, Finn put his own right hand on Brennan's as if to thank him. Brennan felt something being pushed between his fingers. Something small and metallic. He squeezed his fingers together to grasp it.

"Stand apart, gentlemen!" one of the guards admonished. "Sorry, Father."

Finn stepped back, and Brennan stood there with a key secreted in his right hand.

"Time to go, Finn. Take a look around you now. You won't be seein' this place again for a while."

They hustled him from the pub. Brennan followed. He heard a click. It sounded like the shutter of a camera, the kind news photographers . . . there it was again, and there was the photographer. Tipped off by the gardaí. That was low, thought Brennan; they must really have it in for him. The guards opened the back door of the cruiser and pushed Finn inside. He turned to face Brennan. "Get my curate in to tend bar, will you, Father?"

Brennan nodded, but he was barely listening. He had other things on his mind, namely the tunnel beneath the pub and the things Finn wanted removed. Evidence. Proceeds of crime. No doubt Brennan himself would be committing a crime by tampering with the stuff. But Finn was counting on him. And the information — cryptic though it was — had been imparted in the form of a confession. So Brennan wasn't about to break the seal of the confessional by seeking counsel from anyone else. Monty Collins, for instance. He was on his own. And he wouldn't have much time. Surely the gardaí would be planning to search Finn's house and this place, his second home. Brennan didn't like this at all. This wasn't the way he went about things, arseways and in a hurry. But he had no choice.

Finn wanted the bar open, and his assistant bartender in place. Brennan had no idea how to reach Sean Nugent, but he would worry about that later. First things first. He went behind the bar and cast his eyes about for what he needed. The big key hanging on a nail was likely the key to the building; he took it to the door and tried it out. Yes. He then found a pen, a piece of paper, and a thumbtack, and printed up a note. "Closed till noon. Sorry for the inconvenience." He scratched out the Latin cross he signed with out of habit, and replaced it with "FB." Finn would have done better, but there was no time for niceties. Brennan tacked the note to the door, locked up, and looked at the small key Finn had slipped him during confession time. Let the excavation begin.

He headed for the basement door. He saw a string hanging from a light bulb, and pulled it. The light wasn't much, but it was better than subterranean blackness. He made his way down a set of crumbling concrete steps, bracing himself with one hand on the damp, cold walls. Down in the cellar there was one window large enough to admit a barrel of stout and clean enough to provide a bit of light.

It was only when he got to the bottom of the stairs that Brennan remembered being down here as a child, he and two other young fellows. He had sneaked them in when his grandfather was occupied at the bar. Told his friends there were secret items down there, and they could borrow them and play war with them. He hadn't thought of that in years. When he had led the other two into the tunnel, he heard an ungodly roar come out of his father's mouth. Declan and Finn were down there with a wrench and a big wooden crate. Brennan didn't see what was in it because his father threatened to give him a toe in the hole, and no football for a month and a half, if he didn't get his arse up those stairs and out of this building and take those two little gobshites with him before the oul fellow counted to five.

Out of that ill wind had come knowledge that stood Brennan in good stead now: he knew where to find the entrance to the tunnel. It wouldn't have been obvious to a casual visitor to the cellar, if one could imagine a casual trip down here. All that met the eye were kegs, taps, glasses, and other paraphernalia associated with the running of a bar, along with several large pieces of furniture. Nowhere in the walls or the visible parts of the floor was there anything that looked like the door to a tunnel. But Brennan headed right for it. He was grateful to see a flashlight on a shelf near the window. And it worked. He grabbed it and picked his way through the clutter to a filing cabinet resting on a shabby Oriental carpet. The trap door was under there. He shoved the cabinet aside and lifted the carpet to reveal the door, which was made of planks. A padlock secured it to a sheet of metal bolted into the stone floor. He inserted the key into the lock, gave it a twist, got some resistance, and wrenched it around again. The lock sprang open. He lifted the wooden door on its hinges and eased it back against a chair.

The tunnel was accessible by a ladder, which had seen better days but served the purpose. Brennan climbed down and found himself in a passage about six and a half feet high and five feet wide. He cursed his decision to set out for the day in his black clerical suit, which was now grey with dust. He'd have to send it to the cleaners. But he put it out of his mind for the time being. The walls of the tunnel were made of stones and bricks, and the ceiling was covered with sheets of plywood, propped up by posts along the sides. He shone his light ahead and tried to estimate the tunnel's length. It was hard to tell. About twenty feet from where he stood, the floor seemed to slope upwards. Not surprisingly it felt damp, and he could hear water dripping somewhere. But he didn't have time to stand there and soak up the ambience; he had a job to do. Good thing he wasn't claustrophobic, given that he was enclosed in a jerry-built confined space several feet under the ground. It was like being in the catacombs in Rome, except he didn't expect to see any saints buried down here. He walked forward a few steps and noticed an opening in the wall to his left; he peered in and saw some old uniforms and caps wrapped in clear plastic. And ammunition belts, the kind worn diagonally across the chest. He moved ahead and found another opening on his right. Well! That one was interesting; there was a stash of rifles in it, a couple of pistols, and an old-style machine gun. A Thompson? There was a nickname for those, he seemed to recall. What was it? Something from the Al Capone days on the other side of the Atlantic. A "Chicago typewriter," that was it. Interesting find, but Brennan couldn't claim to be surprised, in light of his family's history. He continued his exploration. He came to a part of the wall where the bricks were loose, and he removed one to take a look. His light didn't show anything, but he put his hand in anyway and felt around. Nothing.

The next opening contained a collection of stone Celtic crosses, statues that had a pagan look to them, and others that brought to mind St. Patrick. Other images were of women in robes: Druids perhaps? Many of these items were unfinished, eyes or hands yet to be carved. The tools of the trade were there as well: grinders and power saws of some kind, and jugs of chemicals. One statue, of a young woman whose fingers were missing, was clean and new-looking on one side, drab and old on the other. Being restored? No. Brennan looked more closely. It was the opposite. Brand new items were being doctored to look ancient. The words of the arresting officer came back to him: ". . . forgery, using a false instrument . . ." It wasn't long before he came upon what must have been the false instruments, if that meant, as he now suspected, false documents. In the next hole in the wall were papers piled on a wooden crate, along with a fountain pen and a packet of green paper discs, the round seals you see on the bottom of official documents. Brennan saw a heavy black object with a handle and what appeared to be a round stamp; he had seen this kind of thing in lawyers' offices. A notary stamp. He picked up a piece of paper and saw that it was a title deed with no details filled in. He affixed one of the green seals to the page, slipped the paper into the black notary stamp, and pressed down on the handle, then read what had been impressed upon the paper: "James Shackleton-Gore, Notary Public, City and County of Dublin." All of this would be of great interest to the gardaí. But the guards weren't going to see it.

What was Brennan supposed to do with all this stuff? He couldn't transport it in a cab; might as well wrap it up in a big red bow and present it to Garda HQ. But first things first; he needed bags to pack the stuff in. There were burlap sacks in the basement and, if those did not suffice, he was sure there must be bags of some sort upstairs. He would climb up and check. But first he wanted to make sure he had everything. He walked deeper into the tunnel until the floor began its upward slope. The ceiling didn't rise at the same level, so he had to crouch as he made his way forward. Then he came to a dead end, a big slab of concrete. The foundation of another building? No. Brennan could see gravel and hardened lumps of cement on the floor. The slab had been formed down here and put in place to close the underground passage. Evidently, the tunnel had originally continued and, given the upward angle, opened somewhere outdoors. This tended to confirm what Brennan had heard in whispers when he was growing up in Dublin: that there was an escape route built underneath the old IRA drinking spot.

An hour later Brennan was upstairs, standing inside the doorway of the pub with several extra-large, very heavy plastic rubbish bags full of statues, uniforms, papers, other miscellaneous items, and guns. There was nothing left in the tunnel. He had closed and locked the trap door, replaced the carpet over it, and heaved the filing cabinet back into its spot on the rug. But his work was not yet done. He had to find a place to stash the goods. He didn't have a car with him; he had arrived on foot. So he looked out the window and surveyed the territory. Across the street was a church known as the "black church," which, he knew, was no longer being used. There was a pile of rubbish bags and debris beside the wall of the building. That might provide at least a temporary holding place for Finn's things. The police would likely search the entire area, particularly if they found nothing in the pub itself. But they would start with the pub. Brennan decided that was his only hope for now. He hoisted two bags onto his back and was about to open the pub door when he saw two men approaching.

He flattened himself against the wall inside. And felt like the villain in a bad vaudeville production; all that was missing was the cheesy moustache.

"Closed till noon," one of the men read aloud. "It's past that now."

"Fuck! As if I didn't have a thirst on me that would drop a camel. Well, there's nothing for it but to come back later."

"Or go to Gallagher's."

"No, we'll stick with Christy's. Finn had to run out somewhere. He'll be back."

Brennan heard them walking away. A few seconds later, the coast seemed clear. He opened the pub door, stepped outside with his bags, glanced to the left and to the right, and tried not to look any more shifty and vaudevillian than necessary. Best to present himself as if he lugged heavy loads of rubbish, or illegal goods, out of Christy Burke's pub every day of the week. He crossed the street to the side of the church, where he saw an old table with a broken leg, a scarred, paint-spattered bookcase, even a badly dented deep freezer with bags of garbage piled on top. There was other refuse littering the ground. People were obviously using the old church property as a rubbish tip. Brennan dropped his load on top of the pile. His bags were clean and shiny; the others had dust and leaves and bird shite on them. He wished he could age the bags the way Finn had aged his newly manufactured "ancient" artifacts, but he didn't have that option. He did the best he could and walked away. As far as he could tell, no one had observed him. But there was no way of knowing whether curious eyes watched from the windows of the other buildings in the street. He was nervous when he had to make a second run with the long, awkward parcel of rifles under his arm. They shifted within the bags, and started slipping out, and he nearly lost the whole consignment in the middle of the street. But he managed to keep them covered, then deposited them with the other objects in the pile of debris at the old church.

He was just straightening up when a car appeared at the corner. Brennan tried to resist looking at it, but he couldn't help himself. The occupants paid him no mind, and he walked away with relief coursing through him. He went back for the rest of the bags and dumped them in place.

He returned to the pub, satisfied that there was nothing else he could do to clean up the crime scene. He checked his watch. More than two hours had passed since Finn's arrest. It was time to open up. And he didn't have a barman, didn't have young Sean's number. But Brennan himself knew his way around a glass of porter and a jar of whiskey. He could pour a proper pint if called upon to do so. Not, however, while dressed in a dusty, dirty clerical suit and Roman collar. It wouldn't do to be seen covered with dust and dirt even if he didn't have a job to do and an obligation to look presentable while doing it. He called Monty Collins at his hotel room.

"Hello?"

Brennan sent up a *Te Deum* that Collins was there to take the call. "Monty. How quick can you get moving?"

"What's happening?"

"I'll fill you in when you get here."

"Here being?"

"Christy's. Can you go over to my place first? Tell them to let you into my room. Get me a T-shirt and a pair of pants, and bring them to the pub."

"Should I even inquire why you are stranded without clothing this early in the day, Father? I've known you to be *déshabillé* following a night of debauchery, but . . ."

"I'll explain when you get here. Oh, and bring me my soap."

"You and your soap. Bless me, Father, for I have sinned. It has been three hours and twenty minutes since my last shower. Were you toilet trained too early as a child, or what? I've never met anyone so —"

"Fuck off and get over here." Brennan hung up the phone and looked around the bar to see what he should do to prepare for the day's custom. By the time Monty arrived, twenty-five minutes later, he had everything set to go.

"Thank you," he said to Monty, as he grabbed his soap and clothing and made a beeline for the men's room. "I'll be right out, and we'll open up."

"We?"

"You heard me."

He left Monty in a state of bewilderment, went in to the loo, stripped down, gave himself a thorough soaping and a good rinse, then put on the black T-shirt and casual pants Monty had provided. He emerged, drying his hair with a handful of paper towel, and said,

"All right. Open the door and remove the sign I put out there. Oh! Hold on."

Monty waited while Brennan went back into the jacks. There, hanging over the door to one of the stalls was his filthy clerical suit. Evidence that would tell against him if it were left on the premises. He grabbed it, balled it up and carried it out of the washroom and over to Monty. "Shove this in a bag and take it up the street. You'll see St. Joseph's Convent School. Stash it out of sight somewhere on the property."

Monty looked at him, gobsmacked. "This is getting weirder by the minute. This is your suit? A spoiled priest outfit, by the look of it. What happened to it? And why do you want —"

"Go along with me on this, Collins. I'll explain it all to you later."

"Yes, Father."

Monty took the suit, turned, and went to the door. He opened it and announced that Christy's was once again in business. Then he departed on his unlikely mission with the spoiled priest outfit, and the spoiled priest got on with his tasks.

"What does a man have to do to get a drink in here?" The voice came from a short, unkempt fellow standing by the bar.

"What'll you have?"

"I'll have a pint of Guinness. That is, if you're able for it."

"I am," Brennan assured him, and took his place behind the bar that had been manned by a Burke since Anno Domini 1919.

Brennan picked up a pint glass and set it under the Guinness tap at an angle of forty-five degrees, reached for the tap handle, pulled it all the way back, and poured about three quarters of a pint, then put it aside to settle. When he decided the time was right, he put the glass straight under the tap, poured until a dome appeared at the top, and handed it to the man. A perfect two-part pour.

He served a couple more patrons and found himself adapting quite comfortably to the routine.

Monty returned following his errand, looked towards the bar, and gaped at his friend. "Brennan! After a fraction of a second of astonishment, I now see this as completely normal. Why wouldn't you be behind that bar? You look utterly at home there."

"I am. What can I get for you?"

"I'll have a Singapore Sling with a cherry and a twist."

"Coming right up."

He poured a Guinness and, when it was ready, handed it to Monty. "Here you are, my lad. That will be 170p."

Monty pulled out a five-pound note and said, grandly, "Keep the change, my good man."

"I intend to." Brennan stuck the bill in the cash register.

"Now. Will you tell me what the hell is going on? Where's the previous generation?"

"My uncle is indisposed today."

"Would a hair of the dog cure his ills?"

"Nothing I can do for him here. You may be able to help."

"Not legal difficulties!"

"He was arrested this morning. But I can't get into it now . . . What can I do for you, sir?" he said to an elderly gentleman who was waiting serenely by the bar.

"Tullamore Dew, if you'd be so kind."

"Certainly."

He turned to the array of bottles behind him and poured the man his drink. He took the payment and made change as if he had been doing it all his life.

"How many bartenders do you figure have their doctorate in theology, Brennan?" Monty asked.

Brennan smiled. "They're all theologians, I'm thinking. All the good ones anyway. Philosophers, psychologists —"

"Good heavens!" Now it was Michael O'Flaherty. "Brennan! What's going on? I couldn't reach either of you on the phone so I thought you might be here. But I never would have guessed . . . Why are you behind the bar? But then, why wouldn't you be? You fit right in there!"

"Where's Finn been hidin' *you*?" The speaker was a young woman — well, younger than Brennan; she may have been forty — with short curly black hair, freckles, and bright blue eyes.

"He's had me in training," Brennan answered. "It took a while for me to get the hang of it. I've been out of things for a time."

"You mean the kind of time Finn himself goes away for, couple of years at a stretch, that sort of thing?"

"You said a mouthful there."

"Ah. So is there anything else you've been missing? Are you in need of a refresher course in life's other pleasures perhaps?"

"Well now, there's a story there as well. I —"

He was cut off by a crashing noise, then a shout. What now? The door was opened and a squad of guards poured in. Again. This time the lead man was brandishing a paper.

"Everybody out! We have a warrant to search this place. The officers will accompany you outside. Don't take anything with you except your own belongings."

"You!" one officer addressed Brennan, who scowled back at him. "Open the cash register."

"A robbery, is it?"

"It will all be returned to you, every punt accounted for. Open the cash and step away from the bar."

Brennan looked over at Monty, who was reaching for the cop's paper. Monty said, "Could I have a look at that, guard? I'm a lawyer and, for the time being, I'm Christy Burke's solicitor. I'd like to see the warrant."

The guard hesitated, then handed it over.

Monty skimmed it, frowning, then handed it back. He looked at Brennan, who nodded, *Yes, Finn's in the soup.* The cop folded the paper and stuffed it in his pocket. "All right, everybody. Make your way outside."

Everyone filed out under the watchful eyes of the gardaí, then gathered outside in the bright midday sun. Brennan, Michael, and Monty passed the evicted drinkers, some of whom were peering in the windows, trying to see what the police were up to.

Michael started to speak but the young woman with the curly hair got there first. She was looking up at Brennan with a smile playing about her lips. "Now which one of the Burkes are you?"

"Brennan. Declan's son."

"Declan would be . . . Finn's brother?"

"Right."

"So where have you been? More important, where might you be tonight?"

"Probably behind the bar if the guards leave us in peace."

She noticed Michael then, and said, "Who's this fine fellow now? Another new face in the neighbourhood."

"This is Monsignor O'Flaherty. Visiting from Canada."

"Hello, Monsignor." Then to Brennan, "How do you know the monsignor?"

"I'm his curate."

"Well, yeah . . ."

"I mean curate in the true sense of the word. He's my pastor, I'm his priest."

"You're having me on."

"I'm not."

"No!" she cried.

Brennan nodded.

"I'm gutted," she said. She shook her head and walked away.

He smiled after her for a second or two, then took the opportunity to ask Monty about the search warrant. "What are they looking for?" He tried to sound casual as he contemplated the fact that whatever they were looking for, he had snatched it from their grasp before they could make their move.

"Guns," Monty replied, "and artifacts of some kind, manufacturing or craft-making equipment, a variety of things."

"Ah." There wasn't anything else he could say, because everything he knew had come from Finn's half-arsed confession.

"I wonder why they didn't have the warrant when they made the arrest. They must have received new information. Maybe he opened up when they got him to the station. Hard to imagine, though, from what I've seen of him."

"Wouldn't happen."

"Well, we'll see how it plays out. Has anyone been in touch with him?" Monty asked.

"Not since I watched them drag him out of here in handcuffs." He wasn't about to go into details.

"Where would they have taken him?" Michael asked. "Up the street to Mountjoy Prison, I suppose."

"Not yet, I don't imagine," Monty said. "Police station first, most likely. They'll process him, take him before a judge, who'll either release him or order him remanded to Mountjoy or some other institution."

"I should go find him," said Brennan.

"He'd probably prefer that you stay with the ship, Brennan," Monty advised.

"They'll let him out on bail, though, right, Monty?" Michael asked.

"I don't know Irish law but, to the extent that it's similar to ours, they'd have to hold a bail hearing. Whether he'd be released would depend on a number of factors. Including his history. If it's not his first offence —" Monty looked at Brennan, who gave a quick shake of his head "— then that might affect his chances. And if, for instance, he's on probation or on parole already, it won't go well for him."

Nobody got a drink at Christy Burke's for the rest of that day or evening. The pub was cordoned off as a crime scene. The pub regulars were indignant and convened an emergency meeting to decide where they would go for the rest of the day. They voted to take their business to Dec Gallagher's and headed down to Dominick Street to their temporary headquarters.

"I'm going to stop in at St. Francis Xavier's Church in Gardiner Street and say a prayer for Finn," Michael announced.

"Thanks, Mike," said Brennan. "I'll do the same when I get back to my own parish."

"What are you fellows up to this evening?"

"I can't speak for Monty, but I've had enough excitement for one day."

"I can believe it. See you tomorrow, perhaps." With that, Michael took his leave.

Monty was showing no inclination to leave. "Well, Brennan, what now?"

"Off to the convent, I guess," Brennan replied.

"Oh, yes, the convent. They're giving away clothing to the poor and the defrocked today."

"Bless them."

"I'd better accompany you on your shopping trip, in case you want to try something on. I'll tell you whether it makes you look fat or not."

"How d'yeh think yeh'd look with a fat lip?"

"Like if somebody punched me in the mouth, you mean? Instead of doing that, why don't you tell me what's going on? Start with the suit."

"The suit's the end of the story."

"Which is?"

"I did some cleaning up."

Monty looked him in the eye. "You cleaned up the pub. Somehow I find it hard to believe that even someone as fastidious as you would make cleanliness a priority, given the events of the day. So I am left to conclude that you cleaned *out* the pub. In anticipation of the police."

"I shall not attempt to influence what you think."

"And whatever you found you can't talk about."

"I had a very short conversation with Finn while the guards where there."

"How did you get away with that?"

"I was attired in the garb of a man of God."

"They let him talk to his priest. A confession, perhaps."

Brennan made a "maybe, maybe not" gesture with his left hand. "Come on, let's get to the convent school."

They began walking up Mountjoy Street, and Monty continued his interrogation. "You and Uncle Finn had a chat that may or may not have been a confession, which led you to clean out the pub. And you got your clothes dirty in the process, which suggests that you were in a part of the building the rest of us don't get to see. Because what we get to see is a nice, clean pub. So then you were clever enough to realize that if the police had a look around and found nothing incriminating but did find a very dusty suit of clothes, they would wonder whether someone had been hard at work sanitizing the place. Good thinking. I've always been impressed by how much more intelligent you are than the rest of my criminal clients."

"Thank you."

"Of course, anyone hearing this story . . ."

"Nobody's going to hear it. Right, Montague?"

"Not from me. But having heard it myself, or tantalizing bits of it, I can only speculate as to the whereabouts of the things removed from the pub, if there were any things removed from the pub."

"It's all been taken care of."

"I see."

"Ah. St. Joseph's."

They stood before a large brick building with a statue of the saint in a niche and a cross on top.

"You won't make me go on a scavenger hunt, I hope."

"No. Just around the corner there."

Brennan went around the corner and retrieved the bag containing his suit.

"Good. I'm going to head back to my room, then stop into the church for a bit. You?"

"Back to the hotel, then out for a little sightseeing."

They set out for the Christchurch and Liberties area of Dublin where they had their respective rooms.

"Why don't I take the suit to the dry-cleaning service at the hotel?"

"Good plan. Thank you."

"Think nothing of it. I look at this as just another in a series of bizarre episodes that seem to occur any time I go on vacation with the Burkes."

Burke nodded. What could he say?

When he awoke the next morning, the first thing he did after showering was collect the newspapers. Sure enough, there was Finn being led away from Christy's by the guards. One paper even called him a "reputed crime boss." The dark glasses and the insouciant expression on his face did nothing to dispel that suspicion. And it turned out that Finn was on parole for a previous offence, a money-laundering charge. Not only that, but the gardaí claimed he had breached the terms of his parole by leaving the country, that is, slipping across the border into Northern Ireland, so that was another strike against him. Finn wouldn't be pouring pints at Christy Burke's tonight.

And the paper carried a photo of Japanese passengers getting off a plane at Shannon. Brennan recalled seeing them in an RTÉ newscast, before his uncle had struck the television dumb with his fist. The Japanese stood smiling at the photographer. Christ almighty. Every single one of them had on a tall hat with a brim and a buckle. A crowd of Irish-Japanese leprechauns. "Father, forgive them. They know not what they do," Brennan intoned. Then he saw the next photo, the whole crowd of them standing forlorn in what looked like a bog, each with a piece of paper in his or her hand. The article said:

> Mr. Burke is accused of defrauding a group of Japanese nationals in connection with a land purchase scheme. The one hundred forty-four Japanese people say they each paid anywhere from five to ten thousand pounds for plots of land here in the Republic. They chartered a plane and travelled here to visit their land, only to find

there are no such plots of land. Mr. Burke is said to have made as much as one million pounds in the fraudulent scheme. No court date has been set for the hearing of the charges.

†

Finn Burke's new living quarters weren't much of a hike from his pub. Walk up Mountjoy Street, which becomes Berkeley Street and leads to the Mater Misericordiae Hospital, which fronts on Eccles Street. Eccles is famous, or at least the house at number seven is, as the fictional home of Leopold and Molly Bloom in *Ulysses*. But Brennan's destination was more in the nature of infamy. Behind the Mater is the North Circular Road, and across the road is the Mountjoy Prison. After the charges were read out in court, Finn had been remanded to the Joy, and he was about to have his first visitor.

From where Brennan stood he saw a complex of red brick and grey buildings, and two huge octagonal chimneys. He crossed the street and approached the gate. It took a while but, after a bit of bureaucratic procedure, Brennan Burke, dressed as a priest on a mission to the incarcerated, was facing Finn Burke, the incarcerated, in a prison visiting room. A long, wide table ran down the centre of the room, with a foot-high divider separating prisoners from visitors. Two officers, one at each end of the room, kept watch over the proceedings.

"Welcome to the Joy, Father. Make yourself at home."

"Thank you, Finn. I'll make an effort to fit in and enjoy my time here."

"As will I."

It was the first time this trip that Brennan had seen Finn without his dark glasses on. A pair of grey-blue eyes fastened on him from across the table.

"Will they soon be releasing you, Finn?"

"I'm settling in quite comfortably, let's say, Brennan."

Brennan took that as a no.

"I hope the guards treated you gently after they removed you from my sight."

"They didn't give me a thumping, if that's what you mean. But my old nemesis Inspector Feeney, who has attempted to thwart my career at every turn, was there to greet me with a whole host of slanderous, unproven allegations. They nicked me for land fraud, but Feeney would have egged them on about everything from fake little artifacts that never hurt a soul to automatic weapons . . . I take it they went back to the pub with a warrant?"

Brennan nodded.

A prison warder walked past them, and they fell silent. When he was gone, Brennan asked, "Who is James Shackleton-Gore?"

"You're lookin' at him."

"Will you be fighting the charges?"

"I'm always up for a good fight. Be sure to get yourself a seat in the Four Courts when I make my speech from the dock."

"I wouldn't miss it. What will be the theme of your speech, if I may ask?"

"Redistribution of wealth, Brennan. This is not a rich country, as you know. They keep saying that's going to change, that we're going to reap huge benefits from the European Union, that the 1990s will be the decade when the Irish economy takes off at long last. Well, so be it. In the meantime, in my own small way, I do what I can to improve our balance of trade."

"You're doing good works."

"I am."

"But surely you don't give away all the money you make from your endeavours."

"You've seen my home, Brennan. A nice enough house but it's plain to see I haven't been spending the money on high-tech items, swimming pools, or luxury automobiles. And I pay all taxes owing to the Republic of Ireland, God bless it and save it. Don't be looking skeptical there, Father, I pay up like clockwork every year."

"Does it give you pause at all, though? Taking these people's money?"

"People who are willing to spend money on supposedly stolen sacred artifacts, or wee plots of land in someone else's country just so they can say they own a bit of the oul sod, people like that have too much money on their hands. And I feel very little compunction about relieving them of it. Particularly since the vast majority of Irish people do not have that kind of money to throw around."

"Didn't people find out after they bought the crosses and statues and things that they were fake, or at least questionable?"

"None of them came whinging to me about it."

"But wouldn't they look into it?"

"They knew they were dealing with a crook, Brennan, somebody plundering and desecrating ancient burial grounds and stealing the contents for profit. Or at least that's what they thought they knew. In fact, there weren't any burial grounds. Just my little craft shop in the tunnel of Christy's pub. We claimed there were three, or was it four, sites, known only to me and my people. Sites we could visit only in the dark of night. Just a bit of *codology* for the tourists; they lapped it up. They were complicit in the crime. They didn't want anyone probing it. And they didn't want to acknowledge they'd been had. Feck 'em."

"And the land scheme. How did that work?"

"Worked fine, till the whole feckin' crowd of them got together and decided to land here at the same time. Most of the people who buy land just stay home and wave the deed around their local on St. Patrick's Day. They don't get on a plane and fly all the way over here to stand on a few square feet of bog. But the Japanese! Jaysus!"

"These plots of land," Brennan began, and then wondered if there really were any plots of land. "Or the descriptions on the deeds. What location are we talking about?"

"Well, there's land up in County Mayo. Most of it's bog, but there's a small part of it that's green and scenic and has some hedgerows and stone walls on it. The occasional sheep wanders by, when my lads can corral one of the creatures into their lorry and transport it to the field and give it a smack on the arse and get it to stand up and look into the camera. It all looks brilliant in the brochures. I got hold of the land years ago. And I've been selling it ever since!"

In spite of himself, Brennan had to laugh out loud. He asked, "What are your chances, do you think?"

"Well, now, that will depend on whether the guards find any evidence linking me to the crimes."

Brennan looked around him, then spoke *sotto voce*. "I don't see how they will."

"Because there's nothing there to implicate me."

"I'm sure you're right."

"Even though they've searched."

"Correct."

Something flared up in Brennan's mind for an instant, then it was gone. Something about the tunnel and the items that had been stashed down there. He'd have to try to bring it to mind later. For now, he focused on the man sitting across from him. He said to Finn, "Lovely old neighbourhood. My old neighbourhood and yours. But a bit run down. You'd wonder sometimes why the city doesn't take better care of some of the properties there. The church, other buildings. Old furniture, rubbish not picked up, that sort of thing. Shame, really."

Finn looked into Brennan's eyes. After a few seconds, he said, "The black church. A fine landmark." Brennan nodded in agreement. In collaboration. "Well, Bren, I'm sure you have better things to do than spend your day in the Joy. I appreciate your visit, and I hope you'll come back and see me again. The time is long in here, and I get a bit lonely. You know, another fellow I'd be pleased to see is Larry Healey. Works out on the Naas Road. Perhaps you could tell him I'd enjoy a visit."

"I'll do that. And I'll be back to see you myself."

"Thank you. Here, now, before you go, have them show you around. I imagine you were too young to visit the place last time you had a close family member incarcerated here. O'Reilly!" Finn shouted to one of the guards. "Show my confessor some hospitality, would you?"

"I'm on duty now, Finn. I can't be leaving the likes of you to your own devices."

"Where's Doyle then?"

"He's just coming on."

"Good. Have him give Father Burke a little tour. And make sure he sees the helipad."

"You and your helipad! You're living on past glories, Finn. We're in the nineties now."

"Thank you for the reminder, O'Reilly. The twentieth anniversary will be coming up next year in October. Halloween, to be exact. I think I'll put on a costume that day."

"Oh, you think you'll be choosing your own wardrobe by then, do you? More likely you'll still be sitting in here, wearing the same prison fashions as all the other fine citizens in this place."

"No, no, I'll be out for good behaviour, but you needn't shed any tears at my departure. I'll be sure to drop in for a visit. Keep an eye out for me that day, O'Reilly. I'll be dressed as a prison warder, and I'll have my face painted a bright, glowing red!"

Finn turned to his nephew. "Do you know what we're on about, Brennan?"

"Would this be the helicopter escape in 1973? It made the news in New York."

"Sure it made news around the world. And I, the humble prisoner you see before you today, was right here on the ground when it happened."

"Were you now."

"Yes, I was here. For a short stint on trumped-up charges, then as ' now. I was in the exercise yard when I heard the rotors of a helicopter approaching. Never to my dying day will I forget the sight of it. I'm looking up. We all are. And we see it coming out of the sky towards the prison and, Jaysus, isn't it heading right for us? It's going to land! Right here in the prison yard. And the most comical thing about it is that the man in charge of the prison that day thought nothing of it, thought it was Paddy Donegan, the minister of defence, paying a visit by helicopter. It's right there in the parliamentary debates. Jack Lynch got up in the Dáil the next day and said, 'The officer can be forgiven for thinking it was the minister of defence flying in by helicopter, as the minister is wont to use helicopters as other ministers are wont to use state cars.' So I'll be dressed as that poor, red-faced prison official on the anniversary."

"You're a part of history, Finn!"

"I am indeed, but as a witness only. I was as gobsmacked as everyone else when the helicopter landed in the yard, and three IRA men got on board and were lifted into the skies above the jail. What a sight!"

"How could they orchestrate such a thing? Where did they get the helicopter?"

"Hijacked it. Told the pilot no harm would come to him if he did as he was told, fly into Dublin without alerting air traffic control, and there he was before he knew it, hovering over the Joy and coming down in the yard. Kevin Mallon directed him down using semaphore! Mallon, J.B. O'Hagan, and Seamus Twomey were airlifted out. Twomey was chief of staff of the 'RA at the time. The rest of us, when we caught on what was happening, blocked the screws from getting in the way."

He turned to the warder. "You wouldn't bring us a pint to celebrate that day of glory, would you, O'Reilly?"

"Sorry we can't accommodate you in the manner you're used to, Mr. Burke."

"Ah! The memory of it. Guess who I got a call from that day? Long distance."

"Would it have been my oul fellow? You should have seen the smile on his face when that item of news came on the television."

"And you should have heard him on the phone that night, Bren. He was beside himself with excitement, wanted to hear every single detail, minute by minute, who was where and who did what. And it has to be said, he had run afoul of the 'RA himself, hence his exile in America, but his heart was in the right . . . well, he was still interested in the comings and goings, and the flyings, of his former comrades."

"All right, all right, wrap it up, Finn," the guard said. "No offence, Father, but Mr. Burke's history lesson is over for now. Here's Doyle."

So Brennan was shown around by Doyle, who seemed friendly enough. Not every guard, or prisoner, they came across was as genial. But the other officials did nothing to stop them, and Brennan saw the cell blocks radiating out from the centre, the tiny, cramped cells, and the place where young Kevin Barry was hanged in 1920, at the age of eighteen, for his role in the War of Independence. Brennan wondered which cell his own father had been in, back in the 1940s, a few years prior to his midnight voyage to the Americas.

"A lot of history in this place, Father," Doyle said. "A great many patriots were executed here during the Troubles in the twenties. Well, you probably know all that. Doesn't happen anymore. The last was in 1954."

"Glad to hear it, Mr. Doyle. Thank you so much for taking the time to show me around."

"You're welcome, Father. I'll show you out now."

✝

The Naas Road. That was the location of the other family business, Burke Transport. Larry Healey must be connected with the company.

Brennan decided to hop on a bus rather than pester his cousin for a loan of his car.

It wasn't long before he was standing in a parking lot in an industrial estate off the Naas Road, dwarfed by several enormous tractor-trailers, at the headquarters of Burke Transport Company. There were vehicles of every size, ranging from eighteen-wheelers to utility vans. Most bore the Burke logo but a couple, he noticed, were plain white and had no licence plates on them. He looked into the open door of a garage and saw a green van undergoing a paint job; the new colour appeared to be a flat black. He headed for the door of the office building to ask after Larry Healey. A young red-haired girl at the reception desk smiled at him and said she would page Mr. Healey. She did, and a minute later a short, muscular man in his forties came into the foyer, wiping his hands on a rag.

"Gentleman inquiring after you, Larry."

"What can I do for you, sir? Em, Father? You'll understand if I don't shake your hand."

"That's quite all right. Call me Brennan. I'm Declan's son. He was before your time, but you may have heard the name."

"Oh, yes. The name's well known to us here. He ran the company in the 1940s."

"That's right. Could I speak with you for a bit?"

"Sure." Healey nodded in the direction of the parking lot, and the two of them went outside.

"You may know, Larry, that Finn has landed himself in a spot of trouble and is currently a guest of the warders of Mountjoy Prison."

"I'd heard that."

"I was in to see him and he said he'd be grateful if you'd pay him a visit. He finds the time long, you know."

A smile flitted across Healey's face. "Is that right? Well, I'll be sure to pop in and say hello."

"Thank you, then, Larry. I won't keep you now."

"How'd you get here, Brennan? You came from the city centre, did you?"

"I took the bus."

"No need of that." He gestured to all the vehicles standing in the lot. "I'll grab a set of keys and run you into the city."

Healey returned with his keys and directed Brennan to one of the white utility vans. They got in and drove to the centre of town, engaging in small talk about Dublin and about Larry's extended family, some of whom had immigrated to various places in Canada and the U.S. Brennan thanked Larry when he let him off.

"Don't mention it. I'll swing round to the Joy now. I expect Finn will want to see me without delay."

Chapter 4

Michael

Young Nugent was tending bar when Michael walked into Christy's on Friday.

"Ah! Sean. They found you."

"They didn't have to, Michael. I heard the news and reported for duty."

"You'll have a lot of hours to cover with Finn off the job."

"I'll put in a bit more time than usual, but I've been talking to Brennan; he and I will spell each other off till Finn returns, or, well, till we see what's going to happen. Brennan tells me he's doing some teaching up at the seminary in Maynooth; his work here will be a bit of a change of pace for him."

"It will indeed. Where are your regular customers today?"

"They'll be making their way in soon, I expect."

"Well, I'll have a glass of juice, if you'd be so kind."

"Orange?"

"That would be grand."

Michael took his drink to a table and sat down. He lost himself in the mix of horror and foolishness that provided fodder for newspapers all over the world.

"Michael!"

Michael looked up and saw Father Leo Killeen standing at the bar with a newly poured pint in his hand.

"Leo! Will you join me?"

Leo sat, took a sip of his pint, and nodded at Michael. "I thought I'd stop in and see if Brennan was here. Take a walk up the street and pay Finn a visit."

"He's not here, but I'd be happy to accompany you if you like."

"Very good. We'll wet our throats for a few minutes, then head out."

The two priests indulged themselves in a bit of church chat. What parish was Leo in? Aughrim Street in Stoneybatter, in the northwest part of the city. Church of the Holy Family. Did Michael know it? He had been to the church once. Beautiful stained glass and a lovely altar, and he knew they had an Irish-language Mass. Yes, it was Leo who usually said the Irish Mass. How long had Leo been there? Since the Vikings landed, or so it seemed. Did he live in a parish house? He lived in a house owned by the parish, on the same street as the church, but not a rectory as such. Where was Michael staying? A bed and breakfast owned by people he had met in his role as tour guide.

"Why don't you move in to my place in Stoneybatter? There are just two of us there now. We've got a vacant room. Our third resident is away in the missions."

"Well now. Are you sure? I have to confess I've been feeling a little guilty, taking up a room at the B and B in prime tourist season. My hosts have been so kind. But I'd like to free the room up for them."

"It's settled then, Michael. Let's go."

"Now, you mean?"

"What better time? We'll do our prison visit and then get you relocated."

"Thank you, Leo!"

So they took their places in the visiting room at Mountjoy Prison and made small talk with Finn Burke. As cordial as the meeting was, Michael got the impression that there were things the other two men wanted to discuss, and that Michael was an inhibiting presence. So he made his excuses and left them together. He waited out on the pavement until Leo emerged a few minutes later. They proceeded to Michael's lodgings, packed his few belongings and, after Michael thanked his hosts lavishly, they took a taxi to Stoneybatter.

Michael's new spot, close to the Aughrim Street church, was a terraced red-brick house with two windows up and one down, beside a door with a demi-lune fanlight. Michael and Leo went inside into a small foyer, where on one side there was a coat stand with several rain jackets hanging on it, and on the other a bureau with an oval mirror. Piled on the bureau were a couple of tweed caps, a Roman Missal, an Irish-language New Testament, and a biretta. Not hard to tell who lived in this house. The place had three small bedrooms, all now occupied. Leo introduced him to the housekeeper, Mrs. O'Grady, who assured him that if he needed anything, all he had to do was ask. She gave him the key to his room, which was airy and bright with a west-facing window. The furnishings were a wardrobe and dresser, table and chairs, and a narrow but comfortable-looking bed with a crucifix on the wall above it.

After depositing his belongings, Michael went to Leo's room for a visit. Leo put a pot of tea on to welcome Michael to his new home, and cleared his table of papers and church bulletins, so they could sit across from one another with their teacups. They talked about parish work in Ireland and in Canada, and Leo asked about Michael's earlier travels to Ireland. They sat in comfortable silence for a few minutes, then Leo said, "I hear Finn has set Brennan on the trail of the vandal who's been defacing the pub. And you may be assisting him with his inquiries."

"Oh, they slag me about missing my calling as Sergeant O'Flaherty, but I don't imagine I'll be of much use to Finn. I'd like to help him out, though."

"A word of caution, Michael." Leo paused to make sure he was listening. "As has been said in another context, a little knowledge is a dangerous thing."

"The investigation is pretty low key. So far all we've done is sit and gab with the Christy Burke Four."

Leo's eyes narrowed a bit. "The Christy Burke Four? Have I missed something?"

"I mean the pub regulars."

"And those would be . . ."

"Well, there's Ed Madigan, Jim O'Hearn, Frank Fanning, and Tim Shanahan. Those are the four main players so far. They're certainly the people who would know most about what goes on around the pub."

"Which makes them the four men most likely to be implicated in any slurs sprayed on the pub walls, given how closely associated they are with the place."

"But it's hard to imagine them as, well, criminals, or whatever the vandal meant to imply. Even harder to imagine them as killers! They're a genial lot, or so they seem to me."

"They're pleasantly plastered most of their waking hours, if they spend all their time in Christy's."

"Do you know them at all, Leo?"

"I'm acquainted with them. I don't know any of them very well. I just want to urge you to be careful, Michael. If somebody in the pub is the target of these accusations, that individual will notice before long that you fellows are nosing around in there. If he has something to hide, he'll feel threatened by your activities, and then you might be in danger. Don't tell me you haven't thought of that yourself."

"I have, but I'm sure Brennan is treading softly."

"I hope so."

"Of course that's partly because Brennan is not a man for poking his nose into the business of other people."

"Unlike somebody else we could name, perhaps, Michael?"

"If by any remote chance you are referring to me, I will state only that I stand ready to put my inquisitiveness to work in the service of others. So: have you any idea what this graffiti could be about, Leo? You're obviously concerned. Any suspicions? You haven't by any chance had a confession in connection with this, have you? You can't reveal it to me, of course, but . . ."

"I've had no confession, I can tell you that much. But I do know a thing or two about the political situation on this island. And the . . . well, our culture here. People have long, long memories, Michael, and an injury done years ago, decades ago, can still flare up today. And old bones like to stay buried. I wear more than one hat here, as you may know."

"A biretta and a balaclava, you mean, Leo?"

"If, by that, anyone meant what I think he meant, let him be anathema."

"Just codding you, Leo."

"I'll let it pass this time. But this business gives me cause for concern."

"While we're on the subject of serious matters, I'll tell you something else that has me worried: this Protestant minister, the American, who has disappeared. It's hard to escape the conclusion that he has been kidnapped. Or, well, it could be even worse, obviously. But assuming somebody has him, as a hostage, say, I wonder if a show of solidarity from the Catholic clergy, or even a committee made up of —"

Leo put both hands up before Michael finished his thought. "Stop right there, Michael. Get it out of your head."

"You sound like Brennan."

"You floated this suggestion to him, did you?"

"Yes. I have to say he wasn't encouraging."

"There's a reason for that, Michael."

"I just feel I'd like to make some effort, however minor, on behalf of that poor man."

"There's nothing you can do for him."

"You're knowledgeable about the . . . the politics here, Leo. What do you think is happening?"

"This man is a very public figure, a television preacher in the U.S. He was photographed in Belfast with the Reverend Ian Paisley, who I'm sure you know is a firebrand in the North. There has been a great deal of news coverage here and in the States. The stakes are high. The fact that there has been no word from or about him for over a week . . . I see this as a bad situation that could get much, much worse. Hear me on this, Michael: you do not want your name or your face made public in connection with this. End of story. Now, about this graffiti investigation you've taken on. That, too, could lead you into trouble."

"Do you see the vandalism at Christy Burke's as a political matter?"

"I see it as a possible occasion for, or a reflection of, strong feelings."

"Strong feelings can erupt just as easily in the personal realm as in the political. I don't have to tell you that."

"Let me show you something, Michael. In confidence. Man to man, priest to priest."

"Certainly, Leo."

Leo got up and went over to his dresser, opened the top drawer, and brought out an old brown leather notebook. Michael could see papers protruding from it, yellowed and brittle with age. Leo sat down, flipped through the papers, and drew out a photograph, which he slid across the table. "There's an unholy trinity for you, Michael."

Michael moved the grainy black and white photo into the light and peered at it, and told himself not for the first time that the day had come when he should invest in a pair of spectacles. But he could see the three men well enough. They were gathered around the open cargo door of a large truck. One of the men stood guard with a machine gun held sideways across his body. His eyes were obscured behind a pair of dark glasses. Finn Burke, several decades younger than he was now and, Michael thought, rakishly handsome. Another fine-looking fellow, with light-coloured eyes, was glaring straight ahead; he had an armful of weaponry. They were obviously unloading a shipment of guns. The men bore a strong resemblance one to the other.

"That's Finn," Michael commented. Leo nodded. "And would that be . . . it has to be his brother. Is it Declan Burke?"

"Right. Brennan's oul fellow."

"And that . . . is that you, Leo?"

"That's me, and those two were under my command."

Michael said to him, "Now, you seem well acquainted with Brennan Burke . . ."

"I am, yes, ever since New York. A brilliant and talented young man, and a very dedicated priest."

"True, without question. But not exactly a humble, pliant little lamb to be herded about at will by his shepherd."

"And that task falls to you as his pastor. Lucky man that you are, Michael."

"Oh, I am a lucky man to be in ministry with Brennan. Don't get me wrong."

"No, I understand you very well. I would be happy to work with him myself, any day of the week."

"But what I'm getting at is . . . from what I hear, his father is even more of a . . . forceful personality."

"That's one way of putting it."

"And you say you were his commanding officer. How on earth were you able to exercise authority over such a person?"

"What you see before you today, Michael, is a milder, gentler Leo Killeen than the Leo Killeen who was Officer Commanding of the

Third Battalion, Dublin Brigade of the Irish Republican Army. What you are seeing now is the New Testament version, perhaps I could say."

Leo Killeen was as wiry then as he was now, with cropped dark hair and dark eyes. He had an intense look about him. The expression on his face, and his posture, bespoke command. No question, Killeen was in charge.

"Who took the photograph?" Michael asked.

"Someone who should have stayed home that day."

"Oh?"

"An informer."

"So you fellows got caught with the guns?"

"No. We didn't."

Michael was silent for a moment, then said, "What happened to the man with the camera?" He looked into Leo's brown eyes, which didn't flinch.

"He should have known better," was all Leo said.

That was all he said, but was there an underlying message? That this is the kind of situation one might find at the end of the search for the Christy's vandal? Or the televangelist from the U.S.A.?

"How long after this incident did you enter the priesthood, Leo?"

"Oh, it would have been ten years or so after that. I've been a priest for over thirty years now."

"How do you reconcile what you did then with what you do now?"

"That's why there's a sacrament of reconciliation, Michael, so we can put ourselves right with God. No matter what we've done, as long as we are truly repentant."

"Are you, though, Leo? I get the impression you still have your hand in, or at least are still connected with the Republican movement."

"Nothing wrong with being sympathetic to the goal of a united Ireland. Nothing wrong with ministering to those still active in the movement. I regarded myself as a soldier in a just war, Michael. A war against those who occupied our country. But do I approve of the violence and the killing that are being done in the name of the movement? No, I do not. Am I repentant about some of the actions I myself took in that war? Yes, I am, and I am most grateful to the man who was my confessor and spiritual director in those years of transition from soldier to priest. And I wasn't the only one by any means,

Michael. There were several former Volunteers who became priests or brothers. It was a strongly Catholic movement after all."

They drank their tea in silence.

Brennan

Something looked different at the black church, Brennan noticed when he arrived at Christy Burke's on Friday after a morning of prayer with the Augustinians. It took a second for him to realize what the difference was. All the rubbish bags that had been piled up around the building were gone. Brennan smiled as he pictured a white, or maybe a black, unmarked utility van pulling up to the site, and a short, muscular man heaving bags of rubbish into the cargo hold before taking off for parts unknown.

As soon as he closed the pub's door behind him, he heard his name called from the bar. "Hello, Brennan!" Sean said. "I have a message for you here."

"You know you're spending too much time at your local when they start delivering your mail to you there!"

"True enough."

He handed Brennan a folded slip of paper. Brennan opened it and read, "Request visit with Father Burke. Finn."

"I've been called to assist one of my parishioners," he said. "I'll have to take a stroll up there before the day's out."

"Em, it sounded a bit more urgent than that, Brennan, the way Finn spoke on the phone."

"Ah. I'll go right now. Thank you, Sean."

Brennan left the pub and took a brisk walk up the street in the sunshine to the Mountjoy Prison. He stated his business when he got there, and once again found himself in the visiting area across from his uncle Finn. Finn looked tense. A man in uniform hovered nearby.

Finn addressed his visitor. "Thank you for coming, Father Burke."

"All part of my calling, Mr. Burke."

"It keeps my spirits up, seeing visitors."

"I'm sure it does."

"My friend Larry came to see me, after you kindly provided him with my change of address."

"Good."

"Larry's a great help around the place. Tidies up, hauls away old rubbish . . ."

"Right, yes."

The prison guard walked to his perch at the end of the room. Finn leaned forward in his seat, looked at Brennan intently, and spoke in a voice Brennan could barely hear.

"When you went to the black church, what did you see there?"

"Nothing of note."

"You carried the sacks of . . . rubbish . . . from the pub and deposited them by the church." Brennan nodded, keeping his eyes on the man across the way. "You thought that looked like a good place to leave the bags."

"I did, yes."

"Because . . ." Finn prompted him.

"Because there was nobody around and . . ."

"And?"

"It couldn't do much harm. The yard looked more like a rubbish tip than the grounds of a church. A few more bags wouldn't look out of place. What are you getting at, Finn? Is there a problem?"

"What else was there?" Finn's voice was so low now that Brennan had to rely on lip-reading to follow the conversation.

"There was . . ." He pictured the scene in his mind, then shook his head. "Just old, broken furniture, other bags of rubbish. Looked as if nobody had cleared the place out in recent times."

"And there was an abandoned refrigerator, or freezer . . ."

Yes, a banged-up freezer with refuse stacked on top of it. Brennan had added Finn's things to the pile.

"Right."

Finn stared at him for a few seconds, then said, "And you don't know what was in it."

"No. The lid was closed, weighed down by all the bags. I didn't give it any thought. At the time." He was giving it some thought now.

"Brennan."

Brennan was perfectly still. He didn't like where this seemed to be going.

Finn said, "Pay attention to me here. You must promise me, you must swear to me, that you will say nothing about this conversation.

Not to anyone. Do you understand me?"

He stared at his uncle without speaking.

"Not to the gardaí." He stopped and waited for Brennan's assent.

Brennan responded with a single nod of his head.

"Not to Leo Killeen."

Brennan hesitated. Finn waited.

Finally, Brennan said, "All right."

"Not to Michael O'Flaherty, not to Monty Collins, not to a living soul."

What was coming? But Brennan had a very good idea of what it was. And if Finn, if anyone, was going to entrust his secrets to him, he had to give his assurance that the matter would remain confidential. He made a vow. "You have my word, Finn."

Finn looked at the prison warders and at his fellow inmates. Their attention was elsewhere. He said to Brennan, "The vandal is dead. His body had been stuffed into that freezer."

Brennan had known it was coming, but it was still a shock.

"Nobody is to know about this until I find out what is going on, who this man is, or was, and who had the motive to put two bullets in the back of his head."

"This is dreadful."

"Larry Healey found the body when he picked up the items you placed there. He put all the bags in the van, then took the precaution of looking inside the freezer. I'll spare you the description he gave me. He has transported the body . . . elsewhere. For now. That is how it's going to be, until you hear otherwise from me."

Brennan stared at Finn, his mind racing. He was aiding and abetting someone in the commission of a criminal offence. Whatever it was called, it was a crime. And there was a moral dimension that he would have to sort out as well. But for now . . . was there any chance his uncle was wrong? "Finn, how do you know this was the man who defaced the pub? Couldn't it be some other . . ."

"The body was badly decomposed — Healey had quite a time with it! Wrapped it up in big sheets of plastic — packing material we have in the vehicles — and got it into the van. But the man's clothing was splattered with green paint. It's him, Brennan. I don't know his name, but he's the vandal. We have to find out who he was, who he was writing about, and who executed him and dumped him there.

The killer obviously chose the side of the church for the same reason you did: piles of rubbish left there, the freezer, and nobody interested in it. I have no idea what's going on, but it involves my pub and my clientele. I want to know this before the peelers do. There's not much I can do from here, and I can't have anyone else knowing about it."

Brennan had just been promoted from property crimes to the murder squad. The assignment was even less palatable to him now, but he could no longer entertain thoughts of staying on his bar stool and leaving it all up to Michael O'Flaherty. Brennan had no illusions about his own qualifications for the job; he had been inches from the body and had not even known it was there.

He had to make an effort to concentrate when Finn began to question him again, after checking once more to see who, if anyone, was paying attention. A few glances came their way. Finn waited until they refocused on their own affairs. Then he opened a new line of inquiry. "When you did the cleaning up for me . . ."

"Yes . . ."

"Downstairs, the cellar, all that. Did you happen to notice where a couple of bricks had, em, come loose?"

"I'm not sure whether I noticed that." Brennan tried to get his mind off the dead man, and to recall his exploration of the tunnel beneath the pub. Yes, he could picture the loose bricks now.

"There was something in there," Finn said, then mouthed the words, "A gun. Black."

That struck a chord with Brennan. He had heard something about a black gun. What was it? He tried to remember, as Finn watched him intently from across the table. Then he had it: Kevin, the young fellow who used to do maintenance work at the pub in the mornings, had with some reluctance told Brennan about a gun, black in colour, which had been hidden in the tunnel. Kevin had been curious about it and had looked for it the day after one of the graffiti incidents, but it wasn't there. Well, there was no point in getting Kevin in trouble by telling Finn about the young lad's interest. The gun was gone, and Kevin McDonough hadn't been the one to take it.

All Brennan said was "There was nothing like that in the cellar. Nothing in that cubbyhole. It wasn't there."

The news was not well received. Finn looked disturbed, and continued to be preoccupied until Brennan got up and took his leave.

"Either your mirror is being kind to me, or I really do look quite handsome for an oul fella." It was Saturday and Michael was on a shopping excursion. He looked over his shoulder at the sales clerk, a young woman with wavy brown hair nearly to her waist.

"Sure, the colour sets off your eyes, sir," she said.

"Father."

"I'm sorry?"

"I'm Father O'Flaherty. I'm usually dressed in black."

"Ah. Well, the light blue in the shirt. It suits you, Father. And the tweed jacket has the blue and the grey, like —"

"Like my hair, you're thinking. Admit it now."

"No, I wasn't thinking that, honestly. The grey goes well with the blue, that's all."

"True, it does. And my hair's as white as . . . where could I get myself a white flower for my lapel?"

"Just round the corner. At Morley Bloom's. I'll pop over there and get one for you, Father, if you could mind the shop for a bit."

"Lovely! I will, yes."

Michael moved over to the counter and assured a couple of arriving customers that the "boss" would be back in a minute. It wasn't much more than that when she returned with a white rose in her hand. She attached it to his lapel, patted it into place, and stood back.

"The perfect touch," she announced.

"Thank you, my dear! I'll just stuff my old clothes in the shopping bag. Now, what are the damages?"

Well, that cost me a packet, Michael said to himself as he emerged in Nassau Street late that afternoon. But it was worth it. And wasn't it kind of Morley to send him the white rose as a gift! Everyone was kind over here, God bless them and save them. And it had been years since he had treated himself to a little sartorial elegance. Brennan and Monty would have something to say about this, and they'd be sure to tie it in with the evening ahead. Yes, they were just like two little brothers. Best to ignore them. The three men and Kitty Curran had plans for an evening of music together. In fact, Monty was going to provide the music himself. Michael hailed a cab and asked the driver to take him to Christy Burke's. The driver was nearly the same age as

Michael by the look of things. *No retirement for some of us.*

"Mountjoy Street," the fellow said.

"That's it."

"Bit of trouble over there lately. There's no respect for property these days. But I suppose Finn's grateful it's not something worse."

Before Michael could formulate a reply, the driver leaned on his horn and swerved suddenly to avoid a lorry taking a wide turn in front of them. Michael was thrown against the door.

"Are you all right there?"

"I'm fine, no worries, thank you," Michael assured him.

"Where would you be from now, sir? You sound Irish but there's a little bit of something else there."

"You are correct. I live in Halifax, Nova Scotia. A few short hours away from here on a seven forty-seven."

"Sure, you're right. It's just the next parish over!"

They kept up the chatter until they reached Christy's and Michael bade him a warm goodbye. He went inside and found Brennan and Monty seated at a table near the door.

"Michael!"

"Good afternoon, Brennan."

"We nearly gave up on you. Sit down. What will you have?"

"Em, let me see now."

"Well, aren't you going to sit?"

"Certainly, yes, yes. I'll put my order in and join you in a jiffy." *Nothing to say about my attire?* "Good day to you, Monty."

"Hi, Mike. What have you been up to?"

Wasn't it obvious? Or did he see Michael O'Flaherty dressed in Donegal tweed every day of the year?

"I've been shopping!"

"Oh! What did you buy?"

"Are you two blind, or are youse blind drunk? I have a new suit of clothes."

"We know, Mike, we're just taking the mickey out of you," Brennan said. "You look very dashing. And, I would guess, you'll be next to irresistible in the eyes of any persons of the opposite sex who catch sight of you tonight."

"Oh, go on out of that! I was due for some new garments, so might as well go for quality, eh? Are you not teaching today?"

"I did, this morning. The schedule varies from day to day, which suits me fine." He raised a glass of whiskey and smiled.

Everyone was in place again, Michael noticed. But then, he was becoming a regular himself! He was greeted by O'Hearn, Madigan, Fanning, and Shanahan. The four targets of investigation.

Frank Fanning scoped out Michael's new look, then cast a critical eye over Monty and Brennan. "You're making your companions look a little shabby there, Michael."

"Can't be helped, Frank. Some of us are meant to stroll the boulevards in splendour!"

The Cobblestone pub was in Smithfield Plaza on the north side of the Liffey. The area was a mix of rundown Georgian houses and jarringly modern buildings. The pub was on the corner; the upper storeys were a cream colour, the ground floor a dark green with multi-paned windows. Michael and his friends squeezed their way inside. There was a traditional music session underway, with fiddlers and a mandolin player sitting around a table between the end of the bar and the front windows. Brennan kept walking, so Michael and the others followed him. A blues session was taking place in the back room, where there were a few dozen people seated and others standing. Monty had met some of the musicians earlier and, one way or another, found himself invited to be in the spotlight with a borrowed guitar and the harmonica that accompanied him everywhere he went. Unlike Michael, he knew the dress code. Michael was the most formal person in the room, in his new ensemble, with a skirted and white-bloused Kitty a close second. Monty was wearing a pair of faded jeans and a grey T-shirt and he looked as if he hadn't shaved for a day or two; he didn't look out of place. Brennan's appearance was much the same. Well, no matter.

They all ordered drinks. Monty got up, introduced himself, and expressed his appreciation for the opportunity to perform. He announced that he would be doing a few numbers by a fellow by the name of Muddy Waters. This met with approval from the people scattered throughout the pub, so the name must have been well known. Monty's first song was "You Can't Lose What You Ain't Never Had." It was hard to think of Monty as a respected barrister and solicitor while he was singing this earthy music. Michael particularly enjoyed a sad song called "St. James Infirmary." Things got down and dirty after that, when Monty launched into "Hoochie Coochie Man."

Michael realized he had been gazing at Kitty while the blues wailed on in the pub. What a lovable face she had, full of mischief and fun. She could look very serious too at times, very thoughtful. She must have been a pretty girl in her day and she was pretty now. Mid-fifties, he knew. A good fifteen years or so younger than Michael himself. His mind wandered to a place he rarely allowed it to go. What would his life be like now if he had not given himself, body and soul, to the celibate priesthood of the Catholic Church? What would it be like if he were a "regular guy" and had met Kitty Curran, and she had not become a nun . . . *Go on out of that, O'Flaherty; this is your last whiskey of the night!*

He looked over and saw Brennan's eyes on him. Now *there* was a man who knew a thing or two about the world of women. A fine priest he was; Michael wasn't judging him. Brennan had come to the priesthood a very worldly young man, unlike Michael; hard to give it up once it becomes a habit. But Brennan had undergone a profound religious experience recently after an episode of unchaste behaviour, and he seemed to have embarked on a new life of priestly purity. God had handled the Brennan Burke situation masterfully, in Michael's opinion. Michael sent a little *mea culpa* to the Man Above, for being so presumptuous as to pass judgement on His actions. Brennan had gone on a road trip to Italy with Monty and had fallen into the arms of a woman when he was there, breaking his priestly vows. This wasn't the first time but, to be fair to Brennan, he had had very few of these lapses in the quarter century he had been a priest. And the guilt that was invisible to others, thanks to Brennan's cool exterior, was evident to Michael when they had become well acquainted. When Brennan came home to Halifax after his Roman holiday, he was haunted by his sinful actions and seemed fearful that he had put his priesthood in jeopardy. A talented musician, Brennan had been composing a new setting of the Mass, the *Missa Doctoris Angelici*, dedicated to St. Thomas Aquinas. After the Italian adventure, he seemed to have lost his ability to write music. But God had a surprise in store for him. Instead of punishing him, and taking away his musical gift, He did the opposite. He showered upon Brennan His love and grace, and enabled him to compose music of unearthly beauty, as if to say, "There. That is what I have given you. What have you given Me?" That was the way to handle Brennan Burke. Michael had come upon him on his knees, arms straight out as if on the cross, in silent prayer and repentance, when he thought he was alone before the altar at St. Bernadette's. His knees must have been black and blue for weeks, so much time did he spend kneeling and thanking God and promising never to fail Him again! Michael had faith in Brennan. Well, time would tell.

As for Monty, he was the object of admiring gazes from young ladies all around the pub. A good-looking lad, no question. Talented as well. Michael had heard the blues from time to time, of course, but this was the first time he had ever attended a blues session. A *gig*. And it wasn't half bad. But it made you think and feel a certain way. About life. About women, if you weren't careful. Michael's mind veered away from the kind of thoughts that would be inappropriate, to say the least, for a man with four decades invested in the priesthood.

Chapter 5

Michael

It was cloudy and dull when Michael awoke the next morning in the priests' house in Stoneybatter. He turned on the television to see if he could find a weather forecast. Ah. An electrical storm. He'd be sure to carry an umbrella. He was about to switch off the TV when a news item came on about the missing American preacher, the Reverend Merle Odom. The man's tearful wife, flanked by supporters, stood before a bank of microphones and spoke in a strong South Carolina accent. She pleaded with persons unknown to release her husband unharmed. The scene switched to the most famous face in Ulster, the Reverend Ian Paisley, thundering that the visiting evangelist was obviously a victim of the IRA. And if the Royal Ulster Constabulary could not protect the people of Belfast and their guests, others would step in to fill the gap. An RUC spokesman urged calm and stated that there was no evidence that Merle Odom had been captured or harmed by the Provisional IRA or any other group. The police were working around the clock to find the man and restore him to his family. Michael felt helpless watching the crisis unfold; he wondered what his fellow minister was going through, wherever he was. Fathers

Burke and Killeen had warned Michael against making statements on behalf of the missing man, or making any kind of gesture of support. They were obviously less than optimistic about the outcome for the American, but Michael clung to a sliver of hope. He said a prayer for the minister and his wife.

He decided to spend the day in a manner suited to his vocation. He caught Leo Killeen before Leo left for the day and offered to hear confessions and say Mass at the Church of the Holy Family, the Aughrim Street church. He enjoyed meeting the parishioners in the magnificent old building, and came away feeling he had assisted several of them with their troubles.

On his way back to the house, Michael debated with himself about going over to Christy Burke's for a pint and a bit of companionship. And perhaps a bit of sleuthing while he was on the scene. He had met the regular clientele, though he had to admit he was unable to form even a preliminary opinion as to which of them, if any, might have been the inspiration for the graffiti on Christy's walls. But there had been other names mentioned as well. What were they? What had Kevin McDonough told them that night at the Brazen Head? Michael wondered how much investigating Brennan was doing. Well, whatever he was doing, he had asked for Michael's help, and Michael was more than happy to assist. So he had better start keeping track. A notebook. That would be just the thing. He made a detour on the way home to buy a little black book and a couple of ballpoint pens. When he got to his room, he wrote down everything he had learned so far. The act of writing prompted his memory, and he came up with the name McAvity. The man had a nickname. Nursey? Nurse McAvity. Kevin had identified him as a former patron of Christy Burke's who had taken his limited business elsewhere because he felt uncomfortable among the heavy drinkers at Christy's. What was his local now? Michael couldn't recall.

He picked up the phone and called Brennan. "The Bleeding Horse," Brennan remembered, and said the fellow's name was Bill.

"That's it," Michael said. "He may have some useful information. He'd have been sober all the time in there. That would have given him an advantage the others didn't have."

"Why don't you see if you can track him down then, Michael?"

"Me?"

"Sure. If he's going to open up at all, it would be to a kindly gentleman like yourself, not one of the Burkes from the drinking establishment that made him feel like *persona non grata*."

"You're assigning me the task then?"

"Make it your own. I'll be expecting a full report."

So that was how Michael ended up on a mission to the Bleeding Horse in Camden Street. He and Brennan remembered from their conversation with Kevin that McAvity used to arrive at Christy's exactly at five forty-five. If he was that regular in his habits then, he probably was now. So Michael timed his trip to arrive just before six o'clock. Umbrella in hand, he set off in a southerly direction for Nurse's new local. The weather had cleared, and it was sunny out. No, here was a drop of rain. But, yes, the sun was still shining. The sun shower did nothing to put Michael off his stride; he always enjoyed walking through the city, and he was used to the sudden changes in weather and the odd combination of sunny skies and falling rain.

The Bleeding Horse was an enormous pub in a two-storey building of its own, with exposed brick and wood beams inside. There was a second-floor gallery behind a railing that looked distinctly ecclesiastical. Well, it wouldn't be the first time fittings had made their way from a church to a guzzling den. The pub offered a range of seating, from stools to banquettes to long and short benches, in large open spaces or in tiny snugs. A sign warned the patrons to beware of pickpockets and loose women. Michael took note.

He waited till the barman had a free second, then asked him whether Mr. McAvity might be on the premises. The bartender confirmed that he was indeed in house, and he gave a discreet nod in the direction of a man sitting alone at one of the copper-topped tables on the first floor. Michael ordered a Guinness, then approached the table where McAvity sat with a half pint and a copy of the *Irish Times*. He appeared to be in his early sixties, slightly built with thinning grey curls and wire-framed glasses.

"Excuse me," Michael said. "Mr. McAvity?"

The man looked up. "Yes?"

"Good afternoon, Mr. McAvity. My name is Michael O'Flaherty and I won't pretend I am here by accident."

McAvity registered the Roman collar then, looked a bit alarmed, and asked, "Father? Is something wrong?"

"No, no, not at all. I just dropped in, hoping to find you here, and I'll tell you why. I'm a friend of the Burke family, Finn and his nephew, Brennan, and I'm over visiting from Canada. You may have heard that there has been some vandalism at Christy Burke's."

"Yes, I heard about that."

"Well, Finn's concerned about it, afraid someone may be targeting his clientele, but he, well, he doesn't want to make waves by asking too many questions. Doesn't want to upset his patrons. But I'm not from here. I don't have any patrons! So I've been asking a few questions, on the QT, hoping we might get to the bottom of this thing, and bring an end to it. Would you mind if I joined you for a bit?"

"No, have a seat, Father, by all means."

"Call me Michael, if you prefer."

"All right then, Michael. And I'm Bill."

"This is quite the operation," Michael remarked, looking around the pub.

"That it is," McAvity agreed. "Some of the plotting for ninety-eight took place right in this building." He meant the rebellion of 1798, so the pub had a long history. "And James Joyce was said to have misbehaved here in his day."

"Imagine that! Is this your local now, Bill?"

"It is, and it was. I used to come here, then I sort of tagged along with a friend to Christy Burke's, and I went there for a few years. But I like it here, so I came back."

"How did you like it at Christy's?"

"I didn't appreciate the way I was treated there, Michael, to tell you the truth."

"Oh? By the management, you mean?"

"No, I'm not talking about Finn Burke. A fine publican, and you'll hear no complaint about him from me. No, it was some of the gentlemen who frequent the premises there that made me feel unwelcome. I suspect you may have heard the name they call me there."

"Yes, I did hear it. If a man is subjected to name calling because he doesn't overindulge in drink, that man has my full sympathy, Bill. Nothing wrong with staying sober and keeping a clear head about you!"

"My thinking exactly, Michael. Thank you."

"Would your aversion to drink be a reaction perhaps to past troubles with the bottle?"

In Michael's circle of acquaintances growing up in New Brunswick, the only people who didn't drink were alcoholics, fellows who were trying to get off the stuff! There was one exception, Michael recalled, who was apparently considered such an oddity that his parents invariably referred to him, every single time his name came up, as "Mark Donnelly, doesn't take a drink." A bit like Nurse McAvity here, perhaps.

"I'm not a drinker," Bill said. "Never have been. The fact that certain people at Christy Burke's found that incomprehensible, or endlessly amusing, finally drove me out of the place. Did you know that over twenty percent of adults in this country don't drink at all? That's a higher percentage of abstainers than in most of the countries of western Europe."

This was news to Michael. "I'd never heard that, Bill."

"No. Everyone thinks of Irish people as drinkers. That's because so many of those who do drink, drink too much. Excessive drinking, binge drinking. But you rarely hear about the segment of our population that is always sober! In my case, I don't like the way alcohol makes me feel, and I don't particularly enjoy the taste. But my wife works evenings, and I don't like to be alone. So I come to a pub."

"When did you make the switch back here to the Bleeding Horse, Bill?"

"It would have been two years ago, a little more."

"So what do you do? What line of work are you in?"

"I'm a mechanic and I have my own business. McAvity Auto Service. I live in the city centre but my shop is out in Rathcoole."

"How long have you had the business?"

"Oh, thirty years now. You can always count on cars to rust or break down, so I'll never be out of work!"

"True enough."

"They still bring their cars out to me."

"They . . ."

"The fellows at Christy's. They say I can't drink, but nobody says I can't fix a motor. And they need the work, the cars and trucks those fellows drive. Jim O'Hearn, Frank Fanning. Well, Frank doesn't drive. But he has an old banger that he maintains. Keeps it for a rainy day, he says. 'Lots of days like that in Dublin,' I used to tell him, and he'd say, 'You keep it tuned up for me, then, Bill.' He gets his son to run it out to me once a year. The son's a piece of work, let me tell you. Doesn't appreciate running that little errand for his da, not one bit. Lane Fanning doesn't have *time* to help his father out. Too important. And it burns his arse to be seen in anything less than a brand new BMW. What if one of his posh friends from Ballsbridge catches sight of him?

"Who else from Christy's? Not Finn himself, because his family runs Burke Transport. He has a fleet of lorries at his command, and they're serviced out there on the Naas Road. Who else? Eddie Madigan. I saw him a couple of months ago and he said he was looking around for a little truck or a car; he'll bring it out when it needs work. Sounded as if he was looking for something fairly new, though I don't know how he'd afford it, him being out of a job. Old Joe Burns used to drive a big Toyota Hilux, but he's pretty well off the road these days. His health is gone. I suppose his son has the truck now. Oh, and Tim Shanahan. He doesn't have a car but his younger sister does. He borrows it when he needs it and brings it out here for servicing. Now there's a fine man, and not one to be slagging others about their drinking habits."

"I agree with you. Tim seems like a fine fellow indeed."

"He has his troubles, to be sure. He's not working but I don't know the history there. He spent some time overseas, Africa or someplace, and they say he was never the same man when he came back."

"Oh, what a shame." Michael pictured the mild, bespectacled man and wondered what misfortune had befallen him. But he had questions about the others as well.

"When you said Frank Fanning doesn't drive, what did you mean? Never learned? Though I suppose if he has a set of wheels, he must have driven it at some point."

"Oh sure, he did. Then he just stopped. Driving about like everyone else, then one day he wasn't driving."

"What's behind that?"

"Lost his licence is what I heard, for drink driving. Someone said he had a spot of trouble in the North, and never sat behind the wheel again after that. But I don't know anything about it."

"I see. What does Frank do for a living?"

"He works in a printing shop. Not full time, I don't think. But enough to keep him in, well, drinking money."

"Jimmy O'Hearn, now, what does he do?"

"I'm not really sure. Something to do with boats. I once heard it said that Jimmy or his family lost a fortune. Some investment or business operation, I don't know."

"Well! I wonder what that was about."

"Whatever it was, he doesn't make a habit of discussing it over the bar at Christy's."

"And did you say Eddie Madigan is out of work?"

"Out of work is putting it mildly. Got sacked from the Garda Síochána. Now that would be bad enough for any man. But for a Madigan . . ." McAvity shook his head at the enormity of it. "Old Eddie, the grandfather, fought in the War of Independence. When the treaty was signed and the Irish Free State established, Old Eddie was an officer in the Dublin Metropolitan Police, and when the DMP was incorporated into the Garda Síochána in 1925, he was promoted to the rank of inspector. His son, John, made his career in the guards, too, as did our Eddie. John rose to the level of superintendent. The police history in Maureen's family was nearly as illustrious. A grand wedding it was, Eddie and Maureen's, with all the uniforms present. People joked that it was the best day to commit a crime in Dublin because every garda officer in the city was at the wedding.

"You can imagine what a scandal it was when Eddie was turfed from the guards for — supposedly — taking payoffs. Maureen's family disowned him, she booted him out of the house, and the Madigans themselves have had little time for him ever since."

"Who was paying him off?"

"They say it was drug dealers. I find it hard to believe, to tell you the truth. He's a bit of a hard case, but I never would have thought that of the man."

"Well, an allegation like that would put the kibosh on his career as a policeman."

"It would indeed. Seems it's one thing after another with the Madigans. I know there was bad blood between the Madigans and the Brogans. But that family of Brogans have all died out, the older generation at least. The young people wouldn't care about whatever it was that went sour between them and the Madigans. They've moved across the sea to England. Only Brogan left is an oul one by the name of Irene. And she doesn't leave her council flat."

So chances were the old lady was not out there vandalizing the pubs of Dublin.

Michael chatted with Bill a while longer, then said his goodbyes. He had learned a great deal in his time at the Bleeding Horse. What it boiled down to, and what he told Brennan on the phone when he called to report on his talk with McAvity, was that all four of the Christy's regulars had their troubles.

Brennan

Brennan Burke had found a new calling, and it seemed as natural to him as his vocation to the priesthood. Some might say more natural. He was on the job at Christy's once again, pouring pints as if he had been doing so all his life. The regulars and other customers seemed to take him in stride; he was Christy's own grandson after all.

Michael O'Flaherty, dressed as usual in his Roman collar, was seated at the bar with the four daily communicants, gostering away about nothing in particular until Jimmy O'Hearn announced that he had to leave.

"Where are you off to at this time of the evening, Jimmy?" Frank Fanning asked him.

"I have work to do."

Work? Brennan had never thought of the bar stool boyos in the place as being on the payroll anywhere; they punched the clock so regularly at Christy's, he wondered when they had the time, or the sobriety, to carry out more onerous responsibilities.

"Where do you work, Jimmy?" Michael asked him.

"On the high seas, Michael. I take people out fishing. Usually, of course, in the morning, when the fishing is best, and the drinking is best put off until later! I don't do it every day. Some of my mornings are a little too painful. In this case, though, I promised a crowd I'd take them for an early evening run. So I'm signing out." He lowered his voice. "But not before hailing Mary and the Five Sorrowful Mysteries."

"You say the rosary before you set sail?" Michael asked, surprised.

"No, just a little word with those ones at the table behind us."

He was referring to five women who had come in earlier. They were middle-aged to elderly and, when they had seated themselves at their table, they had looked to the bar expectantly, and one made a signal to Brennan. He caught on: they were to be provided with table service. He went to them immediately and took their orders, pints of the black stuff for all but one of them. They were attired in dresses or trouser suits in pastel colours, and looked as if they had just had their hair styled. There was a scent rising from them that was familiar: hair spray? Each had a cigarette burning in an ashtray. Now they were deep in conversation, and it was almost time for a refill.

Jimmy O'Hearn whispered to Michael and Brennan: "They'd talk the ears right off your head, and every word of it would be bad news. They don't call them the Five Sorrowful Mysteries for nothing. But good souls, all of them. They do the stations of the cross every week, and . . ."

"Oh, which parish are they in?"

"Well, they're in different parishes, but I don't mean the stations in church, Michael. I mean they do a bit of a pub crawl, you know . . ."

"Sure they're on the piss, like the rest of us. Come in for their vitamin G!" Frank Fanning whispered and winked at O'Hearn.

"They start off at the Parnell Mooney," O'Hearn continued, "and drop in here, so we see them regularly. They put away a good few pints before they set out for their next stop, or a couple of them do anyway. They never have the money for a taxi at the end of their outing, so the guards usually give them a lift home."

Michael whispered back, "They look as if they were lifted right out of the Catholic Women's League or one of the bridge clubs in my home town of Saint John!"

"Sure we're all the same people, separated by a mere ocean of water."

O'Hearn went over to the women and greeted them, and they said hello. After a few seconds chatting, O'Hearn invited Michael to their table.

"These fine ladies are dying to know who you are, Michael. A new priest in the local, and them not informed about it! Ladies, this is Monsignor O'Flaherty from Canada."

"Don't be listening to him, Monsignor," one of the women said. "But now that you're here, I'm Mary Daly, this is Mary O'Brien, Kathleen O'Rourke, Eileen Sullivan, and Beatrice Walsh."

O'Flaherty called each by name and said he was pleased to make their acquaintance. They offered him a seat, and he joined them as Jimmy O'Hearn waved goodbye and left the premises.

Brennan could hear the conversation at the Five Sorrowful Mysteries' table and was glad he wasn't a part of it. He heard O'Flaherty commiserating with Mary Daly about the herniated disc in her lumbar spine. The pills she was on for pain counteracted other medication she was taking so, if she seemed a little spacey, that was why. She had to avoid alcohol. Mary O'Brien should be walking with a cane but someone in her block of flats needed the cane more than Mary, so she went without. There were plenty worse off than she was. Kathleen O'Rourke was being given the runaround by the medical establishment — she wouldn't mention any names — who kept telling her there was nothing wrong with her. Did she look stupid to Monsignor? No, she did not. So of course there was something wrong; she knew it, but the doctors in this city weren't willing to expend the resources necessary to diagnose and treat it. Eileen Sullivan had a shoulder so bad she couldn't wash her walls or ceilings, and her home was a disgrace. So as much as she would like to invite Monsignor to dinner some evening, she could not in all conscience have him in her home. Beatrice Walsh was waiting for surgery, and had been waiting for months. She wouldn't be so indelicate as to describe her trouble in mixed company, but listeners were left with little doubt that the problem was not quite life-threatening but gruesome nonetheless.

O'Flaherty must not have wanted to impose on their girls' day out any longer; he excused himself and returned to his place at the bar.

Brennan wondered about Jimmy O'Hearn, heading out on a fishing trip with a considerable amount of alcohol on board. He was about to seek reassurance from his cronies when O'Flaherty relieved him of the task.

"So Jimmy's gone fishing, eh?" Michael said to Frank.

"Yes, odd time for it, but he's off."

"Will he be all right, do you suppose? After, em, being in here . . ."

"Sure he'll be grand. You'll never see Jimmy O'Hearn legless, with drink or otherwise! He lives on a boat. He can walk like a man on deck and on land."

"Lives on a boat, here in Dublin?"

"He does. It's docked at Ringsend."

"A houseboat, is it?"

"No, a regular sailboat. He's rigged it up with all the mod cons."

"Beats paying rent, I'd say."

"Well, he pays a docking fee of some kind. And he does odd jobs about the place. The marina. But I hear they gave him a special deal because of his history."

"Oh?"

"Ever hear of the O'Hearn Yacht Company?"

"Well, no, but that's no reflection on the boats or the family name. It's just me. I grew up in one seaport, I now work in another, and I spend a couple of weeks here in Dublin every year. Yet I've never been a man for boats. I couldn't tell you why."

"Don't let Jimmy talk you into one of his fishing charters then. He'll have you halfway to Scotland. But anyway, he's one of the O'Hearn Yacht O'Hearns. The family has an illustrious history. Or they did have. For over a hundred years the family business was building boats. More like a hundred and fifty years. I think it was the 1840s when Old O'Hearn — this must have been Jimmy's great-great-grandfather — started up the business. World-renowned they were for it. It was quite a thing to own an O'Hearn boat; not too many in Ireland could afford one, but they sold well in England and Europe, and then in America. Every boat was different, and each one had a distinctive — what would you call it? — a bowsprit? No, a figurehead, I think it was. O'Hearn would do a little individual carving for each boat. Might be the owner's profile, or that of his wife, or some little joke. Anyway, when you had an O'Hearn boat, you had one of a kind. They don't have the company anymore, but Jimmy's never lost his taste for it."

"Never lost his taste for what? A pint of porter?" Michael and Frank turned to face a short man with dishevelled grey hair who had just come in the door. Brennan had seen him before, but they had never met. Must have been before he assumed his duties behind the bar.

Frank Fanning nodded at the newcomer. "Blair," he said in greeting.

"Evening, Frank," the man replied, then turned a pair of small, glittering eyes on Michael. "Who's this now?"

Frank offered the briefest of introductions. "Michael O'Flaherty, Blair McCrum."

"O'Flaherty. A new face. Father O'Flaherty, I should say. Where'd you drink before now, Father?"

"He's Monsignor O'Flaherty, Blair," Frank Fanning put in.

"Other side of the Atlantic, to tell you the truth, Mr. McCrum, er, Blair. I'm here on holiday."

"But you don't sound like an American at all, Monsignor."

"I'm not an American. I'm Canadian, but all my people came from here."

McCrum did a double take when he noticed there was a new face behind the bar as well.

"Well! This is the day for surprises. Who is this, standing in for Finn Burke while he is a guest of the state? Again."

"This is a direct descendant of Christy Burke, so govern yourself accordingly, Blair," Tim Shanahan warned him.

"Direct descendant? How's that? What's your name? What's your father's name?"

"I'm Brennan Burke, son of Declan, grandson of Christy."

"And where did you come from, just in time to save the day for your unfortunate Uncle Finn?"

"Finn had me flown in by helicopter from Canada for the occasion. We touched down in the exercise yard in the Joy just to say hello. That raised holy hell, let me tell you. Then I was dropped off here."

The man glared at him, floundering for words. Served him right. Brennan didn't like his manner, whoever he was. McCrum? Right. "What can I get for you?" he asked him then.

"I'll have a Powers if you'd be so kind."

Brennan poured him his whiskey and took his cash.

When he had his drink in hand, McCrum leaned towards Frank and spoke quietly. "Well, young Nugent will be grateful that this man has stepped into the breach." He gestured to Brennan with his glass.

"Is that so?" Frank said, indifferently.

"You know what they say. All work and no play makes Jack a dull boy."

"I'm not quite following you, Blair." But he didn't appear to care much; he stretched around McCrum in order to have a word with Michael.

But McCrum hadn't finished. "You'll never guess who I saw in O'Connell Street this afternoon."

"You're right, Blair, you've got me stumped. So, Michael, how long are you —"

"A certain young lady from this very neighbourhood." He waited. "A certain young lady who is sometimes seen in the company of one Sean Nugent, apprentice barman of Dublin City! Sean the sweet lad who works two jobs and studies for his degree when he can, one course at a time, so he'll have a future to offer this young female who obviously is less appreciative than she might be of Sean's efforts to make something of himself. I hear they haven't been keeping company as of late. Did you hear anything, Frank?"

"Where would I hear something like that, Blair?"

"Well, what's being put about is that, after all the attention Sean has lavished on her, not to mention the money that he works those long hours to earn, she's taken up with a young fellow about five years her junior and the arse out of his pants. There's a lesson in that for all of us, boys; save your money, some women are just as happy with scruff from the slums. The lad's got the same bit of equipment in his trousers as the rest of us, and that's enough for her. Anybody with eyes in his head could see that about her."

Brennan was of a mind to pick the offensive man up and throw him out the door without even opening the door first. But he wasn't about to start evicting Finn's clientele. At least, not this early in his career.

Frank Fanning seemed to have succeeded in tuning McCrum out and directed his attention to Michael O'Flaherty's questions about the photos displayed behind the bar. Frank pointed to this or that picture and gave a little spiel on the people portrayed in them. Christy Burke in his Volunteer's uniform. Various participants in the Republican struggle, some well known, others who had fought without attaining glory.

"And if you know where to look in there —" Frank's gaze went beyond Brennan to the deep recesses of the bar "— you'll see a picture of Christy, Finn, and Finn's son, Conn, all behind the bar together, the three generations. Finn cherishes that photo. It was taken by Finn's wife, Catriona, shortly before Christy died. You look at the three Burkes lined up there and you'll see photographic proof that the apple doesn't fall far from the tree. They look like the same person, at different ages."

"And where's Conn now? I don't see him stepping in to ease the burden now that Finn's out of play." McCrum again.

"Conn's in London, Blair," Fanning replied. "He's working there."

"The Brits had better watch their backs with that young hothead on their territory. But Catriona was a lovely soul. Died too young. Not sixty years old and her heart went on her. Such a shame. There were a few lonely years for Finn after that, with the children grown and on their own. But he hasn't lacked for female company in recent times, isn't that right, Frank? A handsome older man in good health, physically and financially, well that's a draw to a lot of women, no question. But you have to be careful who you take up with."

"I'm sure you're careful yourself in that regard, Blair," was all Frank said.

"You're right on the money there, Frank. Nobody is going to be Mrs. Blair McCrum unless she passes muster with my dear mother and my uncle Diarmuid. And nobody has! They've saved me from the pitfalls more than once, let me tell you!"

He stopped long enough to take a sip of his whiskey, then got his second wind. "But none of that is news. The news of the day is that Finn is pleading not guilty to all the charges. Well, what would you expect? And he'll go to trial some time in the fall. He's got his lawyers working on the bail hearing. So you might see him here any day now."

That was good news, even if it had issued from the mouth of a nasty piece of work like McCrum. Brennan would have to stop in at the Joy, see when Finn expected to get out.

"Well, I have to be off," McCrum declared. "Take care of yourself, Frank. Pleased to meet you, Monsignor. Brennan."

Brennan and Michael nodded at the man, who put his glass down and left the pub.

Michael turned to Frank and asked, "Is he a regular patron here?"

"No, no, he makes the rounds. Stops in here once in a while, then moves on to the next place."

"I didn't appreciate the tone or the content of his conversation!"

"Motor Mouth McCrum, they call him. Pay him no mind. Nobody does."

The company was more pleasant after that, and Brennan was kept on the hop, so to speak, as the pub filled up in the late afternoon. And here came the curly top who had gone away disappointed from his first session at the bar.

"What can I do for you today, my dear?"

She gave him a mournful look and said, "Not much, as we established here the other day. So just give me something to drown my sorrows, Father. Blot out the pain."

He laughed. "What would work for you, do you think?"

"A John Jameson and make it a double."

"Ah. Certainly. My own drug of choice, as it happens."

"Star-crossed in every way," she lamented, and took her glass to a table near the window.

Next up were several members of a local hurling team and, just when he had taken care of them, he heard a familiar voice.

"Lord t'underin' Jesus, b'y! Would you look at that!"

Brennan's head jerked up at the sound of the over-the-top Cape Breton accent. The MacNeil. Monty's perennially estranged wife, Maura MacNeil. Brennan had known she was coming to Dublin, but hadn't expected to see her so soon. He started to formulate a greeting but, as always, she got ahead of him.

"Brennan, I've seen you in a bar, at a bar, crawling towards a bar, clinging to a bar, slumped over a bar, too many times to count. So why should I be surprised to see you behind a bar? Now you've got the perfect opportunity to get your face under the taps and suck the place dry. Well done."

"Now there's a skinful of abuse!" the curly top exclaimed. "Sounds as if she crossed the ocean just to denounce you in a public place."

"You have no idea," Brennan replied.

Then he heard the voice of a child. "There he is, Mum! What's he doing? Selling *booze*?"

It was Monty and Maura's little girl, Normie. Every head in the pub swivelled to the child and then to the bar. But Brennan didn't have time to respond to their curious stares because Normie launched herself towards him. He went out to meet her, picked her up, and twirled her around.

"Normie! Bless you. It's wonderful to see you in Dublin. I'm so glad you're here." He put her down and ruffled her auburn curls.

Then she went to the door and took custody of a baby stroller; she pushed it towards the bar. Little Dominic raised a sleepy head and caught sight of Brennan. The baby's eyes widened and he emitted a peal of joyous laughter and stretched his arms out to Brennan to be picked up. Brennan scooped him out of the stroller, held him aloft and wiggled him in the air. The baby giggled and grabbed two fists full of Brennan's hair.

Everyone in the bar enjoyed the scene, and one of the Five Sorrowful Mysteries exclaimed, "Isn't he a dote! Look at all the dark hair, and those black eyes. He's the spit out of his father's mouth! And the little coppernob. Would anyone believe I used to have red hair just like that? She's an angel."

Maura MacNeil spoke up again. "I'd ask what you've been up to, Brennan. But at least I can see you've found employment."

It was all too much for the Jameson-loving woman with the curly hair. "Your man's been behaving himself, I can attest to that," she said to MacNeil. "You wouldn't believe the line he gave me when I engaged in a bit of harmless flirtation with him. He was having none of it. Sent me packing. You'd have been proud of him." She turned to Brennan. "Lovely children."

She picked up her Jameson, downed it, waved in the direction of the bar, and headed for the door.

Shite! Brennan called after her, "No, wait, you've got it all wrong. Really . . ."

But she was gone.

Maura MacNeil raised her eyebrows and regarded Brennan with amusement.

Michael O'Flaherty looked as if his head was spinning. Brennan saw him direct an uncertain smile at MacNeil. "Hello, Mrs. MacNeil! Welcome to Dublin. Brennan is standing in as his uncle's curate, you might say. Doesn't he look as if he was born to the job?"

"He missed his true calling, Monsignor. But I guess we all knew that."

"My true calling has never looked so good, celibacy and all," Brennan retorted. "Imagine having someone like you tormenting me from morning till night. At least I've been spared that, *Deo gratias.*"

She said to him, "So do your job. Pour me a drink. I'll sit quietly with it and promise not to torment you until I need another. How's that?"

"Best result I can hope for, I suppose. What can I get you?"

"Harp?"

"Pint?"

"Half. I have the children to think of."

"Me too!" Normie piped up. "Can I have a glass of beer?"

Affectionate laughter greeted the child's words.

"How about ginger beer?"

"Is it good? Do you drink it?"

Laughter again.

"Em, well, I'll have a glass of it now, with you."

"Great!" She turned to her father, who had just come in the door. "Daddy! I'm going to have ginger beer!"

"Good idea, sweetheart."

He leaned down and kissed his daughter on the top of her head, and she grinned up at him.

Brennan looked at them and felt the same exasperation he always felt when he contemplated the Collins-MacNeil family and their troubles. He didn't have to look at Maura MacNeil again; he was well familiar with her fine qualities. Was Monty daft? What more could a man want? What was it going to take for him to get off his arse and return to the fold? Gentle priestly counselling hadn't been effective. Giving out to Monty and calling him a bonehead hadn't brought results either. What would Brennan have to do to smarten the man up? Take him by the throat and roar into his face? Brennan had to concede that reconciliation had become a little more difficult when MacNeil learned she was pregnant with Dominic, and Monty not the father . . . But still. Life is short. Work it out, and get on with it.

In the meantime, Brennan poured the little one her ginger beer. He poured one for himself and for Monty, and a Harp for the Mac-Neil. He raised his glass to them all. *"Sláinte!"*

Chapter 6

Michael

"Not often I can say this, lads, but I've been invited to Belfast." Brennan made the announcement to Michael and Monty when the three of them met at Monty's hotel before heading out for the evening on Monday.

"You don't say! What for?" Michael asked.

"They're putting on a concert for peace. It's being organized by a committee made up of Protestants and Catholics, moderate Loyalists and Nationalists, and those in between and all around. The music will be a mix: everything from traditional Irish to rock to opera and classical. The performers will be donating their time to the cause of sanity in the North of Ireland. Leo Killeen is involved. He gave me a call and rather grudgingly asked if I'd like to take part."

"Why grudgingly?" asked Monty. "Doesn't he like the sound of your voice? Is he afraid you won't waive your usual exorbitant performance fee?"

"Those could be factors, but I don't think so. He himself has little choice about attending, but I got the impression he's reluctant to drag the rest of us into it."

"Why? Is he worried?" Michael asked.

"He didn't say as much, Mike. He's just back from there, and wanted to pass the word along."

"Back from where, Belfast? What was he doing there?"

"Didn't talk about it, except for the concert."

"What will you be singing?" Monty asked.

"I'll be doing 'Comfort Ye, My People' from the *Messiah*. They'll pair me up with a Protestant cleric, who'll be doing another number right before me."

"Well, now," Michael said, "that's quite an honour. I look forward to hearing you. When do we go?"

"I told Leo nothing short of the *real* Messiah returning to earth would keep you from attending, so the plan is we'll head up there the day of the concert, Sunday the twenty-sixth, spend the night, and come back the next day."

"Leo's got me pegged already!"

"You're an open book, Michael."

"True enough. So . . . this is the twentieth. It's only six days away. Should we be making reservations for a place to stay? It's high season, after all."

"It's Belfast, Mike. And Leo is going to line up accommodations for us."

"Lovely. What else can we look forward to by way of music?"

"We can look forward to — and this will explain why I so readily agreed to attend — Leontyne Price as the headline performer. I've only seen her once before, in New York, and I am very, very keen on seeing her again. She'll be brilliant."

"Great," said Monty. "Count me in. As a member of the audience. Something tells me this wouldn't be the right gig for a lot of 'ain't got no hope' blues numbers."

"Em, no. That would be sending the wrong message, as they say."

"There *is* hope," Michael insisted, "and this concert will prove it! Or, at least, events like this will demonstrate that people on all sides, ordinary people trying to get on with their lives, want peace, want the various factions to back off and let the wounds begin to heal. Wouldn't it be grand if whoever captured the American minister made the first gesture of goodwill by releasing the man, and issuing an apology to all concerned."

Michael saw Brennan and Monty exchange a look. Michael could read it all too well: *Wouldn't it be grand if there was more than a snowball's chance in the fiery furnace of hell that the preacher will be released, and peace will reign.* Well, hope was one of the three theological virtues, along with faith and charity. Michael would continue to hope for the best, no matter how hopeless the situation might appear to others.

But for now, another night on the town. This summer's vacation was turning into a social whirl for Michael O'Flaherty. He and his friends would be attending a dance that night. Not a disco by any means, but a dance at the clubhouse of St. Peter's church in Phibsborough. Maura MacNeil would be coming with them. She and her two little children were staying at the convent with Kitty Curran. But for this evening Kitty had arranged to have someone, a niece of one of the sisters, pick up the MacNeil kids and take them to her home to play with her own youngsters, so Maura could attend the dance.

There was trouble between Monty and his wife, Michael knew. They had separated some years back. She had become involved with another man after that, and Michael had little doubt that Monty too had enjoyed some attention from the opposite sex. It was Michael's understanding that Monty and Maura had been close to a reconciliation when, at the age of forty-two, she discovered to her consternation that she was carrying a child from the other relationship. The baby was born last summer. That had put the kibosh on the reconciliation, at least so far. None of that was the fault of the little lad himself, of course. Dominic. An angel down from heaven, no matter the circumstances of his birth. Monty and Maura had two older children, Tommy Douglas, who was in his late teens, and Normie, who had just completed grade four at the St. Bernadette's Choir School in Halifax. If their parish priest, Father Burke, had his way, Monty and Maura would put their problems behind them and move back in together and carry on from there. But that wasn't likely to happen on this trip; Monty had his hotel room, and Maura and the children were staying with Kitty Curran at the convent. Well, Michael would keep them all in his prayers.

In the meantime he was looking forward to the dance. The event was to raise money for the church's service to the poor. Brennan said his uncle Finn supported this charity with regular donations.

However ill-gotten his gains might be, Finn must have been using at least some of his money to redistribute wealth in his corner of Ireland. So Michael and his friends could do a good turn at St. Peter's and have a bit of fun while they were at it. They would have a couple of drinks at Christy's first, then head over to the clubhouse at St. Peter's.

The gentlemen set out on foot for the convent to meet their "dates." The place was just off Parnell Square, not far from Christy Burke's. In these more liberal times, they had no trouble getting admitted to Sister's room, where they were greeted by Maura MacNeil. Maura was not as thin as a fashion model by any means but nobody should be, in Michael's opinion. Michael wouldn't have called her overweight either, just comfortable. Her hair was to her shoulders, soft brown with a few silvery threads. Her eyes were grey and had a bit of an almond shape to them. A sweet face, though he knew her speech could be a little pointed at times!

Michael asked her about her plans, and she said she was finishing up her maternity leave and would be returning to her job as a professor at Dalhousie Law School in September. So this was the perfect summer for a leisurely trip to Ireland. She would be in Dublin for three and a half weeks. Normie was having the time of her life so far. The older boy, Tommy, was home in Halifax, spending a lot of time on the road with his band. Dads In Suits, Michael thought they were called.

Maura asked what had been happening, so they filled her in on the misadventures of Finn Burke and his pub.

"Very well then, let us get on with things. Kitty and I were preening ourselves for the evening ahead. Where were we, Kitty?"

"How do you like it?" Kitty twirled around to show off a flowery skirt and pinky-coloured blouse. "It's not often I shop for new clothes but it's so warm, I just had to get something lighter. Shouldn't have left my summer wardrobe in Rome, but who knew oul Dublin would be so steamy?"

"Tell me about it. It's hotter than Scotch love over here," Maura commiserated. "Now let me see this, Kitty. You look *fabhulous*, dahling! And I have just the thing to complete the outfit."

She picked up her handbag from Kitty's desk and rummaged inside it. "Here we go. I got these in Grafton Street. They're clip-ons. I bought them for Normie, but they are *you*!"

She clipped an earring on each of Kitty's ears, and everyone laughed, because they were indeed kitties, little silver kittens stretching their paws up for balls of wool that were the clip-on part of the earring. They were sweet; Michael hoped she'd get to keep them. Perhaps Maura would find another pair for her little girl. Maura stepped back and regarded Kitty again.

"You're all buttoned up here. Let's loosen you up a bit. Unbutton this one and expose yourself to the four winds! You're with friends here." Well, Kitty did look a little stiff with only her top button undone. Another one open would not offend modesty.

Maura reached over and playfully undid the second button on Kitty's blouse. Kitty's hand shot up to her chest, and she fumbled with the button.

But not before Maura saw what was there. Michael saw it too. He recognized the marks for what they were: burn scars that must have been made by the tip of a cigarette.

Michael felt faint. He'd heard Kitty had endured some tough times during her foreign postings, but he'd had no idea it was this serious. He didn't know what to do or say.

Maura looked appalled. "Kitty! I'm so sorry. I . . . ." She put her hand on Kitty's arm and was obviously struggling for words.

"Oh, no worries," Kitty said, but not in the voice Michael was used to hearing. He stared at her, but she wouldn't meet his eyes. As if she were ashamed! What is wrong with this world, when someone who has been the innocent victim of brutality is made to feel shame and humiliation on top of everything else? Whoever had done this to Kitty should be on his knees in shame and repentance from now to eternity.

Fighting tears, Maura turned to Monty and gave him a look Michael couldn't read. But Monty could. He said, "Gentlemen, why don't we go downstairs and wait until the ladies are ready to join us."

"Yes, certainly. Good idea, that's what we'll do," Michael babbled, then wanted to bang his head on the doorpost for being so gauche.

The men left the room. Brennan closed the door quietly behind them. They went downstairs and out of the building, then stood awkwardly on the grounds of the large stone convent. Brennan lit up a smoke.

They stayed silent for a few long minutes. Then Monty spoke up. "What happened, Brennan?"

No reply. Brennan smoked and stared into the distance.

Michael asked, "Was it something in Africa? I know she's done a few stints in the missions there."

"Well," Brennan answered with obvious reluctance, "it's true she had some rough postings in Africa, but for this injury we have to turn to the death squads in El Salvador. They hurt her very badly. She was raped and abused. Several nuns were. Some were murdered. As you probably know from the news stories a few years ago."

"Oh, God help her and save her. Did she tell you this, Brennan?"

"No. I was visiting in Rome at the time, and I saw her when they brought her back. The sight of her, the look in her eyes, it will haunt me till I draw my last breath. She knows I know, but she doesn't talk about it."

Michael wished he were alone so he wouldn't have to put on a brave face in front of the other guys. How could any human being be that vicious and depraved? A sister of the church, serving in a foreign country, trying to help its people. Well, that was the problem, wasn't it? Helping the poor and disenfranchised didn't sit well with those in power. Michael couldn't help but wish Kitty had confided in him. As a friend. But he was a man. He hoped she didn't think men were all the same, brutish and out of control. No, of course she didn't. But it was perfectly understandable that if she were going to confide in anyone, it would be a woman.

They fell silent again. Fifteen minutes or so later, the women emerged. Maura signalled with her hand that the men should go ahead, so the three males made off for Christy's pub. They went inside, found a table, and ordered drinks for all. Not long after they were settled, the women came in, Kitty's eyes dry and clear, Maura's red from weeping. Michael wanted to say something but he couldn't think of anything appropriate so he sat there like a dummy.

Kitty smoothed things over. "All right, that was a long time ago. Let's not sit here with long faces on us."

Nobody knew what to say. Kitty continued, "And I've had my therapy. With, may I add, a very handsome Roman psychiatrist. Dr. Sandro Sabatini!"

"I know Sandro," Brennan said. "I can see where a woman's gaze might alight upon him and rest there a while."

"Of course he looks like a turnip compared to the fine specimens of manhood gathered around this table," Kitty declared loyally.

"Well, you don't need him here. You're on safe ground in holy Ireland," Brennan replied. "But let's not leave the subject of your foreign travels entirely. Tell them the one about Africa, the priest, the bishop, and the great fecking bug."

Michael noticed that one of the regulars seemed quite attentive to their conversation. Tim Shanahan. Michael could not escape the notion that Shanahan was a priest; he had a priestly air about him. If he was, this tale should be of interest to him. Maybe they should invite him to join them. Michael was about to raise a welcoming hand when Shanahan caught Michael's eye, reddened, and turned away.

Kitty embarked on her story. "You'd have to know Charlie Kehoe and Vincent Walsh to really appreciate this. Charlie and Vince were two priests serving with me a few years ago in a small village in Tanzania. They were devoted men of the church but they were also practical jokers, each with the other as his primary target. The latest development up to this point was Charlie's coup at the football stadium. Vince Walsh is an Irishman who grew up in London. He was, and is, a devoted supporter of the Arsenal football club and not at all enamoured of rival clubs, particularly Manchester United. Well, somehow Arsenal and Manchester United arranged to take part in a goodwill tour to sub-Saharan Africa, exhibition games, what we call friendlies. Leaving out apartheid South Africa, needless to say. Charlie Kehoe got wind of the fact that some of the players would be making an appearance at a village near ours, where there was a rudimentary football stadium in the works. Charlie told Vince it was Manchester United coming, and he just happened to have a Manchester jersey on hand. Would Vince like to wear it as a friendly gesture towards the visiting team? The last thing Vince wanted to do was don a Manchester United shirt, but, what the hell, he was nowhere near England, and none of his fellow Arsenal fans would catch him out, so why not welcome the Manchester fellows decked out in some of their gear? The two priests gathered a bunch of young people from the village and drove to the stadium.

"Vince nearly had a stroke. There on the field was the Arsenal football club, kicking a ball around, giving tips to the local lads, and signing autographs. And who did Charlie Kehoe wave over but Spider O'Leary? Like Vince Walsh, David O'Leary was of Irish background and living in England. O'Leary was Walsh's hero. If it weren't for our Lord Jesus Christ, Spider O'Leary would be the Son of God for Vincent Walsh. And there Vince was, meeting him in the jersey of archrival Manchester United. O'Leary ribbed him about it, Walsh stammered, Kehoe snickered from the sidelines.

"After this, Vincent bided his time. That time came when the local bishop was scheduled to visit our village during a period when we were desperate for support and money to keep things going. The bishop was a godly man, but not a humorous one. Now Charlie, as devout and dedicated as he was, was not a fellow who took naturally to life in the wild. A city boy through and through. I don't think he had spent a day outside the city of Dublin until he went out to Africa. Anyway, there were aspects of life in the tropics that Charlie had trouble with, things that gave him the heebie-jeebies. I'm thinking particularly of some of the fascinating and colourful creatures that inhabit that part of the world.

"So the bishop was coming, and Charlie would be saying an outdoor Mass for him and for the local people. The Mass was to be celebrated at a beautiful spot on a hill a few miles away from the settlement. Magnificent view, a place to give thanks for God's marvellous creation. A place chosen by Vincent Walsh. Charlie wanted to do a good job, impress the bishop with all the good work our group was doing. He was especially proud of the way the people exhibited such reverence at Mass. Vince shared these goals but he had another goal in mind: revenge on Charlie Kehoe.

"We had two ancient Jeeps, probably World War Two vintage. Every part of them by this time had been replaced, jury-rigged, wired or taped together. They barely functioned, but we got there. Everyone was in place. The altar was set up on the hill, with a lovely altar cloth decorated by the local women. The tabernacle, the chalice, all of gold. The priest's vestments immaculate. It was so hot that all Charlie had on under the vestments was a tropic-weight black shirt and his collar, his underwear, and sandals on his feet.

"Charlie begins the Mass. Vince is nowhere to be seen, but that doesn't register with Charlie. At least, not right away. When Charlie gets to the point where he is to deliver his homily, carefully prepared to inspire the faithful and the bishop, he hears a noise behind him. Sounds like a toy helicopter. It's coming towards him. Brrrrr, this loud noise gets closer. Charlie turns his head, sees something flying in his direction, jumps and gives a little squawk. Vince has planted a big bowl of ripe fruit behind a nearby tree and has released into the air a bunch of Goliath beetles. I don't know whether you're familiar with them."

"I think I can speak for us all when I say no to that," Maura said.

"Right. I didn't think so. This is, as far as I know, the largest beetle in the world, grows to over four inches in length. It's so heavy, it makes that helicopter noise when it flies. And the male has a big horn on its head."

Michael looked over at Monty and Maura. The expression on their faces showed that they shared his opinion of the giant flying insect. Brennan, who had heard the story before, didn't look much better.

"So Vince has released a bunch of these monsters, hoping that at least one will fly in Charlie's direction on its way to the stash of food. In fact two of them follow the desired flight path. Charlie hates bugs, is terrified of them, especially the great enormous things that populate the African tropics. He wants to continue his sermon, but he can't concentrate. Finally he reaches up and swats at the things, and one of them falls on his foot. That has him dancing. The people are smiling about this, all except the bishop, who doesn't crack a smile. Charlie gets through the Mass, just barely. The whole time he's sneaking glances above his head, down to his feet, fearful the beetles will get on him and climb up his legs. He's got a hand going like a windmill at all times to ward them off.

"Finally, Mass is done. But the ordeal isn't over yet. Vince has another surprise for Charlie. A post-Mass meal prepared by the local church ladies. And I'm not talking crustless sandwiches and little cakes. No. Among the delicacies presented to Charlie and the bishop were Mopane worms, which are very colourful and edible caterpillars. And edible stink bugs."

"Oh, God!" Michael croaked. He couldn't help it.

Kitty continued, "Charlie reels at the sight of them, clutches the table. All the while, Vince is behind him, speaking in a low voice, giving a running commentary. 'Please take a moment to savour these delightful morsels, brought in specially for the occasion from Limpopo. The Mopane worm. Spiky, yet succulent. The edible stink bug. Note the piercing mouth parts. Perhaps you've noticed that the animal has glands between its first and second pair of legs that produce a foul-smelling liquid. That's for defence purposes, of course, and can safely be ignored while consuming them.' He goes on and on. Charlie can't take it. He's the palest white man Africa has ever seen. He comes up with an excuse for leaving, and casts pleading looks in my direction for support. Suddenly, he has to be back in the village to administer a dose of regularly prescribed medicine to an old woman who had to stay behind. I take pity on him and excuse myself.

"Well, Charlie and I hop in one of the Jeeps and we can't get it started. We open the bonnet and fiddle with the motor and the alternator or some such thing. Charlie is pouring sweat by this time, and I'm not much better. Of course everyone back at the Mass site can hear us trying to start the vehicle. So they come over to help, led by Vince, who kindly bears a doggy bag full of treats for me and Charlie. Charlie says to him, 'Fuck you, Walsh, and all belonging to you!' And the bishop hears it, and purses his lips preliminary to delivering a lecture. But Charlie finally gets the Jeep going and starts down the hill. I'm hanging off the side by my fingernails. I assure the crowd we'll be back to pick them up, and off we go. If you could have seen the face on poor Charlie.

"So," Kitty said, "my time abroad has mostly been a career of busted motors, large and terrifying insects, and embarrassing outbursts of inappropriate language. Don't know that I accomplished anything in all those years, but I've seen a lot of the world and met thousands of lovely people, and — believe it or not — had all kinds of fun and foolishness along the way. I'm after them to put me on the road again."

The voice of Sean, the barman, brought them back home. "Your change, Tim!"

Michael looked over and saw Tim Shanahan heading for the exit, looking ill. Sean was waving an Irish pound note at him, but Shanahan ignored it. He gave Michael and his companions an anguished glance and left the pub.

"Paid too much and didn't even stay to finish it," Sean muttered, as he removed Shanahan's near-full pint glass from the bar and wiped beneath it.

†

"I hope you're able for it now, Kitty. Michael is a divil for the dancing," Brennan said when they arrived at the dance in Phibsborough.

"We'll see who's able for it, Burke. But if he wears me out, there's a whole room full of women here who I'm sure would love to do a turn around the room with Michael O'Flaherty."

"And well they should!" Michael exclaimed, he who had been known all over Saint John, New Brunswick, for his prowess on the dance floor. He still loved to kick up his feet whenever somebody rolled up the rug. No wallflower was Michael O'Flaherty. You wouldn't know it to see him now but he had been quite the eligible bachelor in his day; he had courted more than one young lady before he entered the sem. After his ordination, well, he had fallen for a pretty face, or a kind heart, from time to time. Resisted the temptation to act, of course. And then there was the occasional church lady who had become infatuated with him. Some of the flirtation directed his way was over the top, in his view. He did nothing to encourage it, God knows. In fact, he was embarrassed for those women, if the truth be known. He said nothing, and kept them in his prayers. Now, though, the band was warming up. Michael loosened his tie. *Who knows — before the night's over, I may yank it off entirely.*

The band played a set of fast modern numbers. Michael sat out the first few of those. If you couldn't do a jive or a jitterbug, what was the point? But then they did a couple of pieces from the big band era, and Michael was on his feet. Kitty did a pretty good job of keeping up with him. Michael was having a ball, and Kitty looked as if she was enjoying it every bit as much. Monty offered a round of drinks and headed to the bar. Brennan and Maura came onto the dance floor just as the band struck up its next number. An old Strauss waltz. Very romantic! Michael took Kitty in his arms, and Brennan did the same with Maura, but not before looking over at Michael and Kitty and saying in a stage whisper, "She'll only break your heart, Michael."

"And she yours," Michael retorted.

"Nah, she's too busy breaking something else; I won't say what they are. But the woman abuses and torments me from morning till night. And that one backs her up!" he said, pointing at Kitty.

"You fellows are no match for the pair of us," Kitty responded. "Now give your gobs a rest and listen to the music. It's heavenly."

Heavenly, it was. After the Strauss, there was a break and they all rested their feet and had a drink. The band returned with a new tempo, a series of jigs and reels that had the whole crowd on its feet. Then the fiddlers stood to become first and second violin, and the opening chords transported Michael back to his childhood, when his father used to play this very song on their old Victrola. John McCormack singing "Macushla." Not everyone appreciated the Irish tenor voice, but Michael did, and never more than tonight. It made him ache for a time that was forever lost, and ache for the present time, his time with Kitty, which would be all too fleeting. He held her close and she smiled up at him as they danced around the room.

Macushla! Macushla! Your sweet voice is calling
Calling me softly again and again.
Macushla! Macushla! I hear its dear pleading
My blue eyed Macushla, I hear it in vain.

✝

"I don't see Mr. Shanahan here this afternoon," Michael said to Frank Fanning the next day at Christy's. Eddie Madigan and Jimmy O'Hearn were poring over the hurling results in the paper. Sean Nugent was tending bar.

"Howiyeh, Michael," Frank said in greeting. "No, I haven't seen Tim yet today."

"He was here last night, but he left looking a little distressed."

"Is that so?"

"He left without finishing his pint!"

"Must be terminal, Mike!"

"He seems like a good soul."

"He is. A fine fellow, is Tim. He's a professor, you know, teaches poetry and literature. A Yeats scholar is what he is. Knows everything there is to know about William Butler Yeats and his poems. And it's a shame what they've done to him."

"To whom?"

"Done to Tim. They sacked him from his job because of the drink."

"Oh! Where was he working?"

"At the college. UCD." University College of Dublin. "And a brilliant professor. His students loved him. So what if he missed a lecture from time to time? D'you think the students don't miss a day or two themselves? And for the same reason?"

"I'm sorry to hear it, Frank. He's a young man still. Lots of years left in him."

"That's right. He toils away part-time in a library now to meet his expenses. He's overqualified for that sort of work, to put it mildly. Not making use of his talents at all."

Michael hesitated for a moment, then said, "You know, Frank, to me Tim has the look of a priest. That's something I'm quite familiar with, as you can imagine."

"Ah, yes. He doesn't speak of it, but he was indeed a *sagart*. Still is, in a way, I suppose. Isn't that what you fellows say, 'Once a priest, always a priest'?"

Michael nodded. "Something like that, yes."

"But he doesn't practise his vocation now. I don't know why. He'd make a fine man of the cloth. But he never talks about it, and nobody wants to annoy him about it."

"Do you suppose he'd be open to some help about his drinking?" Michael asked.

"Help?" Frank looked puzzled. "Taking the pledge, that class of a thing?"

"Not so much that as counselling, you know. I've done some of that in my time as a priest."

"Well, I'm sure he'd appreciate the thought behind it, Mike. Not sure how much good it would do. I mean, does he want to give it up, you have to ask yourself."

"Well . . ."

"My wife's always after me to take the pledge," Jimmy O'Hearn piped up. "Says I can move back in with her if I go off the drink. But to tell you the truth, I don't think she means it. I think she's happy with things just the way they are. She put the run to me when our youngest daughter moved out to get married. I pay Mrs. O'Hearn a visit once in a while and we get along great, and the rest of the time she has the place to herself. Suits her just fine."

"Suits the both of you, I'd say," Frank remarked. He looked at Sean Nugent, who was wiping the far end of the bar. "What would you do, Sean, if the whole crowd of us here took the pledge?"

"Sure I'd be out of work in short order, Frank, but I'd wish you all the best even so!" He smiled, folded his cleaning rag, and disappeared behind the bar.

"Now there's a fine lad," Frank said.

"Yes, a most personable young man, and he handles things very well here," Michael agreed. "He told me he had an uncle who lived in the town where I come from, in Canada. Grand-uncle, I guess it was. Dead now. I'm thinking I may have met the fellow."

"Right. Sean's grand-uncle. Born back in the 1890s and married late in life. Let me tell you something about him. He did his part for Ireland, even though he was on the other side of the ocean. Smuggled guns over to our boys. On ships coming out of Canada. He and his brother, as soon as they got word of the Rising in 1916. He resisted the call to fight in the Great War. Refused to fight for the Brits, was the way he looked at it. Trained to become a doctor, and that kept him out of the army's sights. So he was able to direct his efforts to assisting Ireland in her hour of need."

Sean reappeared with a couple of bottles of John Jameson in his hands. He saw Fanning looking at him and asked if it was time for a refill.

"I wouldn't say no, Sean. You, Michael?"

"No, but thank you anyway, Frank."

Sean put his bottles on the shelf and began to pour Frank a pint of Guinness.

"We were just talking about you, Sean."

"Nothing too terrible, I hope."

"Not at all. I was telling Michael about your grand-uncle in Canada. You must be proud of him."

"I am, Frank, but you know . . ." He leaned towards Frank as he passed him his pint. "Sometimes I wonder if it's our family name that accounts for the way we get held up at customs and border crossings in the U.K."

"Could be, Sean. Those fellows on British territory have long memories. Or it could be that somebody else in the family has been carrying on the tradition."

Fanning winked at Nugent, and the young fellow gave a quick little smile. Fanning took a long draft of his pint.

Frank Fanning was obviously a man with a keen interest in history and politics. Little wonder he found Christy Burke's such a congenial spot to drink and socialize.

But it was another regular, Tim Shanahan, who was on Michael's mind. "I wonder what made Tim rush away last evening. I was with some friends — well, they'd be familiar to you by now — Brennan and Monty and his wife, and Sister Curran, and Sister was regaling us with some highly entertaining stories about her time in Africa. I noticed Tim was kind of listening in, and then he . . . well, he virtually fled the pub."

"Tim spent some time in Africa himself, I know. Maybe the good sister's stories made him homesick!"

"What was he doing in Africa?"

"I don't know. It may have been back when he was wearing the collar, I'm not sure. He never mentioned it himself. It's just something I heard. But don't be worrying yourself about him, Michael. I imagine he'll turn up as usual tomorrow."

The next day was Wednesday, and Brennan had scheduled an extra couple of lectures at the seminary in Maynooth. Michael was having breakfast in Bewley's Café with him before he left for the day. Monty, after taking a few minutes to admire the Harry Clarke stained-glass windows that adorned the place, joined Brennan and Michael at their table overlooking Grafton Street. They ordered a pot of tea, and all three of them ended up gorging themselves on Bewley's rich cakes and pastries instead of anything one would consider a traditional breakfast.

They occupied themselves with their meal for a few minutes, and then Michael asked, "Now what is it you'll be speaking about today, Brennan?"

"The trinitarian treatises of St. Thomas Aquinas. A comparison of what he writes in the *Summa Theologiae* and the *Summa Contra Gentiles*."

"You're not going to scare off a crop of young recruits, are you?"

"No, this is for the lads who are a little farther along. Only fitting, wouldn't you say? What goes around comes around. St. Thomas himself, the Angelic Doctor, was taught by an Irishman."

"How did he manage that?" Monty asked. "Came up to Dublin for a stag weekend and stumbled into a monastery on Monday morning?"

"Em, no. The Irish were imparting their wisdom to continental Europe by the early Middle Ages, as I'm sure you know. So why should anybody be surprised that there was an Irishman on the faculty of the University of Naples when Thomas Aquinas was a student there in the thirteenth century? Petrus Hibernicus. Peter of Ireland. Peter helped form the mind of our great medieval theologian. And that mind was appreciated back here by none other than James Joyce, who said that Thomas Aquinas just might have been the most clear, the most keen mind the world has ever known. And it falls to me to impart some scraps of Thomas's wisdom to the angelic baby priests of Maynooth."

"Well, I know you'll be clear in your presentation of a very deep and complex subject. Best of luck!"

"No worries. I've been speechifying on this topic for years. So what are you two planning today?"

"There's a traditional music session at Christy's this afternoon," Michael replied. "Would you like to take that in, Monty?"

"Great. I'm off to meet the MacNeil for some sightseeing now, but I'll join you at the pub later on."

✝

Michael was at the bar next to Frank Fanning, enjoying a piece played on the uilleann pipes, when Monty arrived. Christy's was jammed, but a group of young people at a table near the door invited Monty to join them. That was just as well because, as much as Michael enjoyed Monty's company, he had something else on his mind today. Seeing Brennan head off to teach Thomistic theology to a group of seminarians made Michael think of Tim Shanahan, a priest out of uniform who had been a professor of literature before losing his job, a job he must have treasured. Once again, he was absent from the pub.

When the piper took a break, Michael said, "I see Tim's AWOL again, Frank."

"Sure I'm asking myself what's got into him!" Frank replied.

"True. Let's just hope he's all right. Another thing I'm wondering about is why Tim left the priesthood. A priest inevitably wants to know why another gave it up. Did Tim leave to get married? Was that it?"

"Now I can't help you there, Mike, because I don't know myself what happened. He's not married, though. Lives alone as far as I'm aware. I can tell you this much: it can't have been a loss of faith. The man goes to morning Mass at St. Saviour's every day without fail. Well, I say without fail, but he missed the last couple of days. I know that because Father Ryan, that's the Dominican father who says the Mass, was in here for a wee drop — just one, mind — and he was asking me if I'd seen Shanahan. He wasn't at Mass today or yesterday, and that was a fact notable enough to draw the attention of Father Ryan."

"He came in especially to look for Tim?"

"No, he stops in once in a while for a quick one. He just mentioned it because he knows we see Tim quite regularly here."

"Does Tim live nearby?"

"He's not far at all. Corner of Henrietta Street and Henrietta Lane. It's a little confusing, so I'll draw you a map." He grabbed a Paddy Whiskey coaster off the bar and drew a little sketch. "Big red-brick house, second one in, ground floor flat."

Perfect. Michael would stop in to see him. He could tell Tim he'd heard that people were concerned. He'd heard as well that Tim was a priest so Michael was naturally interested in his story. Tim would understand that. And if it turned out that he was ill, perhaps there was something Michael could do for him.

He stayed on for a few minutes longer, then left the pub and headed down Mountjoy Street with Frank's map. A couple of twists and turns brought him to a row of four-storey brick townhouses that had seen better days. And likely would again. Michael recalled reading somewhere that this had been one of the finest streets in Dublin back in the day. There was a bell push that seemed to go with the lower flat, but nobody answered. He rang again. He heard footsteps, and a hard-looking young woman with blue-black hair came to the door. Loud, insistent music blared from the recesses of her flat.

"Are yeh lookin' for Tim?"

"Yes, thank you. Is he home?"

"I think he's in there. Go ahead. Door on the right. It's never locked."

"Em, well, do you think I should?"

"Sure, go ahead. He never complains." She turned and trotted back into her apartment.

Michael opened the door and entered the building. A grubby

paper name plate on the right-hand door said "T. P. Shanahan."

He knocked. "Tim?" he called out. No response. He opened the door and called again, a little louder. "Tim Shanahan?" By this time, Michael was in the tiny living room. Or, to be more precise, the library. Bookshelves covered every bit of wall space except for the front window and the door. Yeats, Joyce, Synge, O'Casey, Wilde, Heaney, Hopkins, Shakespeare, Dante, Blake, Aeschylus, Ovid. Michael gazed about him. This was the home of a man in love with literature and poetry. He was about to call out again when he heard a sound coming from another room. He followed it. His nose wrinkled up. There was a foul smell coming from somewhere in the flat.

Then he saw him: Tim Shanahan lying on his back on the floor of his bedroom. He was in his undershorts, and they were badly soiled. There was a pool of vomit at the side of his head. His eyes were closed, and his thin, handsome face was shiny with sweat. Michael was about to announce his presence when Shanahan sneezed, and sneezed again. His eyes and nose were runny, and he raised a languid arm to wipe them. All he succeeded in doing was to smear mucus all over his face. His right leg kicked out, and Michael moved away. The leg moved again, and Shanahan's whole body began to shake. Michael had seen the DTs before — delirium tremens, the symptoms of alcohol withdrawal — but never this bad.

"Tim!" The man's eyelids fluttered open, and the dark blue eyes stared vacantly at Michael. "Tim, it's Michael O'Flaherty. Father O'Flaherty from, well, from Christy Burke's. I'm going to help you. Let me get a cloth and clean you up a bit, then I'll put you in your bed. I'll call a doctor for you."

"Call my . . ."

Michael leaned down to hear him. He thought Tim said "dealer," but was it "healer"? His doctor?

"Who should I call, Tim?"

"Number's there." Tim tried to lift his arm. He seemed to be pointing to his bedside table. There were books on the table, and Tim's eyeglasses were perched precariously on a volume of Yeats's poetry. There were a few sheets of paper scribbled with notes. One was a phone number. Michael picked it up and recited it. Tim nodded and embarked on another bout of sneezing.

Michael found the telephone and dialled the number. It rang so long he almost gave up, but then a man answered. "Yeah?"

"Hello, this is, em, I'm calling from the residence of Tim Shanahan. He asked me to ring you. He's not well."

"How bad is he?" The voice on the phone sounded familiar somehow, but Michael couldn't place it.

Michael glanced at the poor man lying in vomit and excrement on the floor. No point in painting a pretty picture. "He's in bad shape, and he needs help immediately. Are you a doctor? Should I give him water?"

"I'll be there. Twenty minutes." Click.

"He's coming right over, Tim. I'll see what I can do to make you a little more comfortable."

Michael found the bathroom. A sickening sight, but this wasn't the time for housekeeping. He found a small towel and wet it, then picked up a cake of soap and returned to the man and the shambles he had made of himself. Michael had seen a lot of alcoholism over the years and had spent countless hours at the bedside of patients in hospital. He wasn't squeamish, not like some. He reflected briefly on one of the many differences between him and his fellow priest Brennan Burke. Brennan would rather spend a week ministering to murderers and rapists and drug pushers in the local lockup than a day in a hospital room where people were squatting over bedpans or hawking up gobbets of blood and phlegm. Michael and Brennan complemented each other in that way: Brennan could have the psychopaths; Michael had an affinity for the infirm and feeble, and he put that to work for him now.

He knelt beside Tim Shanahan and gently wiped his brow and lips. He saw a flicker of recognition in Shanahan's eyes. Michael wiped his chest and arms, then his legs. On the insides of Tim's arms, Michael saw reddish marks. A rash? The marks almost looked like puncture wounds from a needle.

"You're sweating to death in here, Tim. I'll open a window for you once I get you cleaned up. I think I should remove your underwear, give you a bit of a scrubbing, and put a clean pair of shorts on you. Would it be all right if I did that?"

Tim nodded weakly and tried to speak. Michael saw tears forming in his eyes.

"Don't you be worried now, Tim. The doctor's coming over, and we'll put you to rights."

Michael did what he had to do to bathe his patient, and he found a clean pair of shorts in the top drawer of the bureau. He got them on him.

"Are you able to get up now, Tim? Just to the bed? It looks fresh and clean, and you'll be comfortable there."

Michael pulled down the grey blanket and white sheet. Shanahan's trembling subsided enough that he could get himself up and, leaning on Michael, made his way to the bed and collapsed. Michael went to the kitchen, found a tumbler, and ran the tap till the water was cold. He held Tim's head up so he could drink.

"Thank you," Tim whispered.

"Sure you're welcome, Tim."

The floor couldn't be left in such a state, so Michael rummaged under the kitchen sink for a rag and cleaning fluid. He was just finishing up when he heard the front door open and a man's voice calling Shanahan's name.

Yes, the voice sounded familiar. As indeed it was; into the room stepped the ex-cop from Christy's, Eddie Madigan. He looked from Michael to Tim and back without speaking. Then he got down to business. He reached into his jacket pocket, produced a syringe, took the protective cap off it, pulled out a rubber tourniquet, wrapped it around Tim's left arm, and injected something into his veins.

Within seconds, Tim's demeanour changed entirely. He looked like a man who was gazing upon the face of God Himself. Michael marvelled at the euphoria the drug had induced in the ailing man. As the seconds passed, Tim seemed to settle into a sense of well-being. He smiled.

"What is it?" Michael asked Eddie. But he knew.

"I've been trying to get him on methadone," was all Madigan said.

Michael had a lot to think about after his visit to Tim Shanahan's flat. The poor man was a heroin addict. And Eddie Madigan, a former officer of the law, was his drug supplier! How could Madigan live with himself? Michael hadn't taken it up with Madigan before he left the flat; that could wait. Tim had reached up and taken Michael's hand in his own. "Thank you, Michael. Thank you so very much for your kindness." Michael had assured him that he was welcome. He made the sign of the cross over him, gave his blessing, and left the apartment.

He wasn't in the mood for more drinking at Christy Burke's, not that he ever indulged in more than two pints of stout, so he headed to his new digs in Stoneybatter. Perhaps Leo Killeen would be in residence, and Michael could probe him for news about the TV evangelist who was missing. Anything to get his mind off Shanahan. And Madigan. Leo wasn't home, however, and neither was the other resident priest, so Michael had the house to himself. He picked up a book of Chesterton's Father Brown mystery stories, which he had been meaning to read ever since his holiday began.

He became engrossed in his reading and didn't notice the time passing. When the room grew dusky, he reached over and switched on a light and kept reading, abandoning himself to Father Brown and his insights into the criminal mind, which the priest-detective had developed in the confessional. Lights flashed against Michael's window, and he got up to see if one of his housemates had come home in a car or a taxi. Maybe he'd have company enjoying a nightcap before settling down to sleep. He pushed the curtain aside and peered into the darkness. There was a car idling in the street, but nobody got out of it. After a few seconds, it backed up and continued a ways down the street. Its lights went out. But it stayed there, and nobody emerged. So much for company, Michael thought, and turned away from the window.

He went into the bathroom, washed his face and brushed his teeth, and was about to get undressed for bed when he heard a sound outside the house. He walked to the window again and peeked out. Was it Leo? No, it looked like Father Grattan, who occupied the room downstairs. Just as Michael was turning away, he noticed the small car he'd seen earlier turn into the driving lane and move slowly along Aughrim Street in the direction of the house. It still had its lights off, which struck Michael as a shade sinister. But then again, he had been reading crime fiction all evening long! The car slowed in front of the house, then moved out of sight. Michael heard Father Grattan come in and open the door to his room. But he would make a point of socializing with Grattan another time; he decided to go to bed and put crime and creeping automobiles out of his mind.

Chapter 7

Brennan

"Can you understand how it might be a little embarrassing for me, Burke? Look at him."

Brennan and Monty were in Monty's hotel room waiting to set out for a stint at the Brazen Head on Wednesday evening. Maura MacNeil had gone out for a mother-daughter shopping excursion with Normie and had dropped little Dominic off with the men. He was sound asleep in a little baby basket of some kind. She had been gone awhile, and Monty and Brennan were most of the way through a bottle of Jameson. Brennan had, perhaps unwisely, launched yet another salvo in the campaign to get the Collins-MacNeil family back together, and to secure a father for Dominic.

Look at him? Brennan didn't have to look. The baby boy, with his black hair and black eyes, looked nothing like Monty. He looked like the child of an Italian father, which presumably he was. The MacNeil's ex-boyfriend, Giacomo. But the baby also resembled . . . Brennan's mind flashed back to a scene he wished he could purge from memory, a bit of burlesque performed by Beau Delaney in Halifax. Delaney was a client of Monty's, but he was also a lawyer himself. One day when Brennan was looking after the baby, Delaney showed up at the MacNeil residence. Taking a look at the baby and then at Brennan, Delaney had embarked on a mock cross-examination after Brennan had imprudently let it be known that someone — it was in fact the MacNeil — had accused him of drinking too much. "If you don't have a problem," she had said, "prove it. Give the stuff up. For a while, at least." Which he had done. Without any trembling, withdrawal, or any other symptoms of addiction. No surprise there. He liked a drink, he didn't need one.

Yet it was careless of him to have reported that little episode to the lawyer, Delaney, who counted back to the time of the baby's conception, then said, "And where were you, Brennan Burke, on the night in question? Let the record show that the witness is unresponsive. Father Burke, earlier in these proceedings you admitted that you have been accused, by someone, of heavy drinking. Is that correct?"

"Have you no other way of amusing yourself, Mr. Delaney?"

"I'll ask the questions here, Father. Have you ever, on any occasion, consumed so much Irish whiskey that you blanked out, to use a layman's term, and were unable to remember what you did whilst under the influence of said alcohol? You *have* thought of this, haven't you, Brennan? You see this little dark-eyed, black-haired baby and you wonder . . ."

Well, no, he hadn't wondered about that. Not really. What grown man in his right mind would even consider the possibility that such a thing had happened? He had to acknowledge privately that there had been the odd time in his life, his past life, when he had consumed so much alcohol that he could not exactly recall what he had done under its influence. But surely he'd remember if he and the MacNeil . . . *Get a grip, Burke*, he told himself. Even if he were stocious with drink, he would never have lost all moral sense to the point where he would get up on his best friend's wife. And, besides, if anything like that had happened, she would have let him know in no uncertain terms. He paled to think how excruciating — "excruciating" from the Latin for "from the cross," that is, the agony of the cross — how excruciating such a conversation would have been, with her giving out to him without mercy and him sitting there taking it, like a gobshite. *Get a grip*, he admonished himself again. He eyed the glass of whiskey in his hand. He put it down. That was it for the night, and maybe the next few nights as well.

He looked at Monty, who had pinned him with his sky-blue eyes. Lawyer's eyes, which had seen it all. Could he read Brennan's mind?

Brennan shook off the idiocy that had come over him and went on the offensive. "Has anyone, friend or relative or colleague, ever made a disparaging remark to you about the baby and his parentage?"

"Eh?"

"Has anyone mentioned it?"

"There is no need to mention it. *Res ipsa loquitur.*"

Brennan sighed. *The thing speaks for itself.* A legal concept, no doubt. He didn't take Monty up on it. Instead he said, "The pregnancy wasn't planned. I think we can all agree that's an understatement. The two of you were separated. She had a relationship, you had female company yourself, so you were both involved with others. Anyone viewing the situation would grasp that reality, so this embarrassment you feel, although a perfectly human response —"

"I know all that, Brennan. Now, I've had enough of this conversation."

They sat in silence for a while, then Monty asked about one of the sites he and the family were planning to visit. Glendalough. This was an ancient monastic settlement where priests had been offering the sacrifice of the Mass as long ago as the sixth century. Brennan was describing the settlement in loving detail when mother and daughter returned with their shopping bags. They stayed for a chat before lifting the sleeping baby from his basket and taking a cab to their room in the convent. Brennan and Monty set off for the Brazen Head to take in a session of well-played traditional music. Brennan stayed off the whiskey, though he didn't say no to the voice of Arthur Guinness calling him from the taps.

He fell into a boozy sleep and was restless all night. Vaporous images arose in his mind's eye. A dark-haired infant being baptized. Then the child's progress through the sacraments. Then the child, who obviously now was Brennan, was standing in a classroom or a hall being called upon to recite the seven deadly sins. His mind went blank except for greed, probably the only one he hadn't himself committed. He was suddenly grown up, and he had a new assignment: to refute the proposition of his superiors that he was unfit for the priesthood. He stood in a cavernous room before unseen authorities.

Question 1: Whether Brennan Xavier Burke is fit to be a priest.

Objection 1: It seems that the man drinks too much.

Objection 2: Further, the man has made a habit of breaking his promise of chastity.

On the contrary, with respect to Objection 1: "Too much" drinking would be that which culminates in illness, irrational or abusive behaviour, or alcoholism, none of which consequences have beset Father Burke. He has never claimed to be an ascetic, a monk in a cell. Besides, it is a known fact that the monks themselves make liqueur, some of the finest in the world. And he is not a member of one of those sects that despise the world and its pleasures. Catholics celebrate the physical world; just look at the sensual works of art in the Vatican. Catholics see the created world as a sacrament, revealing the presence of God here on earth.

With respect to Objection 2: As for the "habit" of unchaste behaviour, "habit" is a word that implies frequency and a regular pattern of behaviour, whilst Father Burke can count on the fingers of one hand (and, if memory serves, still have his thumb left over) the number of women with whom the deadly sin of lust had been fulfilled but the priestly vows had not. Brazil, Rome, New York, Rome again, on that road trip with Montague Collins . . . Father Burke acknowledges that his incidents with women were wrong not only because they represented the breaking of a promise, but because they were acts of selfishness. Taking for himself the most intense of physical pleasures instead of denying himself, as he should have done. Celibacy means that the priest is a person set aside, someone who is to love not just one person or one family, but everyone. He is supposed to live the way the Lord Jesus Christ had done, making a total gift of the self. A daunting task, but Father Burke is working on it. Let it be known that he has spent countless hours on his knees in repentance. After the most recent of his failures, he renewed his promise that he would live up to his vows. And he has done so (though he acknowledges that it has only been half a year since that renewal). He submits therefore that a practice, even if one were, for the sake of argument, to accede to the use of the word "habit" to describe the practice, ceases to be a habit if given up.

I answer that Brennan Xavier Burke is fit to be a priest because of his penitence and true remorse for his failings; his devotion to his calling for over a quarter of a century; his love of God the Father, the Son, and the Holy Spirit; his celebration of the Holy Eucharist; his ministry to the poor in spirit and body; his love for his fellow man, which, whilst not always self-evident, can be deduced from . . .

Reply to Objection 1: What objection? What? Am I awake now? Was I ever asleep?

Sleep overcame him again.

He tried to shake the whole thing off when he awoke for good. He didn't know whether to laugh or cry over the fact that his Scholastic training was so deeply ingrained that he could not even escape it when he went into a dream state. What was it the Jesuits used to say? *Give me the child for his first seven years, and I will give you the man.*

He headed out for a bit of breakfast but was drawn instead to the Church of St. Augustine and St. John, locally known as the John's Lane church because of the side street going by it. Brennan had also heard it called the Fenian church, in reference to all the Fenians who had worked on its construction. He was in awe of the great Gothic cathedrals of Europe; this was a Gothic revival with soaring arches and brilliant stained-glass windows, some by the local man Harry Clarke. There were twelve statues in niches on the tower, made by James Pearse, father of Pádraig and Willie Pearse, who were numbered amongst the slain patriots of 1916. Brennan stood at the back and blessed himself, making an effort to ensure that his worship was directed to the Divine Architect and not to the architecture.

He approached the magnificent high altar and knelt before it. Bowing deeply, he recited the *Confiteor* over and over. *Mea culpa, mea culpa, mea maxima culpa.* He thought back over his life. Although he was the first of Declan Burke's four sons, he was the last of those sons that anyone would have suspected of, or credited with, having a vocation. The call came in the form of a cross burned into his chest in the midst of a fire that claimed his closest friend at the time, in New York. Brennan had answered the call. And in spite of it all, after twenty-five years he was still here. He would not trade the priestly life for anything on earth, not the pleasures of the flesh, not the love of a wife, not even . . . a little black-haired, black-eyed baby boy.

Michael

On Thursday afternoon Michael was back at Christy's. When he saw Eddie Madigan coming through the door, he got up and intercepted him before Madigan made it to the bar.

"How could you do it, Madigan? A brilliant young man like Tim Shanahan, a scholar, a teacher, a priest, now a helpless drug addict wallowing like an animal in his own filth. And others too, young people no doubt, all of them precious in the eyes of God. Peddling drugs to them, getting them hooked."

"It's not like that, Father O'Flaherty. That's not the way it started and that's not the way it is now."

"I saw you with my own eyes, injecting the man with what must have been heroin."

"It was."

"Well?"

"You'll have to hear it from Shanahan if you hear it at all. I'll not be slandering the man in the process of exonerating myself." Michael shook his head in disgust. "Now let me in so I can indulge my addiction to whiskey along with all the other addicts in this place."

Michael stepped aside and then, on impulse, left the bar. He couldn't bring himself to sit and drink with the likes of Madigan. Michael set out for home in Stoneybatter, anger punctuating his steps all the way.

When he got to his room, he sat down to read Chesterton. At first distracted, he finally got into his book. An hour or so passed, then he heard a knock on his door and got up to answer. Tim Shanahan was standing there, scrubbed and immaculate in a black golf shirt and grey pants. Shanahan's mild blue eyes looked at Michael through his rimless spectacles.

"Tim!"

"Hello, Michael. I found you through Leo Killeen. May I come in?"

"Certainly! Please do."

"I'd like to talk to you about yesterday."

"Did Eddie Madigan send you to plead his case for him?"

Tim looked at him blankly, then caught on. "No, no, he didn't. I haven't seen him yet today. Though I will later. May I sit?"

"Yes, have a seat. Should I wet the tea?"

"That would be lovely, thank you. And I can't thank you enough for your help and patience yesterday. You can imagine how ashamed I am, to be seen like that, filthy and disgusting. I'm sorry, Michael. More sorry than I can possibly say."

"We all have our weaknesses, Tim. All of us. So much the worse when our fellow human beings prey on us for their own —"

Tim held up a hand. "Let me tell you a story, Michael."

"All right. I'll get the tea first."

When they had mugs of tea in front of them at the table, Tim began to speak.

"I want to tell you about a girl I knew in Africa."

Ah, here it comes, thought Michael. *Cherchez la femme!*

"She's about this high." He put his arm out, indicating a person about four and a half feet tall. "I was working in Togo, in western Africa, running a small parish there. I'm sure it's dawned on you that I was — I am — a priest." Michael nodded. "We built a tiny church, a wooden shed really, and the local men built us a steeple. They were great about pitching in and helping after I fell from the roof and broke my leg! It was obvious to everybody there I wasn't much of a carpenter. Anyway, the church: it wasn't Chartres, but it was ours! There was an adjoining building, made of corrugated steel, which served as a school for girls. There was already a local academy for the boys. I was the parish priest and principal of the girls' school. There were two other teachers, a nun named Sister Josephine and a young woman named Rosalie who had completed part of her education degree at Alexandria University. Both were Togolese, as was Father Amegashie, a newly ordained priest who did sort of a circuit around the area. Wonderful young lad. Bright and fearless. Not afraid to stand his ground with the powers-that-be in the region.

"Anyway, the young girl. Sabine. Skin the colour of milk chocolate, great big dark eyes that stared in wonder at the world around her. She had a gap between her two front teeth that made her adorable whenever she had a grin on her face, which was often. She had her hair up in two pigtails high on her head, so they looked like horns. I made the mistake of saying to her, when one of my superiors was visiting, 'I see you've got your devil horns on again today.' Father Lafitte admonished me for comparing this African child to the fount of all evil. But she got a kick out of it when I said that. I started calling her Beelzebub, which cracked her up because of the sound of it.

"Not only was she sweet and funny, she was a top student at the school. She became a whiz at math, she had a flair for science and experimentation, and she wrote beautifully in her own language and in English. Her composition and her handwriting were excellent. We also taught the students life skills. As out of fashion as it sounds, the girls were taught to cook and sew and care for young children. But we also taught them some accounting, some carpentry, a lot of things that were considered the prerogative of the men and boys. We gave them a smattering of politics and economics. Had to tread carefully there. But the idea was to help the girls grow into capable, independent women who could fend for themselves and resist being dominated and exploited. We weren't always popular.

"Sabine, as I say, was very good with words. She began to write poems and stories. Said she wanted to write a book. I thought we could put together the kids' stories and poetry in a volume and publish it. Self-publish it, I mean. Send it away to a printer and then sell the copies to earn a bit of money for the school. The project was going well until it came time to choose an illustration for the cover. As bright as she was, Sabine had no talent as an artist. She was terrible. All the girls were asked to contribute a picture, done in paint or crayon, for the cover. We made a contest out of it. Their names were on the back, so you couldn't tell by looking who had done which picture. Then the girls were to vote on the best one for the cover. Well, some were excellent, some mediocre, and Sabine's was atrocious. The worst by far. We had them all spread out on a table, so the children could look them over and cast their votes. Sabine kept pointing to hers as the best, and she tried to convince the others. When another little one laughed at the picture and said it was horrible, Sabine pushed her down and ran out of the school.

"But later that day, Sabine came back and said to me, 'My picture is bad-arsed, banjaxed, God-awful, isn't it, Father?'

"I started to laugh, couldn't help it, and made a mental note to be more careful in my speech around the students. Sabine started laughing too. Then she said, 'But I'm good with letters, right?' I allowed as how she was. 'So can I write the title on the front?' I said she could.

"Well, we got it ready for the printer. I looked it over, checked her title for spelling and all that, and sent it off. Only after it came back did I hold it in a certain light, and look at it a certain way, and discover that she'd scattered letters about that you could barely see. But if you did, they spelled out 'Beelzebub.' Jaysus and Mary be good to us, I thought, imagine if the bishop or the head of our mission or somebody sees that, I'll be crucified. I waited in fear, but nothing happened. And the little divil never said a word, just gave me an angelic smile every time the book was mentioned or passed around. I loved her for it. I loved her anyway. I thought of her as a little sister, almost a daughter.

"Now skip ahead a year or so. I was lying in my bed one night, fast asleep, having a dream. The kind of dream we all have, I'm sure, Father, even — or especially — if we live a celibate life. There was a hand between my legs, and it wasn't my own. It took me a few seconds to wake up and realize there really was somebody with me. A girl, stark naked. I jumped away from her and saw her face in the light. It was Sabine."

"Stop right there!" Michael commanded. He felt as if he'd been kicked in the stomach. Hearing about this dear little child from a man who loved her as a father. Now the man turned out to be a child molester. And it sounded as if he was about to blame the victim! And he thought Michael would want to hear this pornographic story? He got to his feet and looked down at Shanahan.

"Bear with me, Michael, please!"

"I don't want to hear any more of this filth. Have you no shame about yourself at all?"

Shanahan stared at him. He looked as if he was about to be sick. Then he got up and bolted from the room without looking again at Michael. He yanked the door open and fled down the stairs. Michael stood in the centre of his room, trembling with anger and disgust.

†

Michael wasn't in the mood for the daily boozers at Christy Burke's, or not for half the contingent anyway, but there was good news, and he didn't want to be churlish enough not to celebrate it. Well, good news was a relative term in these circumstances. Finn Burke, he who was scheduled for trial several months down the road on charges of fraud and other criminal acts, had been released on bail. And he had invited the Halifax crowd to his house for dinner that evening. Brennan said he would pick up Michael at Christy's for the party.

So Michael stopped and purchased a nice, though economical, bottle of red wine and proceeded to Christy's to await Brennan's arrival. He said hello to Jimmy O'Hearn. There was no sign of Frank Fanning, which was unusual, but it was the other pair — Shanahan and Madigan — that Michael was concerned about. And he was relieved to see they weren't on the premises. Michael signalled to Sean that he wouldn't be having anything, and he sat at a table by himself.

Oh. There at a table in the back was Tim Shanahan. *Father* Shanahan as he was and always would be. Ordination confers an indelible stamp on the man who becomes a priest; no matter what happens after that, no matter what shabby or evil deeds the man commits, that imprint is there for all time. Thou art a priest forever. In this case, it was a man who had taken advantage of a young girl in his care. It was almost incestuous. And if anything happened in that bed, given the child's age, it was statutory rape. Had Shanahan blurted out his tawdry tale in the hearing of someone at Christy Burke's? Had the listener been so revolted that he spray-painted lines about guilt and perpetrators on the walls of the pub? But even as low a specimen as he was, Shanahan could not be termed a killer. No doubt Shanahan had destroyed or killed the little girl's spirit in a sense, but Michael could not imagine the graffiti artist being that sophisticated in his accusations. It was all beyond Michael at the moment, and he wished he could put it out of his mind. He would not be able to recount this squalid story to Brennan; he would feel soiled even repeating it. He'd tell Brennan that Shanahan had some kind of difficulty in Africa. Period.

And there he was, drinking whiskey, and he had obviously had a skinful. He was with a man and a woman. He spotted Michael.

Would there now be a scene of drunken belligerence? Michael was all too familiar with that scenario, people who couldn't hold their liquor and revealed themselves as mean drunks. Michael turned away and hoped for the best.

Things were quiet at the Shanahan table for a few minutes, then Michael heard Tim's voice. He looked over, but Tim was not addressing Michael. He was regaling his companions with poetry, and Michael could see a pink bundle on the woman's lap; a tiny fist emerged from a blanket. The woman brought it to her mouth and kissed it. In profile the woman bore a striking resemblance to Shanahan. A younger sister? As Michael tuned in to Tim's words, he recognized the poem by Yeats, "A Prayer for My Daughter," and Michael had to admit he had never heard it recited so beautifully:

> I have walked and prayed for this young child an hour
> And heard the sea-wind scream upon the tower,
> And under the arches of the bridge, and scream
> In the elms above the flooded stream;
> Imagining in excited reverie
> That the future years had come,
> Dancing to a frenzied drum,
> Out of the murderous innocence of the sea.

How could a man like Shanahan make Yeats's poetry come alive in such a way; how could he pray so eloquently for a little baby girl, when his own history with a young girl might be counted among the storms and screams that Yeats saw as threats to his daughter as she grew?

Michael decided to wait for Brennan outside. He got up and left the pub without a word to anyone.

Chapter 8

Brennan

Brennan borrowed his cousin's car to transport the crowd to Finn's house. After adjusting the radio to his liking — no sooner had he started than he had to come to a screeching halt to change channels and spare himself the unbearable sound of a singer whose voice cracked in a jarring attempt to switch to a falsetto — he made the short trip to Christy's to pick up Michael O'Flaherty. Michael climbed aboard, and they headed for the convent, where they were to meet Monty, Maura MacNeil, and the children.

Mike was uncharacteristically quiet in the car. A few minutes passed before he said, "So, will you be reporting to Finn on your investigation tonight?"

"I'm not sure, Mike. I guess it will depend on whether the opportunity presents itself. Tonight or later; we'll see. I've got all the bits of information stored in my head, such as they are. Have you picked up anything new since you spoke with Bill McAvity?"

"Em, no, well, not much of anything."

One glance at his passenger told Brennan that Michael O'Flaherty had something on his mind.

"What is it?"

"Just something I heard. That Tim Shanahan had difficulties in Africa."

"What sort of difficulties?"

"I don't know. Not really."

Whatever it was, Mike knew and didn't want to discuss it. Well, Brennan was not about to interrogate the man on the way to a dinner party. It could wait.

But Mike spoke up again. "I got the impression there might be drugs involved."

"How do you mean?"

"That Shanahan may have a drug problem."

"What makes you think that?"

"It's just that, em, you know what Bill McAvity told me about Madigan — that there are rumours he was taking payoffs from drug dealers."

"Right."

"It could be true, that he is involved in the drug trade."

"I see. And Shanahan? Where does he fit in?"

"Could perhaps be using drugs."

"Supplied by Madigan."

"Could be."

"What class of drugs are we talking about?" He looked over at Michael again. The man looked miserable. "Something more than a bit of weed on the weekends, I take it."

"I suspect so, yes."

✝

The Collins-MacNeils were waiting outside when Brennan and Michael arrived, and little Normie waved excitedly when she spotted the two priests in the car. A dear little girl she was, with her auburn curls and beautiful hazel eyes. She wore a delicate pair of eyeglasses, and Brennan was well aware that it was considered indelicate to mention them. The baby, Dominic, was fast asleep in his mother's arms.

Women and children were given priority for the available seat belts; Dominic had a special seat of his own, which his mother rigged up in the back. Michael and Monty squeezed into the car, and they proceeded to the dinner party.

Finn's place was in Drumcondra, a neighbourhood situated roughly north of Christy Burke's pub, not too far away but not so close that Finn would be looking at "the office" every time he stepped outside his front door. He lived in a semi-detached red-brick house with a flower garden in the front. Brennan pushed the door open when they arrived; no formality in this family.

Michael and the others followed Brennan to the front room, where they saw Finn practically knee to knee in conversation with Leo Killeen, who was in his black suit and Roman collar. Their chairs were facing each other; there were glasses of whiskey on a table beside them. The two men turned at once when the others entered the room, and tension was visible in their faces. Finn made an obvious effort to break the mood. He stood and moved towards the visitors.

"Come in, come in. Have a seat. I'll get you something to drink. Oh! Who's this now? Some new faces."

Brennan made the introductions. "Maura MacNeil, wife of Monty here. This is Normie, and Dominic." Normie greeted Mr. Burke, and the baby, awake now, stared at him with wide-open dark eyes.

"A pleasure to meet you, Maura, if I may call you Maura."

"You may indeed, Finn."

"And what a charming young lady you have here. And a handsome little boy."

"Thank you, Finn. I am delighted to have the children in Dublin with me. Oh! Leo! Wonderful to see you again."

"You know this gentleman?" Finn asked, surprised.

"Leo and I will always have New York. Eh, Leo? We met in the big city, Finn, when your brother had his trouble at the family wedding." When Declan got shot, and Leo went over to sort out some ancient history, is what she meant.

"Ah, yes," was all Finn said.

Leo had risen and was holding his arms open to herself. They embraced and then stood apart, smiling at each other.

"Some changes in your life since I saw you last, my dear."

"Oh, yeah."

"How old is he?"

"He'll be a year next month."

"Ah. Well, hello there, Dominic. Hope you're enjoying your stay in Dublin."

"He's having the time of his life, Leo. And you remember Normie."

"I certainly do. You're a world traveller, Normie. I met you in New York. Now I see you in Dublin."

"I've seen a whole lot of the world, Father Killeen. I love seeing new places."

"That's the way to be, Normie, good for you. What have you liked on this trip?"

"We went to a place called Glendalough, and there's this little church made out of stones and I want to build a tiny one just like it in my backyard when I get home."

"Excellent idea. You build it and get Father Burke to bless it."

"Okay!"

Turning to her mother, Killeen asked, "How long are you here, Maura?"

"Till the middle of August."

Finn went over to Michael. "Welcome to my home, Monsignor O'Flaherty. I've come up in the world since you saw me last. A little more space here than in my previous, rather cramped quarters. But there's nobody bringing me three meals a day, so I've had to order out! Where's Sister Kitty this evening? I thought she might be with you."

"She's feeding the poor in spirit and body tonight, Finn, working at a soup kitchen run by the nuns of her order."

"Well, let's see if we can save her a few scraps, and you can drop them off to her."

"Oh, that would be grand. Lovely place you have here. I'd never have taken you for a gardener."

"And you'd have been right, Michael," Finn replied with a little smile. "The one next door takes care of that. She wants my half to look as good as hers. I pay for the flowers; she does the work. Everybody's happy."

Brennan wondered briefly whether he should give Finn a little report on what he had learned so far: the whiskey glass and the signs of a vehicle outside the pub the night of the latest graffiti — like Finn, Brennan knew it was the *last* graffiti — scraps of information about the regulars from McDonough and Nurse McAvity, which Finn likely knew anyway. And O'Flaherty's vague allegations about Madigan, Shanahan, and drugs. But it was Finn who held the most concrete information, held the evidence in the form of a corpse. What had Finn done, or ordered done, with the body? Brennan did not want to go into the whole thing now. And it looked as if Finn had other things on his mind, things to be hashed out with Leo Killeen.

But this was a social occasion, and Finn was the host. He took orders for drinks, and Brennan helped him serve his guests. Soon everyone was seated in the front room with glasses in hand.

"So, Leo," Maura asked, "will you be entertaining us with tales of the old days the way you did in New York? I don't live on the edge myself, so I have to get my excitement second-hand, from guys like you and Declan."

"Ah, that was just an oul fellow shuffling down memory lane," Leo said to her. But for Leo, Brennan suspected, memory lane was maybe just around the corner.

Brennan saw Michael turn to place his drink on the table beside his chair and pick up a news clipping that had been lying there. It was a photo of Father Killeen saying Mass in Endastown with the massive armoured vehicles looming over him from behind.

"Did you see this, Maura?"

Michael handed her the news photo. Normie peered over her mother's shoulder at the picture; Maura's mouth dropped open at the sight.

"Oh my God!" she exclaimed. "What are those, tanks?"

"Armoured personnel carriers," Leo answered.

"Is that you, Leo? It is!"

"Mmm."

"And look over to the side, Maura," Michael said. "Who do you see?"

"There's a woman, higher than everyone else. What's she standing on?"

"The base of a light pole."

"She's reading something. Wait a minute! That's not Kitty!"

"It is. And Brennan is the altar boy. You can just see the back of his head."

"Right. I see him now. But what was Kitty doing standing up there?"

"There was a flap about the eulogy the boy's family and comrades wanted read at the funeral. Too inflammatory, wasn't that it, Leo? And who was that fellow who handed the papers to Kitty?"

"I had to do some negotiations to get this funeral approved," Leo said. "One thing the bishop would not allow was the eulogy as first written, filled as it was with accusations that the British Army and the security forces in County Armagh connived in, or carried out, political murders, including that of Rory Dignan himself. And Dermot Cooney, a young Republican firebrand, was expressly forbidden to read the statement. He tried to, as you may recall, Michael, but I ordered him to stand down. That's when he shoved the papers into Kitty's hands to be read. Bless her, she had just hopped up there to signal to the crowd to be quiet. She had never seen the statement before but did her best to edit out the inflammatory bits."

"A glimpse of the real Ireland, 1992," Maura remarked.

"The North of Ireland, anyway. Just across the border."

"I'll stay on this side of the border, thank you very much. Though I have to ask: has there been much spillover from the Troubles here in the South?"

"One of the worst atrocities of the current Troubles, *so far*, took place right here in Dublin," Leo replied. "Well, here and Monaghan. Eighteen years ago, 1974. A bombing operation that was remarkably sophisticated and well-coordinated, particularly for its time. So we can draw the conclusion that it wasn't done by a crowd of amateurs. Four bombs. Thirty-three people, thirty-five if you include two babies in the womb, were killed by UVF — Protestant Loyalist — car bombs. Three hundred were injured. Terribly injured, some of them. But you're right, it's the North that is living this hell day after day."

"This much I know: the atrocities are not all committed by the one side."

"No."

They sat in silence for a long moment.

Then everyone's attention was caught by Dominic, who let out a wail, whereupon his mother produced a little set of colourful toy keys from her bag, and the baby sat on the floor and busied himself with those. His sister joined him and kept him company.

Monty had got up and was standing by the mantelpiece looking at a bunch of photos. Finn invited him to take a closer look, and

Michael joined them. This was his family, Finn explained to them, his wife, Catriona, and their four children. Catriona had died eight years ago, and the children were grown and living on their own. There were pictures of Finn's grandchildren as well. Michael expressed condolences for the death of Catriona. Another photo, in black and white, showed a man and woman with five children, ranging from a babe in arms to a girl of eleven or so.

The photo was well known to Brennan.

"You know that fellow, Mike." Leo pointed to a little boy of nine or ten with dark hair and dark eyes; he was dressed in shorts and a jersey.

"It's got to be Brennan. Is it?"

"It is. In his Gaelic football attire. They couldn't get him to wear anything else, if I remember correctly."

"Were you any good at it, Burke?" Monty asked.

"Wasn't half bad," Brennan replied.

"He was good," Finn confirmed, "but not as good as the lad down the street from him. Sammy Coogan. They played together in the neighbourhood and at school. Sammy's the football manager for the Rebels now. Well, I'm sure you're aware of that, Brennan. Won the All-Ireland Finals two years in a row."

"I've been following Sammy's career. Brilliant!"

"Who are the Rebels?" Maura asked. "In the sports context, I mean!"

"Cork senior footballers. Have you ever been to the People's Republic of Cork, my dear?"

"Not yet. But next trip for sure."

"Anyway, that's young Brennan with the family. Declan and Teresa and the five children, just before they immigrated to New York. Their youngest, number six, was born over there."

"And who's this?" Michael asked. "He sort of looks like Brennan, if you could imagine Brennan with a great big grin on his face and a bouquet of flowers in his hands, but this was obviously before his time."

"Nineteen twenty-two," Finn replied. "That's my uncle Davey. What a character he was!"

"He looks it."

"One of his friends snapped this picture the day his bride, Maisie, was due home from England. She'd been working over there, saving some money, and was expected back at Christmas time. They were planning a Christmas wedding, and Davey was fixing up an old house he'd bought for the pair of them. But with her away and distractions at home, namely his cronies on the hurling team and in his local pub and some other, em, activities, well, the house took a while to get itself renovated."

"I hope those activities didn't include squiring another young lady around town while Maisie was away," Maura said.

"Oh, no. There was only one girl for Davey. He was crazy about her. But he was a little on the slow side getting the place done up. Well, word came by telegram that she was coming home a couple of days earlier than expected. Panic set in. He had cupboards to refurbish, floors to refinish, walls to paint, curtains that were supposed to be made from fabric she had chosen in the summer. You can imagine. So Davey drafted all his teammates and his drinking pals and got them to work on the house. He yanked his sister away from her job in a typing pool someplace and set her up with their grandmother's old sewing machine, trying to get the curtains done. Him standing over her grabbing the pink curtain material as she stitched it up, him going at it with the iron, scorching it no doubt, then trying to get it in place over the windows. Can't you picture him at the ironing board, breaking into a lather of sweat? And there was drink involved. Half the lads were scuppered and making a bollocks of the job. And the clock was ticking away, and the ship was making its inexorable way across the Irish Sea with Maisie aboard.

"This picture is him standing in front of the house. If you look behind him, you can see the curtain rod and the curtains sagging in the front window. Something had gone wrong there. And here's Dave with a bouquet of flowers ready to present to her along with all the excuses he had ready to go about why the matrimonial home was a shambles. For now. But how it would be fit for a queen in very short order."

Everyone had gathered in front of the photo during Finn's recital of the young bridegroom's woes.

"Looks as if he maintained his sense of humour, though," Michael remarked. "You can see a twinkle in those eyes."

"Oh, she'd forgive him anything, by the look of him. Who wouldn't? What a sweetheart!" Maura exclaimed.

"God love him," Finn muttered.

"So, how did it go? What happened when she got home?" Michael and Maura asked at once.

"He was dead."

"What?" Everyone turned to Finn in disbelief.

"Two hours after that photo was taken, Davey was scraping old paint from the front door, and he was shot in the back."

Maura had her hand to her mouth; she looked as if she were about to cry. Michael obviously felt the same way. "God rest his soul!" Michael murmured. "A lovely young man like that. What a terrible waste. Who shot him?"

"The Free Staters. It was during the Civil War."

"How terrible!" Maura exclaimed.

"It was a revenge killing. IRA fellows from Davey's street had done the same to a Free State man, father of five, the week before. That's the way things were during the Civil War."

In a country that had endured its share of tragedy over the course of hundreds of years, the Civil War may have been the worst tragedy of all, as Brennan saw it. The old IRA had fought the War of Independence and, against all odds, prevailed against the British Empire. The British withdrew from Ireland for the first time in seven hundred and fifty years. The country was granted the status of a free state, like the Dominion of Canada. Ireland, at long last, had a government to call its own. But there was a price to be paid. The country was still within the British Commonwealth, and members of the new government were required to swear an oath to King George V of England. Not surprisingly, that was utterly unacceptable to diehard Republicans. And six of the thirty-two counties were excluded from the deal. Michael Collins, in signing the Anglo-Irish Treaty in 1921, believed he had signed his own death warrant. And he was right. General Collins was assassinated by his former comrades in 1922. The Civil War between the anti-treaty IRA and the fledgling Irish Free State — the Irish Republican Army versus the National Army — raged for nearly a year, pitting Irishman against Irishman.

"Your neighbour, your drinking companion, your brother," Finn said, "you never knew who would be next."

"Someone fundamental to your world was gone from the world in an instant," Leo agreed. "Happened all the time."

Everyone was silent after that. Until the jangle of the telephone made them jump. Finn rushed into the kitchen and grabbed the receiver.

"What?" he barked into the phone. He listened for a few seconds, then said, "No. We haven't. That ought to tell you something." He slammed the receiver down.

Leo Killeen's eyes followed him as he came back into the front room. Finn returned the look, then sat down, picked up his glass, and polished off the whiskey.

"What's going on?" Brennan demanded.

Finn looked from his nephew to his other guests.

"You can trust everybody here, Finn."

"I know that, Brennan. It's . . ." He glanced at Leo. "It's the Merle Odom situation. The television preacher who was . . . who disappeared from Belfast."

"What's happening?"

"Nobody knows where he is. *We* don't know where he is."

Brennan had his own speculations as to who was included in that "we," but he was not about to ask. Not in front of the guests. The implication, though, was that Finn Burke and Father Leo Killeen would be expected to know where the American was, to know who had snatched him from the street.

"So," Brennan said, "you haven't heard anything that might explain his disappearance."

"Not a thing."

"The repercussions of this —"

"Have already begun. There are pitched battles going on in the streets of Belfast right now. A church near the Falls Road was fire-bombed. People retaliated by setting fire to a shop in the Shankill area. Rival gangs are going at each other all over the city. Leaders on all sides are trying to put a lid on it."

"All sides?" Leo inquired, with an edge to his voice.

"Well, some of the para leaders are egging their people on. What would you expect? And I hear there is a great deal of pressure being brought to bear on the authorities here and in the North, pressure from the Americans to get this solved."

"I'm going up there," Leo announced.

"You're *what*?"

"Finn, this has got to be contained. The man has to be found.

Whoever has him must be convinced to produce him, alive, now! I don't want to think about the forces that might be unleashed if he's found dead."

"If we don't know who has him, Leo, we can hardly persuade them to do the right thing."

"But I'm thinking if I go up there, and put the word in a few ears, and the word spreads around, to splinter groups . . ."

He wound down and stared at the wall.

Brennan looked at Michael O'Flaherty. Michael's eyes were pinned on Leo Killeen. Dying to hear more about Leo's mission but fearful for his safety; it was all there in Michael's face. But Mike was smart enough to know he was far out of his element, and wise enough to keep his questions and his fears to himself. Brennan could see that every person in the room felt the same way. Even little Normie appeared disturbed. She was a sensitive child; her eyes went from Finn to Leo and back, seeking understanding, or perhaps reassurance.

Only Dominic was oblivious; the baby was playing happily with a set of brightly coloured plastic rings. He stuffed them in his mouth, found them to his liking, then crawled over to Leo, reached up and offered them to him, with a word that sounded like "Da!" Leo laughed and ruffled the child's dark hair, and the tension was broken, at least for the moment.

"You'll be wondering where dinner is, I expect," Finn said. "It's due to arrive any minute, from the Greek place down the street. In the meantime, let me refresh your drinks." He did, and the food arrived and was plentiful. When the meal was over, the dinner guests thanked Finn for the evening and said goodnight. They dropped Maura and the children off at the convent with a plateful of Greek delicacies for Kitty Curran.

Michael

Michael O'Flaherty went to the Aughrim Street church the next day, Friday, for morning Mass. When he got to the *Confiteor*, when he confessed that he had sinned "in what I have done and what I have failed to do," he thought about himself as a sinner, and about the sinners who came to him to make their confessions. Depending on what he heard in the confession box on any given day, his feelings ranged from amusement to exasperation to outrage, but almost without exception he felt compassion and pity for the people whose transgressions he absolved. He thought about this as he made the short walk home, and he realized he had recently acted in a manner unbefitting a man of his calling. The only person who would understand was another priest. When he got to his room, he gave Brennan a call and asked to see him. He said he'd take a walk over to Brennan's place, but the younger man quickly offered to come to Michael.

"I failed a man the other day, Brennan," he told Father Burke when the two were seated together in Michael's room.

Brennan looked at him and waited for him to continue. "A man came to me for, well, I wouldn't say he came to me for help. He came to thank me for . . . a small kindness I had shown him. And then he started to tell me something. Something dreadful that had happened, that he had done. And I cut him off, refused to hear it."

"You're not saying you were his confessor during this encounter, are you, Mike?"

"No. Or at least I don't think he saw it that way. He knows the drill and would have made it clear, if that had been his intention."

Brennan nodded as if he understood. Had he caught on that Michael was talking about Tim Shanahan?

"I can't condone for a minute what he did, Brennan, but . . ."

"What was his attitude? Was he callous about it? Was it something he was boasting about? Or was he unburdening himself, so to speak?"

"I don't think he was boasting. If that was his intent, I never let him get that far. But, no, I don't think so. I think he wanted to talk it through, and he might have thought I would be sympathetic, given the . . . situation I had found him in, and the assistance I had provided. A simple act of goodness that I then repudiated and undid by my arrogance in refusing to let him speak!"

"You couldn't stomach whatever it was he started to tell you."

"That's correct. But now I feel I let him down. I know I did. If it had been a confession, I would have listened to whatever he had to say and then decided whether or not I could grant absolution. Instead, I gave him the brush-off, turned him away. Spoke some harsh words while I was at it. He is so obviously a man in need that, no matter what he has done, I should have heard him out, and tried to direct him as best I could."

"I know what you're saying, Michael. We all make mistakes. We all do things we're not proud of. And there comes a time for most of us when we need someone to hear us out. You've done that for me, you've done it for thousands of others, and something tells me you're going to do it for this poor devil as well."

"I am." Michael stood up. "I'm going right now."

†

Less than twenty minutes later, Michael found himself once again at Tim Shanahan's door. He knocked and waited. Not a sound from inside. He tried again. This time he heard footsteps, and the door opened wide. Shanahan stood there with a book in his hand. Dante, in Italian. He was wearing a pair of blue gym shorts and a grey UCD T-shirt, which was too big for his thin frame. His black hair was clean but dishevelled, as if he had been running his hand through it while reading. He stared at Michael in silence. After a few seconds, he stepped back and made room for Michael to enter the flat. An armchair was bathed in soft light, and there was a cup of tea on a small table beside the chair.

Tim Shanahan sat in his reading chair, and his guest perched on the couch beside him. Michael said, "Bless me Father for I have sinned."

Shanahan looked at him in astonishment, but Michael continued: "I committed the sins of pride and anger. And intolerance. I failed to carry out my responsibilities as a priest and as a man. Please forgive me. Grant me absolution, and allow me to make up for what I have done."

Shanahan stared, almost, it seemed to Michael, with apprehension.

"Father," Michael prompted him.

Shanahan started to raise his right hand, then faltered and let it drop. "I haven't . . . it's been years . . ."

"Go ahead."

The man then sat forward in his seat, raised his right hand, and made the sign of the cross over Michael. He spoke in a voice that was barely audible. "I absolve you in the name of the Father and of the Son and of the Holy Spirit. Amen." After speaking, he fell back in his chair as if exhausted, his eyes closed.

"I'm here today to listen," Michael told him. "Please tell me your story." He eyed the cup of tea. "Could I, em . . ."

"Tea? Certainly. I've a potful out there." Shanahan seemed relieved to turn to mundane matters, and got up and headed into his tiny kitchen. He was back in a trice with a cup of tea, cream and sugar.

He looked at Michael and opened his mouth, but nothing came out.

Michael got the conversation going. "You told me about the young girl who was your student, a very engaging little child. Before I cut you off so abruptly that day, you said she was in bed with you."

Shanahan cleared his throat. "Yes. I awoke to find her in my bed. She certainly hadn't been there when I went to sleep! She had left the school a year or so before this. One day, the class filed in and Sabine wasn't there. I never heard from her or her family; I went to their home a couple of times to inquire but nobody answered my knock. Anyway, on this occasion, I woke up to find her, unclothed, in my bed with . . . her hands on me."

Michael steeled himself not to react.

"It was at that point, the other day, that you decided you'd heard enough. I have to warn you. It gets a lot worse, though not in the way you're expecting."

Michael sat silently and waited for things to get worse.

"I reached for my clothes, held them against myself and went outside the room to dress. I returned to the bedroom and grabbed my bedsheet, wrapped it around her from behind, picked her up and placed her on the chair in my room. She looked up at me as if nothing untoward had happened. 'Victor told me you'd like it,' she said to me.

"'Victor is wrong, Sabine. This is wrong. You know that. Go out there and put your clothes on. I'm taking you home.' The sooner I got her out of there, the more likely Victor would realize nothing had happened."

"Who was Victor?"

"Her brother."

"Oh!"

"I took her home, all the way trying to persuade her that this kind of behaviour was wrong, it went against everything she'd been taught, she was better than this, it would ruin her life, on and on. I knocked at her family's door. No response. But they were in there, I could tell. Finally, I opened the door and gave her a gentle shove into the place, then left.

"I learned soon afterwards, however, that it wasn't her home anymore. She had a new place of residence. But her family would have delivered her there, I knew. Her brother, you see, with the connivance of their mother, had sold her — *sold her!* — to a child trafficker. To be his whore and his slave, whatever he wanted her to be. He owned her; he could sell her if he chose to. He pimped her out and took the profits. A thirteen-year-old girl. Naturally, they had taken her out of the school. That was the end of higher education for Sabine. She still saw her mother and brother. No problem for them. Well, they had gained great riches from the sale of her. They got a television, and the mother got a cordless phone. Which didn't work, of course, but she had it on display. The brother got a brand-name sweatshirt and a pair of track shoes. The pimp tarted Sabine up in trashy western clothing, hung jewellery on her, and made her the envy of some of the other girls at the school. So we had a devil of a time trying to keep the other girls in school and out of danger.

"The whole episode — that man buying the girl — tipped the balance of power in the area. This thug, who owned Sabine, was in ascendance. He was making a name for himself in child-trafficking circles in the region, and was making enemies along the way. One of those enemies was a powerful figure in our community who had acted as a protector of our parish; we could not have functioned without the goodwill of this individual. Now he — our man — was forced into a defensive position. Violence erupted sporadically and looked as if it would get worse. I was so disillusioned by it all, by a mother selling her child for a couple of shoddy western consumer items, and by the lack of appropriate reaction in so many members of the parish, I fell into a depression, took to drinking — something I had a weakness for but had always controlled until then — and I walked out on them. Just left them. Feck 'em, was my attitude.

"I think I told you I broke my leg while building the church. The fracture took a long time to heal, and I developed a bone infection. It got so bad I started taking a morphine derivative for the pain. I obtained the drug from the mission hospital and kept it in a very secure location while I was there, and that's all I took with me when I left. My supply of drugs. I got on a freighter to Lisbon, started drinking, and went on a months-long bender. I couldn't get a prescription for my medication but it was no problem getting heroin on the street. That was the beginning of my addiction to smack. Eddie Madigan keeps me supplied. At my request. Otherwise, he doesn't deal heroin. At all. I'm desperate to get off it. I've tried methadone, but I'm a backslider. I hope to try it again."

"Tim, I am truly sorry. About Sabine, about your mission there, and about your addiction. I apologize again for the way I treated you the other day."

"Michael, don't even think about that again. Little wonder you stopped up your ears when I began that sorry tale. I can't bear to hear myself repeat it. You were so kind to me when you found me in my flat, lying there in my own filth." Tim's voice broke, and he looked away. Then he got up from his chair, stood in front of Michael, and put his hand out for Michael to stand. Tim put his arms out and embraced him. "Thank you, Michael."

When they were seated again, Michael said, "How can I help you, Tim? I mean help you take up your vocation again."

"Oh, they're not on fire with the Holy Spirit over at headquarters when it comes to reinstating Father Shanahan as a parish priest. Drinking priests are one thing; heroin users are quite another. And if I ever succeeded in getting off that, there's still the Africa shambles on my record."

"But surely they understand that wasn't your fault."

"It's not that simple to them."

Michael had the impression that there was more, that Tim was being evasive, but he was not about to interrogate the man after all he'd been through. He did, however, offer a suggestion. "I'm wondering, Tim, if being a priest, celebrating the Eucharist and performing the sacraments, would build up strength in you. The grace of our Lord working in you to help fight your demons, so to speak."

"It's a lovely thought, Michael."

"Are there any other complications in your life? Besides those we just discussed?"

Tim smiled. "Aren't those enough? But if you're asking whether I've hooked myself up with a woman, the answer is no. The temptations have been there, but no."

Because he still saw himself as a priest, now and perhaps more fully again in the future.

Michael got up. "I'll leave you now, Tim, but I'll see you again soon. On familiar ground! Was that by any chance your sister and niece in Christy's yesterday? A family resemblance, I thought."

Tim's face lit up. "Yes! My sister Meg and little Susie. She's a dote, isn't she?"

"I'm sure she is. All I saw was a tiny fist outside the blanket."

"I'll introduce you next time she's in."

"Wonderful. All right, then, Tim. See you soon."

"Pray for me, Michael."

"You don't even have to ask."

Michael would indeed pray for Father Tim Shanahan. But he would do more than pray. That same afternoon, he was on the bus to Drumcondra to see the Most Reverend Thomas O'Halloran. When he spotted his destination, he got off the bus and headed for the brick palace, as it was known: the home of the Archbishop of Dublin. He had called ahead and introduced himself to the receptionist on the phone as a visiting priest, and had secured an appointment for two-thirty. He walked under the rounded arch of the entrance with five minutes to spare and gabbed with the receptionist, Marian, until it was time to be shown into the bishop's office.

Thomas O'Halloran was a giant of a man, nearly a head taller than Michael and maybe seventy pounds heavier. His face was beefy but handsome under his thick grey hair. The bishop was dressed in a black clerical suit, light grey shirt, and Roman collar, with a pectoral cross on a silver chain. He waved off Michael's approach to his ringed hand and bade him sit in a comfy chair by the window. Michael gave a little spiel about his frequent visits to Ireland, and they shared a laugh over the things tourists wanted to see and local people never did.

"I'm going to Belfast on Sunday," Michael said. "Not as many silly tourists up there. You may have heard about the concert they're putting on, for peace."

"Ah, yes. You'll want to watch yourself while you're in Belfast, Monsignor. We're all on edge over the disappearance of the American minister."

"I know. I've been very concerned. If this follows the usual course, Catholics will be targeted in response."

"That may be happening already."

"Yes, I've seen the news coverage. The riots, the violence —"

"I'm referring to something a little more specific than that."

"Oh, no! What's happened?"

"There may have been another disappearance. We're not sure. We're trying to find out, but it's difficult."

"Another disappearance? A Catholic, you mean? Kidnapped as a swap for Mr. Odom?"

"We don't even know that. There is a person who has not been heard from since around the time the American vanished. But it's not at all clear. The situation is 'fluid,' as they say. If it's true, it could be just the beginning of reprisals and counter-reprisals — Catholics, Protestants, people at risk on both sides. It's unbearable to think about."

"Who is it, the person who is missing?"

"Oh, I can't tell you that, Monsignor."

"Of course not, Your Grace. I apologize. People tell me I'm too nosy for my own good, and they're right."

"No apology necessary, Michael. I understand your concern. It's just that none of this is public and the . . . the family wants it kept that way. These things spiral out of control once they turn into a media circus."

"They certainly do."

"Please keep this confidential, Michael. I shouldn't even have mentioned it, but it's in the forefront of my mind."

"I won't say a word, I promise you."

The archbishop returned to small talk for a few minutes, and then it was time to bring the conversation around to the real purpose of the visit.

"I've met an interesting man this time out, Your Grace. Tim Shanahan."

"Ah."

"I understand he's a daily communicant at St. Saviour's."

The bishop nodded, then sat silently, waiting for whatever was to come.

"He strikes me as a good man in spite of his difficulties. And I believe he is still utterly committed to his vocation."

"So you're here to plead his case, are you?"

"I confess that I am, Your Grace."

"The situation with Shanahan is complicated. You mentioned his difficulties, by which I take it you mean his addictions."

"Yes, I'm aware of his dependence on drugs."

"Where did you meet him, Michael? At Mass? Or . . ."

"Em, well, we actually became acquainted at an establishment owned by the family of . . ."

"You met him at Christy Burke's."

"Correct."

"That doesn't do him a lot of good in terms of appearances, as I'm sure you can appreciate, Michael. Christy's is a popular spot. Many's the Dublin man and woman who sees Father Shanahan, day after day, at his regular place at the bar."

"But if he were to resume his position as a parish priest, that would cut way down on his pub hours. The man needs company, and he finds it at his local. Like so many others. I just think being accepted again by the priestly fraternity would help motivate him to work very hard at overcoming his troubles with the drink and the drugs."

"But that's not the only problem with Shanahan. There's the political angle as well."

"Oh? What would that be now?"

"There was a fiasco in Africa. We had a great deal of fence-mending to do there after he abandoned his mission. Walked out on his congregation just as they were making great strides. Left his church, his school, and disappeared into the drug dens of Lisbon. The Africans were less than happy, and some major diplomatic efforts were called for as a result."

"Wouldn't the furor have abated by now, though?"

"Do you mean it's time they got over it?"

"Well . . ."

"All those deaths? I wouldn't expect them to get over it any time soon."

"Deaths?" What was the bishop talking about?

"Ah. I see you haven't been provided with the full story, Michael. I'll leave it for Tim Shanahan to enlighten you, if he sees fit. Then perhaps you'll understand the position I'm in. Otherwise, I hope you'll have a pleasant and a grace-filled stay in Dublin, and perhaps I'll see you at the Pro." St. Mary's Pro-Cathedral was labelled "Pro" because it was only serving as a *provisional* cathedral for the Catholics of Dublin. They had been turned out of their "real" cathedral, Christ Church, when it was taken over by the Protestants at the time of the Reformation. "Provisional"— for five hundred years!

"Yes, I hope to see you there, Your Grace."

"Thank you for coming in and introducing yourself, Michael, and be assured I do appreciate your efforts on your friend's behalf."

And with that, Michael was back on the street in Drumcondra. Wondering who had died in Africa, and what role Tim Shanahan had played in "all those deaths."

Brennan

"Tell me about solicitor-client privilege."

"Well, I see we're not going to waste any time on small talk today," Monty said to him.

Burke waited. He and Monty were seated in Bewley's, having a spot of breakfast on Friday morning and watching the people passing by on Grafton Street below them. Or at least Monty was people-watching; Burke had something else on his mind.

"Remember when you were my client?" Monty asked him. "Does that ring a bell in the steeple for you?"

"I'm getting an echo of a distant chime, yes. Was that the time I was charged with two murders I didn't commit? And you didn't know me very well then and you thought I might be a serial killer?"

"That would be it, yes."

"Oh."

"Well, anything you told me while I was representing you is covered by the privilege, so I can't reveal it."

"Good."

"Why good? You never told me anything! I was flying blind, had to do my own investigation into your background. Remember that part of it?"

"Em . . ."

"Anyway, if you *had* told me anything, it would be privileged."

"So if I were your client now, whatever I tell you, or ask you, remains confidential."

"Right. So, what is it you want to tell or ask me?"

"Nothing."

"What? History repeats itself all over again. He still tells me nothing. I'll say this for you, Burke: you're consistent. Nobody will ever accuse you of being flighty, changeable, flexible . . ."

"Thank you."

"Anything else I can do for you today?"

"No."

Burke had what he wanted. He had been reassured that he could go to a lawyer and request some assistance and not have to worry about the whole thing going public. What he wanted was information about missing persons. He wasn't getting anywhere, not yet anyway, with the Christy Burke Four and their connections, if any, to the graffiti. He suspected that Michael O'Flaherty, with his gentle conversational abilities, would make more progress than would Burke himself. He also suspected that Michael knew more about some of the regulars, Shanahan and Madigan in particular, than he was letting on.

But Burke had one big clue: the dead vandal. He was constrained, however, by Finn's insistence that he not utter a word about the man's death and the removal of his body. He could not, therefore, go to the Garda Síochána and ask for their missing persons list. Even if he made up a cover story, it would fall apart once the guards found the corpse and connected it with Finn's pub. Out of the question. But he could approach a lawyer with a cover story, and ask if he or she would have access to the names of people who had gone missing in, say, the last year and a half. If any of them sounded promising, he would hand the details over to Finn and see if one or more looked familiar.

So that was his plan. He did his best to ignore Monty's probing stare and switched the conversation to sports and booze.

A couple of hours later, he had secured an appointment with Estelle Adams and was seated across from her in her solicitor's office overlooking the River Liffey. He was wearing a sports jacket and a shirt with no tie and had left off the "Father" when introducing himself. Said he was over from Canada at the request of his sister in Dublin; the sister had been unable to locate her son in over a year. The guards weren't taking it seriously, as the young fellow had been in trouble with the law on occasion, and had been out of touch with his family for months at a time. So it might be just more of the same, but she wanted to rule out — he stopped himself from saying "foul play" — anything too dire.

Estelle Adams said this was not the sort of thing she dealt with, but her firm had good relations with the guards, so she might be able to acquire some information informally.

"Stop by late this afternoon. I should have something by then."

"Grand. Thank you."

✝

At four forty-five that afternoon, Brennan was sitting in a small conference room in the law office with a photocopied list of missing persons, names blanked out, but with sufficient other detail that, if he really had a nephew missing, he should be able to recognize him on the list. That might not work quite as well for a man he didn't know, but the time frame could certainly narrow things down.

The list was for Dublin only, so if the vandal had been resident somewhere else at the time he vanished, he wouldn't show up here. The last bit of graffiti — the last graffito? Was the word ever used in the singular, or was graffito a technical term of some kind? He couldn't recall — whatever the case, the last message had been found the morning of the third of July. Finn got himself arrested in the middle of the month; Larry Healey discovered the body in the freezer soon after the arrest. Given the condition of the body and the green paint on the clothing, it was a fair assumption that the man had been killed while making his last stand at Christy's. But, depending on his home life, he may not have been reported missing until later. There were sixteen people who had disappeared so far in 1992. Five were female. Scratch them off. Three were just boys, one of whom had been reported missing earlier in the month. Finn didn't say it was a young fellow, but perhaps the condition of the body made it difficult to determine. Chances were, however, that the individual who had a grudge against someone at Christy's had been around awhile, so Brennan ignored the three young lads. That left him with eight men, only four of whom were recent additions to the list. One was an oul fellow in the throes of senility. The document said that he tended to wander off and had been missing on previous occasions as well as now. The graffiti could conceivably be the work of someone whose mind was going, but a person like that was unlikely to have made a clean escape every time. Brennan was down to three. One was a man of forty-eight, divorced, who had been reported missing July seventh; he had a spotty employment record and often left the Republic to find work. Didn't say where he went. He had been in Dublin for two months before disappearing. A young man of twenty-three had been reported on July twelfth and had not been seen for nearly a week before that. He was known to have bought a round-trip train ticket to Belfast on July sixth; the report did not say when he was supposed to return. Might have gone north to march with the Orangemen. Or he might have gone to jeer at them and come to grief as a result. The last person on the list was thirty-four years old, single, with a petty criminal record and a history of drug use. He had been living on and off with a girlfriend. She reported him missing July sixteenth but, given his habits, he may have been gone before then. Brennan circled the three possibilities.

Not much to report to Finn. His nemesis could be on the list of the missing, but how would anyone know from such scanty information? Nevertheless, Brennan would pass the paper along for what it was worth.

✝

Finn put the list down on the bar, removed his dark glasses, and peered at the information provided.

"Could be any of the three I've circled," Brennan observed.

"Could," Finn agreed.

Brennan had expected him to shrug and dismiss the research as useless, but something had caught his attention. He tapped his forefinger on the paper.

"This fellow. He may be . . . this fits in with something I heard. But I'm not sure who that rumour was about. It's not going to be me following it up." He raised his eyes to Brennan. "Fancy an afternoon of football?"

"I would love an afternoon of football."

"Good man. Thought you would. We're playing Cork tomorrow. Stop by here and pick up your pair of tickets from young Nugent."

"Brilliant. What did I do to earn a day at the park?"

"There's a man there who will be interested in this lad who took the train up to Belfast and didn't come home."

"Which of the sixty thousand people in the stands will be my contact?"

"He won't be in the stands. You've been following the career of your old friend Sammy Coogan?"

"Avidly, and with great envy."

"Isn't that a sin?"

"One of the seven deadly. I pray the *Confiteor* every time I see a Cork match."

"Save your prayers for Dublin. Or pray that Coogan will leave Cork, come home, and be hired as the manager here. He's done well for himself, and for Cork. When's the last time you saw him?"

"When's the last time I played a match on Irish soil? When I was ten years old?"

"Well, you'll have a lot of catching up to do. But first things first. When you see him tomorrow, show him those notes."

"All right. I'll let you know what he has to say."

"You won't have to. If there's anything of significance in that list, I'll be hearing about it."

Finn was a man with several deep channels running at once, apparently.

"How will I get near him?"

"Speak to Sean tomorrow."

He would, and he would speak to Monty today. A man on his first trip to Dublin couldn't do better than to learn a bit of history and watch a little football at Croke Park.

Chapter 9

Michael

Michael O'Flaherty was not about to grill Tim Shanahan about deaths in Africa, not after their soul-baring conversation the day before. Michael didn't know the whole story — perhaps he would never know — but he did not think for one minute that Tim was a killer, let alone a mass murderer. Eddie Madigan, well, Michael wasn't sure what to make of him. Bill McAvity had tipped Michael to the rumour that Madigan had taken payoffs from drug pushers. If it was true, what did that say about the man, a garda in the pocket of drug dealers? Well, he'd been sacked for it, if the stories were accurate. But Michael believed Tim when he said Madigan was not a heroin dealer himself.

Whatever the case, Michael was a little more enthusiastic about dropping in to Christy Burke's than he had been yesterday. He looked forward to seeing Finn behind the bar again, and chatting with the daily communicants in the pub. But when he walked into Christy's in the middle of the afternoon Michael thought there must be some mistake. Had he sleepwalked into the wrong pub? There was only one man sitting at the bar, someone he didn't know. Oh, and there was that annoying fellow who had unleashed a foul tide of slander the last time Michael had seen him. What was it they called him? Big Mouth? No, Motor Mouth, that was it, Motor Mouth McCrum. Well, there was no gostering out of him today. Nothing to say, or too small an audience, perhaps.

The regulars weren't in sight. And neither was Finn. Sean emerged and greeted Michael.

"It's nearly deserted in here today, Sean."

"Sure they're all at the funeral."

"Oh? Whose funeral is it?"

"Old Joe Burns." That sounded vaguely familiar. "Used to drink here," Sean explained.

"Well, that narrows it down!" Michael said, and Sean laughed.

But it seemed somebody had mentioned Burns way back, if Michael remembered correctly. "Isn't it nice," he said, "that they all went to see the man off. Did Finn go too?"

"Of course he did. He'd be with the family, so."

"They were related?"

"Well, Finn was his publican." He said it as if it were the most natural thing in the world: the publican at the old man's local would stand with the family at the funeral. "Here they are now."

Michael looked up and saw Jimmy O'Hearn coming in the door, wearing an ill-fitting black suit. The lone drinker at the bar, who had been sitting on Jimmy's regular bar stool, got up without a word and retreated to a table. Jimmy took his place without comment. Shanahan and Madigan came in afterwards, as did a number of other people. Finn brought up the rear.

"They'll be coming by any minute now," Finn said.

And sure enough, within minutes, everyone stood and raised a silent toast. Michael looked out the window to see who had arrived, and saw a long black hearse idling in front of the pub. It stayed for a few seconds, then slowly moved away. Last call at Christy's for old Joe Burns.

"Good day to you, gentlemen," Michael said to O'Hearn, Madigan, and Shanahan once the ceremony was over, and they returned the greeting. If Madigan bore any ill feeling about the way Michael had spoken at their last encounter, he did not show it.

Michael asked them about the funeral, and they filled him in on the priest, the music, and the number of rear ends in the pews. They lamented that the tradition of the pub, and the publican, playing a role in the funeral ceremony was dying out.

"The local and the church," Michael remarked with a smile. "Seems we've narrowed our lives down to the essentials: churches and pubs!"

O'Hearn returned the smile. "Is there anything else?" he asked, and signalled for service.

"We even have a church that's named after a pub, Michael," Tim put in. "Did you know that?"

"No!"

"It's really Immaculate Conception but everybody calls it Adam and Eve's because people used to have to sneak into the church by way of Adam and Eve's pub when our Mass was outlawed. This was during penal times." Tim affected an English accent: "Right-o, Your Lordship, everything's under control. Those Irish savages are at it again, drinking themselves blind, but at least they're not involved in all that popish carry-on in the church! Splendid, splendid, Major! Well done, men!"

"Shower of shites!" Madigan muttered.

"Well, I'll have to go see the place."

"Merchant's Quay, the Franciscans."

"Good. I'll make a point of sneaking in!"

Michael realized something then, something he hadn't taken in earlier because of his concern for Tim Shanahan. Frank Fanning wasn't in the pub, and hadn't been for the past couple of days.

"Where's your companion Mr. Fanning? I haven't seen him in a while."

Michael saw out of the corner of his eye that Motor Mouth McCrum had got up from his table and was heading for the door. He lingered by the bar for a few seconds, his eyes on the three regulars. When nobody answered Michael's question, he departed.

Once he was gone, Jimmy O'Hearn spoke up. "We haven't seen Frank, either."

The regulars exchanged glances.

"Unusual for him not to stop in," Michael observed.

"Sure Frank is in here every day," said O'Hearn. "Rare that he misses a shift."

"Except those first Fridays," Shanahan remarked.

"True enough," O'Hearn agreed. "Frank misses a day every month, and we noticed after a time that it always seems to be the first Friday of the month. I don't have to tell you about first Fridays, Father O'Flaherty."

No. That was familiar territory to Michael. Traditional Catholics tried to attend Mass and receive Holy Communion on the first Friday of the month as a sign of devotion to the Sacred Heart of Jesus. Michael wondered how many of the faithful kept up the practice in this day and age. Well, maybe Frank Fanning was among the devout.

"Good of him to take the whole day off," Michael said lightly. "Going to his confessor, perhaps, and preparing himself for the Eucharist. That's my kind of Catholic!"

"Not to take anything away from Frank," Jimmy O'Hearn said, "but he must have been attending a church out of town. I remember a couple of Fridays I saw him going into the train station."

"May have been travelling up to Armagh to take communion from the man in the red hat!"

"A fellow could do worse, Tim. Maybe that's it!" Michael responded. The Cardinal Archbishop of Armagh was the highest-ranking churchman in all of Ireland.

"Well, if that was it," said O'Hearn, "he was being modest about it. Because the times I saw him, I got the impression he didn't want to see me. Or didn't want to be seen. I remember slagging him once years ago, saying he must have a woman stashed away somewhere. 'You're not a married man, Frank,' I said to him, 'so there's no need to sneak around!' And he came back at me saying she was married herself, to the Lord Mayor of Dublin. Frank having a laugh and putting me off the questioning."

"A bachelor, is he?" Michael asked.

"A widower. He lives with his sister. His wife died a long time ago."

"Ah. Did they have any children?"

"One boy, Lane. He's done very well for himself, has Lane."

That struck a chord with Michael. What had he heard about Frank's son? Self-important, that was it, Michael recalled from his talk with Nurse McAvity. All he said was "That's good to hear, Jimmy. I hope Frank is all right. Hasn't taken a turn or something." Then he dropped a hint into the conversation. "I suppose his sister would know."

Tim Shanahan picked it up. "I'll ring her and see." He got up and went to the phone at the back of the pub.

Michael ordered a pint from Sean and was having his first sip when Tim returned, looking worried.

"Nora Fanning says Frank hasn't been home the last two nights. She doesn't know where he is."

"Did she notice whether any of his things are missing? Clothes, shaving gear, or anything like that?" Michael asked.

Tim shook his head. "Nothing out of the ordinary. When he left the house on Wednesday, he said he'd be back at the usual time. Closing time here, I expect he meant." Tim stopped for a moment, then said, "I remember him here Wednesday afternoon, but not in the evening."

"So, Wednesday evening to today, Friday . . ."

"But today's not a *first* Friday, so he's not following that pattern. Whatever it means."

✝

"Any word from Frank?" Michael asked Tim Shanahan when he dropped in to Christy's the following day. Tim shook his head.

"And his sister didn't know anything when you called her yesterday."

"She didn't know anything when I called her today either."

"Who else does he have? His wife is dead, God rest her . . ."

"There's just the son. Lane."

"Maybe the boy has Frank over at his place."

Eddie Madigan scowled. "Ha! Not unless Frank just won the lottery. But you could try. If nothing else, you'll get a lesson in what this country is coming to!"

"Well, I think I'll do my priestly duty and inquire after the welfare of one of my new parishioners," Michael declared. "Where would I find Lane?"

"Don't be wasting your time trying to see him at his house in Ballsbridge. He and the wife have got themselves barricaded behind some class of security system. As if the ambassadors in Ballsbridge are going to waste their time breaking into Lane's house. Try his office; he's always there. It's on Grand Canal Street."

"But it's Saturday."

"Makes no difference. He's always at the office."

Michael got cold feet at the thought of hunting down Frank Fanning's son and giving him a phoney explanation of why he was there asking questions, particularly if it turned out something had happened to his father. If someone more official came along, say, a close relative of Frank's publican, Michael might feel a bit more comfortable on his mission. But Brennan Burke demonstrated a distinct lack of enthusiasm for the task. Little wonder: he and Monty Collins had procured tickets to a football match at Croke Park. So Michael hit upon the idea of asking Leo Killeen to accompany him. Leo knew all the Christy's regulars — not well, but at least he was acquainted with them. Perhaps he'd be willing to come along and hold Michael's hand. Or was Leo in Belfast? That's what he'd said Thursday night at Finn's, that he was going up there. Michael hadn't seen Leo around the house yesterday but, then again, Michael had been out most of the day. Easy enough to find out. He picked up the phone at the back of the pub and called the house in Stoneybatter.

Leo was there and listened politely to Michael's plan, then gave voice to the opinion that Michael and the "other" drinkers at Christy Burke's might be overreacting to the absence of one of their number. But there didn't seem to be much harm in speaking to his son, so the two priests made arrangements to meet and go see Lane Fanning at his office.

Their walk took them through the cobblestoned quadrangle and Palladian splendour of Trinity College, then along the less-than-splendid Fenian Street. They chatted a bit about their surroundings, then Michael looked at his companion and asked, "Did you go to Belfast, Leo?"

Leo kept walking without meeting Michael's eyes. Just when Michael concluded that no response would be forthcoming, Leo replied, "I did."

"What happened?"

"Nothing."

"You spoke to people up there about the missing preacher . . ."

"I made inquiries in various quarters, yes. All to no avail."

"Were they stonewalling you, putting you off?"

Leo shook his head. "No. They're in the dark as much as the rest of us."

Did they know there might be a Catholic missing? Did Leo know? Michael had promised Archbishop O'Halloran that he would not say a word about the rumour that a Catholic might have been kidnapped, so that avenue of discussion would have to remain closed. All he said was "So no luck, I guess, Leo."

"I've a couple more irons in the fire. I'll see how it goes tomorrow."

"Tomorrow? Oh, of course, the peace concert. We're all looking forward to that, and a bit of sightseeing as well. Monty has never been there. I guess you'll be attending to other matters while we're on tour."

"I will."

"Tell me this, now, Leo. Are you a well-known figure in that part of the country? I mean, do you take precautions against being spotted or followed or . . . well, I don't know what."

"Some of the places I go, some of the people I meet, would tend to generate interest on the part of certain individuals or organizations that do not share the goals of those I meet. I don't parade through the streets of Belfast wearing my rose-coloured Gaudete-Sunday vestments and biretta, you can be sure of that."

"Em, who would these people be that you spoke to? Not their names, but, you know, what kind of organizations or groups are we talking about?"

"We're not. We're not talking about them, Michael."

That was as far as he was going to get on that subject, Michael knew. He was surprised he got that much out of Killeen. The two of them had another enterprise to attend to now.

They reached Grand Canal Street, where Lane Fanning had his headquarters. The building was a large rectangular block with one corner recessed and fitted with a glass tower.

Lane Fanning had done well for himself indeed. He was sleek and tanned, with stylish tawny hair and clothing Michael would have associated with a "sharp operator." Fanning rose from behind an enormous blond oak desk and came to greet them. Everything but the desk and chairs was white or chrome or glass. A series of metal frames held a collection of abstract paintings. Purchased as a set, Michael guessed. There was a line of wall clocks showing the hour in Hong Kong, Frankfurt, London, New York, and Los Angeles. On a side table was an architect's model of a group of ghastly modern buildings.

Leo introduced himself and Michael and explained that they knew his father. He said that Frank's friends were concerned because this was Saturday and they had not seen him since Wednesday.

Leo asked, "So, have you seen your father? Do you know where he might be?"

"I haven't seen him. I rarely do."

"Oh? Why would that be now?"

Lane's reply was delivered in a voice that had barely a trace of his father's working-class Dub accent. "Why would that be? That would be because the man is inebriated from noon till night, every day, every week, every year of his life. The fact that you're alarmed because he has missed a few shifts at Christy Burke's bar says it all, doesn't it?"

"The man takes a drink, yes, but —"

"Takes a drink! He guzzles twenty pints of Guinness a day! He's known as one of the greatest — most notorious, to be more accurate — pintmen in Dublin. That's his claim to fame. Legendary pintman Frank Fanning. He's so legendary for his drinking they wouldn't take him in the IRA. He didn't meet their standards, such as they are. Security risk. They frown upon pub gossip and operational secrets being passed on through drunken blather. They figured the only thing he'd shoot off would be his mouth. So he's missed the war. I mean the one that's going on to the north of us right now. Da sits on the sidelines and mopes. If only he could take part in the struggle — the shootings and the bombings, I guess he means — we'd be a thirty-two-county Ireland. All this patriotic claptrap. Who cares anymore? It's the nineties, Da. Move on!"

"You don't share his vision of a united Ireland."

"Any hope of a united Ireland went out the window in 1921. My attitude is, get over it."

"That must go over well with your father," Leo remarked.

"It goes in one of his ears and out the other. He doesn't listen to a word I say on the subject. Oh, he has plenty of time to listen to — what's his name? — Nugent over there at Christy's, behind the bar. Sean. 'Brilliant young lad, good Republican family,' blah, blah, blah. The son Da never had! The fact that places like Christy Burke's are still in business . . . well, it says it all about this country. What Ireland needs — to be more accurate, what the individuals living in

Ireland need — is prosperity. A dynamic economy. Foreign capital. An aggressive body of entrepreneurs."

"Ah, the 'greasy till,'" said Leo. "'Romantic Ireland's dead and gone; it's with O'Leary in the grave.'"

The young man looked at him blankly.

"Yeats," Leo prompted.

"Oh, right. Well, as I was saying, we have to develop a business world view. I do business with Northern Ireland every day. I don't care whether they're Catholics, Protestants, or Satanists. All the same to me. I do business with the Brits every day. I don't care what church they attend or whether they vote Tory, Labour, or Loony Party. Borders are becoming meaningless." The telephone jangled, and Fanning picked it up. "Yes? No! Close the deal! I couldn't care less! *Close-the-deal!*" He slammed the receiver down, looked at his visitors, and rolled his eyes.

"Where was I? Oh, yes, my father the armchair warrior. You can imagine how stilted our conversation is when we do meet. Last time I rearranged my schedule to have coffee with him he spent the whole hour rabbiting on about Sean Nugent and Finn Burke and vowing revenge for the death of some woman who died fifteen years ago in Belfast! It was the anniversary of her death. Her name was Drumm or something. I never heard of her. Da thought it would be appropriate to mark the anniversary with a violent outburst of some kind. I shudder to think what he had in mind. Fifteen years, who cares? Well, I'm sorry, but I'm too busy to sit and listen to that."

"Would this have been Máire Drumm, the civil rights leader who was ill and lying in her bed in hospital in Belfast and was shot dead by Loyalist paramilitaries disguised as doctors?" It was clear from his tone that Leo Killeen still cared after fifteen years even if the young Turk across the desk did not. "Is that who he was talking about?"

"Yeah, sounds right."

"And that was the last time you saw your father? That would have been in October!"

"Right, well . . . I know it's a cliché but it's true: time is money. At least for those of us with work to do."

"What exactly is it that you do here, Lane?"

"I move money, Leo!"

"Move it where?"

"Wherever it can make more money. I'm an investment banker."

"So does your father do his banking with you?"

The young man laughed. "I'm not that kind of banker. And this isn't one of your local banks, as you can tell by the name. It's a U.S. outfit." Fanning set about describing his work. ". . . collateralized bond obligations . . . commercial paper . . . asset vehicles . . ."

Michael's mind drifted off to his own interests. Leo had invited him to concelebrate the next Irish-language Mass at the Aughrim Street church. He was looking forward to that, a chance to brush up on his Irish by listening to the experts. And the peace concert tomorrow in Belfast, which meant going on a road trip with Kitty Curran. And Brennan and Monty too, of course.

He tuned back in when Leo spoke. "Is that your family?" Leo was looking behind Lane's desk at a photograph showing a fashionable blond woman and two well-dressed children posing in front of a sailboat.

"Yes, my wife, Victoria, and our kids, Imogene and Bradford." He gazed at them with admiration.

That gave Michael an idea. "You wouldn't happen to have a picture of your father here, would you, Lane?"

"I doubt it. Why? You're not going to call in the gardaí, are you? He's probably gone on a bender in some other drinking hole."

"Well, we don't know that. And his friends are a little concerned." *Even if his son is not.*

"Hold on, let me look. The kids brought some old pictures over to be photocopied." Lane yanked open one of his desk drawers and pulled out a bag of photographs. He flipped through them with a look of distaste. "Let's hope these never see the light of day. Oh, here he is. Stewed as usual." He handed the photo to Michael.

It wasn't the most flattering picture of Frank Fanning. He did look as if he'd had a drop or two. But it would do.

Lane turned his attention to the computer on his desk, then leaned forward. "You know what the next big thing is?" Michael and Leo shook their heads. "The information superhighway!"

"Where would that be, now, Lane?" Michael asked.

"Here, there, everywhere! In cyberspace."

"Science fiction, that class of a thing?"

"No. Computers. The nineties will be all about computers. Pretty soon you'll be able to do *everything* from your own computer: shopping, banking, investing . . . you'll do it all without leaving your desk."

"Ah, well," said Leo, "we have different views of what constitutes 'everything,' my lad. But be that as it may, good luck to you. Would you like to join us for a pint across the street?"

"I don't drink. Some of us don't, you know!"

"Perhaps you should take it up. We'll be on our way now. Thank you for your time."

"You're welcome. Really. If there's any way I can help, just give me a buzz."

Leo shook his head as they descended in the lift. "Sad, Michael, isn't it? All that education . . ."

Where was Frank? One answer was "It's nobody's business." The most sensible answer, Michael supposed. But the other drinkers had looked worried. Rightly so, perhaps, given that an individual with a can of spray paint had made serious accusations against somebody at Christy Burke's. Had the accuser gone a step further and caused harm to the accused? Was Fanning the target? Michael knew from his talk with Bill McAvity that Fanning did not drive. So Michael would do some detective work to find out whether anybody had seen Frank Fanning leave the city by train. If he struck out with the trains, he would try the buses. There was no need to bother Brennan with this little plan, no need even to mention it.

So, after saying goodbye to Leo, Michael set forth with the photograph of Frank Fanning in his pocket. He made his way through what used to be the red-light district of Dublin, known as the Monto, to Connolly Station. He had always found the nineteenth-century building a bit bizarre, dominated as it was by an Italianate tower poking up in the middle. He was more than a little self-conscious; would he look like an eejit flashing the picture and questioning possible witnesses? Should he have left his clerical collar at home? *No use second-guessing yourself now, O'Flaherty — get on with the job.* He chose the ticket counter with the shortest queue and waited patiently until he was facing a young girl with short, spiky blond hair seated behind the glass.

"Excuse me, I'm wondering whether you can help me."

"Where to, sir, em, Father?"

"Well, I don't actually need a ticket. Not today. I have a question for you, if you don't mind."

She looked at him warily. "What kind of a question, like?"

Michael drew the photo from his jacket pocket and showed it to the girl. "Would you have seen this fellow in the station, do you recall?"

The girl gave the picture a cursory glance and shrugged. "Lot of oul fellows look like that."

Well, I suppose a lot of "oul fellows" look like me, too, Michael thought. *Would she remember me if someone showed her my mug shot tomorrow?* "He doesn't look familiar to you then?"

"No. Sorry."

"All right. Thank you for your time."

She was already looking at the next person in line by the time Michael pocketed his photo and moved aside. He told himself not to be discouraged after striking out with the first ticket agent; there were plenty of others. He got into a queue on the other side of the room and waited patiently again for his turn. This agent was a middle-aged woman with faded auburn hair and a friendly expression.

"Where would you like to go today, Father?"

"Oh, I'm not going anywhere. But I was hoping to ask you a question, if I could."

"You ask me anything you like. How can I help you?"

He brought out the picture and asked, "Have you ever seen this man in the station here?"

She peered at the photo. "That's not Mr. . . . . No, no, it isn't. I can't say I've seen him in here, Father. Who is he? Is he missing?"

Michael had not prepared for this; obviously he should have. Of course someone would ask who the man was!

"That's right. I'm, em . . ." No, Michael would not, and could not, say he was helping the police with their inquiries. "I'm a friend of the family, and they haven't seen him. He has, em, episodes when he becomes confused."

"So you think he might have wandered off, that sort of thing."

"Right. That's it. But you don't remember seeing him."

"No. But somebody might. If you'll let me have the picture, I'll show it around for you."

"Ah. That would be lovely. Thank you."

The woman put a sign up — "Next Wicket, Please" — and disappeared. Michael heard the grumbling behind him and did not want to turn around. He studied the timetable posted on the wall in front of him and tried to ignore the discontent that was welling in the queue. People shuffled into other lines, some with good grace, some without. But the ticket agent was back in a few minutes.

"You're in luck. One of the lads, Colm, thinks he saw the man in here. He'll come round to see you. Here he is now."

"Thank you and bless you!"

"No trouble at all, Father."

She took down the sign, opened up shop again, and people appeared in her line as quickly as pigeons spotting a piece of bread.

Colm was a young man with a shaved head and a stocky build; Michael could picture him bashing a ball around on the playing fields of Ireland.

"You're askin' after the man in the picture, are yeh, Father?"

"Yes, I am. You recognize him, do you?"

"Sure I've seen him here, and more than once."

"Would he be by himself on these occasions?"

"Nobody with him whenever I saw him. He'd only buy the one ticket, so."

"Ticket for where, do you recall?"

"Belfast."

Belfast. Well, this merited a closer look.

"The only reason I remember," Colm said, "is that one of the days he went, there was a bombing at one of the hotels in Belfast and I said, 'Are yeh sure yeh want to head up there today?' and he just said he'd be goin' anyway, and I sold him his ticket. Said he'd not be staying in any of the hotels, just passing through."

"Oh? He was going somewhere else?"

"Derry."

"Is that right?"

"Yeah, that's what he said. I suppose he'd hop on the bus in Belfast and travel on to Derry."

"I wonder what he was doing there." Colm just shook his head. "All right, then, Colm. I thank you for your help. Good day to you now."

The young man nodded and went back to his work.

So. Belfast and Derry. Well, Michael would be travelling to Belfast the next day. Maybe he would fit in a little trip to Derry as well. He would give it some thought.

Brennan

Brennan and Monty took a taxi through Drumcondra to Croke Park and entered the stadium along with sixty-five thousand other spectators for Saturday's match between Cork and Dublin. In accordance with Finn's instructions, Brennan had stopped in at Christy's, and Sean Nugent had handed him an envelope with two tickets. Nugent told him Sammy Coogan would be waiting for him at the edge of the pitch right after the match. Brennan asked Sean what the missing persons list had to do with the manager of the Cork Rebels, and Brennan believed the young barman when he shook his head and said he had no idea. Nugent said he had met Coogan on a few occasions but, about this specific matter, Nugent was in the dark. Were his previous get-togethers with Coogan related to football? No. Well, that was that. Brennan wasn't about to pester the lad. He had two tickets to Croke Park and was looking forward to the afternoon.

He gave Monty a bit of commentary about the stadium on the way in. "That's Hill 16," he said, pointing to the terrace at one end of the stadium, "named after the Rising of 1916. There's a bunch of rubble buried beneath it, stuff taken from Sackville Street after the battles. Sackville is O'Connell Street now. They say there's even a car under there, belonging to the O'Rahilly."

"The O'Rahilly?"

"One of the men killed in the Rising. His car was used in the building of a barricade in the street. And that's Hogan Stand, named after Michael Hogan, the Tipperary footballer who was shot during the Bloody Sunday massacre in 1920 here in the park. Bloodiest single day of the Tan War."

"Shot by?"

"The Black and Tans or the Auxiliaries; they were both in on it."

"What set that off? There were killings the night before, was that it?"

"Your man Michael Collins had sent his squad out the night before to assassinate a bunch of British undercover agents known as the Cairo gang. Fourteen of them were shot dead. In retaliation, the British forces entered this park and opened fire on the crowd. They killed fourteen people. Innocent people, not spies or combatants in the war. One of them was a man named Thomas Ryan, who knelt beside Hogan and began saying the Act of Contrition in the young fellow's ear." Brennan's voice dried up for a few moments after that. Then he said, "But we're here for the football. And maybe a pint or two while we're at it."

"But you're on a mission of some sort as well."

"Afterwards. One thing at a time."

The sun came out, the stands filled up with fans in blue for Dublin and red for Cork, Monty and Brennan added their voices to the tens of thousands of other Dublin supporters shouting encouragement to the home side and bawling at Cork, and the two sides went at it until Cork battered the home team into defeat. As the crowd began to file out, Brennan and Monty headed down for their rendezvous with the victor.

Sammy Coogan stood just under six feet tall and was muscular without being bulky. His cropped dark brown hair was going grey, and his face was flushed red, from either exertion or exultation.

"Congratulations, Sammy. Well done. I'm gone nearly hoarse from giving out to your players hoping for a different result, but credit where credit is due. Do you remember me at all?"

"Brennan! Not sure if I'd know you on sight. It's been a few years. But I was told to expect you. Good to see you again. Got my start chasing you for the ball."

They shook hands, and Brennan made the introductions. "Sammy Coogan, Monty Collins."

Coogan examined Monty as if trying to place him. "From Cork, would you be?"

"Originally, maybe."

"Chances are," Coogan said. "Collins is a big name in County Cork."

"You said a mouthful there," Brennan agreed. "Could I leave the lad in your care, Sam? Take him home, see if you can find his uncles and his cousins? He hasn't been all that good in finding them himself."

"I'll be happy to take him under my wing, Brennan. Now that I've got myself accepted in Cork."

"Two All-Ireland championships will do that."

"That seems to have done the trick. But staying with Dublin for a bit, I understand you have some information for me." Coogan picked up the end of his jersey, gave his face a quick wipe. At the same time, he looked about him to see who was nearby. Players stopped by for a word and then went in to the dressing room.

Brennan produced the list of men missing from Dublin and handed the pages to Coogan, who read through them quickly. "That's got to be Clancy," he said.

Brennan waited.

"The dates are right. It's got to be him." He looked up. "Still no word?"

"Em, word about . . ."

"How recent is this list?"

"I got it yesterday."

"So Clancy hasn't been seen since the sixth of July."

The sixth. That meant Clancy was the twenty-three-year-old man on the list. Was Clancy the fellow who'd been shot twice in the head, stuffed in a freezer, and then moved to an unmarked grave? All of it stemming from an ill-conceived desire to spray his discontent over the walls of a Northside pub? Who had reported him missing? His parents? Wife or girlfriend? Did he have children?

"So we have a name for our vandal now?" he asked.

Coogan looked at him. "Vandal?"

"The fellow who sprayed the messages on the pub."

"What pub was that? Burke's, you mean?"

"Sorry, Sam, I'd better back up here. You said Clancy."

"I don't know what paintwork Clancy might have done. 'Up the Republic,' I suppose, or 'Brits out.'"

"The dates are right, you said . . ."

"Yes. Just around the time the American was snatched. Was young Clancy all they could get in return, as a hostage? Or was Clancy taken first, and then the American? And why haven't we heard anything?"

What the . . . ? This wasn't about Christy Burke's; this was about the American minister. Odom had disappeared on the eighth of July, and this fellow on the sixth.

"This Clancy, who is he?"

"Well, he's just a young fellow of no particular prominence. Not much of an employment history or anything like that." Coogan looked around again to see who was nearby. "But he's a vocal supporter of the struggle in the North, and he's anxious to make a name for himself in Republican circles. The thinking here is that he's a little too vocal, and he draws unwelcome attention to, em, certain bases of support here in Dublin. Support for the armed struggle. People in Dublin don't want that sort of . . . recognition of their efforts."

"No, I don't suppose they do. Why haven't we heard about him in the press, about his disappearance?"

"Probably because his family's smart enough to know that the stakes rise in proportion to the publicity; harder for people to back down. They've put it about that he's on holiday. Not that he's ever been overburdened with work-related duties, as far as I know. But they're probably right: keep it low-key and maybe a low-key solution can be found. And we in the South can be grateful for that. We don't want this to rebound on us in some way we can't possibly predict."

The three men were silent as they contemplated what this might mean.

"This is all guesswork, though, really," Coogan said. "We don't know what's going on."

Something else we don't know, thought Brennan, *is where Sammy Coogan fits in here.* Coogan must have assumed that Brennan had come from Finn Burke or Sean Nugent fully informed about Coogan and his connections. Typically, though, Brennan was flying by the seat of his pants. *Thank you, Uncle Finn!* Well, he wasn't about to reveal to Coogan the depth of his ignorance. Back to Clancy.

He said to Coogan, "But this — the young fellow's role in the Republican movement — would account for the fact that he'd stand out as a target; he's made himself known."

"That, and the fact that he's the nephew of Pádraig Aloysius Clancy, the Bishop of Meath."

Chapter 10

Michael

The peace concert was scheduled for Sunday night, the twenty-sixth of July. Michael, Brennan, Monty, Leo, and Kitty boarded the train in the early afternoon and headed north. Signs posted in the coach warned passengers not to leave packages unattended and not to attend to any packages they might themselves find unattended. They pulled in to the train station a little over two hours later and decided to rent a car for their stay in Belfast. That arranged, they struck out for the Antrim Road with Leo at the wheel. He had reserved rooms for them all at the St. Clement's Retreat Centre, which, their hosts said, welcomed people of all religious faiths to enjoy a bit of calm in the otherwise strife-filled city. They checked into their rooms, went for a stroll around the lovely tree-lined grounds, then huddled together to plan their itinerary. The concert was not until eight that evening, which left them the afternoon to see the sights.

It was soon apparent that Michael knew the city better than anyone else in the group except Leo, who was staying behind at the centre to meet an unnamed party for an unspecified purpose as a prelude to other mysterious appointments later on. He would catch up with the others that evening at the concert. Kitty and Brennan had been to Belfast the odd time but did not know the city well. Monty had never set foot in the place. So it fell to Michael, who had brought his bus tours here numerous times, to resume his accustomed role as tour guide. They set off again, with Michael at the wheel, Kitty beside him, and Monty and Brennan in the back seat.

Everyone knows Belfast is a city divided. This is true not only figuratively but literally. All around the city are high barriers, made of metal or wire or brick or fencing, separating the Catholic neighbourhoods from the Protestant. George Orwell couldn't have pegged it better: the barriers are known as "peace lines." Michael pointed them out as he chauffeured his companions around the city. Nobody had to ask which side of the peace line was which. Catholic/Republican/Nationalist houses flew the Irish tricolour and, depending on the degree of militancy, some had pro-IRA murals or graffiti on display. Protestant/Loyalist/Unionist areas flew the Union Jack or the Ulster Red Hand; their murals showed machine-gun toting members of the UDA, the UFF, or the UVF, various paramilitary groups dedicated to maintaining union with Britain and defeating the IRA.

"You'll be interested in that place, Monty," said Michael, slowing down and directing their attention to a neoclassical building with eight Corinthian columns topped by a pediment. "That's the Crumlin Road Courthouse. Don't expect a jury of your peers if you're being tried on charges relating to terrorism."

"Right," said Monty, "the Diplock system. Judge alone."

"They figure jurors will be subjected to intimidation, so no juries."

"The barbed wire's intimidating enough!" Monty remarked, pointing to the coils of wire atop the building's fence.

"If you think that's bad, wait till you see the high court."

Michael drove through the city streets until he came to another impressive-looking building, this one made of Portland stone with multi-paned windows and, again, Corinthian columns as part of its design. The high court was surrounded by a massive concrete structure that must have been twelve feet thick. "Blast wall, to protect the place from car bombs."

"And I thought we had a rough crowd back home at the courthouse on Spring Garden Road."

"The police station is insulated by a bomb wall, too. Not without reason."

The B-word came up again when Michael took a cruise past the Europa Hotel in Great Victoria Street, the hotel where the Reverend Merle Odom had been staying before he disappeared. Brennan spoke up then with a little tidbit about the place. "It has the distinction of being the most frequently bombed hotel in Europe."

†

Organizers of the peace concert, which was to be held outdoors, had rejected the obvious venues, such as the Windsor Park football stadium and the cricket ground at Stormont. They wanted a grittier setting for the event; they wanted to hold the peace concert in the war zone itself, on the site of a bombed-out building beside the Lagan River. The rubble, the burnt, twisted plumbing, the cables and wires and misshapen structural steel, all were to remain in place. Stadium seats were brought in for the expected three thousand attendees. Awnings were on standby for the performers in case of rain; spectators were advised to bring umbrellas.

Michael and his friends stood outside the gates, taking it all in, as they waited for Leo Killeen. There was a massive security presence: hundreds of British soldiers and members of the Royal Ulster Constabulary armed with pistols, rifles, and machine guns. There were armoured cars and tanks around the perimeter of the site, and a helicopter flew low over the crowd. Everyone had to undergo a body search to be admitted. Was it Michael's overactive imagination, or did some of the army and police personnel look askance at the Roman collars on Fathers Burke and O'Flaherty? And here came Father Killeen. Leo affected to ignore the armed forces deployed all around him, and greeted his friends. They submitted to the required pat-downs, the men by a man, Kitty by a woman, and made their way to the bleachers. Michael headed into the row first and sat down, followed by Kitty, Monty, Leo, and Brennan. Soldiers and police patrolled between the rows of seats.

"I suppose you need this kind of security to keep the fans at bay when you perform at home, Monty," Kitty said.

"We have all this and more, Kitty, and still the groupies get through. My life on the road . . . you don't want to know."

But the banter died out; nobody's heart was in it. The soldiers, the wreckage around them, the tension that accompanied any public event in Belfast battered them into silence. The relief was palpable when the concert got underway. There was a variety of music, from peace songs in the folk tradition to classical pieces by the Ulster Orchestra. There was nothing Michael would have called traditional Irish music and, God forbid, nothing that touched upon politics or sectarian strife. About an hour into the concert, Brennan rose and walked down to the stage. Another man was introduced before him, a minister in one of the Protestant churches in Belfast. He sang "O God Our Help in Ages Past," and did a lovely job in Michael's opinion; he was met with heartfelt applause. Then it was Brennan's turn and, accompanied by the orchestra, he gave a magnificent performance of "Comfort Ye, My People," from Handel's *Messiah*:

Comfort ye. Comfort ye, my people, saith your God.
Speak ye comfortably to Jerusalem.
And cry unto her . . .

There was a sudden rat-tat-tat sound. Michael gave a start of fear. Distant, it seemed. But there it was again. Closer this time? People in the audience shifted in their seats and looked about them. Michael put his arm around Kitty and drew her to him, wondering even as he did so what good it could possibly do her. A group of soldiers on the periphery of the stadium ran out into the darkness. The orchestra faltered for a beat or two. Not so Brennan. No beats missed on his part. His head turned slightly, towards the orchestra conductor. "The show will go on" was the message.

. . . that her warfare, her warfare is accomplished.
That her iniquity is pardoned.

There was an extra degree of warmth in the applause as Brennan gave a slight bow and walked up to his seat in the bleachers. The distant guns had fallen silent. Michael let out a sigh of relief and withdrew his arm from Kitty's shoulders. She spoke to him in a quiet voice. "Try to imagine what it's like to live with this every single day and night." He just shook his head.

There were a few more performers and then, as the late summer twilight descended on the city, the master of ceremonies announced the star of the show, the highlight Brennan said he had been anticipating from the minute he got wind of the concert, the person he described as the great Verdi soprano: Leontyne Price. A black American woman, brought up in segregated Mississippi, would no doubt bring a certain gravitas to the quest for sanity in a city where the "peace line" still separated the Catholic from the Protestant parts of town.

Before Miss Price came on, a screen lit up at the side of the stage, and the face of Martin Luther King appeared. The slain civil rights leader had been an inspiration to those seeking civil rights in Northern Ireland in the late 1960s and early '70s. Now the Irish audience, sitting in the ruins of a bombed-out building in Belfast, heard Dr. King's famous "I Have a Dream" speech, in which he cast his mind forward to the day "when all of God's children — black men and white men, Jews and Gentiles, Protestants and Catholics — will be able to join hands and sing in the words of the old Negro spiritual, 'Free at last! Free at last! Thank God Almighty, we are free at last!'"

The crowd rose to its feet and erupted in cheers. The King image faded, and Leontyne Price took the stage. It must have been ten solid minutes before the applause subsided.

Her voice soared into the sky over Belfast as she sang a mix of spirituals and hymns for peace. But the climactic moment of her performance, and of the concert itself, was the aria "Pace, mio Dio" from Verdi's *La Forza del Destino*:

Pace, pace, mio Dio, pace, mio Dio.
Chi profanare ardisce il sacro loco?
Maledizione! Maledizione! Maledizione!

Peace, peace, my God, give me peace.
Who dares profane this sacred place?
A curse! A curse upon you!

The crowd was on its feet again. The high note in which the diva cursed those who had profaned the sacred place gave Michael the chills. But he felt a stab of genuine fear when he looked at Brennan and saw the expression on his face. Brennan's lips were parted, and his face was as pale as a spectre; his eyes were not focused, at least not on anything Michael could see. Brennan had his hands up as if to ward something off. Kitty hadn't noticed; she was still applauding the great soprano. Leo seemed to be scanning the crowd: the enraptured audience and the people milling around outside the makeshift stadium. Monty turned to Brennan to make a comment, but whatever he was about to say died on his lips.

"Wasn't she brilliant?" Kitty exclaimed.

When Michael glanced at Brennan again, it was a relief to see him looking more like himself.

The five of them made their way out and stood by the fence, regarding the scene around them: the massive crowd, the police, the soldiers, a British Army vehicle looking fearsome and threatening on the other side of the road, the still waters of the Lagan, the giant Harland and Wolff shipyard cranes rising over Queen's Island to the east of them.

Michael could hear Monty speaking quietly to Brennan. "What happened in there? I got the impression there was more to it than the high B-flat."

"I don't know. A terrible feeling. I don't know . . ."

That wasn't like Brennan, not to know.

"Did you see something?" Michael asked him.

Brennan shook his head. "Nothing clear, nothing I can identify. Maybe I'm just a little too sensitive to music. I know I am."

Michael could see him making an effort to return to normality. Or what passed for normality in Belfast after dark.

A pair of cops hightailed it down the street. Michael peered after them. They bore down on a group of young men, who suddenly scattered. Two of the young fellows came running in the direction of Michael and his friends. The two looked nearly identical, with round shaven heads and light blue eyes. They tossed off some insults on their way by:

"Fookin' Taigs!"

"Fenian bastards!"

An RUC man came along and eyed the three priests. His gaze rested on Leo Killeen, then he spoke in a thick Belfast accent, "Where did I see you?"

"High Mass at the Pro-Cathedral?"

"Not likely. You're not a TV preacher, are you? No, that was somebody else. It'll come to me. See you around." It sounded like *arynd*.

Michael found it all too easy to believe what Archbishop O'Halloran had suggested to him, that someone up here had snatched a Catholic in revenge for the kidnapping of the TV evangelist. Of course, Protestant anger over the matter was understandable. But there was nothing in that understanding that gave Michael any comfort.

Leo Killeen glared daggers at the cop; then he led the group in silent procession from the concert site. Brennan strode ahead to walk with Leo as they made their way to the car.

The old walled city of Derry is situated high on a hill. Michael looked up at it from the bus terminal below. He, Brennan, and Monty had made a snap decision after the concert not to return to the Republic in the morning, but to extend their car rental and drive on to Derry. Kitty had to go back to Dublin, so they dropped her off at the train station. Nobody knew where Leo Killeen had got to. That left three for the excursion to Derry City. Michael was keen on tracking down the lead on Frank Fanning's whereabouts. Brennan obviously considered it a bit of a fool's errand, but why not have a look around Derry? And Monty was up for a tour. Michael had other ambitions as well, but for now he would concentrate on the Fanning situation.

The first round of interrogations was not productive. Michael had shown Frank Fanning's picture around the bus station in Belfast, but nobody could say whether they had seen him. So the trip started out with little promise. But things perked up when Michael persuaded Brennan to drop him off at the Derry bus terminal. One of the girls there recognized Fanning from the picture. She had no idea where he went when he left the station, but one of the taxi drivers might know. It took nearly an hour, but Michael's patience was rewarded. One of the drivers had taken Frank on more than one occasion to the Foyleside Centre for Longterm Care. Michael was pleased to make the announcement to Brennan and Monty when they returned from a drive around the county to collect him at the station.

Most of the population of Derry lives outside the city's walls, Catholics typically Cityside and Protestants Waterside, which was east of the River Foyle. The population was about seventy-five to eighty percent Catholic, which made it an uncomfortable fit inside the border of Northern Ireland. Here, too, there was a "peace line" in certain parts of the city to keep the warring factions apart.

Michael had not spent a lot of time here, but had occasionally included a quick visit on his bus tours over the years. He knew enough to direct Brennan from the bus station to the Bogside, where they reserved a room at the Abbey Bed and Breakfast.

The Bogside, as the name implied, was a low-lying area beneath the walled city. It was a Catholic enclave, where the current Troubles had erupted more than twenty years ago. Michael and his companions checked in at the bed and breakfast, chatted with the proprietors for a few minutes, then went out for a stroll. The area was thick with history. They headed first to Free Derry Corner. In January 1969, civil rights marchers were attacked by a Loyalist mob a few miles outside the city. People believed the Royal Ulster Constabulary had done little to protect the marchers, and rioting broke out when the marchers arrived in Derry. The police reacted with brutality; they entered the Bogside and began beating people up. The Bogside responded by erecting barricades to keep the police out. That's when the famous white gable wall was painted with the words "You are now entering Free Derry." Then, that August, there was the Battle of the Bogside between residents and the RUC after a Protestant group known as the Apprentice Boys marched close to the Catholic area. Things deteriorated to the point where the British sent in the troops. It was a mark of how dire the situation was that Catholics were relieved to see them. At first, anyway. The army had been in the country ever since.

Michael saw where the Rossville Flats had been, the scene of the infamous Bloody Sunday in 1972, when thirteen civil rights marchers were shot dead by British soldiers. A fourteenth person died of his wounds later on. Michael and his friends walked along Rossville Street to the intersection with William Street, "Aggro Corner," where the British Army and the RUC repeatedly clashed with the residents of the Bogside. People had a nickname for the rioting, which broke out at expected times of the week: the "Saturday and Sunday matinees."

The three visitors looked up the hill to the city walls. Just inside the walled city and looming over the Bogside was the Apprentice Boys Memorial Hall, a strongly fortified stone building in the Scottish baronial style, with spires and a tower on the side. A high fence rose from the wall in front of the building to protect it from missiles that might be lobbed from the ghetto below and, presumably, to protect the Bogside from whatever the modern-day Apprentice Boys might want to rain down on the Catholics.

But Michael and his companions weren't there to relive history. At least, Michael wasn't. He had a destination, and that was the Foyleside Centre for Longterm Care. The other two begged off, pleading prior commitments at the Bogside Inn. Michael made arrangements to meet them there in the pub after his mission, then struck out on his own. He had no idea how to find the care centre, so he availed himself of a passing taxi.

When he arrived at the centre and approached the reception desk, he smiled at the large, capable-looking woman sitting there and tried his luck with the name Fanning.

"Excuse me. I'm looking for a patient here, and I believe the name is Fanning. I'm sorry I don't have any more information than that."

The woman eyed him for a few seconds, wondering, no doubt, why he was there if he didn't know who he was looking for.

"I was asked to come," Michael claimed, "by an older lady whose words were hard to make out over the telephone. She had a stroke, and that affected her speech. You know how it is."

"Well, Father, the only Fanning we have is Dolores Fanning and there's nothing wrong with her speech, I can tell you. If she wanted you to visit, you'd be left in no doubt about the matter. And if she didn't, she'd make that perfectly clear as well."

"Oh, it wasn't the patient herself who called. It was a relative . . ." Michael wasn't used to lying. He wished he had Monty with him. Not that Monty was a liar — Michael didn't mean that — but he had a way of using words that could lead the other person to the conclusion Monty wanted to plant in the person's mind. And he could do it with diplomacy. A lawyerly skill.

But the receptionist relented. "Dolores Fanning is in room 128."
She pointed to the corridor. "Just along there. You can't miss it." She
smiled then, and said, "Good luck, Father."

Michael arrived at room 128 and peered inside.

"Who's there?" a female voice called out.

Michael stepped into the room and saw a woman who looked
to be in her late eighties seated in a wheelchair. She was facing the
window, but her knobbly hands worked furiously to turn the chair
around. The woman had thin wispy hair tied up in a bun and wore
glasses with heavy dark frames.

"Could I help you there?" Michael inquired.

"No, you could not, unless you could do something to get my legs
working again. Oh, a *sagart*. Maybe you could take me to Lourdes for
a cure!"

"Em, well, I'm sorry I can't do that. But if there's anything I can get
for you, or any way I can make you more comfortable . . ."

"Not likely, but thank you for asking, Father. That's more than I
get from some, including my own family." Her glasses had slipped
down her nose; she moved them into place and peered at Michael.
"How come I've never seen you here before?"

"Well, I'm not from here actually . . ."

"I can hear that in your voice, Father. Not a northerner, and yet
here you are."

"Are you Mrs. Fanning?"

"I am."

"Well, I'm inquiring after Frank Fanning. I understand that he
comes here from time to time to visit someone. Would that be you by
any chance?"

"It would not. I'm not related to anyone named Frank."

"Oh. And you don't know Frank at all?"

"I do not. You say he comes here?"

"Yes, or so I've been told."

"Let's ask the one down the hall, then." Mrs. Fanning wheeled
herself over to her bed and grabbed a cord hanging near the pillow.
She yanked on it, then yanked again.

You'd think she was ringing the bells at Notre Dame Cathedral.

"Takes her forever to get here. I'll be dead and covered with cob-
webs before I ever see . . . Oh, here she is."

A tall, thin young nurse had come in the door. "Yes, Mrs. Fanning? You rang?"

"I did. Father —" She turned her face towards Michael. "What's your name?"

"O'Flaherty."

"Father O'Flaherty here has a question. He's wondering about a fellow called Frank Fanning. Ever hear of him?"

"Oh, yes. Mr. Fanning comes by to see Donal Fegan in room 220."

"Ah. Thank you," Michael said. "Has Mr. Fanning been in lately, if I might ask?"

"Let me see now. I saw him recently, I know . . ." She thought about it, then said, "I'm sorry, I just can't remember when it was."

"Could I go up and see Mr. Fegan?"

"Certainly, Father. I'll take you to his room. See you after a bit, Mrs. Fanning."

"I won't be here holding my breath. Good luck with your inquiries, Father O'Flaherty. If you happen upon a local priest wandering about the grounds, you might suggest he start making regular visits to the long-suffering Catholics in this place."

"I will indeed, Mrs. Fanning. Thank you for your help, and God bless you."

"Oh, He already has, as you can see. Good day, Father."

Michael followed the nurse out of the room. When he estimated that he was out of earshot, he said, "Bit of a handful, is she?"

"She keeps us on the hop, to be sure, Father. Now a word about Donal Fegan. If you haven't seen him before, a bit of warning might be in order. He's on life support. Well, you may know that."

"No! I don't know anything about the man. I've just been trying to locate Frank Fanning."

"Mr. Fanning has been very good to Donal. He comes to visit every month like clockwork. He's from the South, but he makes the effort to come. Donal doesn't get many other visitors. None, really."

"What a shame."

"Aye, it is, Father. Even though he can't communicate, still, you'd think the members of his immediate family would . . . Ah, I shouldn't be talking out of school. Up these stairs, and we'll find Donal's room right at the top."

She led him to room 220 and went in. "Good morning, Donal.

Somebody here to see you. It's Father O'Flaherty, a friend of Mr. Fanning. I'll leave you now." She smiled at Donal Fegan and at Michael, then left the room.

Lying on the bed was the emaciated form of a man. He had dark hair and a growth of beard; his green eyes were open. He made no response, verbal or otherwise, to Michael's approach or his words of greeting. Michael gently took his right hand. Again, no response. The man was alive but not sentient, what people called — Michael always recoiled at the word — a vegetable. A framed photo on the bedside table showed a rugged young man standing in front of a block of flats, with a large dog at his side. There was also a scrapbook with Donal's picture on the cover. Michael picked it up and opened it. It was filled with greeting cards and press clippings. The articles were testimonials to a promising young man struck down in the prime of his life. Donal was twenty years old when he suffered terrible injuries — severe brain damage and a broken neck — in a single car crash on a country road. The accident occurred in July of 1984. The injuries brought an end to Donal's dream of returning to school to complete his education, after which he had planned to marry his long-time sweetheart and raise a family. He had hoped to start his own business as an electrician. His teachers spoke of a boy who had the potential to be whatever he wanted to be, and his priest said Donal had always been helpful around the church, making deliveries and doing small repair jobs. Michael looked at the shattered figure on the bed and felt the sting of tears in his eyes. He made the sign of the cross over him and began to pray. Donal Fegan couldn't hear him, but it was Michael's belief that his prayers were heard in a sweeter and a better world, a world in which Donal would be received with loving arms. When he finished his prayers, he gave Donal's hand a little squeeze again, then left the room.

God love Frank Fanning, Michael thought, *for travelling by train and bus on the first Friday of every month to sit by this poor fellow's bed-side and give him the gift of companionship.* Frank would be well aware that the Fegan boy didn't even register his presence, but that didn't deter him from making the trip.

It was not till Michael was back in his room replaying in his mind everything he could recall about Fanning that he remembered something that should not have slipped his mind, something he certainly should have twigged to when he saw Donal Fegan lying motionless in his bed. How could he have forgotten? But it was just one of many bits of information he had scribbled down after his talk in the Bleeding Horse with Bill McAvity, and it went something like this: "Frank F doesn't drive. One day, just not driving anymore. Lost licence, perhaps drink driving. Spot of trouble up North. Never behind wheel again." As Michael saw it, Frank Fanning must have been the driver in this accident. If so, his trips to Derry were part compassion, part guilty conscience. A guilty conscience well deserved. Or might there be more to it? All Michael had seen were the news stories pasted in Fegan's scrapbook, stories that understandably would portray the young victim in the most favourable light. But what if Fegan bore some responsibility himself for the accident? Michael didn't know how that could be, if Frank had been at the wheel. Time for a chat with Monty. Michael left the B and B and headed for the big two-storey drinking spot that was the Bogside Inn. It took a few seconds but he found Monty and Brennan at a table with empty pint glasses in front of them.

"Ah. Michael. We were just finishing up."

"Good timing. I've a question for you, Monty." They all left the pub together, and Michael told them what he had discovered at the Foyleside Centre for Longterm Care. "So, Frank Fanning is carrying a heavy burden of guilt. But, Monty, you've dealt with accident cases, have you not?"

"Yes, I have."

"Is it possible someone else could be at fault for an accident, by distracting the driver's attention or something like that?"

"Sure. Might be kind of hard to prove now, with Fegan in the shape he's in. Or they could have been drinking together, Fegan knowing full well how much Fanning had to drink and getting in the car with him anyway. I had a case recently in which the plaintiff, the passenger, was catastrophically injured. Something like poor Fegan. But his damage award was cut in half because of his contributory negligence."

"That could be the case here?"

"Maybe, but sounds as if you'll never know. How long ago was the accident?"

"Eight years or so, back in 1984."

"And even if that is what happened, how could it do anybody any good now to find out?"

"It could relieve Frank Fanning of some of the guilt he's been carrying around all these years."

"But, presumably, Fanning already knows what happened."

"He may not know. He may have been so drunk that he didn't grasp the extent of Fegan's complicity, if that is the case. Frank is still making guilt trips, mercy visits, to Fegan after all this time. He obviously feels responsible. If it could be put to him, privately and compassionately, 'Frank, we know what really happened. You're no more at fault than Fegan. It's time to forgive yourself.' A bit of healing for Frank. That sort of thing."

"And, as far as the graffiti goes, Fanning is not a killer, or not a man who took Fegan's life in every meaningful sense of the word. If indeed the graffiti was about him."

"Which, of course, we don't know," Brennan reminded them.

"Even if it isn't, Brennan, how could it hurt to minister to the man?"

Brennan relented a bit at that, though Michael knew he and Monty were far from convinced that there was anything to gain by pursuing the matter. But Michael persevered to the extent that they agreed to accompany him to his next destination, the offices of the *Derry Journal*. His purpose there was to search for more newspaper accounts of the 1984 accident. There might be something that had not been recorded in Fegan's scrapbook.

The *Journal's* receptionist showed them to a back room, where they began flipping through old editions of the paper. It didn't take Michael long to find what he was looking for, in the July 31, 1984, edition:

Man Severely Injured in Road Accident

A young man was transported to hospital in Derry last evening with very severe injuries, following a single-vehicle accident on the Groarty Road. The injured man has been identified as Donal J. Fegan, age 20, a resident of Derry City. RUC Inspector Lyle Robinson said Fegan was found alone in the car, on the passenger side. The driver apparently lost control, and the car was found upside down at the edge of the road. The car was stolen, Inspector Robinson said, and the driver has not been found. Police were tipped off to the accident by an anonymous caller. A witness told the *Derry Journal* that the RUC removed some "items" from the boot of the car, but Inspector Robinson would not confirm that information. The investigation continues.

Had Frank Fanning left the scene, left his badly injured passenger alone in the wrecked vehicle on the roadside? That would surely add to the burden of guilt. Had the anonymous tip come from Frank himself? Michael would dearly love to question the investigating officer. But that was way beyond his abilities as an amateur detective.

So he went to work on Monty. And Monty agreed to try to secure an appointment with Inspector Robinson of the Royal Ulster Constabulary. Meanwhile, Michael had another destination in mind, beyond the walls of Derry. He intended to board a bus for County Donegal and make the acquaintance of Jimmy O'Hearn's sister at McKelvey's Bar.

Brennan

The last place on earth Brennan Burke wanted to be was at the heavily guarded Royal Ulster Constabulary station in Derry. But Monty was hoping to assist Michael O'Flaherty in his commendable efforts to make things right for Frank Fanning. Talking to the police was nothing new for Monty, but Derry was not Halifax, and the RUC was not the Halifax Police Department. Nevertheless, Brennan acceded to Monty's request that he come along to pose as a kindly priest who had recently come upon poor Donal Fegan and who struggled to understand what had happened out on the Groarty Road in July 1984, which resulted in the wasting away of such a promising young man.

Of course nobody was interested in helping Father Burke and Mr. Collins secure an appointment with Inspector Lyle Robinson. The inspector was out. Then he was in, but he was tied up. Monty counselled Brennan that patience was their only hope. The day the Man Above was handing out the virtue of patience, Brennan Burke had been too impatient to wait in line for it. And the two hours he and Collins had to wait for Robinson gave rise to fantasies of trashing the police headquarters and leaving it a rubble of stone and sticks, with Inspector Lyle Robinson lying in a heap at the bottom of it. Difficult it would be to make the mental transition from this mode of thinking to the mode of mild-mannered priest of the New Testament of brotherly love. But, finally, they were ushered in to see the man who had investigated Donal Fegan's car accident. Monty cautioned Brennan not to mention Frank Fanning's name. As if Brennan Burke would walk into an Ulster police station and start spewing names. But he took the point; they did not know whether the inspector had ever been able to identify the driver in the crash.

Brennan had never seen a man who looked so exhausted. Inspector Lyle Robinson's pale blue eyes were bloodshot, underlined with dark circles. He ran a hand over his close-cropped grey hair, and the hand stayed up, as if he had forgotten it was there. Every movement seemed laboured, as if he was completely drained of energy.

"How can I help you, sir? Father? I'm a wee bit busy now." *Wee but buzzy nye*, it sounded like.

"We won't keep you two minutes, Inspector Robinson," Monty assured him, "and we are most appreciative of your help. Father Burke here is of course a priest, and I am a lay minister." It was the first Brennan had heard of that. But Collins was, as always, convincing. "One of the people we have met in our ministry is Donal Fegan. And, simply put, we are trying to piece together what happened back in 1984."

"Drink driving is what happened."

"Oh! How terrible, and what a senseless waste of a young man's life."

"Aye, it is. But maybe not as terrible as what would have happened if he had reached his destination."

"Oh! Where was he going?"

"He was headed towards the border on the Groarty Road. You'd have to be out of your mind with drink to flip a car on the Groarty Road. Do you know it? Straight as an arrow. Anyway, you may or may not know that they were on their way to pick up a fertilizer bomb to use against a target here in Londonderry."

Ah. Here it comes, thought Brennan.

"No!" Monty protested. "There must be some mistake. His room is full of testimonials to his fine character." Monty spoke as sincerely as if he did not spend every day of his working life inventing bogus testimonials for characters who were anything but fine.

Robinson snorted. "Fegan's family and his admirers and his terrorist brethren can say what they like. Doesn't change what we know about him. Maybe they think exploding a car bomb in front of a building full of people is a mark of a fine character."

"How do you know this?"

"We know." Robinson sighed and sat back in his chair. He looked as if he could drop off to sleep in an instant. "I don't know what your politics are, Mr. . . . . Collins. Or yours, Father . . . Burke, is it?" His gimlet eyes took them both in.

"Our politics don't include murder, Inspector," Monty declared in earnest.

"Well then, that differentiates you from an awful lot of people in this city and in this country. Have you any idea what it's like to be a police officer in this place, knowing you may not get home to your family at the end of your shift because a bomb may go off and blow you to smithereens? Have you had a look at this city? You've heard of fire sales? The shops here have bomb sales. Have you any inkling of what it's like to be a British soldier stationed over here, seeing your companions ambushed by snipers?"

Brennan spoke up then. "I don't condone bombing and killing and intimidation, Inspector, although you'll have to admit Catholics have not been treated as equal citizens in the North of Ireland. I won't go through the eight hundred years since this island was invaded but how can we forget Oliver Cromwell, destroyer of churches and killer of Catholics? Cromwell, who gave the Irish the choice to go west or be killed — 'To Hell or Connacht' — leaving the good lands for the English and Scottish settlers —" He'd better shut up. He had slipped out of character, and was no longer coming across as a simple, kindly cleric in service of the sick and helpless.

"There is truth in all of that, no question," Robinson replied. "But the atrocities have not all been on the Protestant side, as you well know. And that's been true all through our history. But guns and bombs in the 1990s are hardly the way to redress those historic injustices, wouldn't you agree? The Republicans think the whole country should be run from Dublin, that Northern Ireland should not exist. I say, why shouldn't it exist? You mentioned the plantation of Ireland by the English and the Scots. There was some movement in earlier years, but it really got underway in the sixteen hundreds. As you say, the Anglo-Normans arrived nearly five hundred years before that."

Robinson leaned forward and rested his arms on his desk; he addressed himself to Monty. "Where are you from, Mr. Collins?"

"I live in Canada."

"How are the native people doing over there?"

"Not well," Monty had to concede.

"The English and Scots settlers came to Ireland roughly around the time the French and English started settling in Canada. I'd say the aboriginal populations of Canada and the U.S.A. are worse off than the Catholics of Northern Ireland. Does anybody think the French and the English, the Irish and the Scots, the Germans and the Italians should pack up and leave Canada?"

The last thing we need, Brennan thought, *is to get into a sectarian row.*

Monty was obviously thinking along the same lines. He got the conversation back on track. "Tell me about the plan to set the bomb."

The inspector took a few moments to change his focus, then replied, "Do you know what I mean by the Apprentice Boys Memorial Hall?"

Brennan felt a spasm of fear, right to the tips of his fingers.

"Yes," Monty said, "the big stone place with the spires, up on the hill."

"Fegan and his co-conspirators were planning to blow it up."

"Oh, Christ! No!" Monty exclaimed. There was nothing calculated about his response this time.

Derry, or Londonderry as it was called by the Protestants, was the mythic city of Protestant Ulster. It didn't start out that way. Derry had been the site of a monastery founded by St. Columba in the sixth century. And for nine hundred years afterwards, efforts were made to keep it an oasis of calm and contemplation. But the area was a strategic site overlooking the Foyle River; control of Derry meant control over access to the interior of the country. The English built a fortification in the year 1600 and in the following decades proceeded with the plantation of Ulster, the colonization of the province by English and Scottish settlers, and the concomitant effort to displace and subdue the native Irish population. The tables turned in 1641, when the Irish massacred thousands of plantation settlers in various parts of Ulster. When the Protestants were able to regroup, they massacred the Catholics in return. It was a time of horrific violence on both sides. The fear never left the Protestant mind, Brennan knew, that the Catholic Irish would repeat the slaughter of 1641.

Derry's big moment in history came in 1688, when Catholic forces under the banner of James II approached the walled city. Things did not look good for the Protestant defenders until, according to a mixture of legend and fact, thirteen young men — who came to be known as the Apprentice Boys — slammed shut the gates of the city to keep the invaders out. The Siege of Derry followed some months later in 1689 and lasted for more than one hundred days. One hundred days during which the people inside the walls were starving, and would eat anything they could find. Brennan knew the old joke: "A Derry menu: dog, fed on the bodies of papists, two quid." When reinforcements arrived and the siege ended, many Protestants took the view that providence had delivered them from the hands of the popish hordes. The event provided the Protestants of Ulster with their national defining myth. And their rallying cry, "No Surrender!"

The baronial building that loomed over the Catholic Bogside, with its tower and spires — the Apprentice Boys Memorial Hall — was, if not in appearance, certainly in symbolism, the Parthenon of Protestant identity in the city. And Fanning and Fegan planned to blow it up! Even apart from the loss of life and the property damage, the psychological effect would have been incalculable and the vengeance unthinkable. Thank God the plot had failed.

"Did you catch the others involved?" Monty asked.

"Well, there was no point catching Donal Fegan. He's in hospital in a vegetative state. Has been since the accident. As for the others, we have our suspicions as to who was going to provide the explosives. We are keeping an eye on things. Next time they make a move, we'll be ready."

"Was Fegan involved in any previous activities of this nature?"

"Fegan was a louser. Scum. The newspaper coverage — at least in the Republican press — was sickening. Making this clown out to be a model citizen. He was in fact a foul-mouthed, violent petty criminal who couldn't learn a trade or hold a job or his liquor. That may be news to you if you've only come to know the Fegan family recently."

As far as Brennan was concerned, he and Monty had just come to know Frank Fanning himself recently, as recently as the RUC inspector's revelations thirty seconds ago. They, and Michael O'Flaherty, would have to come to terms with what they had learned about Fanning. Frank was now a serious contender as the subject of the graffiti on Christy's wall.

Brennan and Monty thanked the inspector, then returned to the Abbey B and B, rousted Michael from his room, went out for a bite to eat, and gave him the bad news about Frank Fanning. Michael looked like a man who had been betrayed by his dearest friend. They all took a walk around the city walls and polished off the evening with a few pints and a session of traditional music at Peadar O'Donnell's pub. The session was brilliant. The accordion player had a good rolling style of play, and the bodhran provided appropriate and sympathetic support to the rhythms of the pieces, but it was the fiddle that was outstanding: the intricacy and drive of the playing, the exquisite tonal quality, were everything you could ask for. Brennan had no inclination to leave while the music was going on, and his companions raised no argument. By the time they set out for their lodgings, they came across very few people in the dark city streets, with the exception of police and soldiers.

Michael

Michael surprised his companions the following morning by announcing that he would not be travelling with them back to Dublin. His mission now lay in a small town called Ballybofey in County Donegal, where he hoped to meet Jimmy O'Hearn's sister. He knew her place of employment was McKelvey's Bar. If Michael could enjoy a pint in a new setting and find out a bit about another of the Christy Burke Four while he was at it, so be it.

He prayed he would not find out something terrible about Jimmy O'Hearn, the way he had about Frank Fanning. It was nearly impossible for Michael to picture Frank planning an atrocity like the bombing of the Apprentice Boys Memorial. It was Michael's understanding that the IRA generally gave coded warnings to the police to clear a target like that, to prevent loss of life. But that didn't always work out, obviously; just look at the body count. Surely, Frank would have backed off when he realized the enormity of what he had planned to do. Or would he? Well, Michael hoped there was nothing remotely like that in the history of Mr. O'Hearn.

The day was close and muggy, too warm for clerical dress. Michael had a cool shower and donned a pair of khaki pants and a pale blue short-sleeved shirt. He caught an early afternoon bus to County Donegal, which, as far north as it is, is not part of Northern Ireland, but part of the Irish Republic. Michael had a little laugh to himself when he thought of giving directions. "Well, it's in the north of Ireland, but don't call it northern Ireland because it's not Northern Ireland. But it's not north *of* Northern Ireland, nor is it south of Northern Ireland; it's to the west of it. Up north."

McKelvey's Bar was situated in Glenfin Street in the lovely little town. The place looked as much like a family home as it did a pub. It was a large white house with black trim and a black roof with three dormers. Chimneys stuck up at both gable ends. Michael went inside and sat at the bar. There was a young dark-haired girl serving drinks, and Michael asked after Sarah O'Hearn, or formerly known as O'Hearn.

"Oh, that would be Sarah Duffy. She's just out on an errand; she'll be back soon."

So Michael ordered a pint of Guinness and chatted with the young barmaid until the door opened and Sarah Duffy came in weighted down with packages. She appeared to be around fifty, thin with a tired-looking face and fair hair going grey. Michael got to his feet and relieved her of two heavy-looking bags.

"Thank you, sir! If we could just deposit these things in the back behind the bar there . . ." They dropped the bags, and the young one said she would take care of things, since Michael was here to see Sarah.

"Here to see *me*, are you?"

"Yes, I am."

Her face brightened and lost its careworn look.

"It's not often a stranger comes calling!"

"My name is Michael O'Flaherty. Father O'Flaherty, actually, but it's casual day, as you can see. I'm visiting from Canada, basing myself in Dublin and taking a little tour of other parts of the country. I'm on my way to Donegal Town," he claimed, "for a quick visit there. But I knew Jimmy O'Hearn had a sister working in Ballybofey, so I got off the bus to say a quick hello and enjoy a pint."

"Oh! Lovely, Father."

"Call me Michael, if you like."

"All right then, Michael. Let's take a table. So you're a friend of

Jimmy." She poured herself a glass of orange juice, and led him to a table. "How is he?" she asked when they were seated. "We haven't seen him in a while."

"He's well enough."

"I'm worried about him, though. I always am, but any time I hear from him, things are grand, couldn't be better." She leaned closer to Michael. "He drinks too much."

Michael could hardly deny that. He tried to put a good face on it. "He does take a drink. But I've never known him to be ill with it, or rowdy, or to drive a car while under the influence."

"I suppose we should be thankful for that. So, what else brings you to Donegal, Michael?"

"Nothing but love of this part of the country. I come to Ireland fairly often, but I don't get to spend enough time in this area. I had a chance, so —"

"Sarah!"

"Oh, Niall. Come in."

Michael looked over at the man poking his head in the door. He had a pleasant round face with laugh lines at the eyes; he wore glasses with thin silver rims.

"This is Father Michael O'Flaherty, up from Dublin," Sarah said. "Friend of Jim. Michael, this is my husband, Niall. He's here to collect me."

"Good to meet you, Niall."

"How are you, Michael?"

"Fine, thank you."

Sarah said, "Why don't you come to the house for tea?"

"Oh, I wouldn't want to trouble you, Sarah."

"It's no trouble at all. I'd be delighted."

"Well, thank you then. I will."

"All right. Let's be off."

They said goodbye to the girl at the bar and walked to the Duffys' car on the street outside. The vehicle had seen better days, and Michael estimated that those days were fifteen years ago, judging by the style of the car. Amateur bodywork had been done on the fenders, which were grey and lumpy, a contrast to the faded red of the original paint job.

"Just give me a minute to clear a space for you, Michael," Niall said as he reached in and gently pushed aside two violins and a couple of tin whistles in the back seat. "Sarah, why don't you take the back seat and Michael can sit up here with me."

"I'm fine in the back," Michael protested, but Sarah waved him off and gave him the seat of honour.

After a couple of false starts, Niall got the machine moving and they lurched out into the street. They drove for a few minutes, then pulled in beside a cottage-like house outside the town. The place needed a coat of paint, and the window frames were in need of repair, but the property was neat and orderly. The Duffys ushered Michael into the cramped front room, where there were a sofa and chairs, piano and stool. Dampness had blighted the ceiling and the wall around the window. There was a harp, and a big brass horn of some kind pushed into the corner by the piano.

"I give music lessons here," Niall explained. "Doesn't pay a fortune but it teaches . . . well, it teaches the children music, and teaches me the patience of Job!"

"I suppose it does," Michael agreed. "Do you have children of your own?"

"Aye, do we! Three boys and a girl, from age nineteen to twenty-six. And they all have better things to do than come home and keep their old parents company!"

The two men exchanged small talk while Sarah wet the tea. Niall's conversation revealed a gentleness and self-deprecating wit that Michael enjoyed.

Sarah brought in cups of tea and a plate of biscuits. Michael thanked her. He took his cup, walked over to the wall opposite the piano, and stood before a family photograph. It was in black and white and appeared to have been taken in the 1940s. Sarah joined him.

"That's our Jimmy, right there. Isn't he a dote?" She pointed to a little fellow of eight or nine with freckles, jug ears, and a shy smile. "That's me on the knee of my sister, Deirdre. I was three then. And this is Rod, our big brother. And there's Kathleen, Maggie, and Denise. But I can do better than that. Have you time for a home movie? It's only about ten minutes long."

"Oh, I'd love to see it!"

"This was done by the same fellow who took that picture, same day. It was a Yank, wouldn't you know it? You always see them with all the newest gear hanging off them. Anyway, it was an American who came to Donegal on a bus with his wife. He had a great clunky camera, and he went from house to house asking if people would like him to take a movie of their family. A lot of people took him up on it. I can't remember what he charged. A few bob maybe. Anyway he filmed us, and I got it transferred onto videotape last year. Hold on a minute while I set it up." She reached into a shelf under the television set and drew out a videotape, stuck it in the player, and pressed a couple of buttons.

Michael was surprised by the quality of the film. The black-and-white images were clear and sharp. "That's Roddy," Sarah said. Rod looked to be about fifteen and was kitted out in white shorts, dark knee socks, and a dark jersey bearing an inscription in Irish, which Michael translated as the name of the St. Columcille School football team. A makeshift goal was constructed of netting hung from a clothesline and anchored in place by tree branches. It was manned by another lad of around the same age as Rod. Two little boys, one of them Jimmy, kicked at the ball and attempted to move it towards the goal. All of a sudden, Rod came up behind Jimmy, scooped him up in one arm, grabbed the ball with his other hand, zoomed in behind the goalkeeper, and booted the ball at the goalkeeper's rear end. The grin on Jimmy's face went from one ear to the other, and he raised his fists in triumph. There was a roar of approval from the O'Hearn side and some mildly profane protesting from the other. The scene switched to a wharf and a dockside building bearing the sign "O'Hearn Yachts." On a boat tied up to the dock, Roddy stood behind a little girl in a sailor suit. She had her hands on the wheel. She kept saying "ooh" and "whoosh" as she captained the vessel over imaginary waves. Two other little ones stood by with unconcealed impatience for their turn. "Roddy! Me now, me now!"

"The family business," Sarah said. "The O'Hearns began building boats in 1843. My great-great-grandfather founded the business. When you bought an O'Hearn boat, you could be sure you were sailing in the most finely crafted wooden vessel Ireland had to offer. My great-grandfather started a sideline making figureheads. You know what I mean, the carved figure on the prow of a ship. So you could get a yacht with a personalized figurehead showing your wife or your sweetheart, or whatever carving you wanted. Some of them were very witty; one might have features suspiciously similar to those of a local character or a politician. Of course you could buy a figurehead even if you didn't have a boat. We received orders from all over the world for our boats and carvings. Our da lived for his work, but that didn't mean he missed out on family life. We children spent every free minute there. Took our schoolbooks there after classes, went to work with Da on the weekends. Roddy started learning the family trade when he was eleven years old, so he could be Da's partner. Jimmy did the same when he got old enough. We all had some role to play in the boat works." Sarah sighed and reached for the teapot. She poured Michael another cup and pushed the plate of biscuits in his direction.

"Your father wouldn't be living now . . ."

"No, he died in 1981."

"So, I take it Rod has stepped into your father's deck shoes, so to speak, and is running the business?"

She shook her head sadly. "No, Michael. I'm heartscalded to say we don't have the business anymore. O'Hearn Yachts is now based in Miami, Florida. The Americans bought us out."

"Oh!" Michael had heard that Jimmy was no longer in the O'Hearn Yacht business, but he hadn't known the circumstances. "So the family sold it. What brought that on? They gave you an offer you couldn't refuse?"

"I only wish! No. We were the victims of an unscrupulous lawyer, Michael. He took advantage of our trust, got the business into his own name through some kind of finagling — taxes, offshore holding companies, I don't know what it all meant — but in the end, the Americans became the owners, and the money went into the lawyer's pocket. And that was that. We would be celebrating one hundred and fifty years of boat building next year if it weren't for him."

"Oh, Sarah, I'm so very sorry to hear that. How heartbreaking for the family. Rod, especially, perhaps?"

"He never got over it. He moved as far away from here as he could go. New Zealand. He couldn't bear to be here and to walk along the strand and not see an O'Hearn boat bobbing in the waves, not see the boat-building works, not take his place in the boatyard every morning and wave to everyone passing by on the shore."

"What a shame. You must miss him terribly."

"We do. We've tried to persuade him to come home, or at least to visit."

"Maybe he'll soften up over time. Surely he will."

"We hope so. But there's also the fact that, well, things have not gone well for Rod out there in New Zealand. He just never found his way. Reading between the lines of his few letters, we got the clear impression of someone living in poverty. And shame. Finally, he just stopped writing.

"We've often talked about taking up a collection to bring Roddy home for a visit. Costs a packet to fly here from New Zealand, but we thought if we all contributed . . . We'd make up a story: won some money in the sweeps, the lottery, something, so he wouldn't be embarrassed. I know he's ashamed of how he ended up. But surely that would be forgotten if he got home with us all, wouldn't you think?"

"This must be a great worry for Jimmy as well. It's obvious from the photo and the movie that he worships his big brother."

"Adores him. He's forever trying to persuade Rod to come home. Or he was, before we lost contact."

"Don't give up hope, Sarah. You'll bring him around. Rod will get in touch with you someday. I'll keep you and Rod and the rest of the family in my prayers. You can be sure of that."

"Thank you, Father. Michael."

"What happened with the lawyer? Who was he?"

"Carey Gilbert, in London."

"Did you bring charges against him?"

"Oh, no, nothing like that."

"Sue him for damages?"

"No."

"May I ask why?"

"It took a long time for us to realize what had happened, how we had been swindled. By the time we found out, it was too late. The damage was done."

"But surely, there are steps you can take, prosecute the lawyer . . ."

She just shook her head and turned away.

†

Michael did not intend to impose on the Duffys all day, so he thanked them and said he'd be on his way. Would they mind dropping him off at the bus stop?

203

"Where are you headed now, Michael?" Niall asked.

"To Donegal Town. I like walking there, the castle and the ruins of the old abbey, all of that."

"Well, no need to take a bus. I have to see a student down past Ballyshannon. If you're up for a little drive, we could go through Donegal and out into the country for the lesson. I'll enjoy the company. You'll just have to wait a bit for the wee boy to play his scales!"

"I'd love to go along for the drive. Thank you, Niall."

So the two men got into the Duffys' battered little car and, after another shaky beginning, drove out into the Irish countryside. At one point Michael looked down at his feet and saw the highway going by under a hole in the rusted floor of the car. Times were obviously tough for the Duffys.

They drove into Donegal Town, which had always reminded Michael of Mahone Bay back in Nova Scotia, with the addition of a ruined Franciscan abbey and the castle of Red Hugh O'Donnell. Niall found a parking spot near the water and said, "One of our boats is docked here. Come and have a look."

They walked along the shore, and Niall pointed ahead. They drew up beside a magnificent sailing boat, which, in Michael's estimation, was about fifty feet in length. The hull was painted a gleaming black with cream trim; the wood of the deck and masts was in tip-top shape. But the most striking feature was the figurehead. "Look at that, Michael. The boat was built in 1893. The owner's daughter died of a fever. That's her, the figurehead." It was an exquisite carving of a little girl, the folds of her dress billowing in the wind. She was depicted playing a tin whistle, and the artist managed to convey a sense of joy and mischief in the child's face.

"Oh, Niall, she is beautiful! What artistry!"

"That was the work of Sarah's great-grandfather. He knew the family. All of his figureheads were one of a kind. He spent months on them. I'm thinking they don't do that now, in Miami!"

Michael shook his head at the beauty and the loss.

They returned to the car and set out for the countryside. Niall gave Michael a running commentary on the places they passed and told him about the young lad who was having his lesson that day. The child's father had lost his job as people deserted the village in the wake of the recent Troubles; it sounded to Michael as if Niall was providing his services without expectation of payment. They pulled up before a modest bungalow in a quiet rural area. No other cars passed by. It was clear the place was not thriving.

"How far are we from the border?" Michael asked.

"A mile or so, just down that road." Niall pointed the way. "The music lesson is for an hour. You're more than welcome to sit in."

"No, no, thank you, Niall. I'll go for a little walk, and meet you back here in an hour's time."

"Where would you be walking to, Michael?"

"Em, I'll just go for a bit. Get some exercise."

"Be careful, then. Keep an eye out. Never know who's around."

"I won't get into a car driven by a stranger, no worries there," Michael said lightly.

"You won't even see a car, if you're of a mind to go as far as the border. The road's closed to traffic."

Niall went up to the door of the house. Michael stood and had a little stretch, then set out along the narrow road that led to Northern Ireland. There was nobody in sight. The land was boggy, not much good for farming. There were a few houses scattered about, but he didn't see any life around them, not even a farm dog. He'd been walking for fifteen minutes or so when he caught sight of big metal spikes of some sort sticking up in the air. As he got closer, he saw they were attached to an enormous chunk of concrete that completely blocked the road ahead. An ugly sight, a blight on the landscape. Well, it served the purpose of stopping cross-border traffic; that was obvious. But Michael saw a young boy walking past the barrier ahead of him. He decided to do the same.

Within seconds, he was in Northern Ireland once again. Things didn't look any better on this side of the frontier than they did on the other. Michael saw the same forlorn-looking houses scattered about. He kept going, and eventually came to a tiny village. There was hardly a soul in the streets. He stood in what must have been the market square and wondered what to do. Suddenly he jumped at the roar of a motor. He turned to see a big green and black army vehicle bearing down on him from behind. It slowed, and he saw three British soldiers inside, rifles in their arms. They looked him over before continuing on their way. What could they be looking for in this sad little place?

It began to drizzle, and that prompted Michael to move on. He walked up a side street and saw a faint light glowing in a window. Saints be praised! A pub. Just in time, as the drizzle turned to rain. He heard another loud racket and looked up to see a British Army helicopter approaching from the east, flying low over the town. Michael watched till it was out of sight, then walked over to the pub and opened the door. Half a dozen men sat on stools at the bar. Michael smiled and was about to greet them. But the expression on their faces stopped him cold. To a man they ceased their conversation and stared at the newcomer. The outsider. And he wasn't even in his clerical garb. Was there something about his face, his clothing, his demeanour that announced he was a blow-in from the other side of the border? Michael didn't know how they knew it, but they knew. The bartender wasn't much better. He jerked his head up and grunted. Well, Michael wasn't about to turn tail and leave. He ordered a glass of Bushmills, paid for it, and took it to a table in the middle of the pub. Not only did the men not speak to Michael, they didn't say a word to one another. For some reason he thought of Monty Collins and what he would say. "A Catholic priest walks into a bar . . ." He'd make a joke about it. But Michael couldn't come up with a punchline; there was nothing funny about this. He had rarely felt so uncomfortable in his entire life. Was it always like this, or were tensions even higher than usual with the Protestant minister missing in action? Michael finished his whiskey, got up, and left the silent pub.

He practically sprinted through the rain to the hideous pile of concrete and steel that marked the border with the Republic and hurried across. He continued his brisk pace until he arrived, nearly out of breath — Michael wasn't forty years old anymore! — at the young boy's house. Niall was coming out the door when he arrived.

"You're soaked to the bone, Michael! I should have insisted that you come inside. We'll find you some dry things to wear when we get home."

"No, no, I'm fine, really."

"Where'd you go?"

"Just took a little stroll."

"You went to the border, didn't you?"

"Em, yes."

"Pretty grim, isn't it?"

"It is indeed."

They got in Niall's little car and headed out on the road in the direction of Donegal.

Michael thought again about the beautiful boat he had seen. "It's a shame," he remarked, "that Sarah's family lost the boat business. My heart goes out to them. And the fact that they were cheated out of it by a lawyer makes it so much more painful. Outrageous. How some people sleep at night is beyond me!"

Niall looked over at Michael and spoke in a quiet voice. "I suspect the lawyer is having no trouble sleeping these days, Michael."

"You may be right. Still, shouldn't you take steps against this man? Lay charges or at least have him investigated for fleecing his clients?"

"Can't."

"How come?"

"He's gone. Disappeared."

"Really! From where?"

"London. That's where his practice was. Rod tried to go after him and found out he'd vanished. All the law society would say was that there was nobody in their register by that name. Sarah thinks Gilbert did so well for himself in the swindle that he took off for parts unknown and will never have to practise law again as long as he lives." Niall stopped speaking as a lorry rattled past them on the motorway. When it had gone, he said, "But I have other ideas."

"Such as?"

Niall glanced across at Michael. "I'm thinking maybe he's dead."

"Dead!"

"Killed."

Michael turned to stare. "You're thinking he was murdered by . . ."

Niall raised his eyebrows. "Not by your brother-in-law!"

"I have no proof. Obviously."

"Is he the type, you think, to kill a man? Has he ever shown any tendency towards violence?"

"Not that I ever saw. Rod rarely takes a drink, so I've never even seen him in a surly, drunken mood. But he lost everything that mattered to him when the family got screwed out of the business. I just, well . . . It struck me that nobody could find the lawyer. And somebody had a motive to kill him." Niall looked over at his passenger. "I'm probably out to lunch here, Michael. The lawyer is more than likely alive on a tropical island somewhere, surrounded by dancing girls. I'll tell you this much. If I ever find out that my fantasies are fact, I won't turn my brother-in-law over to Scotland Yard! I'll head up the defence fund. Oh, don't listen to me, Michael. There's something about you that encourages people to confess things they haven't even whispered to another human being. Maybe I watch too many of those crime programs on television!"

After thanking the Duffys for their kind hospitality, Michael boarded a bus to Dublin. A beautiful journey through the country-side, but Michael's thoughts were far from idyllic. Had Rod O'Hearn snapped and killed the lawyer who stole the family business? Had someone learned of this and scrawled cryptic messages about it on the wall of Christy Burke's pub in Dublin? That idea didn't make much sense. Unless Michael changed a couple of factors in the equation. Rod didn't drink, but his brother Jimmy did. Rod wasn't in Dublin, but Jimmy was. Jimmy had a boat and took fishing parties out on the Irish Sea. Did he perhaps cross the sea to England? If drink fuelled a vengeful rage in one of the O'Hearn brothers, would it more likely have been Jimmy? Well, maybe not. Maybe something like that would be more likely to occur in a person who was not used to alcohol, someone who couldn't handle his liquor. Jimmy O'Hearn was well able to do that! And Michael could not quite bring up an image of the smiling, pleasantly plastered Jimmy O'Hearn in a murderous rage. Michael had to admit, though, that he didn't know Jimmy very well. But how well did he know any of them, really?

Chapter 11

Michael

He wondered if he was being too bold. Kitty Curran was "just" a friend. Inevitably. But she was a woman friend and — no getting away from it — a beloved one. Michael had it in mind to offer her a little treat, to show her how happy he was to see her in Dublin. Seeing her was a refreshing change from hearing the dismal stories of the Christy Burke's drinkers. Flowers might be going too far, but chocolates would be appropriate, wouldn't they? There was nothing in canon law — or the discipline of celibacy — that said he couldn't give chocolate to a woman! So there he was just before noontime Tuesday in Butler's Chocolate shop in Grafton Street across from Stephen's Green. There was a crowd forming behind him but he took his time. Should he hand-pick a selection or take one of the ready-made boxes? Well, the boxes looked lovely, and he knew every piece inside would be a treasure. Now, how big a box? In other words, how much could he afford to spend after he had splurged on all the new clothes? *Go big or stay home, O'Flaherty!* He chose the large ribbon-bedecked box of truffles, which set him back twenty-three punts. Smiling, he left the shop, sprinted to the corner, and hailed a taxi.

"The Mater, please."

"Nothing too serious, I hope," the cab driver said.

"Well, now, I'm not sure."

"Best of luck to yeh then."

"Thank you."

Michael and the rest of the Halifax contingent had made plans to have lunch at the Stag's Head. Kitty would be coming along as well, but she called to say she had to stop in to visit someone at the Mater Misericordiae Hospital first and did not know how long the visit would take. So the men agreed to meet her at the hospital.

The cab arrived at Eccles Street and pulled up in front of the magnificent stone hospital with its columns and rows of Palladian windows. Michael paid the driver and got out. When he entered the waiting room, he saw his friends sitting with two old people in wheelchairs. The patients both had matted grey hair and blankets across their knees. They could have been brother and sister, husband and wife, or just fellow inmates. The woman was hooked up to an IV on a pole. Michael had to laugh when he saw the face on Brennan Burke. Father Burke had never been able to hide his discomfort in a hospital. Michael cherished his role as comforter of the sick and dying, but Brennan seemed more at home with the homeless, the imprisoned — hard cases for sure, but easier for him to take than the sickly patient in a hospital bed.

Kitty introduced Michael to Fergal O'Herlihy and Mary Whelan. They both gave him toothless grins when he shook their hands. "Now what accounts for your stay in this fine building, Mary? Fergal?"

Mary began, "With me it started as an infection in my gums. Oh, the mess of it, let me tell you. You think you've seen pus! But the smell and the taste of it in your mouth, I tell you it was —"

"Excuse me, would you?" It was Brennan, tapping the cigarette pack in his shirt pocket. Was it a sudden craving for a smoke, or was he not able for a recitation of these people's ills?

"I'll join you, Brennan," Monty said with haste, and the two of them bolted from the room.

Some of us can take it and some of us can't. Michael and Kitty commiserated with the patients until the other two returned and lingered without sitting.

"What's that you have there, Mike?" Brennan asked.

He had spied the chocolates.

"It's a box of candy, Brennan. Butler's chocolates!"

"Oh, for me?" Kitty exclaimed.

"Ah, well, yes, as a matter of fact," Michael replied. He could feel himself blushing. The more so when he realized from the look on her face that she had only been joking. She hadn't thought they were for her at all. There was nothing for it now but to make his presentation. "I thought you might enjoy a little sweet." He handed the box over.

"Lovely! Let's tear it open!" She removed the ribbon, opened the top and, without even looking inside, offered the box to the sick people. Fergal picked one up, put it back, examined another, replaced it, and finally settled on one. For her part, Mary grabbed a handful, shoved one into her mouth, then thrust the handful over at Brennan.

"Chocolate?" she said, then raised a hand to wipe her mouth, from which the brown sweet substance dribbled onto her chin. Mixed with God only knew what bodily fluids.

"No, no, thank you, no," Brennan insisted. Michael could have sworn he heard a snicker from Monty. Michael knew Monty found Brennan a little fastidious and enjoyed slagging him about it.

A couple of nurses passed by then, and Kitty waved the box at them. "Help yourselves, girls!" Finally Kitty took one herself.

Then she was saying her goodbyes. Michael did the same. They rose to go. And Kitty left the chocolates behind.

Michael had meant them as a gift for Kitty, had meant to present them to her with a bit of finesse, at an appropriate time. As it turned out, she had barely accorded them a glance before giving them away to the first taker. They had cost him twenty-three Irish pounds! He immediately chided himself for thinking that way, when Kitty had been so generous. Of course she was the kind of woman who would share whatever she had.

He made the mistake of mentioning it when they were out in the street. "That wasn't much of a treat for you, Kitty."

"Well, I could hardly keep them to myself, Michael. Next time you give chocolate to a woman, make sure you don't do it under the eyes of hungry, sweet-deprived sick people and overworked nurses!"

Oh! That's what he got for venturing into the unfamiliar terrain of plying a lady with chocolate! He hoped the others couldn't see that he was flustered.

"Smooth, Kitty!" he heard Brennan saying.

"What?"

"A handsome, smartly dressed man buys you candy, and you don't even thank him. Or give him a little peck on the cheek. I don't imagine any more Butler's truffles will be making their way to you in the next little while."

"Oh! I —"

"Thy rebuke hath broken his heart!" Brennan was singing to her now. Michael recognized it from Handel's *Messiah*. Oh God Almighty, how could that man sing so beautifully when making a little joke in the middle of a Dublin street? And wasn't the Irish accent appropriate, given that the *Messiah* had had its premiere right here in Dublin? Michael stopped to take in the performance. Brennan stood with one hand on his heart, the other flung out to Kitty. She stared at him with undisguised admiration.

When the aria was done, he put his hands on her upper arms and said, "Now, show the man some appreciation, would you? Yes, we all admire you for sharing the wealth, but nobody in that hospital would be gorging themselves on *theobroma* — the very food of the gods — if it hadn't been for Michael O'Flaherty!"

"Oh, Michael, I'm sorry. It's just that, well, I never get any gifts. It's not 'poor little me,' it's just, well, the way it is."

She moved forward, put her arms around him, and kissed him on the cheek. *All's well that ends well.*

They made their way south along Mountjoy Street. Brennan halted beside a Georgian-style brick townhouse with multi-paned windows and a demi-lune fanlight over the bright yellow door. The house was three storeys high, topped with a large chimney pot. It was flanked by several identical houses.

"This is where I lived for my first three years," Brennan said, "until my mother moved us to Rathmines. To a house identical to this one. She'd had enough of living, as she put it, right next door to the family pub. She made the move when the oul fellow was in the Joy, up there behind us. Bit of a surprise for him when he got out."

Another of the Burkes in Mountjoy Prison. Well, Brennan had alluded to this, without quite saying it, after his father's past had come back to him at the point of a gun in New York City. Michael tried to look as if this was the sort of thing he heard every day. And, since coming to Dublin, that was almost the case.

He said to Brennan, "Would it be fair to surmise that your father was not a man for surprises? Surprises like moving house when he was out of circulation?"

"That would be a fair assessment, Michael, yes. But my mother could always get him sorted."

They walked a bit farther, and Michael pointed to the tall-spired church across St. Mary's Place from Christy's. "The black church," he said.

"Now you're not saying 'black' as a reflection of its Protestant character, I know, Monsignor," Kitty said.

"No, Sister, certainly not. I heard they call it that because it turns black in the rain. Too bad people seem to think they can use it as a rubbish dump. They've piled every old bit of refuse under the sun there. Isn't that right, Brennan?"

Brennan looked a little startled. Must have been lost in thoughts of his own.

"Black in the rain," Michael prompted.

"Oh, right. Mmm."

"Well, it won't be turning black today," Monty said. "How often do you see a perfectly sunny day like this in Dublin?"

"Oh, ye of little faith!" Kitty exclaimed. "We're no strangers to the sun here in Dublin, are we, Brennan?"

"Sure you're right, Kitty. We're not unfamiliar with it," Brennan agreed. "And that makes it a grand day for a walk to the Stag's Head, where we can once again closet ourselves away from the healing properties of the sun and fresh air."

Brennan

When they got to Dame Court, Maura MacNeil and the two children were waiting outside the elegant Victorian pub. They all went in together. The Stag's Head was one of the most sumptuous pubs Brennan had ever seen — and he had seen his share of drinking spots — with its stained-glass windows, rich wood interior, and long mahogany bar topped with Connemara marble. Normie directed her baby brother's attention to the mounted animal heads high on the wall, and the little fellow gazed at them in wonder.

They found a table and got the baby settled in a high chair, then they ordered stew and bangers and mash and pints of porter, and settled in for a relaxing time.

"Do you like my new shirt, Father?" Normie asked.

He hadn't noticed it till now. She was wearing a pint-sized blue Dublin football jersey.

"Oh, that's a great shirt, Normie. Have you joined the team? Should you be at practice instead of hanging around the pubs of Dublin?"

"Ha ha, very funny. I'm not on the team. I got it at a big store called Arnotts."

"Oh. Right. Well it looks very nice on you."

"Thank you. A lot of kids here wear them."

"Yes, they do. You look right at home with your Dublin shirt and your red hair."

"Do you think so?"

"I do."

A sweet little girl she was. Her talk about football, though, brought unsettling memories of the conversation he had with Sammy Coogan after the match at Croke Park. Brennan had passed Coogan's comments along to Finn but he had not heard another word about the young fellow who had disappeared around the same time as the Reverend Merle Odom. The lad was named Clancy, Brennan recalled, nephew of the Bishop of Meath. Brennan had never met the bishop but he knew something of his work; the Most Reverend Pádraig Aloysius Clancy was renowned as a biblical scholar. Was the Clancy family enduring the same agonies as the Odom family, and for the same reason?

Luckily, Normie distracted Brennan from his worries. She was cutting up tiny bits of lunch for Dominic and feeding them to him on a spoon. In between bits she regaled the group with a description of the sights she had seen in Dublin that morning, including her favourite gold jewellery in the world, which had been made four thousand years ago, displayed in the National Museum, and the most beautiful washroom in the world, in the National Library. "It's got tiles on the wall in a pretty pattern and it has green and gold coloured glass, and comfy chairs! We should make our bathroom like that at home!"

"We should open a pub like this at home," Monty said. "Brennan will be the bartender, I'll be his apprentice, and Normie can do the decorating."

"Can we? Please? We can make a fancy bathroom in it. I'll do all the work, I promise!"

"Can't guarantee it, sweetheart."

"Aww, Daddy!"

"What caught your own fancy, Maura?" Kitty asked. "Have you seen anything of interest at all?"

"I wouldn't even know where to begin. But I certainly spent a long time with the exhibits relating to the Rising, the War of Independence, the Civil War. The guns, the caps, the uniforms; I felt I was in granddad Christy Burke's clothes closet! Am I right, Brennan? Did they relocate his closet to the National Museum?"

No. I relocated it myself, from the tunnel to the black church.

All he said aloud was "Did you notice whether it was jammed with skeletons? If so, it may have been Christy's."

"So what do you think, Brennan?" the MacNeil asked him. "All that business about the graffiti. Are you really convinced it has something to do with the Christy Burke Four? Or do you think it's something political, relating to your family?"

He was saved from having to answer by Michael O'Flaherty. "Well, Leo Killeen has warned me to mind myself. He seems to think there is something political behind the whole thing. But I'm not convinced of that. Not everything that happens on this island is political! Particularly here in the South. But, whatever it is, we're not getting very far in our inquiries."

"How long has it been since the last incidence of graffiti?" Monty asked. "Three weeks? Nearly four. Do you suppose the problem might have just gone away, and there's no need for any more investigation?"

"I think we'd best keep at it," Brennan replied.

They all looked at him with interest, obviously waiting for more. But Brennan was not prepared to say any more, not prepared to reveal that the only reason the problem appeared to have gone away was that the vandal had been shot while delivering his last message, and that their project was in reality a murder investigation.

There was a long moment of silence, then Monty spoke again. "Let's get back to politics and history." He directed a pointed glance at Brennan. "I'm sure I'm not the only one in the room who would like to hear from Christy Burke's grandson on the subject. So. Now that you're on your native soil once again, Brennan, where do you stand?"

No getting away from it this time. "I've had to wrestle with that question all my life." He paused to light up a cigarette, inhaled a lungful of smoke — ah! — and let it out. "If I were transported back in time to 1919, I'd have stood with a Collins even grander than yourself, that being Mick Collins."

It was comical in a way. Monty, who was half-Irish, was not interested *enough* in Irish history, while Michael O'Flaherty was *too* interested by half and might get himself into trouble one of these days.

"Collins, when are you ever going to get off your hole and do some research, see if you're related?"

Kitty turned to Michael. "Monsignor, next time you hear this man's confession, be sure to add two decades of the rosary for language displeasing to God."

"Sorry," Brennan said, "but really this fellow is such a bollocks."

"Make that three decades, Monsignor."

"I'll do that, Sister. Last time, I gave him the stations of the cross three times as a penance, but it seems not to have had any effect on him. Incorrigible, I'm afraid."

"Don't be changing the subject, which is this fellow here." Brennan pointed at Monty.

"Leave me out of it, Burke. The subject is you and your politics. Get on with it."

"All right. Where would I have been during the Troubles? I'd have been with Christy, waging war against the Brits until we brought them to their knees. And we did bring them to their knees. The odds against that were astronomical; I still marvel over it seventy-one years after the fact. No question of where I would have stood to that point. But what about afterwards, when the war was over and the treaty signed? Would it have galled me to have to swear an oath of allegiance to the English king? Would it have stuck in my craw to see the six counties excluded from the new country? Of course it would have."

He had only to remember how it had galled him to be stopped and searched by British soldiers at the border in Armagh; on that occasion, it was all he could do to resist the impulse to take that little Tan fucker and kick him back to Coventry. And then he'd had to serve Holy Mass in front of a phalanx of British armoured cars at the funeral for Rory Dignan. Did he wish it was otherwise? Obviously.

"But that was the reality of 1921. We were not going to get out of the oath. Although nobody at the time, at least in this part of the country, thought the border was permanent, we were not going to have the six counties. It's a wonder we got anything. With the treaty, we became the Irish Free State. We had our own government, our own army, our own police force.

"With all that Michael Collins and Richard Mulcahy and the others had achieved, would I then, after fighting at their side to the point of that magnificent achievement, have turned a gun on them because we didn't get it all in 1921? That's what would have been required of me if I were to stay with Christy and the Irregulars after the treaty was signed." Brennan took another lungful of nicotine, expelled it. "Somebody turned a gun on Collins when he was commander-in-chief of our national army. Cut him down before he reached the age of thirty-two. It wouldn't have been me."

He picked up his glass of whiskey and downed half of it. "And it's still going on. I would love to see a united Ireland. But would I blow people's legs off to get it? Same old question: does the end justify the means? How can I say yes to that?"

Monty asked, "How do you deal with this, you and your dad? And Finn?"

"We don't."

"So you make these periodic visits to Dublin, and you see your uncle Finn . . ."

"He's not the only person I see in this city."

". . . and you don't talk about his politics."

The MacNeil came aboard him then. "Well, we shouldn't be all that surprised. How much does this guy ever tell us about himself? And think about his father. Declan Burke. Shot in front of all the guests at a family wedding. And when Declan recovers, and the New York cops try to solve the crime, Declan won't tell them anything. Brennan and Monty launch an investigation on their own; Declan won't open his mouth to help them. Was there an Irish connection to the attempt on your life, Da? Silence. He wouldn't talk about it. So why should it surprise any of us that Brennan visits Ireland and spends all his time drinking in his uncle's pub, a pub steeped in the uncle's Republican history, and they don't talk about it? The men in that family are all cut from the same cloth, as far as I can see." Her eyes searched his face. "But, Brennan, tell us this. How would you and your uncle know, without ever talking about it, that this is something the two of you should avoid talking about?"

"I don't want to talk about it."

After a few minutes Kitty said lightly, "All that painful history, and the politics, and we have all the personal baggage that everybody else has, on top of it all. No wonder the pubs do such a roaring business on this island!"

"I read somewhere that there are a thousand pubs in Dublin now."

"Monty, my dear, that's nothing new!" Kitty scoffed. "'And when Ferdiad was come into the camp, he was honoured and waited on, and choice, well-flavoured strong liquor was poured out for him till he was drunken and merry.' That's from the *Táin*, the *Cattle Raid of Cooley*, one of the classics of ancient Irish literature, a recitation of events that may have occurred as long ago as two thousand years. Another reference to drink in the epic says that 'only' fifty wagons of the stuff were brought to the camp. So we were at it even then. Did you know that by the late seventeenth century there were fifteen hundred taverns and alehouses in this city? A century later the number had doubled! But we needn't feel any guilt. What did Flann O'Brien call our pubs? 'Licensed tabernacles'!"

Michael

Michael O'Flaherty's mind had not been at ease since Wednesday, when he returned to Dublin from the North. He and the others had gathered some distressing information about Jimmy O'Hearn and Frank Fanning, and they would have to figure out how it fit, if at all, with the menacing graffiti at Christy Burke's. And where had Frank gone?

But Michael had a bit of a social event to distract him for now. He and Leo Killeen were entertaining at home that evening. Well, Leo was the host; the gathering was in his room, because Father Grattan was receiving parish visitors in the "good room" downstairs. Brennan, Monty, and Kitty were the guests. Little Dominic had a fever so Maura and the children sent their regrets. But the other five made a festive evening of it. They borrowed chairs from Michael's room, and Michael provided the refreshments: wine, whiskey, tea, and biscuits from a family-owned bakery in the neighbourhood. Kitty, Leo, and

Brennan reminisced about their respective childhoods in Dublin, and the *craic* was good indeed.

But Brennan's childhood memories included the family pub, so the subject of the Christy Burke Four came up once again.

Monty turned to Michael. "Sergeant O'Flaherty, why don't you give us a report on your trip to Donegal?"

So Michael gave them an account of the O'Hearns' loss of the family enterprise. "Imagine the family being swindled by their own lawyer!" he exclaimed to Monty.

"They're not the first to have suffered that fate, Michael, unfortunately. I remember a case in Halifax where the lawyer stole his clients' money, and the clients lost their house as a result. The day the client and her family moved out, the day they had to drag their suitcases down the front steps of their home for the very last time, they met the lawyer coming up the stairs moving in!"

"No!"

"I couldn't make it up, Michael."

"Monty, sometimes I wonder how a fine fellow like yourself can get up and go in to work every day, the things you see in your job."

"Sometimes I ask myself the same question."

"So here we have the O'Hearns who were known far and yon for their boats. They were all brought up at the water's edge. You'd almost think their lungs could breathe salt water, the way Sarah tells it. Their life's work, their vocation, all that history. A hundred and fifty years. And they had it stolen from them. The father of the family must be spinning in his grave. Died of a broken heart, I shouldn't wonder."

"And the lawyer was never prosecuted," Monty remarked. "I find that strange."

"Niall Duffy told me the lawyer has . . . disappeared."

"I see."

"But I'm wondering . . ."

"Yes?"

"Well, the graffiti depicts somebody in Christy's as a killer and, well . . . I guess what I'm saying, Monty, is . . . no, the idea is absurd."

"What idea is that, Mike?"

He looked around the room, then mumbled, "Maybe the lawyer was . . . bumped off!"

"You think O'Hearn killed the lawyer."

"Well, stated as baldly as that, it does sound ridiculous. I'm not thinking it, exactly, just wondering. But if we could trace the lawyer somehow, see where he went, and then find out if he's still breathing —"

"I should be able to help you there, Mike, at least if he's still practising. What's his name?"

"Gilbert."

"Is that his first name or his last?"

"Hold on a second while I get my notebook." Michael went to his room and returned with his little black book.

"Sure you're never off duty, Sergeant O'Flaherty, with your notebook at hand," Brennan said to him.

"Were your notes made contemporaneously with the events described therein, Sergeant?" Monty asked, in the tones of a courtroom lawyer.

"Remind me, Kitty," Michael said, "not to invite my two little brothers along on my next trip abroad. They are nothing but a nuisance, and they do not understand the gravity of the adult matters the rest of us are called upon to deal with."

"Michael, *acushla*, all you can do is ignore them. Eventually, they'll tire of their little games and go away."

"I'm sure you're right, Sister. Carey Gilbert, of London," he announced, after flipping through the pages of the infamous notebook and finding his entries for County Donegal.

"All right. I'll see what I can find out on the phone from the law society over there."

"Oh, would you, Monty? That would be grand."

"Think nothing of it!"

Michael turned to Brennan and asked him, "Have you filled your uncle in on the results of our efforts so far?"

"I've told him we don't yet know who was the target of the graffiti. That's all he'll want to know."

Well, that was that. Brennan knew Finn better than Michael did. They would have to come up with more concrete results.

They took the time to refresh their tea, and the plate of biscuits made the rounds. The talk turned again to the old days, and Leo began regaling them with a tale about someone named Seamus Neary.

"Seamus served with me back in the day. Served time with me, I should say. This was when I was in Mountjoy Prison. More than one person in this room is familiar with the Joy. You probably know from Brennan here that his father, Declan, served time there in the 1940s; we both did."

Michael nodded his head, Kitty raised her eyebrows, Brennan remained impassive, and Monty smiled.

"Anyway, the reason Seamus was serving time was that they picked him up in Kilcullen. He was there to liberate some rifles he knew were in the possession of certain citizens of the town. Weapons that could be put to better use by those of us promoting the cause of a united Ireland. It was taking Seamus a while to build his collection. So Sunday rolled round, and Seamus did his duty as a good Catholic boy and went to Mass. The Garda Síochána were always on the lookout for a new face in the local church. Stranger in town attending Mass for the first time? Could be an IRA man, and should be watched after leaving the church steps. They got him all right. And he wasn't the first caught that way, by any means." Leo paused and took a sip of his tea. "The lads who are active in the North today, well, I wonder how much Mass-going there is amongst them. But back to poor Seamus. His commanding officer sent him a rocket. Didn't tell him to stay away from Mass, mind. But 'get your job done and be home by Sunday, and worship in your own parish. Carry out your patriotic duties on the other six days.'

"Now, Seamus was a comical card and he was in the Joy with us and he stretched a bit of boot leather over a frame and made himself some class of a bodhran to keep time with, and he gave us a song:

Come all ye young fellows who love our dear land.
We need Volunteers to lend us a hand.
The work doesn't pay like the post office grand
But on Sunday your posts don't have to be manned.

The Republic of Ireland won't be built in a day
And not on the Sabbath, our great leaders say,
For at Mass we'll be kneeling on every Sunday
And give only six days to the bold IRA.

"Well, the lads were nearly wetting themselves because what Seamus didn't know was that his commanding officer had just been

221

nicked and was there in the gloom, and Seamus couldn't see him, so he carried on with the song, and it got a bit intimate about the officer, and him there in the dark in the Joy hearing every word of it. Seamus went on about the man sitting at the archbishop's table on Sundays, and them helping themselves to lashings of drink, and it got a bit sacrilegious and the boys were urging him on —"

The ring of the telephone startled them, so immersed were they in the past. Leo was still smiling when he reached over and picked up the phone. "Hello." The smile vanished. "Where?" He listened for several seconds and never said another word into the phone. He replaced the receiver and rose from his seat. He turned his back to his guests, opened his desk drawer and took something out, shoved it into his pants pocket, then addressed his company. "I have to go."

"What is it, Leo?" Brennan asked.

Leo didn't answer, just shook his head.

"Let me go with you," Brennan said then.

Another shake of the head.

"Should we wait for you here?" asked Kitty.

"No."

It was Michael's turn. "Is there anything we can do?"

"No," he answered. Then he said, "Pray."

With that, Leo grabbed a set of keys from a hook by the door and left the room.

The others sat in uneasy silence till Monty spoke up. "It could be anything. But do you suppose it's the preacher?"

"I'd lay odds on it," Brennan replied. "The question is . . ."

"Is he alive?" Monty filled in. "I have a feeling the answer is no. The only thing Leo asked was 'where.' Nothing about his condition."

"I wonder how far poor Leo has to go tonight," Kitty said.

"Far enough so it's across the border, I'm hoping," Brennan muttered in reply.

Brennan

Brennan had no luck reaching Leo the following day, and there was no news, good or bad, on the radio or television about the Reverend Merle Odom. Or, Brennan reflected later, about young Clancy.

Michael O'Flaherty was scheduled to say the noontime Mass in

Irish at the Aughrim Street church, so Brennan offered to serve on the altar. When Mass was done, Brennan commended Michael on a job well done, and they decided to have lunch at Michael's place and then head over to Christy's.

The priests' housekeeper, Mrs. O'Grady, made them roast lamb sandwiches on crusty bread, and she had a chocolate cake on hand for dessert, so they thanked her profusely. When she was out of earshot, Michael brought up Leo's hasty departure of the previous night, and said he had not seen Leo since. What did Brennan make of that?

"That phone call and that hasty departure don't bode well for the situation on this island, I'm thinking."

"So you think it's the Belfast crisis."

"I do. I just hope I'm wrong, but somehow I doubt it."

"You think the minister's been killed."

"Yes, I do."

"Brennan, I can hardly bear to imagine what might happen as a result."

"That makes two of us."

And Michael didn't even know about the Clancy disappearance. If the bishop's nephew had been snatched as well, what hope would there be now for his safe return to Dublin? Of course he may already have suffered the same fate as Odom. If so, were they in for a spate of Catholic-Protestant kidnappings and killings, each one avenging the other? Would the events involve people in religious life, or their families? But this was nothing but grim speculation.

"Something occurs to me, Brennan, as bad as things might be." Michael leaned forward and spoke in earnest. "This could be a wake-up call. At last. If poor Odom has been killed, God rest his soul, surely there will be an international outcry. This man is an American, and you know how they are about their own. Foreigners dying, that's one thing. Too bad, pass the butter please. But an American? Well, that's another matter entirely. The U.S. might bring so much pressure to bear on the authorities in the North, and perhaps the authorities here in the South, to get this sorted . . . I mean if Northern Ireland comes under the scrutiny of the international community in light of this, perhaps something good could come out of it in the end. Not that I'm downplaying what has probably happened to that poor man. But something will break the cycle, something will lead to peace, now or in the not-too-distant future. I'm sure of it."

God love and protect Michael O'Flaherty, Brennan thought. O'Flaherty was a highly intelligent man, with decades of experience as a priest and confessor; in the confessional one hears people own up to the most despicable behaviour. Michael was a man who believed in the existence of evil; he had even assisted at an exorcism! But he had a blind spot, and that was Ireland, his ancestral home.

"Michael," Brennan cautioned him, "nothing good is going to come out of this. It could be even worse than you imagine." *Particularly if it's not just the Reverend Merle Odom, but Bishop Clancy's nephew as well.* "I would like to share your optimism, but I cannot. International attention hasn't deterred the factions in the North from violence in the past, and it's not going to now. It may have the opposite effect; increased publicity may make it harder for people to back down. They'll feel they have to make a point. Only evil will come of this."

Michael looked more and more dejected as Brennan went on. "I suppose you're right, Brennan, but I don't like to give up all hope. It goes against my nature."

"I understand that, Michael, but I don't want to see you setting yourself up for disillusionment. Do you remember the story Finn told us that night at his house, about the young bridegroom Davey? We were all wondering what happened when his bride got home and saw the trouble he'd run into trying to fix the house up for her. What happened was, he disappeared from the story. Took a bullet in the back. A revenge killing, for something he hadn't personally done. Do you remember what Leo said? 'Someone fundamental to your world was gone in an instant.' That's the way it was, and that's the way it is now, in certain parts of this island."

They were silent as they cleared the table, and headed out for the afternoon.

†

Order had been restored in Christy Burke's by the time Brennan and Michael arrived; all four regulars were in place. That man McCrum was seated at a table near the bar, but his mouth was not in gear, a relief to all present, no doubt.

Frank Fanning looked scrawny, and there was a yellowish cast to his skin. Seeing him now, Brennan could not conceive of him as the would-be bomber of the Apprentice Boys Memorial Hall. The whole plot was inconceivable, not to mention what would have happened in the wake of it. But whatever Fanning had done, or tried to do, Brennan's heart had to go out to him today. He looked like hell.

Michael O'Flaherty obviously thought so too. Michael had been rocked by the news of what Fanning had been plotting in Derry, but Brennan knew he had become fond of the regular crowd here in the bar, in each case seeing the man behind the flaws and weaknesses. Michael was looking at Fanning with sympathy.

"Frank!" Michael said. "We haven't seen you in a while, or at least I haven't. You've had us all concerned."

"Ah, well, I was in the hospital, Michael."

"Oh, is that so, Frank? And you didn't tell anyone? Are you all right now?"

"I'm fine. But the doctors don't agree with me. They're saying there's something wrong with my liver. They're saying I drink too much. Not the sort of thing I was going to call in and announce here at Christy's! Doctors these days, they're all about fourteen years old and they don't know a thing about the world or the people in it. Feck 'em!" He took a long sip of his pint, put down his glass, and sighed with pleasure.

"That will put the roses back in your cheeks, Frank!" Jimmy O'Hearn assured him. "It kept many a working man going in this city for years, so it did."

Brennan saw Tim Shanahan exchange a look with O'Flaherty. Whatever his own personal habits, Shanahan wouldn't be a man to buy into the legend that the jaundiced yellow of a liver-damaged drinker would be cured by more drink.

Michael and Brennan sat at a table and were joined by Shanahan, who said, "Good to have our foursome back again." His tone suggested that he was quite aware of how that foursome might appear to the rest of the population.

"Indeed," affirmed Michael, and Brennan agreed.

Turning to Brennan, Shanahan said, "I was wondering whether you were aware of the Russian choir that's performing this evening. I know you're a musician yourself."

"No, I hadn't heard. What's the word?"

"It's the St. Gennady Russian Orthodox Choir."

"I know them; they're brilliant! Didn't even know they were in town."

"They are. You can hear them at the Jesuits' church at seven o'clock." He stopped and seemed to give it some consideration before he spoke again. "I'm going. We could go together if, well . . ."

"Perfect, Tim. Leave from here at, what, half-six?"

"Good. You, Michael?"

"No, you fellows go ahead. The music, and the language, would be wasted on me!"

Shanahan nodded and smiled, then returned to his place in the universe of Christy's pub.

Michael opened his mouth to say something, but everyone's attention was caught by an exclamation from Mr. O'Hearn. "Well, here's a sight we rarely see! Father Killeen!" O'Hearn stood and raised his glass to Leo Killeen as the priest entered the pub and closed the door behind him.

"Jim," Killeen said and nodded.

"What happened, Father? Is everything all right over at the Glimmer Man?"

Michael looked at Brennan and asked, "Glimmer Man? I think I've seen that place."

"Most likely. It's a pub in Stoneybatter. Leo's local. He's not a big man for the drink, but when he has a drop, he has it there."

A little joke at Leo's expense. But O'Hearn's expression was one of concern, not jocularity.

"Have no fear, Jim," the priest assured him. "The Glimmer Man hasn't come to grief."

O'Hearn looked relieved.

Leo caught sight of Michael and Brennan and greeted them. Brennan started to pull out a chair for him, but Finn appeared at the bar and looked at Killeen.

"Good afternoon, Leo."

"Finn." Whatever passed between them did so without another spoken word, and they both disappeared behind the bar.

Frank Fanning said, "It's not often you see Leo Killeen in this place. I tell Finn it's just as well not to have two old soldiers in the same trench in case the enemy comes storming in! Grand fellow, Leo, very dedicated to his vocation. As he was to his previous vocation! He's not a big drinker but he's good company and a fine storyteller if he knows you're on the right side of God and politics. But he can be intense, can Leo. He's been known to leave more than one man trembling in his wake. In church, I mean, in the pulpit or in the confessional. He doesn't even raise his voice. Just has a sixth sense about what you've been up to. Well, he's seen it all, in both his incarnations."

If Leo came rarely, what brought him in today? What were Leo and Finn talking about behind the bar? Brennan didn't get a chance to ask. Leo emerged and walked out of the pub with nothing but a distracted little salute to those assembled.

A party of young women came in then, celebrating the return of one of them from Liverpool, and their high spirits and witty conversation kept everyone entertained. Motor Mouth McCrum's eyes glittered at the girls as he passed by on his way out of the pub. Later on, after the young ones straggled out, Michael finished his drink and prepared to leave. Brennan curbed the temptation to question Finn about the visit from Leo; if either of them wanted Brennan to know what was going on, he'd find out soon enough.

Seconds after Michael departed, the door opened again, and two men entered the pub. One was heavy-set with fair hair buzzed short on his round skull. The other was thinner and darker, with the same close-shaved head. In spite of the mild, sunny day, they both wore dark blue windbreakers and had their hands in their pockets. They peered around at the patrons, then looked at Finn. He didn't invite them to have a seat. He directed his dark glasses towards the two men, and they stared back. After a few seconds of this, they turned and left. It wasn't long before Brennan heard a car start up and drive away.

This time, he got up and approached the bar. "Who were those fellows, Finn?"

"Don't know."

"You don't know them, and yet you —"

"I didn't like the look of them."

"They got the message."

"They'd have been expecting it."

"Whoever they were."

It was the mirror image of the scene Michael O'Flaherty had

described, when O'Flaherty had walked into a pub somewhere on the other side of the border. The locals took one look at him and froze him out. How were people able to recognize each other this way? Natural enemies circling around each other in the wild.

Brennan shook his head and returned to his seat.

†

It wasn't long before Brennan and Tim Shanahan were on their way to the Jesuits' church in Upper Gardiner Street. As they walked along, Tim chatted knowledgeably about the sacred music of the Roman and the Orthodox churches, the use of Church Slavonic in the Orthodox liturgy, the timeless beauty of Gregorian chant, and other subjects dear to Brennan's heart.

Tim looked over at Brennan. "Michael may have told you I'm a priest, though currently out of service."

"He did, Tim, but he didn't have to. I'd have known you anywhere as my brother priest."

He gave Brennan a thoughtful look and said, "Thank you, Brennan." He was silent for a minute or so, then, "I'm not sure whether he told you about the troubles I've brought upon myself . . ."

"He told me you ran into some difficulty in Africa and he made a vague reference to drugs, but he did not go into any detail. And you have my word on that, Tim. Michael loves to chat." Shanahan smiled at that. "But he knows how to keep a confidence."

"I believe that of Michael. He's a lovely man and a very compassionate priest. Since he did not tell you — bless him — I will: I'm a heroin addict, Brennan."

Brennan turned to him, and Shanahan met his gaze, then averted his eyes.

"I'm truly sorry to hear that, Tim. If there is anything I can do to help you, now or in the future, I will. All you have to do is ask."

"Thank you, Brennan. You have no idea how much it means to hear you say that."

Brennan found himself hoping fervently that, whatever the pub graffiti was about, it wasn't about Father Timothy Shanahan.

They walked in companionable silence until they reached the Church of St. Francis Xavier. There was a sign posted outside, giving

228

notice of another event of interest to Brennan, an evening devoted to the spiritual exercises of St. Ignatius Loyola. Tomorrow, Friday. He would try to attend.

He and Shanahan went inside. It was one of Dublin's neoclassical churches, with four Corinthian columns and a pediment at the altar. But the music was about to transport them far from neoclassical Europe. The Russian choir took its place in the sanctuary, thirty men in black suits and white collarless shirts. From their first bass note, it was as if everything had ceased to exist except the sound.

The magnificent harmonies, the dark colours of the music, the drone of the bass, the deep, sonorous timbre of Russian music had a mesmerizing effect on Brennan, and stayed with him as he knelt to pray in front of the Blessed Sacrament after Tim Shanahan had said goodnight and the choir and spectators had left the church. As sometimes happened to him when he was deep in prayer, Brennan had an experience that was not of his making. On these rare occasions, he was presented with realities that could not be grasped with the intellect alone. He realized that he was in the presence of the Blessed Trinity, or it was present in him, in his soul. He felt that he could perceive God as three persons in one, inseparable, equal and of one essence. It was something he struggled manfully to explain to his seminary students, but the truth of it was beyond the power of the unaided human mind, including his own even after these experiences. As St. Augustine said, "If you've grasped it, it isn't God." But he knew with absolute certainty that whatever he was experiencing, it was real. The best he could do was quote St. Teresa of Avila: it was like feeling the presence of someone in the dark. At other times, he was not in darkness, but was flooded with an interior light so brilliant that he knew it was not of this world.

It was music that made him receptive to this state. No surprise there. Augustine again: music was meant to lift the spirit from the corporeal to the incorporeal realities; it prepared the soul for contemplation of eternal truth.

But there was a price to be paid, as there was for everything. Some of his experiences were not of the ecstatic kind. Some were bleak intimations of evil in the world; some filled him with dread. Usually, his forebodings came to naught: the feeling passed, and nothing happened. Occasionally, though — rarely — it seemed his premonitions were of events that would come to pass.

The peace concert in Belfast, the high B-flat, the *maledizione!* What had he seen in his mind's eye that night? He didn't know. But it disturbed him, particularly now, after being in an altered state of mind. Was something going to happen? Was the Apprentice Boys Memorial Hall going to be attacked after all, unleashing unimaginable retribution? Would some other monumental institution be the target? Or would it be something on a smaller scale? Was it the Merle Odom crisis, come to its inevitably bloody conclusion? Could it be a premonition of something personal, something unrelated to the sectarian mayhem in this country? Or was it nothing? Was it just Burke himself, with his deep sensitivity to music, reacting to Verdi's aria as the composer would have wished, with dread and foreboding? Who wouldn't be disturbed, at night in Belfast, surrounded by armed soldiers and police, knowing why such a show of force was required?

But Belfast wasn't the only location that had him spooked. He hadn't liked the look of that pair who came into his uncle's pub that afternoon and seemed to be casing the place. He would have written off the incident, would probably have forgotten it altogether, if Finn had not stared them out of the room from behind those obscuring lenses of his. Finn knew they were trouble. Well, it was time for Finn to speak up. Who were they, and what was going on?

It was just after ten o'clock. Brennan had been on his knees for more than an hour with no awareness of the passing of time. He got up, rubbed his knees, left the church, and headed for Christy Burke's. There was a soft mist, and the air smelled fresh. When he got to the pub, primed to confront his uncle, he found not Finn but Sean Nugent behind the bar. *Shite! Wouldn't you know?*

But wait, what was Sean saying to him?

"If you're looking for a pint, I'm your man. If you're looking for your family, he's down below."

"What would he be doing down there at this time of night?"

"Em, he didn't say, but I expect we'll be seeing him shortly. What can I get you tonight, Brennan?"

Brennan started to speak, then saw the barman's gaze move to the door of the cellar; Nugent gave somebody a nearly imperceptible nod. Brennan turned and saw a big man with thick dark hair and black-framed glasses; he was looking at Nugent as he closed the cellar door.

The man was wearing a long, bulky raincoat, which struck Brennan as being a little too heavy for the mild misty evening. The fellow's eyes surveyed the assembled drinkers before he left the pub.

Sean returned to his duties. "A pint for you, Brennan, or a Jameson?"

"I'll have a pint, if you'd be so kind, Sean. Make that two, would you?"

"Certainly."

He poured two pints and handed them to Brennan. Brennan paid for them, then said, "I think I'll go down and pay a social call on my favourite uncle."

"Oh, Finn won't be long, I'm sure, so maybe you should just —"

"No worries. He'll be pleased that I made the effort."

Something in Sean's expression suggested otherwise, but Brennan was not deterred. Grasping the two pints in his left hand, he went to the cellar door, opened it quietly, walked through, and closed it behind him. He started down the stairs. There was a faint light coming from the nether regions of the building, but the steps and most of the cellar were in shadow. He descended in silence. When he got to the bottom he heard a couple of clicks, then a metallic clanking sound. The sounds came from the tunnel.

He walked to the open hole in the floor, tightened his grip on the two pint glasses in his left hand, grabbed the top of the ladder with his right, and climbed down. He stood in the tunnel and peered down its length. There, with a kerosene lantern flickering overhead, was Finn, shoving a large brick into the face of the wall. He sensed Brennan's presence and whipped around.

"Jaysus! Brennan! Are you fucking daft?"

"Evening, Finn. What's daft about dropping in to say hello to my elders? Save you from climbing those steep stairs. I'm just being thoughtful."

"You are in your bollocks."

"What are you up to? Restocking the shelves? Need any help?"

"Feck off and don't be pestering me here. Take yourself upstairs. I'll be right behind you."

"Too crowded up there, Finn; the place is filled with nosy parkers. You know what they're like. Better to talk down here in private. I've brought you a drink."

"I see that. Talk about what? You've discovered who was the target of the slurs painted on my wall? You've nicked the fellow who killed the vandal? Could that be it?"

"No. We shall persist with our inquiries."

"Well, then?"

"I've learned about various personal difficulties in the lives of your regulars, but I'm assuming you have no interest in any of that unless it points to a solution to the problem."

"Your assumption is correct. So that's all I had to hear from you. Up you go."

"Wait a second now. I intend to settle in for an intimate little chat. And you've got such a cozy atmosphere down here with the gaslight."

He placed the two pints carefully on the floor and climbed the ladder up to the cellar again. He grabbed two bar stools and managed to lower them one by one into the tunnel. "Have a seat, man dear."

"Brennan, you're annoying me already, and I haven't even heard yet what it is that you want to talk about and I don't."

But he sat on one of the stools, and Brennan sat across from him; their knees were touching. They picked up their pints.

Brennan raised his glass. *"Sláinte mhath!"*

Finn kept his glass in his hand, resting on his right knee, and said nothing.

"Something's going on, Finn. What is it?"

"I don't know what you're talking about."

"Yes, you do. What's happening?"

"Brennan, if you think there is something happening and I'm sitting here saying there isn't, that means one of two things: there's nothing happening, or there's nothing happening that I can talk about. Either way, you don't hear anything. That's no reflection on you."

"How could it not be? Are you thinking I'd walk out of here and start rabbiting on about it to everyone I encounter in the street?"

"Of course not. You don't even rabbit on about yourself. No one's saying you're a talker. Change the subject."

"Who are the two goons who came in here this afternoon?"

"Goons?"

"You know who I mean. The two enforcers with the military hairdos."

"You already asked me that."

"I didn't get an answer."

"You got an answer. I said I don't know them, and I don't."

"But you know what they represent, I'm thinking."

"And what would that be, do you suppose?"

"Paramilitary types from the North, is the smell I get off of them. Would your own mind be running along those lines, by any chance?"

"If that's what they are, they won't find anything to interest them here."

"What do you think they are hoping to find?"

His uncle merely shook his head.

"Who, then? Who are they looking for?"

"If they're looking in my pub, they're looking in the wrong place."

"But they came in here. That would suggest they expected to find someone here."

"Well, it wasn't me, was it? Or my patrons. Those two went out the door sixty seconds after they came in. Eyed the clientele and left."

"After you stared them down."

"Brennan, I cannot help you."

"I'm trying to help *you*, Finn."

"I'll survive. Don't think I don't appreciate your concern; I do."

"I think it's high time we talked about the subject we avoid every time I visit Dublin."

"What subject would that be? Whatever it is, we've been wise to avoid it."

"How involved are you still in Republican affairs?"

"Are you asking me whether I've washed my hands of the struggle to unite this country?"

"Has that struggle any realistic hope of success?"

"Your grandfather Christy and those who fought with him in the Tan War had no realistic hope of success. But they succeeded. Partly. I don't know whether I'll live long enough to see the job finished — the six counties included in the Republic — but I know it will happen some day. It will."

"I have no such confidence."

"So, what's the solution? Forget all our boys who are lying in their graves because they fought to the death for their country, the martyrs from '16 who went before the firing squad, the fellows who were hanged during the Tan War? We tell them, 'Sorry, lads, you died for nothing.' We just give up and leave it undone? The way the Staters did in 1921?"

"The Free Staters got as much as they were going to get from the English at the time."

"Like fuck they did! They should have kept fighting till they had it all."

"Have you forgotten the alternative to acceptance of the treaty? England threatened us with 'immediate and terrible war.' The pro-treaty side spared us that. As a result, they had to endure accusations of treason and betrayal from the men they had fought beside, in the IRA, up until the summer of 1921. And what did the people of Ireland get out of all this? Civil war, friend against friend, brother against brother. As de Valera put it, the Volunteers would have to 'wade through Irish blood' to achieve their goal. Well, there's still Irish blood on the ground, but the goal has not been achieved."

Finn remained impassive but Brennan persevered: "Did the Free Staters do regrettable things during the Civil War? Yes, they did. But look what happened when the anti-treaty side got into power. They cracked down on their former comrades in the IRA, just as the Free State government had done, and started throwing them in prison. That's when Leo Killeen was sent to Mountjoy, and my oul fellow too. Lucky for us all they weren't executed! Others weren't so fortunate."

"Declan was sent there for armed robbery, not because he was IRA."

In spite of himself, Brennan had to laugh. "Slandering your own brother to make a point!"

"I'm just putting the facts on the table here."

"Well, you're right about Dec, I'll give you that. He was in for armed robbery, but he'd been raising money for the cause, not for himself."

Brennan stopped to take a few long sips of his pint, then said, "And after all that, it wasn't the Republican side but a Free State politician, John Costello, who declared the country a republic. Bit of irony there."

"A republic minus the six counties."

"We were never going to have them. That's *realpolitik*." Brennan rose, drained his pint and laid a hand on his uncle's arm, and made ready to leave the old rebel's tunnel. He spoke in a softer tone of voice. "Believe me, Finn, I do understand the loyalty to the Republican idea that the IRA has fought for. When I crossed the border and was held up by those Tan . . . those British soldiers, I wanted to get out of the car and give them a bollocking they wouldn't forget. But I didn't. And I wouldn't. I sympathize with your ideals. But not at the cost of any more lives."

Chapter 12

Brennan

Finn wasn't talking, but Brennan knew something was up. And he intended to find out what it was. When he met Leo Killeen last year in New York, Leo had spoken to him freely about episodes in the past. Leo's past and that of Declan Burke. And he had done so because Brennan was Declan's son. Never mind that Declan had never unburdened himself of any of that history to Brennan. Leo obviously felt he could confide in the first-born son of his old comrade-in-arms. Brennan intended to trade on that now. It was late, half-eleven. Would Leo still be up? If not, Brennan would catch him tomorrow. Ah, good. When he arrived at the priests' house in Stoneybatter, Leo's light was on. Better still, Michael O'Flaherty's was not. Brennan knocked at the door and hoped Leo would hear it. No response. He tried again. A few seconds later, he heard footsteps coming down the stairs.

Then Leo's voice on the other side of the door. "Who's there?"

"Leo, it's Brennan Burke."

The door opened a crack, and Killeen peered out. "Are you by yourself?" he asked.

"I am. What's wrong?" Leo didn't reply. "Em, may I come in?"

"Right. Of course, of course. Come up."

Brennan didn't speak again until they were in Leo's room with the door closed behind them. "After you left the pub today, two fellows came in. Finn stared them down, and they took off."

"What did they look like?"

Brennan described them, and Leo seemed to file the information in his mind.

"What's going on, Leo? You made a hasty exit from here the other night without a word of explanation. All you said to us was 'pray.' Next time we see you, you and Finn are in conference behind the bar, and you're gone again. And two individuals who look like paramilitary types appear in your wake. What the hell is going on?"

Leo looked into Brennan's eyes but still did not speak. Then something in his expression changed; he seemed to have made a decision. He gestured to Brennan to have a seat, then he walked over to the television set, picked up a videotape, and quietly inserted it into the VCR.

"What is it, Leo?"

"I haven't seen it yet myself. But I have a fairly good idea. Whatever it turns out to be, when you walk out of here, never, ever let on you saw it. Do we understand each other?"

"Do you even have to ask?"

"All right then."

Leo picked up the remote control and pressed a button, then perched on the edge of a chair near the machine and stared at it.

The screen was blue, then snowy. Suddenly it showed a man sitting on a straight chair, his arms bound behind his back. Sweat was visible under the arms of his shirt. He appeared to be in his sixties, with a full head of straight hair and large, very white teeth. They looked false. The man was to all appearances an American. He had a beard, and his hair had lost the blow-dried, styled look it had in the official pictures. He looked more gaunt than he had in the news photos, but there was no doubt about his identity: the Reverend Merle Odom, from South Carolina, U.S.A.

The setting was an old basement with a stone foundation; grass and earth could be seen in the cracks between the stones. There was a dirty window high in the wall. What looked like a horse bridle hung on a spike protruding from one of the cracks. The room was brightly illuminated, incongruously, by fluorescent light. There was music being played in the background, an accordion and a snare drum keeping a peppy beat; Brennan made out the words "fight" and "north," the names "McKelvey" and "O'Neill."

The captive was not wearing a blindfold. The reason for this became clear a moment later, when a man entered the room from stage left. The man, who looked skinny in his baggy T-shirt, was wearing a black balaclava over his head.

He started in on a conversation that had obviously begun earlier. His voice was that of a fairly young man. "I don't understand why you say such nasty things about the Holy Father. The Pope."

Leo looked over at Brennan. "There's a problem for us, right there."

Brennan nodded. The young lad's accent was Dublin, not Northern Ireland. An international incident.

They tuned back in and heard Odom deny he had ever maligned the Holy Father.

"But I saw you up there with the Reverend Ian Paisley," the Irishman said. "That same Paisley who disrupted the Pope's talk at a grand meeting somewhere on the continent. The European Parliament, I think it was. I watched it on TV. Pope John Paul was about to speak, and Paisley started shouting and held up a sign saying the Pope was the Antichrist! *Our* man, all in white, cool as a cucumber with a little smile on his face, was just standing there waiting for the ructions to die down. Standing there as wise and as patient as God while *your* man made a horse's arse of himself."

"Well, I didn't hear about that particular incident." Odom had a strong southern drawl.

"My question is: what have you and Paisley got against the Pope?"

"Well, of course I have nothing personal against the man himself. It's what he represents, the authority he claims to have."

"Sure somebody has to have authority. Otherwise who knows what's right and what's wrong, what's true and what's false? And there's thousands of churches and they all say different things."

"*Sola scriptura*, my friend!"

"What?"

"The Bible is our sole authority."

"But where does it say that in the Bible?"

"Say what, my friend?"

"Say that the Bible is the only authority, like."

"I think you're under a misunderstanding, brother."

"Well, now, I just mean it can't be the only authority, can it? You say the Catholic Church is wrong and that nobody should follow its teachings, but you're following them yourself. Because it was the Catholic Church way back in time that got together and sussed out which books belong in the Bible and which books don't. If you don't believe that, then you might think some of the books that are in the Bible now aren't really the word of God. And that some other book is out there, that is the word of God and you're missing it. So you must think the church was right about that."

The Doctor of Theology in the dimly lit room in Dublin absorbed the theology lesson, as did the American preacher.

Odom was silent for awhile, then said, "But you don't believe all the fighting and bombing and killing that's going on over here is just about religion, do you? Seems to me there's a lot of politics and history involved that goes beyond people's choice of how they serve their Lord and Saviour."

"When Catholics are oppressed and the Protestants fight hammer and tongs to keep the country divided, then I have to say we're fighting to protect our religion as well as to unite the country under the flag of the Republic! Tea?"

"Pardon me?"

"Would you like tea now?"

"Uh, could I have a cup of coffee?"

"Sure, you can have coffee with your tea."

"But I don't want tea. I want coffee."

"And have it you will. When I come back with your tea."

The young man got up and left. The butt of a handgun protruded from his pocket. The music could be heard again, something about the "lads" and "Crumlin Jail." The American, strapped to the chair, stared straight ahead. Leo pressed fast-forward until the young fellow returned to the scene, bearing a tray of sandwiches and biscuits. Odom's tea. With a steaming mug of coffee.

"Thank you, much obliged!" Odom said.

"You wouldn't think of tryin' anything funny when I untie your hands, so you can eat . . ."

"No, I won't do anything, I swear! I just want to chow down!"

The young fellow bent over the preacher and untied the straps, then retied them around his chest, so he was still imprisoned in the chair. Odom ate as if he hadn't had a meal in days. Perhaps he hadn't.

"Thank you. This really hits the spot."

"You're welcome. You see, Mr. Odom, we don't want to cause you any hardship. Not like the hardship being suffered today and every day by a bunch of fellows who shouldn't be in prison. Fellows who aren't criminals at all, but are soldiers fighting for their country.

"So here's the thing. All we're asking you to do is make a little statement on the tape here, saying you're being well treated and you've got faith you're going to be released, just as soon as the British occupation forces do the right thing and release a list of political prisoners that we will give you to read."

The minister looked at him warily. "But what kind of things did these men do, that got them into prison?"

"They were patriots, fighting a just war."

"But what would happen to, uh, the Protestant population in Northern Ireland if the Catholics take charge of the whole country?"

"Nothing's going to happen to them. They'll have all the civil rights they denied our people all those years. So now it's time for you to play your part in history."

Odom's hand shook as he put it up to brush back his hair. Brennan Burke was overwhelmed with compassion for the man. He looked over at Leo Killeen. Leo's face was rigid with tension.

"What ha —" the American began, then cleared his throat and started again. "What happens to me if they don't agree to release the prisoners? My wife, she's not well. Please, let me go and I'll speak publicly on behalf of any of those prisoners who . . ."

"It doesn't work that way, Mr. Odom. We think you'll be much more convincing speaking from that chair. When your taped statement is played in America, when they see you strapped to a chair looking a little scared and a little desperate, they'll raise a great hue and cry to have you released. The president will give the word, behind the scenes maybe, and . . ."

"My government won't do that. They'll say they don't negotiate with, uh . . ."

"Terrorists, Mr. Odom?"

"Well, I just mean that's what they'll say. That's not my word."

"Your government makes deals with terrorists every day."

"It does no such thing! America stands for freedom around the world. Sometimes in order to give people freedom, America has to —"

"Negotiate with terrorists. It always has done. In your case, your congregation will put the pressure on. They won't care about a few Irish prisoners of war. Let 'em go, they'll say, and send the Reverend Mr. Odom back to us unharmed!"

"How do I know that if I do what you say, you'll let me go?"

"You'll just have to trust us on that. Now you've had enough for tonight. I've got a blanket and pillow for you here. I'll be back tomorrow morning with your lines all written out for you and —"

A loud bang cut short the Irishman's speech. His head swivelled to the left. He took a step back and fumbled for the gun in his pocket.

"Don't even think about it. Stand back against the wall. Now." (*"Nye."*) The voice was low and calm, the northern accent harsh. Merle Odom stared with fear and alarm at this new element in the room.

There was another loud noise. It sounded as if the new arrival had kicked closed the door he had just kicked open. He came into view, the right side of his face to the camera. A man in early middle age, with greying fair hair and light-coloured eyes, he looked as cool and collected as if he had happened upon a tea party. In spite of the warm weather, he wore a bulky jacket.

"Sit *dyne*, Clancy."

Clancy! The fellow reported missing in Dublin, nephew of the Bishop of Meath. He hadn't been kidnapped; he was the kidnapper. God help the bishop if this gets out; God help the boy's family.

"Jesus," Clancy pleaded on the tape, "don't be giving him our names! But never mind: he won't tell. He's a good fellow —"

"Sit down, I said. You're not givin' the orders here. Your name isn't all he knows, is it, Clancy?"

Odom leaned forward in his restraints, perspiration forming on his forehead and temples. "I don't know anything, honest to God I don't!"

"Aye, you *dew*. Unfortunately." The man turned to the prisoner as he spoke, and reached inside his jacket.

Odom's eyes bulged in terror; he struggled frantically in his seat. "I have nothing to do with what's going on here!"

"Aye, you do. Now. I'm sorry."

"I'm just a tourist. I hardly even know Ian Paisley!"

"Fuck Paisley." The man drew a gun from his jacket and held it down by his side.

Odom cried out, "No! You can't do this! I'm an American —"

The shot made Brennan jump. "Oh God!"

When he looked at the screen again, Odom was slumped to the side, a bullet hole between his eyes. A sound of sobbing came from the corner of the room.

"Had to be done, Clancy. Thanks entirely to you, you little Free State bollocks, and your band of fellow gobshites. What the fuck were you thinking, coming up here and snatching the man off the street, setting in motion all this turmoil?"

"We didn't plan it! I went up to Belfast on the train to see a couple of the lads from Dublin, who'd gone up there to work. Me and, well you know the fellow I mean — he had to be up early in the morning because he works in a restaurant, and he'd just got himself a car — so we were out and about early, driving past the Europa, and there he was. Odom. We recognized him from the news picture with Paisley. The opportunity was there for us, too good to pass up! Lift the man from the street and trade him for Donovan and Buckley and Whalen. Get them out of prison."

"Didn't you think of the repercussions of something like this, you bollocks?"

"I didn't expect —"

"You didn't think ahead. And then, when you did some thinking, you came up with a bad idea. You used this house without permission. You brought Odom down into this room, past all the items we have stockpiled right there." He pointed to the door. "Do you think, if we'd let the man go, he would have kept his gob shut about all that firepower that's going to be used against his fellow Protestants in Belfast? I had to kill him. You left me with no choice. I should have made you do it. Now I'm thinking I should give you the same treatment."

"No, Des, don't do it! I won't say a word. For the rest of my life, I won't, I swear it!"

"You're fuckin' right, you won't. Because I've got other plans for you, for the rest of your life."

"Anything! Anything, Des!"

"Good. Get up."

Clancy came into view, no longer wearing the balaclava. His red hair stuck out all over his head. His green eyes were locked on Des.

"Here's the way it is, Clancy. Are you listening to me?"

"Yes!"

"As of today . . . no, as of the eighth day of July, when all this started, you and your fellow amateurs are members of a brand new, hitherto-unknown-to-the-authorities splinter organization. You should be enjoying this, Clancy, you're the latest split in the movement! You're going to call yourselves the 'Republican Irish Volunteer Force.' Like it?"

"Sure. Sure I do, Des."

"Why'd you break away from the mainstream Republican movement, Clancy?"

"Uh, because we, uh, it . . ."

"Because you don't agree with the policies of the Provisional Irish Republican Army, correct?"

"If you say so, Des."

"Because the Provos aren't getting the job done."

"Well, now, I wouldn't want to —"

"Yes, you would. You're out of patience with us. We're a bunch of poofs, and we just sit around pulling ourselves, and you want action and you want it now. And that's why you took matters into your own hands. What are the Provos, Clancy?"

"Um, well, we're . . . I mean they . . ."

"What'd I tell you?"

"But . . . won't I get killed for saying the 'RA are poofs? Or, you know, I'll get punished?"

"Chance you have to take, Clancy. It's a risky business you've embarked on. A great big fuck-up. Now I'll ask you again: what are the Provos?"

"The Provos . . . are a bunch of poofs."

"And what do we do?"

Brennan, watching this, felt he was back in school, with the priest grilling him for answers, a strap nearby if needed. This man had been to the same school. All the Irish had.

"What do we do?" he repeated, when Clancy fumbled his lines.

"Sit around pulling ourselves. Yourselves."

"And what do you want?"

"We want action and we want it now."

"Right. That's your story, and God and Mary help you if you ever forget it. Now assist me in disposing of this poor sad bastard here."

"Oh, my God, Desmond," Clancy sobbed. "I can't bear to touch him. None of this was his fault."

"That's right. You'll think twice next time. Get his legs. Now!"

Leo switched off the machine and looked at Brennan. Neither man spoke. They had just witnessed the murder of the first victim of this boneheaded kidnapping plan, but likely not the last. How many others were now fated to suffer in the wake of this killing? It didn't take long to find out.

Leo jabbed another button on the remote, and the television screen lit up with an RTÉ news bulletin from Newry, a well-known trouble spot just north of the border. The body of the Reverend Merle Odom had been fished out of Carlingford Lough that morning. Because of the location, near the border, there was much discussion on the news as to where Odom had been killed, in the North or in the Irish Republic. He had been shot in the head. The scene switched to the Reverend Ian Paisley addressing a crowd on what appeared to be the front steps of a church. "The Reverend Merle Odom was a man of God, a man of family, a man of courage. I am proud to have considered him a friend. His death is an atrocity. I call upon the authorities to hunt down his killers and bring them to swift justice. How many more murders and bombings will it take before the IRA terrorists are shut down for good?"

The next to comment was the Cardinal Archbishop of Armagh, who offered condolences to Mr. Odom's family and his congregation on behalf of the Roman Catholic Church in Ireland. He expressed confidence that the police would solve the matter and bring the perpetrators before the courts. The bishop was followed by a spokesman for Sinn Féin, which added its voice to the condemnations of the shooting.

There were a few more commentators, then the program moved on to the next bit of unwelcome news. "Rioting broke out in Belfast and other centres today in reaction to the news of the American evangelist's death. A street battle erupted in front of a hastily painted mural in the Shankill Road. Seven people were taken to hospital."

The camera zoomed in on a gable wall on which was painted the picture of a priest in a Roman collar, lifting the chalice during the Eucharist. Except that, when the camera got closer, Brennan could see that the chalice was in fact a pint of Guinness.

"Those fuckers!" Brennan exclaimed. Then it got worse. The cross-hairs of a rifle were shown superimposed on the white square at the priest's throat. *How is this ever going to end?*

The coverage turned to the rioters, some in black balaclavas, some with their faces bare, contorted in rage. Other factions pushed back. One man, in a group held behind a barricade, jabbed his finger in the direction of the mural. "That's fookin' sacrilege, that is!"

The scene switched to another man, with a scarf over the lower half of his face, and an Ulster Freedom Fighters insignia on his jacket, waving a submachine gun around. "This," he shouted, "this is the only language the Fenians understand!"

Back at the news desk, the presenter started to introduce a new item about a by-election in Cork, then said, "Oh! We have just received word of a new development in the Merle Odom story. A group calling itself the Republican Irish Volunteer Force has claimed responsibility for the killing of the American preacher. We have Matt Dempsey on the line. Matt? What can you tell us about this organization?"

"Not much, I'm afraid, Aideen. No one I spoke to had ever heard of the RIVF until this communiqué was issued."

"What does it say, Matt?"

"It says, 'The Reverend Merle Odom was killed because he sup-ported the oppressors of the Catholics of the Six Counties.' The RIVF says it intends to take the struggle for a united Ireland to a new level unless progress is made in the release of political prisoners and the reduction of British troops in the North of Ireland. A Provisional IRA source, who refused to give his name, said that he had never heard of this group, and that the IRA condemned the killing of Odom in the strongest terms."

"Thank you, Matt. And now . . ."

Brennan was overcome with a feeling of dread. He seized upon the notion that his feeling at the peace concert was a premonition of the American's death. It probably was no such thing but if he could think of it like that, he could tell himself that the premonition had already come true, the event had occurred, and there was nothing else to the omen. But never mind that. You didn't have to be a mystic to experience a feeling of dread with all this going on.

He and Leo Killeen prayed together for the soul of Merle Odom, for his family, for Bishop Clancy and his nephew, and for the people of Ireland, then Brennan said a sombre goodnight to Leo and returned to his place in the Liberties.

The dark night seemed endless. Brennan had no sleep. He tried the repetition of prayer. Didn't work. He tried drink. No effect. There was no escape from the images he had seen on the television screen and the images that played across the screen of his own mind: hatred distorting the faces of his countrymen, bullets tearing through their flesh.

Chapter 13

Brennan

There was no rest for him the following day. He had promised to visit some inmates in the Joy and assist them with various difficulties, and he was glad he did, but it took up much of the day and drained the small reserve of energy he had left. There was the evening program he didn't want to miss at the Jesuits' church in Gardiner Street, the presentation on the spiritual exercises of St. Ignatius. It was fascinating, and he did his best to stay sharp and take in what he was hearing, but when some of his fellow priests invited him to a get-together afterwards at a residence near the church, he should have said no. He did say no to the offer of a drink but he stayed on and socialized until nearly two in the morning. One of the fellows called a taxi for him but he waited outside, and it never showed up. He decided he might as well walk till he spied another one. All he could think of was getting to his room. As soon as he got in the door, he would dive onto his bed and pass out. He had not had a moment of sleep the night before. His collar was hot around his neck but he was too lazy to reach up and take it off. His steps were heavy and his eyelids half-closed as he plodded through Summerhill in the blackness. He always had music running in his head; this time it was Mozart's dark, brooding "Kyrie in D Minor."

There were very few people out at this time of night, at least along this route: the occasional drunk delivering himself of a song or a soliloquy, or lurching about in the street, a few drugged-out young lads, or a couple having a snog in a doorway. When he got to the *"Christe Eleison"* in the Mozart, he heard the sound of a scuffle, then a shout and a string of curses. A cry of pain, and more cursing. He peered ahead in the dimness and saw two bodies writhing on the pavement. One staggered to his feet, pulled the other upright, and drove his fist into the fellow's face. Then he put his hands around the man's throat.

"Hey!" Brennan shouted, and ran towards them. "Back off, you!"

He grabbed the aggressor and pulled him backwards. The fellow whirled on Brennan and took a swing, catching him on the left side of his face. The force sent him reeling back against the brick wall of a building. He launched himself off the wall towards his attacker, who had thrown himself down on the victim again. Brennan tackled the fellow, and they ended up wrestling on the ground. The victim of the beating managed to roll over, get up, and scuttle away. Brennan held his attacker down and got a good look at his face. A young lad of about fifteen.

"Settle yourself down there," he told him.

The boy said, "Fuck off, or I'll kick your head in. I don't care what kind of collar you've got on; I'll send you to hell."

"That's not going to happen, so put it out of your mind. Get yourself under control, so I can let you up."

"It's not up to you to let me do anything."

"Under the circumstances, it is."

The young fellow's breathing slowed a bit, and Brennan thought it might be safe to ease up. He started to let go, the kid made a move, and Brennan gripped him again.

"What was that all about? You and that man."

"Nothing to do with you, whoever the fuck you are. I don't care if you're the Pope himself; it's none of your business."

"I make it my business when I see somebody being assaulted."

"The louser deserved it."

"Why?"

"He was trying to take my spot."

"What spot is that?"

"You can't see it, can you?"

Without taking his eyes off his captive, Brennan replied, "I didn't notice anything."

"Right. That's what's good about it. Hard to see. Let me up."

Brennan released his hold on him, ready to apply it again if need be. But the boy just sat up, rubbing his arms where Brennan had held them in an iron grip. Brennan took him by the left arm, gently this time, guided him to the curb, and sat him down. Brennan sat beside him.

"Tell me about your spot."

"Number one, it's hard to see. Number two, it's warm in there at night because there's a heat vent. And number three, it has . . ."

"It has what?"

"Free delivery."

"Of?"

"Dregs from old bottles. Food from the restaurant. They throw out perfectly good food at closing time. Goes into those bins."

Scavenging for scraps of rubbish.

"So this is where I sleep, and nobody takes it from me."

Brennan took a quick glance down the alley where the boy was looking. There was a grimy-looking chip shop and a bar that Brennan would not have entered even if it was selling the last glass of Jameson whiskey on the planet.

He studied the lad. Not a hard-looking fellow at all. A soft face, really, with golden hair and big green eyes. But he was filthy.

"How long have you had this place?"

"Weeks. I got it off an oul nutter that croaked. They took him away, and I moved in."

"Do you have a family here in Dublin?"

"Sure, right over there. See them propped up behind the bins? Oh, no, guess not. Guess I don't have any then."

"What happened?"

"My oul man fucked off, that's what happened. Found a new mot and he's living with her and not with us. Hope she goes on the batter some night and puts the eyes out of him. My ma couldn't afford to keep us all in the place we had, so they put her in a council flat where there's no room for me and the four sisters I've got. Ma took over the big room for her and the new boyfriend, so my sisters have the other room and the sitting room, and even if they didn't I couldn't be in the same house with that fucker she calls my stepfather. Because I'd fucking kill him some night, just like he tries to kill me every time he beats the shite out of me. But what am I telling you this for? You don't give a fuck."

"I do. What's your name?"

"Right. So you can grass on me to the peelers."

"I'm not going to report you. My name's Brennan. Yours is?"

He said it grudgingly, but he said it. "Aidan."

"All right, Aidan. Let's find you something good to eat, and then get you a shower and a bed for the night. Then we'll see what we can line up for you in the morning. Later this morning, I should say."

"And lose my fucking spot that I just had to fight for?"

"What I have in mind is something a little more sheltered than your regular space. The council workers . . ."

"Don't be telling me about social workers. They keep trying to get me back with my oul one in the flat, and I go back and two days later, Ma and the stepfather are roaring at me again that I'm no fucking good, and I have to leave. I'm better off on my own."

How bad must it be, Brennan wondered, that sleeping on the streets of Dublin is better?

"Well, I'm not going to leave you here in the street."

"Yeah. You are. Because it's nothing to you what I do."

"On the contrary, it matters to me a great deal what you do."

"Yeah, right. You're a good Samaritan walking the streets of Dublin City at three o'clock in the morning. I'd say you're out here because you got ossified, and they locked you out of the church house. Right? Now you've got to sleep rough too!"

"Could be." He smiled at Aidan, and Aidan looked as if he was almost ready to smile back, but he beat down the temptation and gave Brennan a sneer instead. Brennan ignored it.

"Let's go find something to eat."

"After you. You stick your head in first." He pointed to the bins.

"How about a change of diet?"

"Fuck off and leave me alone."

"I'm going to go and find us something to gnaw on."

"Us?"

"Yeah. I'm a little peckish myself."

"Go then. There's your exit line. I won't hold my breath waiting for you to come back with the food."

"You're thinking I won't?"

"Do I look like a fuckin' eejit?"

"No, you don't."

"Right. So, sayonara. I won't set the table waiting for the feast to be delivered."

"O ye of little faith. Here, take this. I need it, so I'll have no choice but to come back."

"Your wallet? Are you daft?"

"That remains to be seen. Here. I'll take out enough cash to buy us dinner, and you hold on to this till I get back. Get yourself out of sight there, so you don't get into any more trouble. See you in a bit."

Brennan took out twenty-five punts, leaving two fivers in the wallet. He handed the wallet to Aidan, then pushed himself up off the curb, and walked away without looking back. Was he in fact daft enough to believe the street kid would wait for him and return the wallet when he came back with the food? No. Chances of this fellow being anywhere in sight when Brennan returned were slim to none. But so be it. It was all he had to offer Aidan as a show of faith in him. Brennan wasn't naïve enough to really have faith in him, but he suspected nobody had ever shown him any trust in living memory. Brennan would come back as promised and if, as expected, Aidan and the wallet were long gone, well, he'd call and cancel his credit card in the morning and hope he was right in thinking there was a limit on how much a card holder had to pay in the case of a stolen card. Whatever the case, he'd get it sorted. His driving licence could be replaced, and he could get by without the two five-pound notes he had left in the wallet. Now, where in the hell was he going to find a restaurant or a take-out place open at this time of night? He approached a street light and peered at his watch. Three-fifteen, on his second night without sleep. The image of his bed rose before him like a mirage. His eyes felt as if they had sand in them; he closed them for a moment and wondered what would happen if he fell asleep standing up. But he pushed himself; he had a job to do.

He walked for a few minutes and spotted a pizza joint with a take-away service. It appeared to be closed but, when Brennan put his hand against the window and peered inside, he saw the owner slumped over a table with a bunch of receipts. Brennan rapped on the window, and got a scowl and a gesture from the owner. The message was unmistakable. Get lost! But Brennan waved his money, and persuaded the man — bribed him — to open up and make a pizza with everything on it. Brennan leaned against the building trying to stay awake for the twenty minutes it took to prepare and cook the pizza. He bought two bottles of ginger ale to go with it. There were also cartons of chocolate milk, and he got one of those as well. He grabbed a fistful of napkins, and handed over all the cash he had, twenty-five Irish pounds. Juggling his purchases, he walked back to the spot by the rubbish bins where Aidan made his home.

No sign of him. Well, no surprise there. Why wouldn't he abscond with the wallet and credit card? Whether the boy would ever look back, and recall that a complete stranger had showed some faith in him, Brennan would never know. But for now, he didn't feel like walking away. He didn't have the strength. What he did have was a pizza that smelled delicious. And Brennan realized he was famished. He sat down, with the box on his lap, and placed the drinks on the pavement beside him. He felt his eyelids getting heavy. He could no longer resist. He closed his eyes and sank into sleep.

"Could you not watch with me one hour?"

Brennan heard the words of scripture, and knew he should poke himself awake for the homily. His da would smack him in the side of the head if he fell asleep during Mass again. He tried to lift his head up from the pew in front of him. He turned his head. Hard surface; it scratched his face. He opened one eye and saw what looked like a gob of spit not ten inches from his face. He reared back. And heard laughter above him. Where was he? He blinked at the shadows around him. Jesus the Son of God and Mary the Immaculate! He was lying face down in the street. It was filthy. He bolted upright, and started wiping his hands down the sides of his suit.

The laughter continued. He looked to its source, and saw a young fellow standing there, an expression of pure delight on his face. What was his name? Aidan.

"Some of us can handle sleeping rough, and some of us can't. You look a little confused, Brennan Xavier Burke."

"How do you know my name? Did you just quote scripture at me?"

"Sure I did. Just 'cause I live in the street doesn't mean I'm thick, right? You're not so brilliant yourself, if you can't suss out how I know your name. I've got your wallet, remember?"

"Ah. Right."

"I see you got us some pizza. I don't like anchovies, but I'll pick them off, rather than send you back for a new one."

"Good of you, my lad."

Aidan sat down, and jerked his thumb at the spot beside him. Brennan joined him.

"Don't worry. No slime right there. And it wasn't me who spit on the pavement. But you have to learn to dodge a lot of that, and used condoms, and lumps of dog shite. You get used to it."

Brennan was going to have a hard enough time getting used to the idea of picking up a piece of pizza and eating it without washing his hands first. But he was going to have to tough it out, and not show his squeamishness. They began to eat in silence. Brennan indicated the ginger ale and the chocolate milk. Aidan nodded, and picked them up.

"Want your wallet?"

"Em, yes, sure."

"Here."

Brennan took it and put it in the inside pocket of his jacket.

"Aren't you going to look in it?"

"No."

"I took a fiver out for emergencies."

"Fair enough. This pizza isn't half bad," he said.

"I've had worse," Aidan agreed.

"When we finish up here, I'm going to take you to a friend of mine who'll help you out."

"Some kind of holy Joe?"

"A holy type, but one who doesn't blather on about it."

"Oh yeah? Who's this gaffer then?"

"A sister."

"Carries a big stick, right?"

"No stick, no pain. Sister Kitty will get you fixed up."

"Yeah, right, she's going to —"

"Aidan, shut the fuck up and eat."

The boy looked at him in surprise, then resumed eating. When mealtime was over, he had consumed six of the eight pieces, and the soft drink and chocolate milk.

†

Not long afterwards, they were standing in front of the convent near Parnell Square. It was shrouded in darkness.

"Shite! We can't expect them to be up before the sun," Brennan said.

"Too bad. So I'll just run along now."

Brennan took Aidan gently by the arm. "No, you won't. Hold on."

He remembered being in Kitty's room with Michael and the others. The view was to the east, he recalled; they had walked up to the third floor, and almost but not quite to the end of the corridor. So which window would be hers? Not the last one. Second last? He had no choice but to chance it.

He bent down and picked up a couple of stones. He pegged one at the window. Perfect hit. But no Kitty. He pegged another one. A light flashed on in the room, and a curtain moved. Could she see him?

"Kitty!" he called out. "Kitty! It's Brennan."

He turned to Aidan, who was standing there gaping at him. "We'll just have to wait." And wait they did, with no result. "Might as well have a seat till she spies us. Or comes down."

They dropped to the grass and sat, staring up at the massive old building.

"Only hope I got the right room," Brennan muttered. He was ready to keel over and pass out asleep on the grass. He'd slept on worse. Just a few minutes ago. The situation struck him as so bizarre he wondered if he was hallucinating from lack of rest. Sleep deprivation was a form of torture; it wreaked psychological havoc on the person . . . What was that? A siren in the distance. Trouble again somewhere. Was it coming closer? No. Yes.

"Jesus the Christ and Saviour of the world!" He scrambled to his feet.

"You've put the fucking guards onto me, Brennan, you *amadan*!"

"No, no!" He grabbed Aidan by the sleeve, and pushed him into a hedge at the side of the property. "Stay in there, and keep your head down!"

Brennan got Aidan squirrelled away, and not a moment too soon. A garda car came roaring up to the convent, and two guards got out. At the same time, a light went on over the front door of the convent, and a nun emerged, fully dressed. Fierce-looking. Not Kitty. One of the officers went to speak to her; the other peered into the gloom in front of and beside the building. Brennan emerged and stood in plain view. The guard saw him and shouted to his partner. They both converged on Brennan and seized him by the arms, one cop on each side.

"I can explain," he said.

"You'd better."

The nun called out, "Have you got him? He was throwing stones at our windows and shouting something. I couldn't make it out, but I did hear the name Brennan."

"I'm here to see Sister Kitty."

"Is that a fact?" The nun's eyes bored into him. "If so, I'll have to have a word with Sister Curran about the company she keeps. So, what's your problem, which prompts you to terrorize our community in the middle of the night?"

"I don't have a problem."

"You do now," one of the guards asserted.

Then Brennan heard the voice of Kitty Curran. "What's going on, Sister?"

"You have a gentleman caller, Sister Curran, though 'gentleman' is hardly the appropriate word."

Kitty caught sight of Brennan then, and he watched her expression go from incomprehension to barely concealed amusement.

"Oh, I can take care of this, Sister Ermenilda. Guard, you may release him."

"Do you know this man, Sister? We were given the name Brennan. Is that correct?" The guard looked at Brennan's soiled clerical suit and Roman collar. "Is it *Father* Brennan?"

The other guard eyed the first and wiggled his hand in the well-recognized pantomime of a glass being lifted and lowered.

But Kitty had an answer for them: "No, it's *Mister* Brennan. Please release him, guard. He's harmless. Really. He's known to some of us here."

"If he's Mr. Brennan, why the priest suit?"

"Mr. Brennan did attend the seminary. Didn't you, dear? But the sem is very challenging. Intellectually, if you know what I mean. Not everybody is able for it. But there's nothing wrong with that. We all have different abilities and gifts. And some of us have been touched by the angels. Like poor Mr. Brennan here." She gave him a mawkish smile. "Some of the sisters here in Dublin watch out for him, make sure he has a meal, gets his hair trimmed, takes a bath once in a while. I can see his clerical costume is getting a little shabby again, but we'll fix that up for him. You can release him to me, guard. Honestly."

"You're sure?"

"Oh, yes. Come inside with me, darling."

The guards released their grip on him but stood by warily in case he had to be wrestled to the ground. He returned Kitty's simpering smile, and said in a singsong voice, "Thank you, Sister."

She came forward and patted him gently on his injured left cheek, then took his hand. He began shambling towards the door with her. They went inside. The other nun looked at them uncertainly, then headed upstairs.

"Well, Mr. Brennan," Kitty said to him when they were alone, "do you have something to tell me, or have you really taken leave of your senses?"

"The first thing I have to tell you is thanks for bailing me out. The second is that there is someone else lurking in the bushes outside. If he's still there."

He filled her in on Aidan, and she readily agreed to help. They waited until the guards were well and truly gone, then returned outside, where the day was just beginning to dawn. Brennan sent up a prayer that the young man had not scarpered. But there he was, crouched in the hedgerow where Brennan had left him. He crawled out and stood, and Brennan introduced him to Sister Kitty.

With his eyes on Kitty, Aidan jerked his head in Brennan's direction, and asked, "So, what's the real story? Is he a priest or some sort of head-the-ball, or both? I went through his wallet, and his cards just say Brennan Xavier Burke. Nothing about 'Father.'"

"Have you spent any time with him, Aidan?" Kitty asked.

"A bit."

"What do you think?"

Aidan glanced briefly at Brennan, then looked down and scuffed his shoe along the ground. "I think he's what he's supposed to be."

Kitty had a plan ready for Aidan; she had worked with the poor and troubled when she lived in Dublin before, and she still had connections now. She dug out some clean clothes and sent him off for a shower, then went to work on the phone. She found him a place to stay and set up a couple of appointments for him later in the day. When he emerged pink and glowing from the bathroom, she told him what she had lined up for him, and assured him that she would be going with him to his new quarters. She and Brennan sat with him in a small parlour until one of Kitty's helpers arrived to pick them up. Brennan went outside to see them off.

He held out his hand, and Aidan grasped it. They shook. Brennan wanted to take the poor, unfortunate child in his arms and let him weep the tears of a lifetime. But he would leave that to someone much better in that line than he was. Kitty Curran.

All he said was, "Aidan, if ever you get the urge for pizza at four in the morning, Kitty will know where to find me."

Aidan just nodded, without words. Brennan did not break the handshake until Aidan did. He made the sign of the cross over the boy, gave him a blessing, turned and walked inside the convent.

Brennan returned to the little parlour and sat in an armchair. He felt himself drifting off to sleep. He leaned back and slowly sank beneath the rim of consciousness.

He awoke with the sun beating down on his face through the window. It took him a few minutes to realize where he was. Then the whole long night and morning came back to him. He looked at his watch. Twenty to nine. Christ. He was due to say the old Latin Mass at St. Audoen's at nine. Where was Kitty? She had left with Aidan. Brennan got up and found the bathroom. When he saw himself in the mirror, he could scarcely believe his eyes, which were watery and bloodshot, underscored with dark circles. His face looked grey, and he had a big red gash on his left cheek. His white collar was now brown, with a streak of blood on it, and his suit was dirty and even torn. He worked up a lather of soap and washed his hands and face. His only earthly desire now was to brush his teeth. He would have to stop at a pharmacy and pick up a brush and paste before Mass. He had to go.

Kitty was waiting for him when he came out of the bathroom.

"Brennan, you look as if you haven't slept in a week. And what happened to your face? And your suit? I didn't want to ask with Aidan here."

"I was in a fight, and I slept on the pavement."

"What? How did you . . ."

Brennan shook his head. No time for explanations. "I'll tell you all about it next time I see you. For now, could I annoy you for one other favour?"

"Why ever not?"

"Toothpaste. And is there any chance in the world that you have a spare toothbrush?"

"Did I not just produce clothing out of thin air for another man in need?"

"You did."

"Wait two seconds and I'll be back with toothpaste and a brand new brush."

He waited, she returned with the necessary items, and he went in and cleaned his teeth. When he emerged again, she said, "You still look like hell. Go home and go to bed."

"Mass time. Got to run."

He wrapped his arms around Kitty and held her close. "Thank you, angel."

"You're welcome, dear, simple Mr. Brennan. Young Aidan was very grateful for your help. He kept saying, 'He gave me his wallet to hold. Can you believe that?' What was that all about?"

Brennan waved off the question and left the convent on the fly.

He got to the church with two minutes to spare, ran up the aisle, made a quick genuflection and sign of the cross, and entered the sacristy. He stopped for a few seconds to catch his breath, then vested for Mass. He took care with the white alb, making sure he did not get any blood on it from his face. Then he donned the green chasuble with the gold cross on the back, placed a black biretta on his head, and took a deep breath. It was at that moment that two young boys came barrelling into the sacristy.

"Sorry we're late, Father! The bus . . ."

Brennan held up his hand. "No worries, lads. I'm late too. I'm Father Burke." They caught sight of his wounded face and gawked. "Get yourselves dressed, and we're on."

Father Burke walked up the aisle behind his altar boys. He noticed

Monty and the MacNeil on his left. They did a double take when they saw him. No wonder, with him looking like the wrath of God. But he soon forgot all that, as he became suffused with the divine love that surrounded them all in the neoclassical interior of the church. He sang the Mass as it had been sung for over a thousand years, the Gregorian chant sounding raspy this morning but, as always, perfectly in tune.

He stood at the back of the church after Mass, talking with parishioners and accepting the occasional compliment about the beauty of the liturgy and music. He ignored the curious looks the people directed at his face.

Monty and Maura were the last to file out. They stared at him, and Monty spoke up, "Barroom brawl, Father?"

Burke was too tired to come up with a rejoinder. That gave pause even to the MacNeil, who opened her mouth to comment, then thought better of it. The fact that they were in the church together gave rise to a glimmer of hope in Brennan, and he said, "Come with me." He turned towards the front of the church, and they followed him up the aisle and into the sacristy.

He pulled three chairs out, and they all sat down. The little boys were getting out of their surplices, practically tearing them off so they could get on with their day. "Easy there, boys," Burke admonished them.

"I know, Father, but we have a match starting at eleven, and we've the bus to catch."

"All right. We have to expect that on a Saturday morning. Thanks for your help today. Great job."

"Thanks," they both said, eyes shining. Then they bolted from the room.

Father Burke stood and began removing his vestments, revealing the dirty, damaged suit and collar underneath.

"Are you all right, Brennan? You've been injured. What happened?" Maura asked, genuinely concerned.

Monty joined in, "What on earth . . ."

Brennan held up his hand to forestall the inquiries. He didn't have the energy to recount last night's events, and he could not reveal what had kept him up the night before. But young Aidan, the boy without a home, was very much on his mind.

"I'm fine. Listen to me. Please." They were uncharacteristically silent as he sat again, and faced them. "You two love each other," he said. "There's no doubt in my mind about that."

No response, just wariness on their part.

"Well? I don't have the strength to heave myself out of this chair to go home, so I have all day to wait for your answer, if necessary. Love, I was asking about."

Monty finally answered. "That's never been in dispute."

"Ah. If only Giacomo Puccini were alive today, he would set that to music. One of the greatest, most poetic, most glorious declarations of love of all time. But I'll take what I can get. That's a yes. And you, my dear?" he said to MacNeil.

All she did was nod.

"That's not a problem, then. Your problem, as I understand it," he said to Monty, "is embarrassment. Over the baby, Dominic. You would be embarrassed to be seen raising a child who, obviously, visibly, is not your own."

"You'd be the same way if you were in my shoes, Brennan. You're made of the same stuff. We all heard the stories of the scenes you staged to get your old girlfriend back from another man in your New York days."

"In my youth, long ago."

"You'd be the same way now. I know you. You're the same kinda guy as yours truly."

"Very well. I'm the same kinda guy. And the same kinda guy is pleading with you to get over it, and be a father to that child. And a husband to this woman."

They were listening. Burke knew that much. He had never seen them so attentive, if understandably cautious.

"Monty, I'll ask you this again: has any one of your friends or colleagues ever made a snide remark about you and Dominic and his parentage?"

"Well, no, not to me, but . . ."

"And if they did, you strike me as the kinda guy who'd be well able to handle it." Brennan regarded them in silence for a long moment, then said, "Come with me some night through the streets of Dublin. I'll show you some sights that will put embarrassment in its proper perspective."

"What happened last night, Brennan?"

"Just another boy without a father, without a home, without the love of a family. Nobody could ask for a better mother than you, Maura, but the results are in, and they are dismal. Studies show that children without fathers have higher rates of hyperactivity, antisocial behaviour, aggressiveness, emotional disorders, conduct disorders, academic failure. They are much more likely to be unhealthy, to be abused, to wind up in jail or on the streets. Those are the facts. And it's not just the poor. The research shows that fatherlessness is a risk factor all by itself, regardless of income in the household. And the problems get worse as the child gets older."

"How did you come up with these findings, Professor Burke?" Monty asked, in a clipped voice.

"I got them from you, counsellor. A case involving one of the boys in our after-school program; I sat with him in court. Remember? This was part of your summation."

"And you just happen to recall it word for word."

"Why not? I listen, I record, I recall."

Silence.

"Did I get any of it wrong?"

Silence again.

"Right. So. Nobody in this room wants that kind of future for Dominic. Correct?"

They took that in, then Brennan resumed his mission. "And it's not just Dominic. Normie and Tommy Douglas would feel they had ascended to heaven if you two ever did what you both really want to do, and moved back in together. You've done a beautiful job raising the two of them, even with the separation. But Dominic hasn't had their advantage, a father present in his life from the beginning. Don't let him wait any longer. Don't let yourselves wait any longer."

Brennan closed his eyes and rubbed his temples. Without opening his eyes, he continued, "Life is short. Look around you. Lost children living in the streets. People blowing each other's heads off a few miles to the north of us, leaving women without husbands, children without fathers, parents without sons. The most important people in their lives, taken from them in an instant. Life is short. Don't waste any more of yours or that of your children."

He raised his weary eyes to them. "For the love of God, will you think about it? Please."

Chapter 14

Michael

The news of the American minister's death had broken late Thursday night but Michael had not heard about it until Friday morning. The Irish papers and news broadcasts were consumed with the story, and they relayed the coverage from the United States, where the Irish and the British ambassadors had been called on the carpet in Washington. The Americans were apoplectic, and demanded everything short of a Marine landing to track down the killers and avenge the preacher's death. All day Friday Michael had carried with him an image of the man's body floating in Carlingford Lough. That didn't make for a heavenly rest, but he finally managed to drift off and sleep late on Saturday morning. When he awoke, he rolled off the bed and dropped to his knees in prayer. He was still trying to formulate his petition for peace when the phone rang. What time was it? Oh. Half-eleven already. He pushed himself up and grabbed the receiver. Tried to say hello but it came out as a croak.

"Are you all right, Mike?" It was Monty.

Michael cleared his throat. "I'm fine. Haven't been sleeping well.

The killing of the minister, you know . . ."

"A very sinister development. It doesn't augur well for the immediate future."

"No." Michael remembered Brennan's bleak prognostications
about the fallout should Odom be killed, and Michael's own hope
that, as bad as it would be, an outrage like this might be a turning
point. It was hard to maintain that optimism today.

"But I'm calling on another matter," Monty said. "I checked into
that lawyer, the guy who handled the sale of the boat business connected to one of your suspects. Jimmy O'Hearn."

"My 'suspects,' as you put it, Mr. Collins, might better be described
as my 'targets of slander,' victims of unsubstantiated slurs painted on
the wall of a respectable establishment on Dublin's Northside."

"Well said, Michael. You may want to turn in your sergeant's
badge, and don the robes of a barrister, so protective are you of your
clients' interests."

"Thank you for those kind words, sir. Now, what about the lawyer?"

"I contacted the law society in London. They had nothing on
Carey Gilbert except that he had been struck from the rolls for non-
payment of his dues, and was no longer practising in the U.K. The
woman on the phone put me on hold and came back to say someone
told her he had heard Gilbert left the country. That's all they knew."

"Of course he left the country, Monty! With the O'Hearn family's
money!"

"And you're afraid Jimmy O'Hearn tracked him down and killed
him."

"Well, obviously I'm hoping and praying that's not the case! But
we know the man left the country. Did he leave this earthly life altogether?"

"I'll leave it to you to find that out, Sergeant."

They said goodbye and Michael took to his bed again, but could
not get past the images of the preacher, and hate-filled rioters in Belfast, so he got up and got on with his day.

He stopped in at the Aughrim Street church to offer up prayers
for the soul of the Reverend Merle Odom and for his family. And for
peace, or at least calm, in the North of Ireland. Then he made his way
over to the pub. Michael O'Flaherty's life in Dublin: church and pub.

He hadn't been there long when the door opened, and a man's voice said, "Good afternoon to you, Maureen."

The four regulars turned to face the door and acknowledged the arrival of a middle-aged woman who had a soft, gentle face and silver-streaked hair done in a twist. She approached the bar and said, "Edward. I didn't want to wait until . . . it got too late."

Glances were exchanged.

Eddie Madigan rose to his feet and said, "Hello, Maureen."

"I'd like you to come to the college with me Monday morning. It's about Gwen."

Madigan's voice was sharp. "What about her? Is she all right?"

"She's grand, except . . ." Mrs. Madigan lowered her voice, but Michael heard the words "continue in the summer course," "account," and "fees now." Then she said, "Please come outside, so we can discuss this."

Eddie followed her out of the pub without looking at his companions.

"Well, he's in the soup now, when she tells him to step outside," said the man who had greeted Maureen upon her arrival. Michael looked over at the bar and saw the fellow standing between the bar stools occupied by Tim Shanahan and Jimmy O'Hearn. It was Motor Mouth McCrum.

"She just wants a private word with him," Tim said. "Maureen is always courteous when she stops by. A lovely woman, is Maureen."

"She is. You're right, Tim," O'Hearn agreed.

"It's a shame about Eddie and the wife," McCrum said to no one in particular. "Sad to say, she walked out on him when he had his trouble."

"It was a hard time for them, Blair," Tim said, "but I'm sure they'll get it sorted."

Blair McCrum, that was it. Michael had forgotten his first name. Had known him only as Motor Mouth.

"Hard time!" McCrum exclaimed. "Hard time's not the half of it when a man gets turfed from the Garda Síochána, and him coming from one of the biggest police families in the city. Finn, would you be so kind as to pour me a Powers." McCrum got his drink and paid for it, then turned to Shanahan. "Not a simple matter to get things sorted when you're accused of corruption and you get sacked from the police force. Not that I believe a word of the story that's going around against him. He's a fine fellow, is Eddie Madigan, at least I always thought so, though we all have our weaknesses. Maureen is a fine woman. You can hardly expect her to stand by him in his trouble, her father being a garda himself. Tough times for them now. Didn't I see their youngest in Grafton Street the other day, looking like a tinker in a faded-out dress too small for her, and an old scuffed pair of shoes. She wasn't a patch on the other girls, in their stylish new frocks. But I'm sure Maureen is doing her best. You have to feed them first; buying a decent wardrobe comes a distant second to that. Sad." He shook his head.

"What are you on about now, Blair?" The question came from the back of the room. Michael turned and saw one of the Five Sorrowful Mysteries, twisted around in her seat and giving McCrum a murderous look. As they had been on the other occasion when Michael had seen them, the women were all dressed up with their hair freshly styled. They sat around two tables pushed together.

"Monsignor," the woman said then, "grab a chair and sit down. Let us treat you to a drop of something."

"Well, thank you, ladies," he said, and went over to join them.

"What will you have, Monsignor? Pint of the black stuff?"

"Sure."

The woman signalled to Finn, but Michael was on his feet again. "Don't trouble yourself, Finn. I'll get it myself."

"No worries, Monsignor. You sit tight with your parishioners. I deliver."

When Finn had brought the pint, Michael thanked him and turned to his companions. "Please call me Michael, and would you give me your names again?"

Mary Daly, Mary O'Brien, Kathleen O'Rourke, Eileen Sullivan, and Beatrice Walsh. He would try to keep them straight.

"He's an oul woman," Beatrice said, indicating McCrum with a lift of her chin.

Kathleen took umbrage at that. "You're an oul woman yourself, Bea. So am I. We all are, or we soon will be. Don't be insulting old women in my hearing!"

"We're not old and we're not like him. He's the biggest gossip in Dublin City. Every word that comes out of him is a lie."

"I grew up around the corner from the McCrums," Kathleen said. "We always thought he was a bit God-help-us."

"Oh, I don't think he has that excuse, Kathleen. If he did, people would be feeling sorry for him. Wouldn't be his fault. But I never heard anyone say that. He's just a nasty piece of work and always has been."

"I don't know," said Mary Daly. "He has a lot of connections, people he knows, on the city council and in the guards. Old Motor Mouth must get it right some of the time! Och, he's coming our way."

"Mind if I join you ladies? And Monsignor?" He pulled a chair from another table and squeezed himself in between Eileen and Michael.

"She's certainly keeping him on the carpet a long time today!"

"Who would that be now, Blair?" Kathleen asked, as if everybody didn't know.

"Maureen Madigan — I'm surprised she keeps his name, but I suppose it's for the sake of the children — Maureen is keeping *Edward* from his blood brothers at the bar. They're going to be way ahead of him in the blood alcohol count! Too bad you can't walk into a lawyer's office and get a divorce the way you can in the more lenient countries of the world; Maureen could do better for herself."

"Are you eyeing her for yourself then, Blair?" asked Mary O'Brien.

"Ah, go on out of that, Mary! I am not. It's just that if I were Maureen, I wouldn't throw away my life remaining faithful and true to the likes of Eddie Madigan. He wouldn't do it for her!"

"Oh, he would so, Blair. Who's ever seen Eddie having a snog with another woman?"

McCrum's face took on a sly look. "Nobody's seen them, because guess what?" Nobody took a guess, but McCrum was not deterred. "Because his little bit of crumpet is in jolly old England!"

The women stared at him. Gratified, he smiled and went on, "Or she was. Must be lonely times for her these days, with him *persona non grata* across the pond!"

"What are you talking about?" Mary O'Brien demanded. "Madigan is never in England. The man is here in this bar every day of his life!"

"And he always will be. Now. He won't be sent on any more missions by . . ." McCrum leaned over and spoke in a conspiratorial whisper. "Special Branch!"

"Oh, your bollocks, Blair! Special Branch! You've been watching too much James Bond!"

"James Bond. Is that the fellow that has all the female company and brilliantly wraps up his secret mission at the end of the show? Not like our Eddie Madigan, sent over to do a job at the Public Record Office and getting waylaid — excuse my language, ladies, Monsignor — by a temptress named Abigail, keeper of the records, and getting so distracted he banjaxes his mission and gets hauled back to Dublin in disgrace and loses his job. Edward Madigan, I'm sorry to be the one to tell you this, but you're no James Bond!"

"Are you hearing voices in your head, Blair? There's pills you can take for that, you know! I can give you the name of the man I see, not for voices, but for pain management. He's a specialist, treats all kinds of cases, and he's one of the best!" Eileen said. "A few sessions with Dr. Traynor will get you sorted."

"You can have my pain pills, Blair," Mary Daly offered. "They won't cure what ails you but you won't know the difference, you'll be so spaced out! And you won't be able to remember a word of that fantastical story you just recited about Eddie Madigan. You're the only one I've ever heard come up with that yarn! What I heard, what we all heard, is that Eddie got in with some drug dealers and took a brown envelope from them. I don't believe it of Eddie, I really don't, but that's always been the talk."

"You know what I think?" Blair said. "I think the drugs came later. I think Madigan got sacked after this cock-up in London, then started peddling drugs to support himself. And the rumours that he was taking bribes from the underworld started after that. And the gardaí were content to have that story go round rather than admit that Garda Special Branch hired the wrong man for a sensitive job across the sea."

Michael had no idea what to think. The man beside him was a disagreeable busybody, to be sure, and his story was outlandish. But what if there was a grain of truth in what he said? What if there was a Special Branch angle to Madigan's misfortunes? Speaking lightly, in the hope that nobody would think he considered Motor Mouth McCrum the fount of gospel truth, he asked, "What kind of mission are you talking about, Blair? It all sounds a bit far-fetched, doesn't it?"

"Truth is stranger than fiction, Monsignor, as I've learned over the course of a lifetime, and perhaps you have too. My sources never divulged to me what his mission was, and rightly so. It was very hush-hush, and of course I didn't push."

Of course.

"All I heard was that he was supposed to carry out some sort of operation at the Public Record Office in London, four or five years ago, and he ended up in the soup over it, and there was a Mata Hari named Abigail involved. She worked there and played some kind of role in the failure of his mission. Wore him out and left him weak at the knees, most likely. And there was hell to pay with the Brits, and there were red faces in Garda HQ here, and Madigan was bundled off out of England and sacked from the Garda Síochána." He lowered his voice. "Oh, here he comes now. She's let him off the leash. Have a drink, why don't you, Edward?"

His remarks were met by silence among the Five Sorrowful Mysteries. Like Michael, no doubt, the women didn't like Motor Mouth's attitude but they were left wondering what on earth to make of his tale. McCrum looked about the room, then got up to sit with someone at another table. Nobody said goodbye.

Later on, in his room, Michael gave brief consideration to asking Leo Killeen about the Public Record Office and whether he knew anything about a "mission" there. But Leo wasn't home. Just as well; it wasn't hard to imagine what Leo would have to say about the spy story. Michael was debating how to spend the rest of his day when he got a call from Monty, who was taking the family to afternoon tea at the Shelbourne Hotel. Brennan was coming; would Michael like to join them? He most certainly would. The hotel was established by a Burke (though Michael had no idea whether the illustrious man was connected to the Burkes he knew) and the constitution of the Free State had been drafted there. Did Monty know that? All the more reason to spend time in the place. They made arrangements to meet at the hotel, and Michael hung up the phone. Should he take a cab or walk? It was a bit of a hike to Stephen's Green, where the Shelbourne was located. But taxis cost money, and he had time, so he decided to go on foot.

He went downstairs and opened the front door of the house. As soon as he stepped out on the pavement, the sky opened up, so he turned right around and went back inside, with the intention of going upstairs for his umbrella. But he saw the residents' rain jackets hanging on the clothing stand in the doorway. As far as he knew, neither of the other priests was home, so surely nobody would miss a jacket if he borrowed one. The first one he tried must have belonged to Father Grattan, who was taller and stockier than Michael. He put it back on the hook. Beside it was a dark green nylon windbreaker he had seen on Leo; that would fit, given that they were about the same height and weight. He donned the windbreaker, flipped the collar up, and started out again. It was bucketing rain. He walked, head down, and brooded about the Reverend Merle Odom and the terrible way his life had been taken from him. Michael wondered why there had been no news about a Catholic being kidnapped, as Archbishop O'Halloran had suggested. Had that rumour been unfounded? There was nobody Michael could ask, not even Brennan or Leo; he had assured O'Halloran that he would keep the matter to himself.

Michael had been out for two minutes or so when he heard the squishy sound of tires on the wet pavement. He slowed down as he approached an intersection, thinking the car might be turning. But no, he saw out of the corner of his eye, it was moving at a low speed and did not have a signal light on. So Michael crossed the street and kept on. Rain ran into his eyes, and he wiped it away with his sleeve. He speeded up a bit; the sooner he got to the Shelbourne and out of this downpour, the happier he would be. When he increased his speed, the car seemed to keep pace with him. Maybe it was somebody he knew; a chance for a lift? He turned to look. He saw two men in the front seat and possibly another in the back. The front-seat passenger rolled down his window and peered at Michael. Then the man turned towards the driver and gave a quick shake of his head. The window went up again. The car turned away on the next street and was gone. Michael thought he had seen the man somewhere before, but he could not be sure. A lot of fellows had the same short haircut and, well, it could be anybody. But what about the car? Hadn't there been a car in the neighbourhood before, creeping along? At night? Michael tried not to be spooked. Nothing had happened, then or now. It was most likely a simple case of mistaken identity, fellows out in the rain looking for somebody they knew. Well, whoever they were, they were gone. Out of sight, out of mind.

Brennan

"Brennan! Are you all right?"

The words came at him through the fog of sleep.

"Che cosa?" he muttered.

"Have we come to the wrong place?" Brennan recognized the voice of Monty Collins then. "Or is this our Brennan, living in a multilingual dream world that the rest of us can't possibly —"

"I was in Rome. Dreaming of Rome." But he couldn't remember one thing about the dream. "What time is it? What are you doing here?"

He lifted his head from the pillow. Blood on the pillowcase. What? Oh, right. He touched his face. The fight with the young fellow, sleeping rough on the pavement. And he was still in his soiled clothing.

"We're here because we couldn't reach you. You missed tea at the Shelbourne Hotel. Remember that plan?"

It came back to him. It was Saturday. Still. The MacNeil had called him sometime during the day; they were all to meet for tea at the hotel. But he had passed out from exhaustion. He had heard the telephone at some point, maybe more than once, but had ignored it and gone back to sleep.

"How did you get in here?"

"It wasn't locked. You're slipping. You should get more sleep."

"I should. So goodbye to you."

"Okay, we'll leave you to it."

"No, no. I'll get up."

He heaved himself from the bed and stood up. Good thing he had something on him besides the skin he was born in; the MacNeil and O'Flaherty were also in the room. It was then that he recalled his last conversation with the Collins-MacNeils, in the sacristy of St. Audoen's Church. Nobody alluded to it. Well, they wouldn't, with Michael here.

Monty gestured to Brennan's dirty suit and collar. "Another spoiled priest outfit for the dry cleaner at my hotel? They'll think I'm murdering priests and taking souvenirs."

"Another!" the MacNeil exclaimed. "Are you saying this happened before?"

"Don't ask," Monty replied, obviously remembering a bit too late that the first dirty suit was the result of Brennan's cleaning out the tunnel in his uncle's pub.

"Seems to me there are a lot of 'don't asks' in that family," she said, pointing to Burke.

"*Pòg mo thòn*, MacNeil."

"This is your curate, Monsignor?" she said to O'Flaherty.

"I'm afraid so."

"Can't you do anything with him?"

"Not so far, Mrs. MacNeil, but I'll renew my efforts."

Brennan tuned them out and whipped the bloody case off his pillow, grabbed a fresh set of clothing and his shaving kit, and left his guests for the bathroom down the hall. He had a shower, brushed his teeth, dispensed with shaving, and left the pillowcase to soak in the sink. He was back in his room within five minutes.

But he still got slagged. "Did all that have to be done right now?" Monty asked him.

"Are yeh mindless? What else am I going to do, get out of bed in that condition and not clean myself up?"

"You'd arise from your bed wrapped in the purest of white linen, anointed by the holy angels with purifying oils and unguents, and you'd still go off to the showers."

"Feck off."

"Well, we missed you at teatime, but we're glad you haven't come to grief," the MacNeil said to him.

"Thank you, my dear. Where are the children?"

"We dropped them off with the sitter after tea. I've no doubt Normie will spend the evening designing the tea room she now wants to open in Halifax." She looked around the room. "This is so *you*, darling. The devil-may-care attitude to window treatments, the casual placement of furniture." Affecting the mannerisms of a fussy interior decorator, she fluffed the curtains and relocated his chair. "Crucifix over the bed, Roman Missal and Breviary in Latin on the bureau, immaculate clothing in the wardrobe, piles of books and music, and a pack of smokes, whiskey and glasses in a makeshift bar in the corner. Yes, one would say on entering this room, here lies —

or should I say *hic jacet* — Father Burke."

"Didn't know you had the Latin. Proper thing," he said. "Find a place to sit, all of you. Here." He made the bed up; three of them sat on that, and Michael took the chair.

Which was appropriate, because he had the floor. He proceeded to deliver himself of an improbable tale he had heard from Motor Mouth McCrum. Some daft story about Eddie Madigan, Special Branch, and a siren who had supposedly sabotaged Madigan's undercover mission at the Public Record Office in London.

That was met with great hilarity on the part of Monty and the MacNeil. Brennan felt the same way.

"Only one way to find out, boys," MacNeil said. "Michael, this is a dirty job and beneath the dignity of either of us. But this pair —" she flapped her hand in the direction of Monty and Brennan "— have shown themselves to be less than scrupulous on too many occasions to count."

"Objection!" Monty cried.

"I second that," Brennan said. "When have I ever —"

MacNeil cut him short. "You want I should diss you in detail in the presence of your pastor, Burke?"

"I cannot imagine anything you could say that would cause Monsignor to regard me as anything but his humble and obedient acolyte."

"Is that a yes or a no?"

"It's a *move on.*"

"That's what I thought. Now, let me get it figured out. I'll do the costuming for this production. Monty, I'm going to dress you as a plumber. That worked so well in recent years in the U.S. You'll arrive at this Abigail's little love nest, with its scarlet flocked wallpaper and mirrored bedchamber, in a van painted with the catchy motto 'Wherever you GO, we're right BEHIND you.' You'll wear a cap with those words emblazoned on it. Your task will be to talk your way into her flat, where no doubt she has a cache of secret documents that, if discovered, will blow the lid off the Madigan affair and bring down the governments of two countries. You go into the loo and sit there with your butt crack showing until Burke, who will play the role of cheap seducer, shows up to distract her and lure her into the boudoir. Then Monty goes into action and searches the place. If he has to creep in and burrow under the bed, well, as I say, it's a dirty job."

"Why don't I get to be the seducer?" Monty asked.

"Typecasting," his wife replied. "Burke, on the other hand, saintly and pure as he is, might enjoy playing out an unaccustomed role. So. Burke. I envision a riverboat gambler look for you: a tight, shiny suit with wide lapels, a shirt open nearly to your waist, and gobs of gold chains on your chest. Your hairdo will be a pompadour, and I think a pencil moustache would add to your appeal."

"I'd give anything to see that!" Michael exclaimed.

"No reason you shouldn't, Michael. I can't think of any reason on earth why this plan won't succeed."

The foolishness went on for a bit until the MacNeil said, "I wonder if there really is an Abigail."

"However will we find out?" Monty asked. "Oh, I know. The same way we find out who is calling when the phone rings. Pick up the phone."

"Makes sense," Brennan agreed.

"That was a jibe at me, Brennan. Sometimes I tend to speculate aloud as to who it might be who is calling. It sets Collins crazy. 'Answer it, mystery solved.' But I can't fault his logic. So, who'll make the call?"

"You will," Brennan declared. "If this person exists, she may be lulled into the utterly unjustified impression that a woman calling — you — would be less threatening than a strange man. If only she knew."

"Good. I'll do it. But she won't be at work in the archives on a Saturday night. First of the week we'll find the *femme fatale* of the file room."

Christy Burke's door flew open and banged against the wall Sunday afternoon. The regulars all turned at once, pints in hand, to see who had come in. The young barman, Sean Nugent.

"Have you heard the news, gentlemen?"

At the bar, all the heads shook in tandem.

"They found the man!"

"What man have they found?" asked Eddie Madigan.

"The fellow who was doing the painting on the walls — the vandal! He's dead!"

"Dead where?" Madigan demanded. "When? Who is it? How do they know it's the vandal?"

"Because they found him with the paint on him. Same paint. That's what they're saying."

"Who?"

"The gardaí, on the radio. Well, all they're saying is they found a body. Out past Finglas, by Dunsink Lane. But I ran into Johnny O'Keefe, and his da's a garda. The guards say it's the fellow who's been spraying up the place because he had green paint sprayed back on him. As if he got killed in the middle of doing his dirty work! Executed, more like. Two bullets in the back of his head!"

"Who is it?" Madigan asked in a quiet voice. "Have they given him a name?"

"If they know, they're not telling."

Brennan had been as gripped by the announcement as the others, which meant that his investigative abilities, such as they were, had momentarily deserted him. Belatedly, he looked at the Christy Burke Four to see if any one of them appeared especially rattled by the news. But all of them were focused on Sean Nugent, and Brennan could not pick out anything revealing in the expressions of one or the other. It would have been every bit as interesting to see the expression on Finn's face as he heard the "news" of the body being "discovered." Discovered in the place where Finn and Larry Healey had decided to inter the remains. But Finn remained in the shadows behind the bar.

There was more news on the dead vandal the following day. And wouldn't you know it would come from Motor Mouth McCrum. He had missed the scoop on Sunday; on Monday he was wiping up the rear with some tidbits about the guards. He stood at the bar just after noontime, holding something against his chest and fumbling with a handful of change, while Finn got him a glass and half-filled it with whiskey.

"Things are heating up, at least for somebody, now that they've found the vandal rotting in his grave. The guards are on the move."

As well they should be, thought Brennan, *with a murder on their hands.*

If this caused Finn any anxiety, there was no sign of it in his face or in his eyes, which were, as usual, obscured from view behind his dark glasses.

The town crier went on, "They were spotted in the Bleeding Horse last night. The gardaí. Twice. Place was jammed but all they did was look around and leave. Didn't question anybody. That says to me" — McCrum stopped and took a sip of his drink — "that they were looking for somebody in particular. Somebody they expected to find at the Horse but didn't, because the fellow wasn't there. Making himself scarce, perhaps."

"Or perhaps just not there," Tim Shanahan replied mildly.

"Or perhaps," Eddie Madigan put in, "the guards had a thirst on them, but then they saw Superintendent O'Higgins planted on a bar stool and giving them the eye, so they scarpered."

"Twice though, Eddie?" Blair McCrum replied.

"Sure you've got me stumped there, Blair."

"Who do you think they were after at the Bleeding Horse?" Jimmy O'Hearn asked.

"I have my theories," McCrum answered, "but I'll wait for the evidence."

"Since when?" O'Hearn muttered into his pint.

But McCrum seemed not to have heard. He resumed his speculations. "In the meantime they'll be looking for traces of whoever it was — whoever did the murder. They say a killer never gets away without leaving something behind."

"Yeah, in this case, a pair of bullets left behind in the fellow's noggin," Madigan remarked.

"No, you know what I mean, Eddie. Threads or hairs, something like that, transferred onto the body. Remember that murder that was solved because the victim had been tied up in the killer's truck or his garden shed, or whatever it was, and the guards solved it because they found fertilizer on the victim's clothes?"

"I might fertilize my pants too if I was tied up in a shed with some yobbo holding a gun to my head."

"There's no talking to you, Eddie, and you an ex-guard; you should be telling us all about these things, not me telling you."

"I'll leave it to you, Blair. I'm retired."

"Well, I'm convinced they've got a lead. They'll have someone in the nick before the week's out. And the news has travelled across the sea." Whatever he had been holding when he came in he was now waving around. "Finn, I know you have a video player here. I've seen it on occasion. You might want to dust it off for us now."

"What for?"

"I have a tape to play for youse. Finn, you're famous." Finn clearly didn't like the sound of that. "Well, you're not, but Christy's is. Go get the yoke and set it up for us, Finn. You'll see. And I'm warning youse. You'll not like what you hear!"

Not surprisingly, the patrons expressed their determination to watch whatever the blathering arsehole had with him. Finn, with obvious reluctance, went into the back and returned with the equipment. He set it up, and McCrum handed him the tape.

"This is a comedy routine," McCrum explained. "The fellow comes on late at night and pokes fun at the day's news. It's a British program my nephew always tapes. Normally I don't bother with it, but he put me on to this episode. Roll the film, Mr. Burke!"

Finn pressed play, and a young man appeared on a stage. He had kind of a foolish rubbery face on him, but that would be an asset in a comic. He was talking about death. He spoke in a Cockney accent until he got to the subject of Ireland, at which point he switched to a stage-Irish brogue.

"And speakin' of death. Our Irish friends across the water are big on death. And I can say this, 'cause I'm half Oirish meself, so I am, begorrah and begob! Admit it, all you Paddies out there. You love it when somebody croaks their last. Ever been to an Irish wake? Party! Party! Party! But you can't just die; you have to die right. Worst thing an Irishman can say to another Irishman is 'May yeh die roarin' for a priest!' Worst case scenario for yer Paddy, dyin' without the priest. Anyway, listen to this. According to a news item out of Dublin today, this bloke died because he disrespected his local pub! Oh, they take their drinking holes seriously over there! Dead serious. The bloke apparently got himself murdered. Why? Because he messed up the walls of the pub, put a little bit of graffiti on there. Can't you picture it? The man is tanked to the gills in his favourite shebeen and he's doin' some thinkin', and he says to Pat and Mike at the bar, 'Sure, this place could use a coat of paint, sure it could! What do youse all think of that?' But the other boozehounds, they don't want the place painted. They like it just the way it is. Don't be making changes to an Irishman's pub; you could get yourself killed. And that's what happened to this guy. He stumbles out of the pub, decides to do a bit of a paint job himself, puts a message on the place for the rest of them, shag the lot of them, and they kill him for it! Word is, the coppers over there think it's one of the pub regulars that done him in. I been there, I can believe it! But it's not as bad as it sounds. If it's like every other Oirish pub I've ever been in, there was probably a priest or two on the premises supplementing their meagre allowance of communion wine, so maybe Father O'Toole was on hand to answer the victim's roaring before he breathed his last!

"And the Eyetalians. Death is big on their agenda too. Ever see the old crones all in black? You see one of them coming, it's-a lights out, Tony! Well, the news out of Sicily today is that —"

Finn snapped the tape off. "Fuckin' maggot!"

Frank Fanning was outraged. "They'll be voting him in as prime minister next. That little Tan bastard is just saying what they all think: the Irish sit around all day and drink till they're spiflicated!"

If anyone thought this was an odd remark from one of Dublin's most renowned pintmen, someone who sat in a pub every afternoon and evening of his life, pouring Guinness down his throat and getting spiflicated himself, nobody let on.

A couple of other men looked ready to punch somebody in the mouth. An Irish pub was no place to be calling the Irish down as drunks. Jimmy O'Hearn looked perturbed. Tim Shanahan, too, looked unhappy. The priest in him, perhaps, taking umbrage at the callous way a man's death had been turned into fodder for the television audience.

Eddie Madigan, though, seemed to find it all rather droll. "If youse think the man is full of shite about us, stand up for your principles: take the pledge! Go off with the monks and come back cured." He raised his pint and downed it. "A refill for this Paddy, my good man, or may yeh die roarin' for a priest! Not a problem in this place, though, Finn. Fathers Shanahan and O'Flaherty are on permanent assignment here, and I believe I saw your nephew, Father Burke, offering the sacraments behind the bar not long ago."

Finn belted the video machine and grabbed the tape when it came out. He shoved it at Blair McCrum without a word and busied himself behind the bar. McCrum moved off to a table near the window, where he could survey the comings and goings in the street.

Michael

The admittedly daffy notion to expand the investigation beyond the Irish Sea got a boost early Monday afternoon, when Monty called Michael with another bit of information about the shyster, Carey Gilbert.

"I was thinking again about the English lawyer."

"Oh, yes. You found out he had left the country and had not been heard from again."

"Right. But I wondered whether he had set up shop somewhere else."

"Why he'd ever have to work again, I don't know. He could be living like a lord off his ill-gotten gains. If he's still among the living!"

"Well, his name didn't come up as a partner in any law firm. But I looked at the directories listing practising lawyers in the Commonwealth and the United States. There are two lawyers named Carey Gilbert. By a process of elimination, I finally tracked our Carey down. Alive and well and working in Toronto."

Relief descended upon Michael. The lawyer hadn't been murdered after all. Of course he hadn't. Michael scolded himself for letting his imagination get the better of him. "He's in Canada?"

"Yes. He's an associate in a large firm on Bay Street."

"An associate."

"Right. Not, or not yet, a partner in the firm."

"Hiding his light under a bushel perhaps."

"Perhaps. But why don't you ask him yourself?"

"What? Call him, you mean?"

"Hop on the boat and go see him."

"Boat to where?"

"Old Blighty. He's visiting his mum, in a place called Huntingdon, for a bit of a holiday. I called his firm, and his secretary told me that much. Didn't give me the address or number, of course, but if the mother is Mrs. Gilbert, you may be able to smoke him out. Better not leave it too long, though; he's due back in Toronto on August eighth. This is what? The third."

"Can't leave today though! And it takes the better part of a day to get there. But what do you think, Monty? Are you really saying I should go see him, or are you just winding me up?"

"If you want my honest opinion, I'd strongly advise you to stay out of it, Mike. If this guy is a shyster, a fraud artist, a crook, you're not going to get anything out of him, so what could you possibly gain by confronting him? It sounds to me as if you've gone as far as you can go with this. We know he wasn't murdered. I commend you on your investigative powers, Sergeant, but it might be time to close the file and move on to your next case."

Brennan

"Shall I affect a regional dialect?" the MacNeil asked her fellow conspirators in a very creditable posh British accent.

"Perfect," Brennan replied. "Go ahead."

They had all gathered in Brennan's room Monday afternoon for the phone call to the questionably existent Abigail in London.

MacNeil spent a few minutes on the line obtaining the number of the Public Record Office. Then she made her call. "Good afternoon. I'm hoping to reach a person who assisted me some years ago in your office."

"Good move," Monty whispered, "checking to see if she was there years ago."

MacNeil continued, "I believe her name was Abigail, though I'm not absolutely certain of that. Lovely. Thank you." She gave her co-conspirators a thumbs-up.

Michael said, "She exists!" Then, concerned, "What's Maura going to say?"

"Have no fear, Michael," Brennan assured him. "She's never at a loss for words."

They fell silent and gave their full attention to the telephone.

"Yes? Abigail? I don't know whether you'll remember me or not. My name is Blythe Badgely-Venables."

Brennan had to make a conscious effort not to snort with laughter.

"Rather a mouthful, I know, and you may not recall the name. But perhaps you'll have some recollection of the assistance you afforded me. It would have been four or five years ago. I was inquiring about a man my grandfather had in his employ. Did work about the grounds. Simple sort of fellow by the sound of it, not all there. Sad. Collins was his name."

Brennan smiled across the room at poor Collins.

"There was a scandal. Something to do with the animals, something ghastly, well, the less said the better. And the poor devil had to be dismissed. Those were harsher times, and I've always wondered what became of him. He had a cottage full of children. But pardon me for running on. I had asked you back then about the poorhouse records. Does any of this sound familiar? No? Well, of course, why should it? I can only imagine the number of requests you get in the run of a week. What's that? It was in, uh, Staffordshire. Oh! Blurton, did you say? Splendid! I'll look into it. Thank you so much, Abigail. Cheerio!"

She hung up and faced the men in triumph. Retaining her British speech patterns, she announced, "Abigail Howard is alive and well and working in the Public Record Office and was doing so five years ago. And Collins," she added, giving him a pitying look, "you might find records of your family's unfortunate stay in the Blurton Poorhouse. Lovely word, isn't it? Blurton. Suits you to a T, I daresay."

Brennan began the applause, and everyone joined in.

"Well done, Blythe!" he enthused in an accent matching hers. "Smashing performance!"

"Now what?" she said in her normal voice.

"After all that, we can hardly just leave her there," said Michael. "She's a resource waiting to be tapped. Now that we know she's real, we may have to give some credit to Motor Mouth McCrum for having at least part of the story right. I say we go over and meet her," he urged them.

"We can't gang up on her," MacNeil warned. "One or two of you go, and see what you can find out. And you'll need a cover story."

"I don't suppose," Brennan said, "that she'll fall for Collins getting released from Blurton at this late date."

"I'd say not. She sounded very bright, very precise, and well-spoken."

"Did she sound like a temptress?" Monty asked.

"Not to me, but then, who knows what wiles she'll use on you lot?"

"All right," Monty said, "Brennan and Michael —"

"Oh, not me, Monty," Michael demurred. "If there's a cover story,

I'd never be able to pull it off. I'm not a good liar at all."

"We believe you, Mike," Brennan said.

"Okay. Monty and Brennan go as plumber and seducer, or in some other capacity. You guys figure it out."

"Here's the story," Monty declared. "And it only requires Brennan. Two of us would look as if we're tag-teaming her. Brennan goes in dressed, not as a lounge lizard but as a plainclothes detective." He turned to Michael. "Are you sure you want to duck this assignment, Sergeant O'Flaherty?"

"It pains me to admit it, but I'm sure. Besides, I think she'd suspect I'm a few years past retirement age for a copper. We'll unleash Brennan on her. If she gets out of line, as she may have done with Madigan, Brennan has a more intimidating persona than I could ever work up myself!"

"And," MacNeil put in, "if she tries her feminine wiles on him, Father Burke will be immune to all that, saintly priest of God that he is. That's why we can't send Monty. He'd only lie down on the job."

"You might be surprised to hear that a few young ladies have given old Monty the eye over here, and I have been a model of decorum."

"You're right. I would be surprised. But let's get on with the program. What is Brennan going to say to Abigail?"

"Are you people daft?" Brennan remonstrated.

Monty ignored him. "He's going to say he's an inspector with the Dublin police, the Garda Síochána. How about Detective Inspector Jack McGuire?"

"Yes!" MacNeil concurred. "Put him in a trench coat, stick a fedora on his head and a cigarette in his mouth, and he's definitely a Jack McGuire."

"And he's investigating Edward Madigan on another matter. A sensitive matter but not an international one. We don't want her running to the authorities over there if we can help it. How about this? Madigan is being investigated for a series of incidents that took place over a period of several years in the mid- to late 1980s. We have heard that he may have been out of the country, that is, in England, at the time of one of these episodes. Her name, and that of the Public Record Office, came up in the investigation. We're trying to determine exactly where he was at that time. The whole point is to get her talking about him, see if we can find out what happened, if anything.

Think you can handle that, Burke?"

"Do I get to take Motor Mouth McCrum by the throat and squeeze if all this turns out to be for nothing? Which I suspect it will?"

"The witness is being unresponsive, My Lord. Please answer the question."

"Let me answer your question this way: I don't think there will be anything to handle, and I'll be out of there in five minutes. The reason I'm willing to take part in this absurd little pantomime is that my sister is in London this week, and I'll have a visit with her."

"Brigid?" Maura asked.

"Maire, better known as Molly."

"Where does she come in the family? She's the oldest, isn't she?"

"That's right. She teaches history at the University of London but has been in Monserrat all summer doing research."

"Remind me to put in for a sabbatical studying the legal system in Monserrat when I get home," Maura said. "She's obviously got a good thing going."

"True enough," Brennan agreed. "Now she's home in London for a few days, so I'll have a night on the town with her."

Michael

Michael caught up on all the latest news when he dropped in to Christy's early Monday evening. He knew of course all about the vandal's body being discovered, knew that the amateur investigation Brennan was conducting with Michael's assistance had become a murder investigation, and that he and Brennan were way out of their league. The Garda Síochána were on the job. But Michael had had a little chat with Brennan about it all. Brennan's understanding of his uncle's wishes in the matter was that, whatever was behind the graffiti and the murder, Finn wanted to know about it before the police did. So, in that way at least, nothing had changed. One of the things that piqued Michael's interest was the report that the guards had been spotted in the Bleeding Horse. The way he heard it, they went in looking for someone but did not ask anyone where the person was. A sensitive matter? Maybe, maybe not. It could be something minor or routine. But Michael knew one of the regulars at the Bleeding Horse, so why not stop in for a casual visit and do a little probing? He looked at his watch. Six-fifteen. He knew Bill McAvity worked during the day at his auto repair shop and arrived at the pub after that. Michael decided to take a walk across the Liffey to the Southside.

The barman at the Bleeding Horse recognized Michael and nodded when he entered the pub. Michael looked around, but McAvity was not in his usual spot. Delayed at work, perhaps. Michael sat at the bar and ordered a pint of Smithwick's, which he knew was brewed on the property of a Franciscan abbey in Kilkenny. Wouldn't that be a nice sideline to develop back home at St. Bernadette's! He drank his pint slowly, nursed it so to speak, while he waited for Nurse McAvity to make his appointed rounds. But by seven forty-five there was no sign of him. Michael asked the barman whether Bill had been in. No, he had not. Michael thanked him and went on his way.

He took a turn in the confessional at the Aughrim Street church when he got back to Stoneybatter. A smattering of penitents came and went, absolved of the minor transgressions they believed had besmirched their immortal souls. Some of the words, deeds, thoughts, and omissions reported were so mild that even Michael, with his overdeveloped conscience, would not have taken the trouble to confess them. But then came the Dark Lady of Drimnagh. She was a single mother who got caught peddling drugs and went to jail. Her four children were put in foster care as a result. The day she was released on parole, she went on a bender and got picked up for disturbing the peace. This was a breach of her parole, so she went back in the slammer. When she got out the next time, she attended a meeting with her social worker to arrange the return of her children to her council flat. She left the meeting to walk home and get the place ready for the return of her family, but she stopped into her local, met an old boyfriend, got drunk with him, and they got into a row. She belted him in the eye, and he hit her back, knocking out a front tooth. She stumbled away, spotted a car with its engine running and nobody in it, hopped in, and stole it. Inevitably — it was inevitable to Michael, if not to her — she got stopped by the gardaí and was charged with theft and with drink driving. When she finally served all her time and was reunited with her children, she struck one of them in anger, and the child fell down the stairs; the woman was charged with assault, and the whole cycle started up again. The only surprise to Michael was her presence in the confession box, her apparently sincere craving for forgiveness. In addition to his spiritual guidance, he urged her to seek help and offered a number of suggestions.

Nobody came into the confessional after the Dark Lady left. Michael wondered, as he always did at times like this, how people could let their lives spiral so far out of control, how they kept making the same bad decisions over and over again. Every time there was a fork in the road, they chose the wrong way. Every single time. He said a prayer for the woman but, as strong as his faith in God was, his faith in the poor, sad penitent was fragile. God would rain down His grace upon her, but she was a creature with free will and, if Michael had learned anything about human nature in his long, long life, he knew she would keep taking the wrong fork in every road ahead of her until she died as she had lived, in squalor.

It was part of his job, his vocation, to hear such life stories, but that did not mean he enjoyed it. As he sat there in the silence, gazing into the darkness of the confessional, he thought of the people he had come to know at Christy Burke's. And he felt a twinge of guilt, more than a twinge. He felt guilty because he had probed into these men's lives, behind their backs, and had discovered things they found deeply painful. Oh, it was true that people slagged Father O'Flaherty, saying he was too curious for his own good. Nosy, in fact. But Michael was nosy only for good news, or at least harmless news. He always wanted to know who people were, who their families were, where they came from. He loved to hear there was a wedding in the offing and, all the more, a christening. And he enjoyed a puzzle and a mystery. Hence his nickname, Sergeant O'Flaherty. But he abhorred gossip. He most definitely did not want to hear that one of his parishioners was cheating on his wife, or on his income tax. Michael did not want to hear about "personality conflicts" in parish offices or on committees. Luckily, he and Brennan Burke were a match there. You'd have to pull Brennan's fingernails out with a pair of pliers to get a word out of him about other people, and even then maybe he'd keep his gob shut. How long had it taken for Brennan to reveal that Monty and Maura, his closest friends, were living separate and apart? Come to think of it, Michael had learned that from Monty himself, not from Brennan at all. So neither pastor nor priest was a gossip.

But back to the Christy Burke Four. Michael's part in the investigation had provided him with information he had no right to possess. He had learned their secrets even though, he realized, the regulars at the pub never said a mean-spirited word about one another; they spoke of the troubles each had suffered, but always in a sympathetic manner. They stuck up for each other, in fact, when that man Blair McCrum hissed his malicious gossip into their unwilling ears. They would not have been happy with the insinuations spray-painted on the pub walls but, try as he might, he could not imagine any of them dispatching the painter with two bullets in the back of his head.

Still, Michael had information about the Four, and he wasn't all that pleased with himself on account of it. Was there perhaps something he could do to make up for it, or to ease in some way the distress each of the men was feeling over the turn his life had taken? Michael had tried to step in and assist Tim Shanahan, but his plea to the archbishop had fallen on deaf ears. What about Frank Fanning? Frank had a lot to atone for. There was no way of knowing how he coped with the memories of his foiled plan to blow up the Apprentice Boys Memorial Hall in Derry. But it was clear that the man wasn't callous about what he had done to Donal Fegan; he had been making monthly visits to Fegan's bedside for eight years. That showed remorse. And that opened the door to repentance and absolution. And then there was Jimmy O'Hearn. What could Michael do for Jim? He thought back to his visit with Jim's sister, Sarah, in Donegal. The heartbreaking story of the family business being stolen by the unscrupulous lawyer. The beloved older brother, Rod, a broken man living in poverty in the Antipodes. Well, there it was: Michael knew what he could do for Jimmy and Sarah. He could bring their brother home. That was not beyond the realm of possibility, surely. There must be an economical flight, a seat sale at some time of the year, from — where was it, Australia or New Zealand? If necessary, Michael could pass the hat discreetly to raise money for

Rod O'Hearn's flight. Michael envisioned the reunion and smiled. That just left Eddie Madigan. A harder case, no question — a man who had been sacked from the Garda Síochána. Was it because of drugs, corruption, or some covert mission in London?

Chapter 15

Michael

Michael could scarcely believe what he was doing, even as he stood on deck with the wind whipping his hair and clothing, and scanned the Irish Sea all about him. He was standing next to Brennan on the ferry to England on the morning of Wednesday, August the fifth. Brennan was on his way to see his sister Molly and, with any luck, to interview the Mata Hari called Abigail at the Public Record Office in London. Michael would like to have accompanied Brennan to London so he could meet Molly — they had enjoyed friendly chats on the telephone a few times when she had called Brennan at the rectory back home — but that would have to wait; Michael had business to attend to in Cambridgeshire.

Michael's cover story for the trip was that he thought it would be fun to accompany Brennan on the ship to England and have a little look around. He'd always wanted to see Cambridge, so they would part company when they got onto English soil. They would meet up and catch the ferry back on Friday. But Michael had a hidden agenda. He intended to have a word with the infamous lawyer Carey Gilbert

287

in the hope of obtaining information that might bring the O'Hearn family back together again. If he could accomplish this, at least one good thing would have come out of all the inquiries into the lives of his drinking companions at Christy Burke's.

Michael put the investigation out of his mind for the duration of the ocean voyage and the train ride through Wales, with its green hills and valleys and castles. His first stop, after a series of train connections, was Huntingdon, Cambridgeshire. It was a lovely English town with beautiful old stone buildings that looked mellow and timeless in the honey-toned light of evening. He took a little stroll around the town centre, then checked into his hotel, the George. There was a bit of an awkward moment when the man at the desk began to wax eloquent about the town's historic link to Oliver Cromwell and the various Cromwell sites Michael could visit. Did Michael know the hotel had once been the home of Cromwell's grandfather? No, he did not. Something in Michael's expression or tone of voice, or perhaps it was the Irish-tinged accent, caused the man to falter in the midst of his Cromwellian oration, and he handed Michael his key and directed him to his room. Why, Michael wondered, would anyone promote the Puritan Cromwell to an Irishman, when that same Cromwell and his army had landed in Ireland for the purpose of putting down a rebellion, massacred thousands of Irish men, women, and even children, had singled out Catholic priests for slaughter, had destroyed churches and confiscated the lands of Irish Catholics and turned them over to Protestants? And then called his actions "the righteous judgment of God on these barbarous wretches"! Well, Michael didn't want to start the war all over again. There was nothing for it now but to go to his room, get some sleep, and pursue his inquiries in the morning. Not until he headed out of his room the next morning did he notice there was a portrait of the old war criminal facing him from across the corridor!

But he had a pleasant night and awoke refreshed. He had a shower, donned his clerical clothing, and enjoyed a filling breakfast. The morning staff were more than happy to accommodate his requests for a telephone directory and a town map, and it didn't take him long to find the address of Mrs. Augusta Gilbert. It was only a short walk from the hotel, and Michael was soon at the door of the small, immaculately kept house of the Gilbert family.

He rang the bell and waited for Mrs. Gilbert to answer. Instead, when the door opened, he found himself dwarfed by a man who was about six and a half feet tall and weighed probably two hundred twenty pounds. He had short, dark, curly hair, going grey, and a pair of fashionable eyeglasses.

"Oh! I was expecting Mrs. Gilbert," said Michael.

"Sorry. My mother is over at the vicarage. Is there anything I can help you with?"

"Em, you would be . . ."

"I'm Carey."

"Ah. Well, it really is you I came to visit."

The man looked perplexed, as well he might.

"What I mean is, I looked up your mother's address — or I hoped it was your mother — with the goal of finding you through her. Anyway, here I am."

"You want to see me? Well, please come in then."

He stood aside and let Michael enter the house, then directed him to a comfortable-looking front room and bade him sit.

"Tea, Father, um . . ."

"Oh, I'm sorry. My name is O'Flaherty, Michael O'Flaherty." He would have loved a cup of tea, but he could hardly accept the hospitality of the man he was about to confront with his crimes against the O'Hearns. "I'll decline the tea, thank you. I won't be staying long."

"Very well. How may I help you, Father O'Flaherty?"

"I am here as a friend of Mrs. Sarah Duffy, formerly Sarah O'Hearn. I believe you know the family." The lawyer's expression was as bland as if Michael had commented on the rose garden outside. "They are understandably concerned that they have lost contact with their brother Rod. I don't believe they ever saw him again after the boat company . . . changed ownership."

The reference to the boat company had no apparent effect on the lawyer; his expression was unreadable. Well, it would be, wouldn't it? How many stories had Monty Collins recounted of calamities in the courtroom, when Monty had to maintain an unruffled appearance even while his case was falling apart in front of him? Why would this fellow be any different? And Gilbert had had years to perfect a look of innocence to mask any guilt he might have felt about swindling a family out of the business it had built and nurtured through five generations. Guilt? He probably didn't feel an inkling of remorse.

Well, Michael was not about to let it go. "The boat business, O'Hearn Yacht Company, was a very successful and profitable venture, as I understand it."

"Oh, it was indeed. Still is. More so now, of course, with American capital behind it."

The gall of the man! "It's a shame, isn't it, that the O'Hearns are out of it now?"

"It is, I suppose. But with the brother's problems, it seemed the only thing to do at the time."

"The brother's problems?"

"Yes, the fact that he was mentally incompetent. Well, I expect you know all about that."

What was Gilbert talking about? Was this how he had covered up his deed? By painting the victim of his scam as mentally incompetent? Wherever Rod O'Hearn was, did he know that his former lawyer, who had cheated him out of the family business, was also slandering him and calling him incompetent?

"Are you saying, Mr. Gilbert, that Rod O'Hearn was not competent to manage his affairs, and that is why —"

"No, no, you've got the names mixed up, Father. Not Rod. James of course is the brother who is mentally incompetent. He lives in Dublin, I believe."

"James. Jimmy."

"Oh, you're acquainted with him? So I guess you know what I mean."

Michael stared at the lawyer. Jimmy O'Hearn was no more incompetent than was Michael O'Flaherty himself.

"And the brother-in-law," Gilbert continued. "That would be the sister in Donegal . . . what was her name?"

"Sarah."

"Right. Sarah's husband. With his history, Rod didn't see he had much choice in the matter."

Michael was at sea. "Her husband?"

"Well, you know. Bit of a dodgy character. Criminal history and all that."

No, Michael didn't know. What was this man talking about? The look he gave Michael was shaded with suspicion.

The lawyer said, "I'm surprised you don't know all this, Father, since you say you're a friend of the family. I fear I've said too much. And I'm asking myself whether there's something else motivating this visit."

Michael felt he had nothing to lose at that point. "I'm here because the O'Hearn family was defrauded of its rightful ownership of the O'Hearn Yacht Company. Nothing can be done about that now. But at the very least I would like to help bring about a family reunion. In fact, I'll be looking for contributions towards poor Rod's airfare so he can visit his brother and sisters in Ireland. Naturally, I won't be asking *you* to contribute to the fund."

Carey Gilbert was looking at Michael in open astonishment. "Poor Rod? Is that what you said, Father? You think Roderick O'Hearn can't afford a plane ticket back to Ireland?"

"Well, I understand he was never the same after being cheated out of —"

"What's this about being cheated? I'll grant you this much: Rod was never the same after selling the boat business. And glad of it. But he'd have no trouble paying his way to Ireland if he had a mind to go there. Probably has his own Lear jet, for all I know." Gilbert peered at Michael. "You didn't know any of this, did you? Somebody has sold you a bill of goods, by the sound of things."

There was no point in trying to bluff it out. Michael sat there, mortified. He had blundered into this with the story all wrong. It served him right to be humiliated in front of this man. Quietly, he asked, "What's the real story, Mr. Gilbert?"

"Rod O'Hearn retained me to handle the sale of the yacht company to American investors for what was then, and would be now, a very, very good price. Rod's father had left the company to his two sons. Not to the daughters. We wouldn't do things that way now, but the older generation, well, that's how things were done. Rod showed me documents from the Republic of Ireland certifying that his brother, James O'Hearn, had been declared mentally incompetent. Rod had a power of attorney from James, which gave Rod authority to manage James's affairs and to sign in his name. Rod described in considerable detail the criminal history of his brother-in-law in Donegal, who was a con artist and a small-time crook, and he was afraid this fellow would try to make trouble for the company, for the family. Rod was not willing to continue trying to operate the company with these people cocking things up all the time. The company was Rod's by that time, to do with as he wished. He sold it to the U.S. consortium and made a fortune in doing so. How he compensated his siblings, if he did, was up to him. Rod O'Hearn walked away a very wealthy man. Last I heard he was well set up in New Zealand, living like a country squire. I have not heard from him, or about him, for many years."

Michael sat there, gripping the arms of his chair. There was no question in his mind that the lawyer was telling the truth. It was Rod O'Hearn, not this lawyer, who had made a bundle by stealing the boat business from his family. And he had done so by portraying his brother as mentally unfit and his sister's husband as a crook. Jimmy O'Hearn was an alcoholic, but Michael had never detected anything wrong with his mental capacities beyond that. And Michael had met Sarah's husband, Niall, in Donegal. He was a music instructor who went out of his way to provide free lessons to a child who could not afford to pay. His wife worked in a pub. They lived in a little house that needed work, and they drove an old banger of a car that should be on the scrap heap; clearly they could not scrape together the money for repairs. Niall Duffy was not a con man. Jimmy and Sarah adored their older brother and had spent all these years fretting over his well-being. When in fact he was doing very well for himself, and not sharing a bit of his good fortune with his family. Well, how could he? He had been putting on the poormouth all these years to hide the fact that he had stolen from them their rightful inheritance.

Michael told Gilbert what he knew about Jimmy O'Hearn and Niall Duffy. Should he turn around and tell Jim and Sarah how their beloved big brother had betrayed them? They had a right to know. But was there any point in breaking their hearts with the news? Would they be any better off? Would they be able to confront their brother and demand their share of the fortune? Did they have any legal grounds for doing so? Michael had no idea, and he was not about to prevail upon Carey Gilbert for legal advice! Gilbert didn't owe anyone a thing, and Michael owed him an abject apology.

"Mr. Gilbert, you have been the soul of patience with me today. I am most undeserving of your kindness. I came here today convinced that it was you who had defrauded the O'Hearns of their livelihood."

"Me?" Gilbert stared at him wide-eyed.

"I'm so very sorry. That is what the family believes. That is the story Rod spun for them to cover his own shameless deeds. I thought that's why you left England. Please accept my apology for thinking ill of you and confronting you in your mother's home today."

"No, no, it's not your fault, obviously. I'm reeling from what you've told me. Roderick obviously set me up, too, with falsified papers from Ireland and a series of lies to mask what he was doing. The sale of the company to the Americans was separate from all that; it was in Roderick's name, and so the purchasers have nothing to answer for. I have to make that point. But what he did to his family in order to get to that stage, well, he'll have to answer to them, I guess. No wonder he never set foot in Ireland again! As for me, I immigrated to Canada because I met a Canadian woman, married her, and decided to try life in her hometown. Somebody's gone into hiding, but it isn't me!"

Brennan

Brennan enjoyed his train trip through the magnificent countryside of Wales and England and wondered what the hell he was doing, hunting down Abigail Howard at the Public Record Office. The train was held up for nearly a full hour outside Euston station. The whispers throughout the railcar suggested the station had been evacuated because of a bomb scare; the whispers further suggested this was a common occurrence. Fine irony there, if the thing blew up. "Son of well-known Irish Republican family . . ." Never mind all that. The train rolled in, Euston station was still standing, and Brennan left the station for the short walk to the Harlingford Hotel in Bloomsbury, where he had stayed on occasion before while en route to or from Ireland. He registered at the desk, took his things to his room, washed up and changed his clothes, and then went out and across Marchmont Street to see whether Judd Books was open. He was in luck. As always when in London, he emerged from the bookshop with two armloads of books. He dropped them off in his room and headed out to the North Sea Fish Restaurant for supper.

The next afternoon, dressed in a pair of grey pants, a white shirt, and a navy sports coat — no trench coat, no fedora — he set out for the Public Record Office. He walked to the Russell Square tube station, went as far as Hammersmith and changed lines, and was reminded yet again how big a city London was when he noted that it took more than half an hour to get from central London to his stop at Kew Gardens. He emerged from the station, consulted his notes, and walked from there to the gigantic modern pavilion on the Thames that was the Public Record Office. The lower two floors were of glass; the three upper floors had only a thin line of glass running along the concrete walls, to keep the sun off the documents, Brennan supposed. He asked at the desk for Abigail Howard. There was no intake of breath, avoidance of eye contact, or suspicious stare; Miss Howard would be with him in a moment.

Abigail appeared at first glance to be a little girl, but a closer look suggested she was in her early thirties. She had wavy brown hair pulled up in clips at the sides, small brown eyes, and a pale, thin face. Brennan had the urge to march her out of the office for a good, hearty pub meal. But he was there to seek help, not to offer it. They found seats in one of the large, brightly lit reading rooms on the first floor.

Brennan looked around him at all the heads bent over papers. "British history. It's all here, I expect," he said.

"It's all here," Abigail agreed in a plummy English accent. "From the Domesday Book, our first survey in 1086, right up to the present day. We have sixty-nine miles of shelving up there." She raised her eyes to the ceiling. "People come from everywhere to do research. Fascinating documents on file here, as you might imagine."

"Yet there are some things the public is not allowed to see."

"Precisely. Some things they will never see; some things are embargoed till well into the future."

"Till everyone who might be implicated is dead."

"That's one reason. Political sensitivities too."

"Right."

Brennan cast his mind over the cover story Monty had devised for him: he was Detective Inspector Jack McGuire, investigating a series of sensitive incidents involving Eddie Madigan, and the police had received information that Madigan may have been in England at the time of one or more of the incidents. He, McGuire, had been assigned . . .

He smiled at the young woman across the table. "My name is Brennan Burke. My uncle has a pub in Dublin, and the pub has been targeted with a series of disturbing messages. It may remain a fairly harmless case of vandalism, or it may escalate to something more serious. We don't know."

"A pub. I don't quite see how I can help you, Mr. Burke."

"We think the messages are aimed at one of the regular patrons there, a man who got into a spot of trouble here in your office. There's a story going around about this fellow, and your name came up."

She looked away from him. A party of researchers or perhaps tourists entered the reading room, led by a stunning young woman, tall and dark-haired. She spoke to the group quietly as she pointed out the amenities. She would have been more suited than little Abigail to playing the role of temptress. But Mr. Burke was not distracted. He had eyes and ears only for Abigail Howard.

"What we heard was that four or five years ago this man from Dublin got into some difficulties here."

It was clear from the expression on her face that Abigail knew perfectly well what he was talking about. Good, for two reasons. One, Brennan might not be wasting his time after all. And two, he wouldn't have to mention Special Branch and then not be able to follow up with a sensible explanation.

"I assume you're talking about David. I haven't had many experiences in which foreign men have come into the office and attempted to suborn me in the exercise of my duties."

"Right. That pretty well confirms what we heard about David, that he made an effort to . . . suborn you, as you said." Of course Brennan had no idea what "David" had done.

"Force me, more like. Seduce me, cajole me, coerce me, in that order." Small and frail she might appear, but Brennan sensed a steely character underneath.

"Could you tell me a bit about it, Abigail?"

"I'd be more than happy to. I have no loyalty to *him*, for reasons that will become obvious. And if there are messages directed at him in some drinking hole, well, good. I hope the story gets round. Serves him right. Though I have to say I'm a little surprised to hear that this would be a mark against him in a Dublin pub; it's a wonder they haven't raised a monument to him, or written a drinking song to commemorate his deeds. I'm sorry if that sounds offensive, Mr. Burke."

Brennan waved it off. "Tell me."

"It happened just after I began working here. He started coming in, the man I knew as David Stephens, which I later realized was not his real name. I still don't know what his real name was. But I expect you do."

She waited, but Brennan did not enlighten her. He was not about to inform on Madigan by name — no informers in the Burke family — so he waited her out.

After a few seconds, she resumed her story. "He came in requesting documents about India."

"India."

"India, Africa, then Scotland and Wales."

"What was he trying to do with all of that?"

"Throw us off the scent, that's what."

"I see."

"His real interest, as if I mightn't have guessed from the accent, was Ireland. But no, I shouldn't say that. We have people from all over the world here, to see papers on the most arcane subjects, not necessarily about their home countries. Scholars researching any number of subjects. So I had no reason really to doubt that he was pursuing studies relating to these other places. David always carried a little case with him, with pens, notebooks, and that sort of thing. He read and jotted down notes. Completely immersed in his work. Except when he would take a cigarette break. In addition to his research," she said, making a face, "he also expressed an interest in me."

"Ah."

"I was new on the job, young . . . and unattached, which he was quick to suss out. He was older, and more experienced in these matters. He offered to treat me at the coffee shop, so I said yes. A couple of times. And I joined him on the odd smoke break. It was funny. He had a lighter that showed Sir Winston Churchill smoking his cigar; when you turned the lighter a certain way, the cigar appeared to burst into flames, but Sir Winston's expression didn't change a bit. Of course it seemed so much wittier because I was smitten with David." She pressed her lips together and looked down. "Young and foolish."

"How did he treat you on those occasions?"

"Wonderfully, at the start. And why wouldn't he be the soul of consideration, when he was after something?"

"Sure, I see what you mean."

"He was handsome in a way. Not a cinematic type, but attractive in sort of a rough-and-ready way, I guess I'd say. And he had some riveting tales to tell, about fighting the IRA in Ulster. Mad, bad, and dangerous to know!"

She stopped speaking when the stunning brunette stopped by the table and told her some of the staff were meeting after work for a drink; would she like to come along? Yes, she would. Then she got back on track.

"One day, he asked me out to lunch. We talked about my work. He seemed to be fascinated by the enormous collections of papers we had, priceless documents of great value. He asked what was kept where, that sort of thing. What about records that were still embargoed, papers dealing, for instance, with our relations with the Irish early in the century? The Anglo-Irish War, he meant, 1919 to 1921. Well, I gave him a general idea of where things were. Why not? It's not as if he could get at them! They're not for release, and we don't have people roaming through those collections. Everything in the building is secured. Then the conversation turned more personal. He talked about himself and asked lots of questions about me. Getting to know each other, you know how it is." She peered at Brennan, then looked down at the table. "He asked about my flat, and I said it was a tiny little place nearby, and that I could walk to work. He leaned towards me and put his hand over mine. 'Why don't we go there?' he said. 'What? Now?' I asked him. And he said he'd like to see it; it would allow him to know me better, and all that rot. I'm embarrassed to say I fell for it. So we left the restaurant and walked to my flat. He took my hand as we walked. I saw one of the other girls in the neighbourhood and she gave me the eye, and I have to admit I was chuffed to be seen with him, an older man taking an interest, that sort of thing. Well, we got to my flat and I showed him around, which took all of thirty seconds, it's so small, and that's when he really started to work on me."

Brennan kept quiet and waited for her to continue.

"He had one thing on his mind," she asserted.

Brennan nodded as if to say *Boys will be boys.*

"He pulled me close to him and kissed me . . ."

"Mmm-hmm."

"Only, I pulled away. I didn't want it to happen then, not when I knew I would be late going back to work and would be distracted about that. But more than that, it wasn't a good time . . . for personal reasons."

Brennan had no need to hear those reasons.

But Abigail went on with her story. "You're going to laugh. But the problem was what I had on. Just workaday clothes and, well, a pair of granny bloomers, great cotton things that were clean, of course, but grey from repeated washing. Well, enough said; it was not the way I had envisioned the seduction scene with me and David. If I'd known, I'd have made a bit more of an effort with my hair and makeup and underthings and all that. You know."

"Sure. I know."

"So I put him off. But he wasn't deterred. Oh, he backed off physically but he spoke to me in very affectionate terms. And then he got to the point. He wondered if he and I could stay on in the office some evening so he could carry out his researches without being rushed. If I could just get him into the room with the Anglo-Irish records . . . my presence in the room would guarantee that nothing would go astray. But no, I most certainly could not stay on after hours and sneak him into the room!"

Eddie Madigan had obviously underestimated Abigail Howard if he thought she would succumb to charm or threats, and place her career in jeopardy.

She continued, "His reaction was almost one of panic, for lack of a better word. He tried to bribe me then, with money. Wouldn't I love a larger, more suitable flat? I could scarcely believe what was happening. When I rejected his every effort, he apologized, tried to mollify me, and finally left the flat with a promise to make up for the awkwardness he had caused." She was silent for a few seconds as she looked around the room. "Well, that didn't happen. There was no sign of him for two or three days, until he turned up again late one afternoon. He greeted me coolly, then sat and began reading, and I went about my duties. Just before closing time, he came to me and brought up the lunchtime fiasco and asked me to tell him straight out whether I was really interested in him or was just leading him on! If anyone had been doing any leading, it was him. And not for the reasons I might have been hoping for. I reminded him that he was the one who had insisted on coming to my flat. Anyway it escalated into an argument, and he stormed out! Threw his papers on the desk and left in a fit of pique."

"What sort of papers was he looking at that day?"

"I think they were about Scotland. Battle of Culloden, perhaps. Whatever they were, I dutifully refiled them and finished my work and went home. It was not till the following day that I found out what he'd been up to."

"And that was . . ."

"He hadn't really stormed out at all. He'd set the whole thing up, planning to cause a scene about our earlier encounter. Then he could pretend to be miffed about it, and stalk away. I wouldn't wonder where he was; I would *know* he had left the building in a huff. But in fact he hadn't stormed out in a fit of passion! He'd stayed on in the building, armed with the information he had managed to worm out of me before things went sour, the information about the records and where they were kept."

As Abigail told her story, Brennan tried to imagine the scene. Madigan hiding in the jacks until the office shut down for the day, peering out to see if the coast was clear, sneaking into the corridor, trying to find his way to the storage area where the sensitive Irish records were kept under embargo, looking over his shoulder to make sure he was not spotted by a security guard, feeling acutely anxious. Would he find the right area? Would he be able to get into the room? Would he be caught before he could steal the papers he wanted? Would an alarm go off? Was there any hope of escape? Abigail wasn't sure exactly what happened, but it seemed Madigan — "David" — tried to break into the storage area with some kind of housebreaking devices he had smuggled in with his pens and notebooks. So there's Madigan fumbling at the door with his burglary tools, frustrated and fearful, in a lather of sweat, and suddenly an alarm shrieks and puts the heart crossways in him and jolts him into the air.

"I don't know what happened after that. I believe he was arrested, but I don't think there was a court case. As far as I know, some kind of arrangement was made. Somebody said they traded him for a criminal or a terrorist in Ireland who was wanted over here. At any rate, he was bundled out of the country. Back to Ireland. *They* would probably love to get their own hands on those papers. Maybe they sent him over to do their dirty work!"

"Who?"

"Who knows? Their Secret Service? Special Branch? That lot in Ulster? Even the IRA, for all I know! I don't know who he really was, and I can't say I care. What I do care about is that we have a very effective security system in place here, and the system worked. We caught the bastard!"

✝

Mirabile dictu! The excursion to the Public Record Office had not been a wasted effort after all. Brennan had met with success, most unexpectedly; he would have to think it all through. Later. He put it out of his mind for the rest of the afternoon, as he walked around London and took in the sights of the great city.

Now, as evening descended, he had a most pleasant event ahead of him: dinner with his sister Molly at her flat. He stopped in at his room, washed up a bit, called Molly on the phone, then made the short walk to her place in Gower Street. She was standing outside the enormous white stone and red brick building when he arrived. Molly was the eldest in the family, not quite two years older than Brennan, but the two of them could be mistaken for twins. They were both tall and had black hair with silver strands at the temples, dark eyes, though his were black and hers a deep blue, and similar features, including a typically Irish curve of the upper lip and a somewhat beaky nose. She broke into a big grin when she saw him approaching.

"Bren, my darling, it's pure bliss to see you!"

"Same," he said, kissing her cheek and enfolding her in his arms. He held her for a long time before releasing her.

"Come on up. I've got dinner on."

She led him up the stairs to her modest second-floor flat, with its tiny sitting room and kitchen, bright with the early-evening light coming through the west window. Her few bits of furniture had the patina of age, and the walls were fitted with bookshelves nearly up to the ceiling. She opened a press, pulled out a bottle of John Jameson, and poured them each a shot. She handed Brennan his and sat with her own in hand.

"You're welcome to stay over, as I told you on the phone, but I know you might find it a bit cramped. I took this place when Neville and I parted company. Close to the university, but space is at a premium."

"No, I'm perfectly content at the Harlingford. What are you cooking? It smells wonderful."

"A jolly old English fry-up. Organ meats and all that."

"I said it smells wonderful, not like an abattoir."

"Farfalle al sugo rustico."

"With lamb?"

"With lamb."

"Brilliant! Why don't I go out and get us a bottle of red?"

"No need. I have quite the wine cellar here, which boasts a couple of bottles of excellent plonk you brought here on your last trip."

"Oh?"

"You said a good Barolo should be allowed to age."

"Well! Bring it on." He looked around.

"It's in the cupboard under the sink. If I had the space for a wine cellar, or even for a decent wine rack, I'd have to pay two hundred pounds more a week!" She bent down, rummaged about, then produced the Barolo. She opened it, and left it on the counter to breathe.

"So," she said, when she got seated again, "wouldn't you know I'd be off on a field trip the summer you're on this side of the Atlantic? Otherwise, I'd have gone over to join you in Dublin."

"I know, but at least you're here now. How long will you be in London?"

"Just this week for a conference. Then I fly back to Monserrat for my research."

"How did you manage to snag that assignment?"

"Purely academic reasons. You've heard the expression 'publish or perish.' I'm due to produce another article. So I searched and searched for a topic that would connect Irish history with a tropical climate."

"I thought your area of expertise was women warriors in Ireland."

"Sure it is, from Queen Maeve to the Cumann na mBan and the IRA."

"Have they taken the struggle to the southern hemisphere for some reason?"

"Em, no, they haven't. So I've had to seek out new areas of study."

"What did you come up with?"

"Irish slavery in the Caribbean."

"Will you be studying us as slaves or slaveholders?"

"Both. Though, with respect to the former, the term 'servant' is preferred!"

"Well. That should prove interesting."

"It should. But if it doesn't, if I don't find anything new to say on the subject, who cares? I'll just shove my paper in a drawer. The point is to get me down there in the sun!"

"Good for you. You're enjoying it then."

"Immensely. Terry flew down to Monserrat to see me, and we lifted a few at the local guzzling den." Terry was their brother, an airline pilot who lived in New York. "We were nearly wetting ourselves when we got into the old family stories. You featured in many of them, having been the black sheep of the family for so long. Starting with your first day of school in the U.S.A. The new boy in class, right off the boat from Ireland. Remember the note the teacher sent home? You were doing geography, and Sister Mary Dolores asked you to read aloud. You did fine until you came to a certain lake in South America.

"'I can't say that,' you told her.

"And she said, 'It's pronounced Lake Titicaca.'

"'Like fuck it is!' exclaimed the little gurrier from Dublin.

"That was only the beginning of your career as the boy least likely ever to prostrate himself before the bishop and be ordained a priest. They didn't know what to make of you at the school; you looked and sang like an angel in the choir but you were such a little hellion. Well, really, that's still you, isn't it?"

"The subject of our conversation, I believe, was Monserrat."

"Right. Terry and I in the bar. Once he got oiled up, he started regaling the locals with all manner of tall tales about his adventures in the cockpit. He had them sitting there with their gobs hanging open in disbelief."

"And rightly so. Every word out of him past a certain point in the evening would have been a lie." Terry was renowned for his barroom bullshit.

"Yes, it was great gas. Now, how about you, sweetheart? How have you been?"

"Couldn't be better."

"Good. Although you'd say that even if you'd had three limbs lopped off in the morning. You're like that knight in the Monty Python movie. Everything with you is 'only a flesh wound.'"

"No flesh wounds here."

"What's the news in Dublin? Fill me in while I tend to my cooking."

Molly busied herself with oven and stove, plates and pans, as Brennan gave her a rundown of the summer's events. She was well aware of the missing preacher found dead in Carlingford Lough, and the eruptions of violence in the North as a result. Brennan had to hedge a bit on that. He was not about to reveal that he had seen the video of the man being executed by Desmond somebody in the presence of Clancy, nephew of the Bishop of Meath. Brennan would be forced to live with that secret for the rest of his life. The people of Northern Ireland and the United States, and sympathetic observers like Michael O'Flaherty, would be left wondering till Judgment Day who had killed the evangelist. Without anyone to put on trial, who would be made to bear the brunt of Protestant rage? Brennan was powerless in the matter. All he said to his sister was "I've heard there's a Dublin connection."

"Republicans of Dublin, take cover! Is there anybody in our family mixed up in this? I don't mean any of us would be so stupid as to snatch the man, but I hope there aren't any Burkean shadows flitting about behind the curtains."

Brennan hesitated for a moment, then said, "There may be a degree of Burkean knowledge after the fact. But, as far as I know, nothing more than that."

She waited for more, but he turned the conversation to the summer's other developments: the tank-and-barricade Mass, the graffiti and the Christy Burke Four, the Japanese land scheme and Finn's stint in the Joy.

"Can't you just take a nice, relaxing holiday, Bren? I'm sure you could use one."

"I'd probably be bored rigid."

"But all that carry-on in Dublin and the North . . . And the time you took a trip back to New York, our oul fellow got shot in the chest and nearly died."

"My good friend Monty made a similar observation about holidays spent with the Burkes. He was on hand for the New York debacle as well."

"And he's here for all this now?"

"'Fraid so."

"Whatever does he think of us?"

"What we've got going for us is that he's seen worse. He defends thieves and killers for a living. Defence lawyer."

"Maybe we don't look so bad compared to his clients."

"Well, there again, you may recall, I was one of his clients."

"Of course." She sighed, then stood up. "Let's eat. Give us a Latin grace before we start. Or maybe an exorcism to clear the room of all the dark shades that seem to have come amongst us in the twilight." He made the sign of the cross over her and over the offerings she had prepared, and said a prayer of thanksgiving in the ancient tongue before sitting down, whipping his napkin off the table and putting it in place on his lap, and digging in.

The pasta and lamb, served with a loaf of hard-crusted bread and a green salad, was brilliant, and so was the wine, and he told her so. They clinked their glasses and smiled at one another.

"Darling, tell me, how is life in Halifax? Are you enjoying it?"

"Very much."

"What is your church like? What music are you doing? You composed a Mass, and that went over well, I believe."

He spent the next few minutes, between bites of food and sips of wine, describing his life as a priest and choirmaster in Nova Scotia.

"Good. Work is going well. Now, what about friends? Do you have people to talk to, if you should ever feel the need to talk? Which I suspect would be a rare event."

"Amn't I talking to you?"

"You only see me once every two or three years. So let's hope you have somebody to fill that gap! As tough as you are, or make yourself out to be, Bren, you need other people in your life. It can't just be you and the Almighty."

"You say that as if the Almighty is less than all mighty, less than complete, and needs to be supplemented by earthly —"

"Go on out of that and answer my question. Tell me about your friends."

"Well, there's Michael O'Flaherty. You've spoken with him on the phone. Probably more frequently than you've spoken with me."

"You always seem to be out on the town when I call. Michael says, 'Yer man's at the Grafton Street Mission,' which, upon interrogating Michael, I discover is an institution called the Midtown Tavern."

"I minister to the drinking community there."

"You lead by example, I assume, Father. God bless you. So, there's Michael. A lovely man, if his telephone conversations are anything to go by."

"He is a lovely fellow. And in fact he was caught in a cleft stick coming over here."

"Here, meaning England?"

"Yes, he's here, but not in London. His dilemma is that he would love to meet you, but that would mean blowing the cover story he gave me about his reasons for the voyage to England in the first place. He would have me believe he's always wanted to explore Cambridgeshire. So I kept a straight face on me and went along with it. The man is incapable of deception."

"What is he really getting up to?"

"It has to do with this vandalism at Christy's. One of the pub regulars was swindled, or his family was, by an English lawyer. I suspect the lawyer is in Cambridgeshire somewhere, and Michael is on his trail."

What Brennan didn't say was that he had long held the suspicion that O'Flaherty had a bit of a crush on Molly, arising from their telephone chats; if Michael hadn't made a point of coming to London to meet her in the flesh, that suggested Kitty Curran had turned his head. All the Barolo in Europe wouldn't be enough to make him say that aloud.

"This graffiti business," Molly said, "wouldn't you think it's most likely a comment on Finn himself?"

"It's hard to avoid that suspicion, even though Finn dismisses it out of hand."

"That's Finn's version of events, but keep in mind he was so convincing that enough Japanese to fill an airliner took his word that they owned land in the Republic of Ireland."

"True. But, whatever the case, Michael O'Flaherty is keen to assist in the graffiti investigation, so I've left him to it. I'm sure whatever he learns here in the U.K. will be of no value — the lawyer is hardly going to confess to unethical or illegal conduct — so Michael will have missed meeting you for nothing."

"No worries. We'll make a point of meeting another time. And you told me a while back that he's your confessor. You were a little hesitant when you first arrived there from New York."

"It was just that Mike is so, well, innocent. I didn't want to disillusion him about his new curate."

"You're not a saint. How could you be? Michael's been around long enough to understand that."

"True. It's turned out fine. He's a wonderful priest and a very astute confessor."

"So, you have Michael as a friend. Who else?"

"Some of the other priests are mensches. Good company."

"And this Monty you mentioned. He's a good pal as well. So, you have some blokes to go about with. Now, what about women?"

"What about them?"

"Well, I hope your circle isn't limited to men. Do you have some women friends as well? And I don't mean a gaggle of church ladies who incessantly contrive to attract your attention and who worship the very soil on which you tread."

"You may rest assured that all of my acquaintances fall into the category of not worshipping me or my footsteps or the sacred ground over which I pass. That being said, there are a couple of women at the choir school, teachers, I'm friendly with. And, em . . ."

"Em, what?"

"There's the MacNeil."

"And that would be who? Head of a Scottish clan or something?"

"You could say that, I suppose. She's Monty's wife. Or, well . . ."

"Well what? She's Monty's wife, or she isn't. Which is it?"

"I've descended into gossip here." He picked up his glass of wine, drank it almost to the dregs, then pulled out a pack of cigarettes. He was about to light one, then remembered his manners; he looked to his sister for permission.

"Go ahead." She reached behind with her left arm and grasped a small plate, which she offered as an ashtray. Brennan lit up and inhaled a lungful of smoky relief.

Molly then took up where she had left off. "Brennan, identifying a person as someone's wife, or even ex-wife, if that is the case, hardly qualifies as vicious gossip. It is simply a fact. Neville is my ex-husband. So this couple . . ."

He could see her thinking, then coming to a realization about something.

"This is the couple you told me about on the phone that time. I called, and it was clear something was on your mind, and you gave voice to your frustration over your efforts to counsel a family of your acquaintance. You didn't name them, of course, being discreet as always; you implied that they were members of your parish."

"They are."

"But even then, I had the impression they were more to you than parishioners."

"Is that so?"

"Because halfway through your story, you departed from the standard priestly vocabulary and went on to describe the man as a stubborn fecking bonehead on whom God had wasted the gift of superior intelligence, because if he didn't have enough sense to appreciate what he had in the person of his wife, then he would lose her to some other man who would take the husband's place and be the luckiest man in Christendom, and then where would the husband be, and wouldn't it serve him right, the fecker!" Molly took a sip of wine and smiled at her brother. "Or words to that effect."

"I don't remember that."

"You remember everything."

"Your point?"

"I'm thinking this is your friend Monty that you were ranting about. You wouldn't have been that worked up about someone you barely knew. So, back to the subject of his wife. Your fudging about her status suggests your matchmaking efforts have not yet borne fruit."

"I'm still at it."

"Tell me about her. What's she like?"

Where to begin? He shrugged, and took another long drag of his cigarette.

"A nonentity, is she? A cipher? A bit of fluff? I thought you said she was your friend. You don't usually have time for vapid individuals about whom there is nothing to say."

"The MacNeil is a very strong personality, the farthest thing in the world from vapid or fluffy. She's got a tongue in her head that would slice through the right foreleg of your horse just as it was coming down the home stretch at Leopardstown, and you'd lose the house all over again."

"But there's more to her than that."

"Oh, yes. Great depths beneath all that armour."

"Sounds like somebody I know," she said, holding him in the gaze of her dark blue eyes.

Then she turned up the flames under him. "You know, Bren, at the time of that phone conversation I remember thinking there was a bit of a subtext to it. That you genuinely wanted what was best for this family, no question. But there also might have been an element of temptation, in the form of this woman whom you knew, living apart from her husband, and that the temptation would ease somewhat if he moved back in with her."

His sister could make a bonfire out of him right here in her kitchen and she wouldn't be able to force him into *that* sort of discussion.

"If you met this one, Molly, you wouldn't be able to imagine her tarting herself up as a temptress to lure a passing priest into her clutches."

"That's not what I meant, sweetheart. I was referring to your own state of mind. I'm not suggesting for a minute she's one of these people who comes to the door with her face newly painted, yet still happens to be in her filmy negligee, when you come calling."

"Unthinkable! If she could hear this conversation, she would have me reduced in thirty seconds to a quivering heap of gelatinous matter on the floor."

"Glad to hear it. You've met your match in her."

"On the day I was born, I met my match. In you!"

"Does she have a name?"

"Didn't I tell you her name?"

"No you didn't. You said the MacNeil. What's her name?"

"Maura."

"Perfect. I knew it wouldn't be Tiffany. Well, even though I had to pull it out of you, it comes as a relief to hear about this cast of characters in your life. Because I worry about you. You're a mystic and a man of God, you say a beautiful Mass and your music is brilliant, and the church is damn lucky to have you, and we're all proud of you. But I worry that you're too self-contained for your own good."

"And here I was thinking we already have a shrink in the family, and it's Paddy, not yourself."

"You're my little brother. And since you don't worry about yourself, or talk about your troubles, if you have any troubles, just as you would never admit to any pain when you'd get hurt and bloodied in your old Gaelic football days, and you just a wee boy at the time, and since you haven't changed one iota since that time —"

"Where's that sentence going? You lost me several *since*s ago."

"Don't change the subject, which is that you haven't changed since you were that hard-headed little scrapper in the streets of Dublin."

"My dear, nobody has changed as much as I have."

"Think so, do you?"

"Do you have another bottle of this?" he said, indicating the empty wine bottle.

"I rest my case. And no, I didn't have two bottles of that, but I do have a nice Chianti." She got up and found the wine, opened it, filled her brother's glass, and poured half a glass for herself.

"All right," Brennan announced, "I'm roasted and done. Now let's talk about you."

Molly told Brennan that her divorce from Neville would soon be finalized, that she had kicked him out of the house a couple of years earlier because she refused to allow anyone to treat her with so little consideration, and their son and daughter, who, as Brennan knew, were grown and living in Devon and Oxford, respectively, backed her up. Once Brennan was brought up to date on all of that, he and his sister went back to their childhood and relived old times until Brennan reluctantly parted from her at two in the morning, with a promise to take care of himself and all belonging to him, and returned to his hotel.

Chapter 16

Michael

Michael and Brennan met at the Holyhead ferry terminal on Friday and boarded the ship to Ireland. Brennan filled Michael in on his conversation with Abigail Howard. The incident at the Public Record Office had really occurred, even if not quite in the way Motor Mouth McCrum had reported it. Then Brennan asked how Michael's tour of Cambridgeshire had gone and, of course, Michael came clean and reported on the real reason for his visit. Brennan didn't seem surprised, but he was dismayed to hear that it was not the lawyer, but Rod O'Hearn himself, who had swindled the family. Michael did not know what to do with that knowledge. He would have to reflect on it.

But right now Michael was more interested in what he had just learned about Eddie Madigan. The ex-cop really had been drummed out of the Dublin police force following a disastrous attempt to break into the secret archives in London. The action was considered so serious that Madigan would rather be thought a crooked cop, taking payoffs from drug pushers, than have the truth get out. And his employer, the Garda Síochána, felt the same way. They were saved public embarrassment by making a deal with the British authorities to give up a criminal or a spy — someone they had in custody in Dublin. The exchange satisfied the British and allowed the Irish to keep the incident under wraps. What was in those records that prompted Madigan to take such desperate action?

Michael could puzzle over it till doomsday and be none the wiser. And he could hardly walk into the nearest garda station and ask the sergeant on duty about it. The only person Michael could think of to ask was Leo Killeen, who seemed to be in the know about many shadowy activities in and pertaining to Ireland. He would buttonhole Leo the next day and see what he could find out.

†

"I'm going to have a word with Leo," Michael told Brennan Saturday afternoon. They were sitting in Michael's room having a cup of tea.

"A word about what?"

"Madigan, if you'll be kind enough to excuse me for a minute."

"That's about all the time it will take for Leo to put the run to you."

"Maybe so, but I'll give it a try. Help yourself to some more tea."

Michael got up and went to Leo's room, knocked and was invited inside. After the two exchanged greetings, Michael got down to business. "Now I have a question for you, and don't be taking my head off for asking it."

"Allow me to guess the subject of your question, if I might, Michael. 'Leo, where can a fellow go for a bit of sightseeing and souvenir shopping for the folks back home? Somewhere scenic, not too frantic, so I can slow down the somewhat hectic pace of my visit so far.' Would it be something along those lines, Michael?"

"Em, no, not exactly, Leo. There's a man who interests me in Christy Burke's pub."

Leo sighed. "Yes?"

"Fellow by the name of Eddie Madigan."

"What about him?"

"You know him."

"I don't know him well, but we're acquainted, yes."

"I heard something about him."

"Of course you did. Because instead of contenting yourself with

311

having an occasional pint and touring the country with your friends and saying Masses and hearing confessions — not that I don't appreciate the assistance you've been giving us at the church during the course of your so-called vacation — instead of being content with those wholesome and spiritually uplifting activities, you are turning up little stones all over the city, and what may crawl out may not crawl back in again. I've warned you, Michael, and I'm warning you again, you may get yourself into the soup with some of your inquiries. Politics, loyalties, old enmities, you never know what you might be stirring up."

That of course brought the Merle Odom slaying to the front of Michael's mind. "Leo, about the American preacher, who do you suppose . . ."

Leo put up a warning hand. "Not now, Michael. What is it you came to ask me?"

"Well, most of what we've uncovered so far in the Christy's investigation has nothing political about it. Except perhaps in the case of Madigan." Leo gazed at Michael without expression. Michael continued, "We've uncovered information that casts doubt on the story that Madigan was sacked from the police force because of drug-related corruption."

"Have you now."

"There was a break-in at the Public Record Office in London."

Leo was silent for a few seconds, then said, "Go on."

"It was Madigan."

"And this tells you what?"

"There was something Madigan was so desperate to see in those files that he risked his entire career — risked arrest in England — to try to find it."

"And this is connected to your inquiries about the scribblings on the wall of Christy's pub? Is that what you're telling me?"

"Well, in all honesty, I don't know how it would relate, but . . ."

"But what?"

"I was wondering whether you knew anything about Madigan or the records he might have been looking for. Or whether you could recommend someone I could ask."

"I'll tell you what I don't recommend: raising this question anywhere within the hearing of a garda or a Madigan. Or a pub gossip sitting on a stool in Christy Burke's."

"I had that much figured out on my own, Leo!"

"Good man. Leave it with me. I'll make a couple of calls. If I have nothing to tell you, give it up, Michael! Promise?"

"If you have nothing to tell me, then there's probably nowhere I can go with it anyway."

"That's not exactly the sort of promise I was looking for."

"I'll do my best."

"I guess I'll have to live with that!"

Michael caught Leo glancing at his wristwatch and said, "I've been taking up your time here, Leo."

"No, Michael, it's not you. It's just that I'm expecting someone, so . . ."

"I'll be off then. See you later, Leo. *Dominus tecum*."

"The blessing of God on you, Michael."

Brennan

Michael returned to his room and said to Brennan, "I've made some inquiries. If they pan out, my son, you'll be the first to know."

Brennan nodded absently. He had his head in a newspaper full of rioting and violence in the North of Ireland in the wake of the American minister's death. He and Michael exchanged a few comments about that but Brennan had other things on his mind. It was no accident that he was sitting idly in Michael's room that warm, sunny Saturday afternoon. He was there at the request of Leo Killeen, who had been very enigmatic but said he'd like to have Brennan in the house. On standby, he said. He was expecting a visitor and, if there was trouble, Leo might have to call on Brennan for backup. He also instructed Brennan to leave Michael O'Flaherty out of it. How he could do that, with the pair of them sitting at Michael's kitchen table, Brennan didn't know. He would deal with it if he had to.

After a few more minutes of conversation with Michael, Brennan heard footsteps outside and turned in his chair to look out the window. A youngish priest was striding towards the house, glaring at it as if it might be the wrong address and a waste of his time. He appeared to be in his late thirties or early forties and had an uncompromising look about him; Brennan would not want to blot his copybook in that fellow's catechism class. But then, the same had been said about

Brennan himself. He heard a sharp rap at the door and heard Leo go out of his room and head downstairs.

"Oh," said Michael, "Leo's having company. He told me he's expecting someone."

"Mmm," Brennan replied.

It struck him then that there was something familiar about the visitor. Brennan ran the image of the man's face through his mind like a videotape. Exactly like a video — then he recognized him. The man who had shot and killed the Reverend Merle Odom was here in Leo's house, dressed as a priest.

Michael was sitting in the kitchen chair closest to the wall adjoining Leo's room. Brennan wanted that seat.

"Can you hear that?" he asked Michael.

"Leo, you mean?"

"No, the bells. Where would they be coming from at this time of day? It's not time for the Angelus."

"I don't hear anything."

"Sit here. Maybe you can figure out what church it would be."

So they switched seats, and Michael pulled his chair closer to the window in the hopes of hearing the nonexistent, or at least non-ringing, church bells.

"I don't hear a thing. But your ears are younger than mine. And more acute when it comes to music and bells."

Brennan shrugged and got Michael onto another subject of discourse. Brennan then tuned Michael out because his attention was focused elsewhere, on the sounds coming from the room on the other side of the wall behind him. He couldn't make out a word of conversation but he could hear voices. Voices raised, voices lowered. Raised and lowered. And on it went. What was the man — Desmond, that was the killer's name — what was he doing here? What were he and Killeen discussing so intently in the room next door?

Brennan jumped, startled by a loud noise, and spilled his tea all over his arm. What was that? A loud crash on the other side of the wall. Then nothing. Absolute silence.

Michael sprang out of his chair and started for the door, but Brennan was ahead of him.

"Michael, stay here."

"There's something going on in there! Leo —"

"Michael, I know. I'm going to handle it. For your own good, stay in here with the door shut. Don't show your face."

"But —"

Brennan stopped him with a hand on his chest, then bounded to the door, wrenched it open, and launched himself towards the door to Leo's room. He knocked. No answer. Knocked again. Something had happened in there. But not to both of them, surely. And who was more likely to have had the better of an encounter? The slight, elderly Leo Killeen or the strapping young man Brennan had seen entering the house? Brennan turned the doorknob and pushed. The door opened without resistance; Leo had left it unlocked. There was a man on his knees on the floor and another standing, glaring down at him, eyes blazing. Gone was the hard, arrogant look from the face of Desmond of the Provisional IRA. He was on his knees before Leo Killeen, his expression one of misery and apprehension. Leo was the embodiment of the wrath of God; his intensity was unnerving even to Brennan, standing in the entrance out of harm's way. Leo had things well in hand. Brennan wasn't needed. He backed out of the room and quietly shut the door.

Michael was standing where Brennan had left him, his light blue eyes pinned to the doorway.

"It's all right. Really. Leo's got things under control."

"Who's in there? What's going on?"

"I can't tell you, Mike. And you're better off not knowing. Go and wet the tea. We'll have a seat and wait till the fellow departs."

Not long afterwards, they heard the sound of someone leaving Leo's room and going down the stairs. Michael turned in his chair to peek out the window.

"Michael, turn around. Get away from the window."

Brennan's tone of voice did the trick. Michael whipped around to face Brennan, a look of bewilderment and then fear in his face. "Brennan, what in God's name . . ."

Brennan put his hand on Michael's shoulder, and peered around him. He could see Desmond out on the pavement, with a videotape in his right hand. He walked away, diminished, his eyes cast down, the swagger gone from his step.

Brennan didn't move from the window when Leo came into the room.

Leo dispensed with the preliminaries. "Michael, I'm sorry. I have to speak to Brennan alone."

Brennan followed Leo into the hallway and gently closed the door behind him.

"He found out about the videotape," Leo explained. "Not surprisingly. Young Clancy 'fessed up that he had brought the tape to me for his own protection, so somebody would know he wasn't the one who shot the minister. Of course Desmond couldn't allow that to go unchallenged, given that it was him on the tape committing the murder!"

"Thank Christ he didn't take matters into his own hands and go after Clancy."

"Well, he couldn't, with the tape still out there."

"So he came to Dublin in clerical dress."

"On my advice. He's not the first man to cross the border, in either direction, disguised as a priest!"

"Nobody would look twice at him coming to this house."

"Exactly. But as soon as he's inside, he's effing and blinding, and threatening to kill those two poor goms who snatched the American. Says he knows they're back in Dublin now. Clancy and his accomplice, whoever he is. Where was the videotape? Did I make copies? Well, I had to settle him down in short order. I invited him to tear the place apart looking for a copy. But he didn't. He knew I wasn't lying to him. I had the one and only tape, and I slammed it down on the table so hard I snapped one of the table legs off; that would be when you came in to see what had befallen me."

"I was afraid he'd attacked you."

"No, no, not at all. He's the one who's afraid, for his immortal soul. Killing a man in cold blood, and threatening to kill two others. Well, I got him simmered down. He knows Clancy and the other lad will be going to their graves without telling the story. Those two are painfully aware that if the Desmond name gets about, he'll know they talked. Desmond understands a couple of other things as well. That I'm not about to turn informer, so he has nothing to fear from me. And if he crosses me or causes me any harm, he'll have his conscience to answer to. But more than that, he'll have some earthly beings to answer to as well! Men who wouldn't be up and walking if it weren't for my interventions on their behalf; they 'owe me,' to put it in the crass terms of the marketplace. I put the word out to these fellows, without of course saying what Desmond had done; just said that if I come to grief they should look to Desmond as a possible cause. I got Desmond sorted."

It was clear to Brennan that Father Killeen was as formidable as a man of God as he had been as a commander of the Irish Republican Army.

"So, Brennan," Leo said lightly, "does all this tempt you to take on a new ministry?"

"Not sure I'd be up for that sort of encounter with my parishioners."

"All in a day's work, Father."

"How do you manage it, Leo?"

"Hate the sin, love the sinner, Brennan. Nothing new in that. I'm with them in their goal but not in their methods. Not anymore. And whatever they've done, they know I've done the same. And that my work now is the salvation of souls, theirs and my own."

"I understand you that far, Leo. But Desmond . . . Never as long as I live will I get over seeing him shoot that man in the head. And now, all the rioting and uproar. How will it ever be resolved? They're never going to catch anyone for it." Brennan was silent for a long moment, trying to take it all in. "But then, that's not our job, is it?"

"No, it is not. The Killeens are not informers, the Burkes are not informers. We don't turn people in to the authorities. Brennan, you and I listen to confessions every week. How many grave sins do we hear and carry around with us, knowing we will never utter a word to a living soul, knowing that those sinners — in some cases criminals, even murderers — may never be brought to earthly justice, and will certainly not be brought to justice by you or by me?"

"I know," Brennan said quietly. He too had heard the confessions of murderers in his time as a priest. "I know."

Michael

It was driving Michael nearly to distraction wondering who that man had been at Leo's in the afternoon, and what Leo and Brennan had to discuss out of Michael's hearing. Brennan had left without stopping in to see Michael again, so whatever it was, he did not want to be questioned about it. And he knew Michael would not have been able to resist asking! But Brennan and Leo would not have excluded him without a good reason. That, however, only made it more maddening; what in heaven's name was going on? Well, if he was meant to know, he'd know. Sometime. For now, he would do a bit of laundry and cleaning up, then head for his regular drinking spot later on.

When he dropped in to the pub that evening, it was packed. Nothing like hot summer weather to entice people into a dingy, smoky bar! Speaking of smoke, Brennan was there with a burning cigarette hanging from his lips, almost forgotten by the look of things, as he stared at a Gaelic football match on the television. He had on a pair of faded jeans and a T-shirt that said something in Italian, and he looked as if he had been ensconced in Christy Burke's pub for about twenty years. Everyone was glued to the coverage, including O'Hearn, Fanning, and Shanahan at the bar. Michael didn't break their concentration to say hello. He joined Brennan and two other men at their table and tuned in to the action. Dublin was playing Kerry. Michael arrived just in time for a Dublin goal, and shouts of joy reverberated off the walls of the pub. It didn't take long before Michael too was hooked. A pint of the black stuff appeared in front of him, and he lifted it without taking his eyes off the screen.

Michael became aware of someone standing by his chair and, when there was a break in the action, he looked up and saw Maura and Kitty.

"Oh! Good heavens!" He got to his feet.

"We're not going to get much action out of this pair, Kitty," Maura said. "Holy priests of God that they are and, typical men, sitting in a bar swilling booze and staring at the game on television. Just our luck. Let's dump them."

"Sure, you're right, Maura. Ten minutes after we're gone, one of them will say to the other, 'Did you see that? He picked the ball up directly from the ground. His foot didn't touch it at all, at all! Em . . . wasn't there somebody else here?'"

"'Wha? Not that I ever noticed.'"

"They didn't notice us standing here, they wouldn't notice us gone."

"No!" Michael protested. "Stay. I'll get you a chair. Two, I mean. Brennan?"

"Eh? Oh. Evening, ladies."

Only then did Brennan remember the cigarette, with the ash nearly an inch long on it. He took one last drag from it and ground it out in the ashtray. A roar went up from the crowd on the television as a Dublin player got a yellow card, and all eyes swivelled to the TV. Then Brennan looked at the women again and started to get up.

"You're a wise pair," Maura said then, and turned to grab two chairs from the next table. She hoisted them over the heads of two fellows at the table. They didn't even notice.

"I'll get those," said Brennan.

"I'll help you," Michael insisted.

"Never mind. I have them. We're not helpless, are we, Kitty?"

"Indeed we are not. Nor are we here to while away the entire night," Kitty declared. The women sat down. "I have a message for you boys from Leo Killeen."

"Oh! We saw him earlier today."

"Well, earlier today, Michael, Leo hadn't yet been put on the spot with respect to the music for the Mass at the Pro."

"Mass?"

"You remember Mass, don't you, Monsignor?" Maura put in. "The Holy Eucharist? Historians say it predates the development of the game of football, at least as we know the game today. In fact —"

"No, I mean, yes . . . Em, is there a particular Mass that Leo —"

"Ah," Kitty said. "I see. You haven't heard about the big do happening at the Pro-Cathedral Thursday night. A special Mass for peace. The red hat will be there, and herself from the house in the park" — she meant the president of Ireland, whose official residence was in the Phoenix Park — "and the archbishop and clergy and all the angels and saints. Well, you get the idea, so you won't want to miss it."

"I wouldn't miss it for the world. What a lovely idea."

"Anyway, Leo is tied up with the preparations tonight, but he tried to call you and you weren't there, so he tried me. Thought I might be seeing you."

Michael tried to look nonchalant, but he was pleased that someone would relay a message to him through Kitty, pleased that his friendship with her was an established fact in certain circles in Dublin. "Right. So, what's this about the music?"

Only then did Brennan give his full attention to the conversation.

"Leo's got his knickers in a twist —" Michael's face must have registered his surprise at Sister's language, because she laughed and said, "Let me rephrase that, Monsignor. Father Killeen has raised a question about the selection of music for the liturgy on Thursday night. There will be Latin, all well and good, and English, all right again, but there is nothing on the program in Irish. There will be remarks in Irish, but he thought there should be some Irish-language music. The liturgical director was harried and busy and said to Leo, 'Fine, *Ag Críost an Síol*, but I don't have time to rehearse it. Sing it yourself.' Leo, not being one to back down, said, 'I will.' So, he's on at the Offertory."

"And?" Brennan asked.

"And what do you think? Leo needs you to help him out."

"I will. With bells on. And incense wafting about my person."

"How about you, Michael? Can you sing?"

"Well, I —"

"He can, Kitty," Brennan answered, "and I don't say that lightly about anyone."

"I can believe it!"

"I've heard Michael and I've tried to encourage him to sing parts of the Mass at home. But more to the point, he's a brilliant Irish speaker. Much better at it than I am. Tell Leo, if I don't see him first, that the three of us will sing it. I'll take care of collecting the music, and I'll call him with a rehearsal time. Killeen, O'Flaherty, and Burke will make their debut together at the Pro-Cathedral."

"What'll you call yourselves?" Maura asked. "The Holy Trinity? I guess that's taken."

"No, that would work," Brennan replied.

"Brennan! Say an Act of Contrition before you utter another word!" Michael commanded him.

"All right, Maura, our work here is done." Kitty got up, and Maura did the same.

"Where are you going?"

"To the Abbey, Michael. We have tickets for the theatre."

"Oh! What are you going to see?"

"*A Month in the Country*. A Turgenev play, adapted by Brian Friel."

"Ah." Michael had no idea.

"So, gentlemen, we shall take our leave of you," Maura said. "But we look forward to your performance on Thursday night."

Brennan turned back to the Dublin-Kerry match. Michael did the same, but with mixed feelings. He wanted to see the football, but he would love to have tagged along with Kitty and Maura. Not to the theatre without a ticket, though, so the game it would be.

The peace Mass was something to look forward to, Michael thought as he walked home to Aughrim Street after celebrating Dublin's victory over Kerry in the final seconds of the match. He hoped to find Leo Killeen at home so he could ask him all about it. But Leo was not in residence when Michael arrived. He would have to catch him later.

✝

It was not until after confessions on Sunday that Michael finally had a chance to ask Leo Killeen about the Mass. Leo filled him in on the plans and the list of attendees, which, as Kitty had announced, included important figures in the worlds of church and state.

"If you need any help with the preparations, Leo, just give me the word."

"Thank you, Michael. I will. Em, while I have you here, and since you'll be pestering me about it anyway . . ."

"Yes?"

"I made a call in relation to the question you were asking yesterday."

About Madigan. Good! Who was Leo's source? A policeman? An intelligence officer? Some kind of Special Branch operative? That was a question Michael was not about to ask. He merely said, "Oh! What did you find out?"

"Nothing."

Michael tried to mask his disappointment. "We know the incident happened, though," he prompted.

"Just because something happened doesn't mean people are willing to blather on about it. The person I spoke to, who is knowledgeable about these matters, left me with the unmistakable impression that this incident was extremely embarrassing to the authorities here, and the fact that they had to give something up to the Brits only underscored how embarrassing it was. Madigan was carrying a false passport, had a whole fictional identity set up, but the British authorities found out

321

who he really was. Inevitably. A garda from Dublin trying to blow up a storeroom full of secret files held in England and pertaining to Ireland, well, it's just beyond the pale. Get it out of your head. My man had nothing to tell me and I have nothing to tell you."

But in fact Leo *had* told Michael something he hadn't known. "I understand," Michael said. "Was there any damage from the attempt to, em, blow things up?"

"No, security caught him just after he'd lit the fuse. A makeshift effort, some inflammable material he tried to shove under the security door. It likely would have fizzled out before it did any damage. A desperate manoeuvre. We're not privy to whatever was in that room, so we don't know what Madigan was after. End of story, Michael. Now, could you do something for me? Could you take my noon-hour Mass tomorrow? I have to go out of town."

"Gladly, Leo, certainly. And thank you for your efforts on my behalf."

"I'd like to say you're welcome, but the words would stick in my throat."

"I thank you nonetheless. And tomorrow I'll be at the altar, twelve o'clock sharp. Where are you going?"

"I'm not telling you!"

With a curt nod, Leo turned and went on his way.

Michael now had a new perspective on the Eddie Madigan incident. Madigan had tried to blow up the secret archive! He had done his best to make things go smoothly, establishing a false identity, working on Abigail Howard to admit him to the file room so he could get his hands on the documents. But when it all fell apart, he crossed the Rubicon. He got hold of explosives and went in with the hope that what he couldn't remove, he would destroy. Or had that been his plan from the beginning? Either way, Madigan must have known he himself would be destroyed in the fallout. What was he so desperate to hide?

This train of thought brought Michael to something he had heard a while ago about the ex-cop or his family, that there were strained relations between the Madigans and somebody else. Where had he heard it? He tried to recall. It was Nurse McAvity. That's who had told him. Bad blood, he'd said, between the Madigans and another family. If Michael could find out what that was about, he might be able to explain the bombing attempt. It was time for another interrogation.

It was early evening when he set out for a brisk walk to the bus terminal in O'Connell Street and found the bus that would take him to Camden Street, to the pub where some of the United Irishmen had gathered to plot the 1798 rebellion. Good. There was Nurse McAvity in the same seat he'd been in when Michael had found him before. "Bill!"

McAvity looked around and stared at Michael, as if trying to place him. The penny dropped when he focused on the Roman collar.

"Monsignor . . . O'Flaherty, is it?"

"That's right. Michael."

"Of course, Michael. Have a seat. Can I get you anything?"

"I'll have whatever you're having."

Bill signalled to the bartender and pointed to his glass. A half-pint, nearly full. When Michael had his own half pint, he sat beside McAvity and made small talk for a few minutes. Then he got to the point.

"When we spoke here last time, you were kind enough to provide some background on the people who might be targets of the slander on Christy Burke's wall. And you told me about the bad feeling between the Madigans and another family, but my old memory is not what it used to be, and I've forgotten the name."

"I'd hardly expect you to remember it, Michael. I had a moment when I couldn't recall your own name! The people I was talking about are the Brogans. They and the Madigans would cross the street in front of the airport bus rather than give each other a good morning or a good afternoon. That was the past generation, though. It's not a big family, and the young Brogans have all immigrated to England."

"But did you tell me there's an elderly woman?"

"Old Irene. She's not well at all. She doesn't put a foot outside the door of her flat. I'm speaking literally now, Michael. She doesn't leave the flat. She's in one of the big tower blocks in Ballymun. Her children set her up there before they moved away. It was a good idea at the time. Ballymun was the hope of the future, public housing with central heating. Nothing else around though, so something of a ghetto. Much worse now, with drugs and all the social problems associated with them. Anyway, Irene Brogan stays inside. Has a woman come in and bring her whatever she needs. So that poor soul hasn't been painting nasty words on the walls of Christy Burke's pub."

"I wonder whether she'd have a word with me."

"You never know. She can be fierce, but if you catch her on a good day, well, you never know."

"So, Bill. A bit of excitement in here recently. The guards were here, I understand."

"Yes."

"After that man's body was found."

"Looking for a bit of information," McAvity said, in a tone that invited no further inquiry.

†

Michael was on the buses again the following morning, this time for the ride to the Ballymun public housing estate, which was almost as far out of town as the airport. It took him a while to locate Irene Brogan's name, but he found it in one of several high modernistic towers, which looked as if they had been constructed in the 1960s. Michael didn't much like the look of the place, a mix of high, low, and medium-height blocks of flats. The phrase "brutalist architecture" came to mind. And he didn't like the look of some of the characters lurking around the compound, vacant-eyed young people who gave him the impression they'd run a knife into him as soon as wish him good day. He just had to be on the enormous estate for five minutes to know it was a social engineering experiment gone horribly wrong. And five minutes in the elevator — which stalled on the sixth floor on the way up, trapping Michael with a man who had vomited down the front of his shirt — offered some insight as to why Irene Brogan never set foot outside her flat.

Mrs. Brogan peered out at Michael in answer to his knock. She cast a quick look right and left in the corridor and then returned her attention to Michael. He introduced himself and said he was a friend of a business owner in the city, a man who owned a pub that was being targeted by a vandal. And if he could have a few minutes of her time, he would explain why he had sought her out. She looked at him with the suspicion his story might be said to deserve, and he smiled a bit sheepishly.

"I'm not here to sell you anything. I'm not even going to quote scripture."

She reluctantly admitted him, then banged the door shut behind him. She was a short, wide woman dressed in some sort of lime-green lounging outfit that billowed about her.

"Welcome to the People's Republic of Ballymun, Father. I hope none of my comrades treated you to any disrespect on the way in."

"No, no, Mrs. Brogan, I had no trouble at all. But yourself, are you all right? How long have you been living here?"

"I've survived here for nearly twenty years. I wouldn't call it living."

"Do you have family in the area?"

She raised a cynical eyebrow. "I have no one here. I might as well be in Moscow."

"Who helps you out then? Brings you things you need? Takes you for appointments?"

"There's a young one here. I give her a few bob a month, and she does my errands."

"Is there somewhere else you could go? I'd be happy to help you make arrangements —"

"Would I be here if I had somewhere else to go? I can tell you're a good soul, Father. Thank you, but I'm all right. There are plenty who are worse off than I am. Now let me make you a cup of tea, and you can tell me what's on your mind."

Michael stood at the window, looking out at the bleak scene below. A jet plane roared by, rattling the windowpanes.

Mrs. Brogan returned with the tea, and they sat down. "As I explained, I'm helping a friend who runs a pub in the city. A vandal has been spray-painting graffiti on the place, and the messages seem to relate either to the publican himself or to some of the regular customers there. One of the regulars is a man named Eddie Madigan." Mrs. Brogan's lips tightened at the mention of the name. "Someone told me, and I don't have a tactful way of putting this, that your family and the Madigans do not get on very well."

"Your informant is correct."

"Would you be willing to tell me what lies behind the ill feeling?"

"I don't mind telling you. In fact, I'd be happy to broadcast it on RTÉ if they'd let me. It goes back to June 1920, couple of years before I was born. Denny Brogan was my father's older brother; there was twelve years or so between them. There was Denny and his wife Meg, and Liam and Tippy. They had a place ten miles north of here.

The family ran a creamery. Denny was with the Volunteers, who by that time had joined up with the Irish Republican Brotherhood to become the IRA. Denny was a crack shot with the rifle, and he'd just as quickly pin you with his eyes if he heard a foul word come out of your mouth. There was no 'bloody' or 'eff' or 'damn' in the presence of Denny Brogan. If you were staying at his house — and you'd be welcome to stay as long as you needed — you'd not be missing Mass on Sunday. Nor would you be sodden with drink in his presence. You'd have a drop or two and you'd leave the premises walking like a gentleman. That's what he was, a gentleman and a soldier, fighting under the inspiration of Michael Collins to rid his country of an occupying force.

"And his most trusted comrade in the world was Eddie Madigan, grandfather to the man you'd know as Eddie Madigan today. Those two stood together, took orders together, planned and schemed and fought together. Denny trusted Madigan absolutely. Denny even let himself be subject to a disapproving blast by Mick Collins over some oversight committed by Madigan, which Collins thought was Denny's fault. Some little cock-up, I don't know what, but you couldn't be too careful in those days, and Mick had to keep a tight rein on them. So Denny stood there in front of Collins, who was giving out to him without mercy, and Denny took it rather than breathe a word of the fact that it was his friend Madigan who had banjaxed things.

"Denny's Volunteer service meant he had to be absent from the creamery on a good many occasions. So Meg was left to do the work, and Liam helped as best he could, him being only eleven years old at the time. Heavy work, running a creamery. It's 1920 I'm talking about, so the Tans were here."

"Right," Michael said. The Black and Tans were a ragtag outfit cobbled together by the British, made up of First World War veterans who had returned to England and Scotland in 1918 only to find themselves surplus to requirements. A bunch of ruffians, they were, sent over to restore order in the Irish colony. They got their nickname from the patched-together uniforms they wore. In Ireland to this day their name was synonymous with chaos and brutality.

"Savages!" Irene cried. "Well, they were getting too close for comfort, nosing around for members of the IRA in the village and thereabouts.

"Liam was Meg and Denny's only child. Nobody seemed to know the why of it; they just never had any more children. So, as you can imagine, the sun rose and set on Liam Brogan."

"Oh, well, who was Tippy then? A cousin?"

"No, no, he was a beloved part of the immediate family. A little black and white border collie with some other stuff mixed in, the dearest little dog you could ever hope to see, with a dear, sweet face on him and one ear that flopped over.

"That dog had taken on strange ways with Liam. They had always played together. Liam would throw sticks and Tippy would fetch them, the usual thing, you know. Tippy would run in circles around Liam's feet when they went out walking, yapping and barking and carrying on, and Liam would bend over and grab him gently by the ears and tell him to get out of the way and let him walk, and you'd swear you could see the dog laughing when he looked up at Liam and started running around his feet again. But in the time leading up to the day when the Tans arrived, Tippy was not nearly as playful. He walked at Liam's side, almost but not quite brushing against his leg, not a word out of him. Or not a sound, I mean. When the child would sit or lie down, Tippy would curl up beside him. And never sleep, just stare at the boy with those big brown eyes. It only came out later that Liam had something wrong with him, something terrible the medical tests hadn't been clear on before this happened with the Tans.

"So it was that on a day in June 1920, a motley crew of Black and Tans in their Crossley tender roared up to the creamery looking for Denny. He wasn't there. So what does a well-disciplined army of men do when they can't find the fellow they're after? Set fire to his barn, of course! Which they did.

"Tippy was frantic, running back and forth between the barn and the house, where he thought Meg would be. She was down the road, but she saw the smoke and came running. Old Deirdre O'Hagan was a witness to this from her front window. There were no other houses nearby. Deirdre was all crippled up, and unable to move unless her daughter was there. The daughter had gone into the city to the market. No telephone. So Deirdre was helpless to do anything but watch as the whole thing unfolded. And one thing she knew beyond a shadow of a doubt: the Tans knew the boy was in the barn. Maybe not when they set the fire, but once it caught, they knew. Deirdre saw one of them standing there, pointing his rifle at the barn door. And his head and his lips were moving. He was talking to somebody inside.

"Tans left, with the child still in the barn. Meg met them on the road. She came running up to the creamery and saw the flames. As soon as she caught sight of Tippy being so frantic, she knew Liam must have been in the barn. Tippy ran ahead of her and they both went into the barn, Meg screaming Liam's name. She didn't stop for an instant. Went on in. Meanwhile another carload of Tans had found Denny. They brought him home. They saw what their comrades had done, and let Denny run to the barn. Inside was Liam, trapped in the burning building. Meg and Tippy's bodies were found over top of Liam's. Tans went in and shot Denny in the back.

"Why did all this happen to Denny and his family? Because of old Eddie Madigan. Madigan went on to great acclaim as one of the first crop of officers in our new Irish police force. I've never been inside the home of the Eddie Madigan you know. But those who have seen it tell me the place is a shrine to their family history. An entire wall is taken up with photographs and news cuttings, notes and citations. There's a receipt displayed in a frame, a receipt signed by Collins himself for old Eddie's contribution to the national loan. As you know, Collins raised a loan and everybody got a receipt. He wasn't just a guerrilla war leader; he was a businessman, and a damned efficient one at that. So Eddie got a receipt, and there's a note on it scribbled by Collins, acknowledging his work for the cause.

"What neither Collins nor anyone else in the provisional government knew was that Madigan was a spy for the Brits. It's not known even today. Except by the Brits, I suppose."

And Eddie Madigan, the grandson, Michael noted to himself.

"Madigan passed Denny's name to the Black and Tans, saying Denny was the man who had killed one of their spies, the British spies, the week before. Madigan was an informer and a traitor, and the massacre at Brogan's creamery was the result. Denny Brogan was shot in the back after seeing his wife and son and dog together in death in the barn, the son having been burnt alive and his mother and dog giving up their lives to go with him."

Michael had no way of knowing how much the story might have been overlaid with legend in the years since 1920, but if he were a Madigan . . .

Irene Brogan finished the thought for him. "If a traitor like old Eddie Madigan was your illustrious ancestor, would you want the secret to get out? It would serve them right if it did, every one of the bloody Madigans in County Dublin today!"

"Do others in your family feel the way you do about it?"

"Those who gave a shite one way or the other are in their graves. Those who are alive today are more concerned with partying in the disco than how and why their own flesh and blood were betrayed and murdered. Irish people don't care about their history anymore, Monsignor, especially the young. They go on with their lives as if they just fell out of the sky with no history at all. And don't even mention language to them. Was there ever another language here before English? They look at you as if you're a creature with two heads. They don't care; it's a joke to them."

"I guess you're telling me you don't know of anyone who might be trying to raise the issue now, either publicly or perhaps in a more roundabout way."

"No one has listened to me trying to raise it in living memory; those who listened in the past didn't believe me. If someone is trying to bring it up now, they haven't taken me into their confidence. More tea, Monsignor?"

Michael stayed and chatted with Irene Brogan for an hour or so after that. They talked about history and her family's role in it, Dublin and changes in the city that she had heard about but never seen. When Michael got back to the city centre, he headed to Aughrim Street to say Leo Killeen's noontime Mass, as promised. Then he went looking for a flower shop and, when he found one, he ordered a bouquet of lilies to be delivered to the lonely woman in Ballymun. He asked to have some chocolate included with the order.

But flowers and chocolate were not uppermost in the mind of Michael O'Flaherty that day. His thoughts were on the ex-garda Eddie Madigan and the terrible blight on his family name, or what would be a blight if it ever became public knowledge. Michael had no trouble seeing this as the kind of secret one would risk one's career to cover up. But was it more than that? Was it a secret to kill for?

Chapter 17

Michael

There were a number of old and sickly people at the noon Mass on Monday, and this inspired Michael to spend a few hours that afternoon visiting patients at the Mater Hospital. When he got back to his house in Aughrim Street, there was a note tacked to his door. "15:35. Dropped in to see you, will try church or back here later. TS" Just above the initials was a cross. Tim Shanahan, still signing his name as a priest after all these years. Michael looked at his watch. It was just past four-thirty. Tim might still be at the church, if he hadn't come by again and updated his note. Michael headed out again. He entered the church, which was radiant with the sun shining through the multicoloured glass of the windows. There on the left side near the back was Tim Shanahan, sitting in a pew, gazing at the altar.

Michael slid in beside him. "Hello, Tim. Got your note."

"Hello, Michael. I just wanted to thank you for what you tried to do for me."

"Oh?"

"I saw the bishop yesterday."

"Ah."

"He told me you went to the brick palace to plead for clemency on my behalf."

"Well, I just thought a word in the right place might help. You never know till you ask."

"He wasn't all that receptive, I take it."

"Well, he seemed to be a little fixated on your troubles."

"My drinking, my heroin addiction, my disastrous mission in Africa. You have to admit, Michael, Tom O'Halloran could be forgiven for not begging me to resume my place in the pulpit, telling good Catholics how they should live."

"You do have some obstacles to overcome, Tim. And yet . . ."

"There was a major diplomatic flap when my mission crashed in Africa. I'm sure he mentioned that."

"He did say there was some political fallout."

"I told you about my young student, Sabine, whose family sold her to a child trafficker, and about things becoming destabilized, the balance of power shifting between rival factions, all of that. I was so disillusioned I walked out on my mission and was in a drunken, drug-ridden fugue for months afterwards."

Michael nodded. He remembered all too well the dreadful story Shanahan had told him. He also remembered something Archbishop O'Halloran had said, "all those deaths." Had things been even worse than Tim admitted?

"Six weeks after I left my African parish, Michael, a power struggle broke out between the child trafficker who had purchased Sabine and the hard man who had protected our parish. Our man now considered our parishioners to be allies of his enemy. During my time there, I had developed a bit of a rapport with him; maybe there was something I could have done. . . . But I wasn't there. He and his henchmen went into the school and slaughtered everyone on the premises that day. Seven people. Sister Josephine and our young priest, Father Amegashie, who both threw themselves over the children's bodies to try to protect them. Five of the schoolchildren were killed. All of them hacked to death by machetes. Is it any wonder I'm not allowed to practise my vocation as a priest? The priest who walked out and left his parishioners to be murdered? You asked me the first time we spoke

whether I had no shame. Now you've heard the story, and my role in it."
He held Michael's gaze. "Is that shame enough for you, Monsignor?"

†

Michael was overwhelmed when he got home. And that feeling stayed with him throughout an evening of reading and sipping tea. He became even more disturbed when he tried to get to sleep. The horror that Tim Shanahan had lived through, and still lived with, was something Michael would never be able to endure. Would Michael have turned to serious drinking or drug use if he had gone through that? Who could say he would not? And Tim was not the only one of the Christy Burke Four who had hardship in his life. Eddie Madigan's dreadful secret, Frank Fanning's past, Jimmy O'Hearn's family saga. The case of the pub vandal, however, remained as resistant to Michael's efforts as ever. Who was the vandal singling out in his *J'accuse!* on the walls of the pub?

Surely, it was stretching things to imagine the fellow knew all the skeletons in all four closets. True, Michael and Brennan had learned the men's secrets, but the two priests had set out to investigate the pub regulars. Why would the graffiti artist zero in on four individuals and dig up dirt on them, if he had nothing against them starting out? Other than being regulars at the pub, the Christy Burke Four had nothing else in common, as far as Michael knew. The slogans were painted on the pub's walls, not on the walls of the men's homes. So did the vandal himself have some connection with Christy's? Well, Michael had been over this ground with Finn Burke. And Finn had been unable to identify anyone with a serious grudge against the pub. That was why Brennan had started the investigation by trying to identify the target and work backwards to the vandal, rather than the other way around. And here they were with four suspected targets, men who had violent events in their history, which could go a long way towards explaining why they spent so much time drinking their cares away at Christy's. It struck Michael then that the four men almost certainly knew each other's secrets, even if they did not divulge everything they knew when questioned. Loyalty, Michael assumed. Or, if they weren't privy to the details, they knew at least that each of them had a troubled past. This shared sense of hardship would

332

account for the fact that they were a close-knit group and had been drinking together for years. But Michael had never felt threatened by them as a group or as individuals. Not one of them made him feel he was in the presence of a killer.

How could he and Brennan get to the bottom of the Christy Burke's mystery? It was none of their business, really. None of Michael's, certainly. Brennan at least had a family connection and had been asked to assist. It was no secret that Brennan had taken on the task reluctantly and considered most of what they'd learned useless. No doubt he wished he'd never heard the half of it. As for Michael, he hadn't exactly shone in his role as Sergeant O'Flaherty.

But how was he doing as *Monsignor* O'Flaherty? In spite of the suspicions that had attached themselves to the Christy Burke Four, Michael had become fond of these men, all of them. He wanted to help them, no matter what they might have done. How could he do that, though, really? Why not just give it up, and leave them to solve their own problems? He drifted off to sleep with that thought in his mind.

But he awoke the following morning with a line from Genesis running through his head. "Am I my brother's keeper?" For better or for worse, Michael knew that's what he was called to be. If his brother, his friend, his fellow human being was troubled, Michael felt duty-bound to lend a hand.

The most obvious person to start with, he felt, was Jimmy O'Hearn. There was something Jimmy should know. Michael could not keep the secret of Rod O'Hearn's betrayal to himself. Nor could he stand by while the lawyer, Carey Gilbert, was being slandered, however unintentionally, by the O'Hearn family. Michael got up, showered, ate a hasty breakfast, and went to morning Mass. He would catch Jimmy O'Hearn at home before Jimmy installed himself at Christy Burke's for the day. This was a conversation to be had in private.

It was a soft day, cool and cloudy with a bit of a morning mist, when Michael got off the bus in Ringsend and made his way to Pigeon House Road, where the Poolbeg Marina was located. Michael asked around and was given directions to Jimmy O'Hearn's boat. Michael remembered someone saying it was a sailboat, not a proper houseboat.

It was maybe twenty-five feet in length, rocking gently in its berth. He stepped gingerly onto the deck of the boat and knocked at the cabin door. No answer. He peered into the boat's immaculate interior. No sign of Jimmy. Another time, maybe. When he had hoisted himself back onto the pier, Michael heard a banging noise coming from the shore, and looked over. There was Jimmy, standing in the back of a little truck with a rag and a bucket of water.

"Jimmy!" Michael called out, and O'Hearn started at the sound. He stared in Michael's direction for a couple of seconds, nonplussed, then greeted him.

"Is it yourself, Monsignor? Making your rounds early, are you?"

"I am. But I'm loath to interrupt a man at work!"

"No worries. I'm just finishing up." He poured liquid out of a container onto his rag and gave the bed of the truck a final rub, then jumped down and wiped his hands on his pants. "You get to the point where you can't put off your cleaning any longer. So, Mike, are you out here looking for the floating chapel?"

"Floating chapel?"

"You're too late. Our people came up with the plan for a floating chapel when the English forced all the Irish people out of the city. They came out this way, and that's why you have a neighbourhood called Irishtown in the city of Dublin! They had a church moored to the shore. But they eventually built St. Matthew's. On land. I kind of like the church-boat idea myself, but I'm a few hundred years out of time. Enough of that, though. What's on your mind today, Mike?"

How to begin? "Well now, Jimmy, I've been a little concerned about you. Thought we could have a bit of a chat before the day gets underway."

"Before I check in at Christy's, you mean!"

"I suppose that's what I mean. I'll be checking in myself later on."

"What did you want to talk about?"

"Well, em . . ."

O'Hearn looked at him and waited, then said, "Come inside, why don't you, Mike. Make yourself a cup of tea while I wash up and change my clothes."

"Sure."

So Mike brewed tea for two as O'Hearn got himself cleaned up. They sat down together at the tiny galley table and sipped their tea.

Mike got to the point. "Jimmy, I'm aware of your family's loss of the boat-building company."

Jimmy looked down at his teacup and said in a voice tight with tension, "I suppose it's no surprise you've heard about it. People talk. No getting away from that."

"The story going around is that the lawyer . . ."

The eyes that met Michael's were haunted and filled with pain. It took a while for Jim to find his voice again. Finally, he said, "He cut us out of the business, cut the hearts out of us, then scarpered to parts unknown!"

The look in the man's eyes was enough to disabuse Michael right then and there of any notion that the truth would set Jimmy and his family on the road to healing. Michael could see that the loss of the business, the treachery, was still an open wound. Michael wasn't about to rub salt in the wound by revealing to Jimmy that his own brother had betrayed him and his sisters. The family should be told, no question, but Michael couldn't bring himself to do it.

All he could say was, "I just thought it might help if you talked about it."

"Thank you, Mike, but I said all I have to say on the subject a long time ago. And there's nothing you can do to make it better. I do appreciate your concern, now, don't get me wrong there."

"All right, then, Jim. I'll be off. See if I can do any better on my next stop!"

"Thanks all the same, Mike. I'll see you later today, I expect."

And with that, Mike was off, his pastoral efforts come to naught.

Brennan

Brennan was the barman at Christy's again on Tuesday afternoon. He had received a call from Sean Nugent, passing along a request from Finn: could Brennan take over bar duties today?

"I could and I will. Nothing wrong with Finn, I hope? Or yourself, of course."

"No, not at all. We, em, he has to go off somewhere, so."

"Ah."

"I have to bolt now. Thank you, Brennan."

"No worries."

So here he was. And there was a little girl on the bar stool opposite him, her legs swinging high above the floor.

"You're leaving us, Normie."

"Yes, I'm afraid so, Father. I really like Dublin; it's not that. But Kim and her mum and dad have rented a cottage at the beach back home, and they invited me for a sleepover for a whole week at the cottage! I really miss Kim."

"And I'm sure she misses you. You'll have a brilliant week together."

And, Brennan hoped, Monty and little Dominic would have a brilliant few days by themselves. Days brought to them in part by Brennan Burke. The Collins-MacNeil family's original plan was to stay in Dublin till Saturday. But Monty received an urgent call from the office; an important client was in trouble, and the firm wanted Monty to handle it. Immediately. All the talk about him going home made little Normie homesick, and she called her best friend, Kim, and this resulted in the cottage invitation. Brennan saw it all falling into place. Here were a few days — or evenings at least — for Monty and Dominic to spend together, get to know each other, be father and son. With a bit of lobbying, ostensibly on behalf of Normie and Kim, Brennan saw the project through: tickets home for Monty, Normie, and Dominic. They would fly from Dublin to London tonight, and to Halifax tomorrow. This would give the MacNeil time with Kitty without the kids, before Kitty departed for Rome on Friday. Maura would stay on till Saturday as planned. Brennan was pleased with the arrangements.

"I miss Tommy, too," Normie said of her older brother. "He's going to look after Dominic in the daytime before Daddy gets home from the office. Tommy's picking us up at the airport. I told him to bring Lexie in the car. I hope they get married! And if they do, you can do the wedding, and sing at it!"

"Thank you, angel."

Perhaps there would be a wedding some day. But, before that, Brennan intended to see the father and mother of the groom reconciled. They still had not spoken to him of the guerrilla "counselling" session he had offered them after his long night on the street, but he would be patient until they were all back in Halifax. Then, surely, they would see the wisdom of his advice.

Distracted by the little girl at the bar and by the Man Above, to whom he was beaming up prayers for a successful family reunion,

Brennan nearly missed an order from the very object of his machinations. Monty was standing in front of him with a look of amusement on his face.

"Did you hear the one about the mystic who walked into a bar? He took the place over and nobody could get a drink. Ever again, for eternity. Which was fine for the mystic, who experienced eternity as one ecstatic moment in time. But it was a lot longer for the thirsty patrons, who —"

"Pint of the black stuff?"

"If you would be so kind. And make it a good one."

"Sure I'll pour yeh de most dacent of points," Brennan replied in an exaggerated Dub accent.

"Good. 'Cause it'll be my last drop on Irish soil. It wouldn't do to have me staggering onto the plane with the two kids. That would disappoint their mother, and I wouldn't want to do that."

"She'd have you peeled, the flesh hanging off you in bloody strips."

"Not for the first time."

"I heard that!" The MacNeil. "Pour me a Harp if you can do it without adding any barroom commentary."

Brennan poured them their pints. "Are you packed and ready to go?" he asked Monty. "I regret that I can't borrow a car and give you a lift but, as you can see, I'm on duty here."

"No problem. The kids will enjoy the airport bus. Everything's an adventure at their ages. Of course, now that I think of it, even at my age life is an adventure. Particularly on those occasions when I've spent my vacation in your company and that of your family."

"Don't be going on about that again."

"Speaking of adventurers, though, I didn't have a chance to say goodbye to Leo Killeen."

"Well then, ring him at home and get him over here." Brennan found a scrap of paper and wrote out Leo's number. "It seems I've always been able to reach him at this time of the day."

Monty went to the phone at the back of the pub but was soon back with the news that Leo was not in at this time of the day after all.

"Give him my best when you see him."

"I will."

Over the next little while, the Christy Burke Four filed in and took their places at the bar. They all wanted the television on, and Brennan obliged them. Looking for more news on the pub vandal murder, perhaps? Was it old news for one of them? Impossible to tell. To Brennan, they all looked a little tense today. But the place was jammed, and he was busy, so he didn't have the chance to talk to them beyond greeting them and ministering to their libational needs.

Later on the Five Sorrowful Mysteries hobbled in and waved to everybody at the bar. One of them — Brennan couldn't be sure of her name — was using some sort of aluminum walking unit. From his observation, she didn't seem to be relying on it, but rather booting it ahead of her as she walked. The five women settled themselves at a table, and he took their orders. Two of them could have nothing but water today, unfortunately. Did he have anything distilled? He had something distilled but it was a long way from water. Unless you looked to the origin of the word "whiskey," *uisce beatha* in Irish, which meant "water of life." But no, they'd take theirs from the tap. Would they like a slice of lemon or lime? One would. The other could not take citrus; it irritated something or other, the lining of a body part he'd never heard of. That prompted a discussion of what the other Sorrowful Mysteries were unable to consume. It would have filled a good-sized botanical text. He brought them their drinks, such as they were, and assured them that anything they needed, they could get it from him. He prayed they wouldn't require medication, although he had plenty of placebos on hand.

"Thought I might find you here but not *there*." It was Kitty Curran, just in the door. She pointed to him behind the bar. Then she spotted Maura MacNeil and directed a remark about Brennan to her. "Nothing would surprise me about this fellow."

"You've found me, love," he said to Kitty. "Now what can I do to brighten your day?"

"It's about Aidan."

A sliver of fear jabbed Brennan's heart. What had befallen the poor homeless child now? "Is he all right?"

There must have been something in the tone of his voice; the MacNeil looked in his direction and didn't give him the evil eye at all. She came over to the bar, gave Kitty a quick hug, and glanced from her to Brennan.

"Nothing's amiss, darling," Kitty assured him. "Put your mind at ease."

"What's the story then?"

"I've found a family for him. Foster parents."

"Ah."

"Who's Aidan?" the MacNeil inquired.

Kitty turned to her. "Brennan didn't fill you in on his long night out? Fighting, sleeping rough, being reprimanded by Mother Superior, being detained by the gardaí, any of that?"

Maura MacNeil was gobsmacked. "No, he did not!"

"Did you notice any wounds on his face at all?"

"Right. We did. But, typically, he didn't say much about it."

"Most likely he never will. Poor Mr. Brennan; he'd hardly be able to tell it properly, with his limited abilities." Another astonished look from the MacNeil. "So I'll give you the story myself. But not now. We haven't the time."

Maura MacNeil said, "We'll talk later, Kitty," and returned to her seat at the end of the bar.

Kitty provided Brennan with an explanation. "Here's the thing. We have a foster family. They've been vetted and have an exemplary record. They've taken in children before, after raising five of their own. There's no problem with them. Lovely people. But Aidan, well, this is all new to him. His experience of family life has not been one of joy and merriment. So. He wants them checked out. By you."

Brennan stared at her, not sure what she meant.

"He thinks the world of you, Brennan. He has faith in you, just as you had in him."

Suddenly, Brennan didn't trust himself to speak.

"So I told him I'd track you down. Didn't tell him how easy you are to find!"

"Good of you, Sister."

"But of course it didn't occur to me that he'd see you pouring booze" — she looked around the crowded pub — "for the entire population of Dublin City."

"Em, what will we do?"

"Nothing for it but I bring them in here. We won't let on to them why." She slapped her hand down on the bar. "Don't go away."

In less than an hour Kitty returned with a middle-aged couple in tow. The man looked athletic and had good-humoured crinkles around his eyes. As did his wife. She was a bit oversized and had kindness written all across her face. They looked about the pub, lost in bewilderment. Kitty led them to the bar.

"Mr. and Mrs. Conlon, this is Father Burke."

Their bewilderment deepened as they tried to match the title with the job.

Mrs. Conlon spoke up, "I, em, I understand you're a friend of Aidan and you can tell us something about him." So that was the cover story Kitty had given them. "But really, there's no need. We've met Aidan and we'd love him to make his home with us."

"Well! That's . . . that's grand. Have a seat, why don't you."

They sat on bar stools and kept their eyes on Brennan. Should he offer them a pint? How did one proceed in a situation like this? He was saved by a young voice in the doorway.

"Brennan Xavier Burke! Where's your good suit? Still at the cleaners?" Aidan. His skin looked fresh and clean, his golden hair light and glossy, his clothes in good order. "Wait a minute. You're not . . . are you working here?" He caught sight of Kitty. "He's a man for surprises, so he is."

"Always has been," she agreed.

Aidan came up to the bar and nodded at the Conlons. Brennan noticed Monty and the MacNeil at the end of the bar, looking on warily. The Christy Burke Four were attuned to things, as well.

"I should explain," said Kitty. "Father Burke, first name Brennan, is the nephew of Finn Burke, who owns this pub. Finn is off today, so Brennan has kindly offered to tend the bar for him."

"Ah," Conlon said, and reached across the bar to shake Brennan's hand. Brennan held on to his hand for a couple of seconds and looked into his eyes. Nothing but good that he could see or feel. It was the same with the wife when he took her hand in his.

"Well, well, well!" Another new arrival. "Isn't this interesting? Newcomers in the place, and right up at the bar, too! Don't you know you have to pay your dues in time and in coin before you get a place of honour there? And who are these children? Have they changed the drinking laws since I was here last?"

No! Not now. McCrum.

The prying creature had come forward and fixed his eyes on the Conlons. "Wait a minute. I know you people. I've never known you to be drinkers. But after all those childer, some of them not the full shilling — God love you for taking them in, when no one else would — maybe you've finally been driven —"

This was not going to happen. Personal matters were not going to be hashed out in the presence of Motor Mouth McCrum.

"Mr. McCrum," Brennan said.

"Yes, Mr. Burke? Or do you go by your other title? I wonder what the archbishop would say if a little bird stuck a beak in his ear and told him —"

"There will be no little birds sticking their beaks in anywhere today."

"I beg your pardon!"

"Could you step outside with me for a moment?"

"Step outside?" McCrum looked about him and announced to the room at large, "He's asking me to step outside!"

Brennan came around the bar, grasped McCrum by the arm, and gently but firmly guided him to the door.

"What are you doing, Mr. Burke?"

"I'm escorting you from the premises."

"This is outrageous!"

Brennan got him outside.

McCrum blustered at him, "Unhand me, you impertinent man, and allow me to go about my business in the pub."

Would you listen to the highfalutin' language coming out of the creature? "Don't tempt me," Brennan warned, "to go beyond impertinence and put my hands around your throat. You'll not be doing any more of your business in Christy Burke's pub."

"Wait till I have a word with Finn about this!"

"Finn's not here. I'm the man in charge. Be off with you."

McCrum put out his elbow and tried to shove Brennan out of the way. Brennan grabbed the elbow, spun the man around, and pushed him towards the street. "Go. And don't let me hear your poisonous remarks or your black-hearted gossip in this place again."

"I don't know what you're talking —"

Brennan opened the pub door, then turned and said over his shoulder, "Fuck off. Consider yourself excommunicated."

Christy Burke's erupted in cheers and the thumping of tables. Brennan returned to his place behind the bar. He acknowledged the ovation with a little bow and got back to pouring drinks for a queue of drinkers waiting patiently for service.

Aidan was staring at him. "You're a hard man, too. I wonder how many other sides there are to your personality!"

"You don't want to know, Aidan, you don't want to know."

When the patrons had all been served, Aidan spoke up again, this time to his putative foster parents. "So. Do you think you'd be able to put up with me? I can be a little hard on the head at times."

"Aidan, dear," Mrs. Conlon said, "we've had our heads hardened by a houseful of children for nearly thirty years."

Something caught Aidan's eye at a table nearby, and he pointed. "You'd rather have *him*, wouldn't you?" Little Dominic was on the floor, peeking around the legs of the table, big eyes on the gathering at the bar.

The Conlons saw the baby and smiled. "Isn't he a dear little lad!" Mrs. Conlon said.

"Yeah, right," said Aidan. "He is. So that's what people want. Not someone as old as me."

The attitude was cocky, as if he couldn't care less who was wanted and who was not, but Brennan didn't buy it for a minute.

"Are you out of nappies, Aidan?" the woman asked him.

"I am."

"Well, so are we. What's the expression? We've been there and done that. Someone who can go to the toilet by himself, pick up his own fork, pour himself a glass of milk, that would be just the boy for us!"

"Is that so?" Aidan looked at Mr. Conlon.

"Whatever herself says. I follow orders." Everyone laughed. "I will say I don't miss the nappies, and I do like company watching the football."

Aidan eyed them for a while, then issued another challenge. "Do youse love me?"

Brennan didn't know where to look.

But Mrs. Conlon caught the ball and manoeuvred it to the goal like a master striker in the World Cup final. "Love takes a little while. We don't know you yet." She looked at him and smiled. "But there's something about you, Aidan. I've a feeling that a couple of nights with you in our home, maybe your second day at our breakfast table, I'm going to fall in love with you, my new son, and there'll be no getting away from me after that!"

Aidan clasped his hands together on the bar and looked down at them.

"Brennan?" Kitty prompted him.

Brennan wasn't a man for declaring his feelings at every whim and fancy. But this occasion called for it, so he spoke the truth. In his own way. "Wouldn't take two nights, I'm thinking. One long night and pizza for breakfast with him did it for me."

Aidan kept his eyes on the surface of the bar, but it was obvious that he was taking it all in. Brennan smiled at the boy and turned to Mr. Conlon. "How about you, sir?"

"Me? I'm as soft as shite. If herself falls in love with the lad two days in, I'm already there, worrying myself about the day he gets old enough to leave us. That's what I see for Aidan; I'll be missing him already, and him not two days in the house!"

Nobody spoke for a good fifteen seconds.

Then Aidan, in a subdued voice, said, "Good. If youse had said you loved me now without knowing me, I'd have taken you for eejits or liars."

"We're not either of those, I promise you," the missus said.

"Sister," Brennan said to Kitty. "Why don't you find a table for yourself and Aidan? I can't offer him a pint, him not being of age —"

"Aw, Brennan, it's not like I never —"

"You want to get me sacked from my job, Aidan?"

"No, barkeep, stay on the job. It keeps you off the streets."

"That's what I thought. You have a seat, and I'll bring you a pint of orange juice. For you, Kitty?"

"I'll have the same."

Brennan spent the next half hour or so chatting with the Conlons. They kept turning around to see Aidan, as if afraid he would disappear. But he didn't. By all appearances, he and Kitty were deep in conversation, which ranged from the intense to the hilarious, if their body language was anything to go by. Aidan's eye caught Brennan's every once in a while, and the boy would look away. As for the Conlons, there was no doubt in Brennan's mind that theirs was the place for Aidan. There would be rough times ahead for the lad, given the pain he had endured for so long in his young life. Nobody gets over that in a hurry, if they ever do. But the Conlons would provide a soft landing whenever he came home restless and troubled.

"Well, we should be off," Mrs. Conlon declared. "Have to pick up some things for our tea. For three of us, I'm hoping."

"I'm thinking there will be three of you at the table." Brennan sent a quick glance in the direction of Maura MacNeil and Monty. She smiled. He raised his glass. They knew a thing or two about human nature, and they appeared to be satisfied that the young fellow was in good hands.

The Conlons headed out, and Kitty Curran followed, after bidding goodbye to Monty and telling the MacNeil she'd see her back at the convent.

Aidan lingered in the doorway. "Brennan Xavier!" he called out.

Brennan looked at him, and the boy came over to the bar. "What d'yeh think of them?"

"If I weren't stuck behind the bar here I'd be trying to get in there ahead of you."

"No worries. I'll make up the spare room for you any time you like."

"Grand. And I'll make sure you have my phone numbers, the one here and the one overseas; that way, we can check up on one another." The boy nodded. "Mind how you go, Aidan. The blessings of God on you."

The lad's eyes held Brennan's for a moment, then Aidan turned and walked quickly from the bar. Brennan carved a sign of the cross at his retreating back.

Chapter 18

Michael

Michael sat at the table in his room Wednesday and read all about the plans for the special Mass for peace at the Pro-Cathedral the following night. The newspaper said the Archbishop of Dublin, the Cardinal Archbishop of Armagh, and the Bishop of Meath would concelebrate the Mass. The cardinal would give the homily. There would be a few short remarks by political leaders and clergy of other faiths. The church's Palestrina Choir would sing the Mass. A beautiful service, by the sounds of it. But what was this? The paper made a point of saying that Father Leo Killeen, the "well-known Republican priest," would not be speaking. Well, most people would not be speaking. Why single him out? Michael wondered if Leo was in his room. He thought he'd heard a radio in there. He got up and went next door, knocked, and was greeted by the well-known Republican priest himself.

"Afternoon, Michael. You just caught me. I'm on my way out."

"Are you ever in for more than the flash of a second? We called you yesterday from Christy's. Monty's off home and wanted to say his goodbyes."

"Ah. I'm sorry I missed his call. I'll see him next time, here or maybe over there. Who knows? So what's on your mind today?"

"I've just read that you're not speaking at the peace Mass."

"I never was going to speak at it. Wasn't going to sing at it, either, but now I'm doing that!"

"The reporter makes it sound as if you got a belt of the crozier and were refused permission, or got turfed from the roster, or something like that."

"None of the above."

"Well, I don't think much of that style of reporting!"

"Thank you for being concerned, Michael, but don't give it another thought. I've endured worse."

"I'm sure. Well, I'll let you go, and I'll send my blood pressure skyrocketing by reading the rest of the article."

"It will be a brilliant event, the peace Mass, no matter what the press says about it. Or about me. And to make it even more brilliant, Brennan has scheduled a little rehearsal for us this evening, seven o'clock. At the Aughrim Street church."

"Perfect. See you then."

Michael returned to his room and his paper. The news article was accompanied by the now-famous photo of Leo saying Mass in front of the British Army tanks in Northern Ireland with the crowds kneeling on the pavement for the Consecration. Soldiers and Orange Lodge marchers were visible in the background. Then there was an article rehashing all the troubles that had erupted after the death of the American evangelist.

Michael headed out just before seven o'clock that evening and walked down the street to the church to join his fellow choristers for rehearsal. Leo joked that he and Michael, who were both about six inches shorter than Brennan, should have chairs to stand on to even things out. "Isn't that what the matinee idols used to do in the talkies, to make themselves tower over the women?"

"We'll just give them a big voice," Michael replied, "and we'll be tall in their eyes as well as their ears. I'll stand here, Leo, just in front of the maestro, and you —"

"You'll stand where the sound dictates, lads. So let me hear the two of you before I join in." Brennan handed them the sheet music, then stood back to appraise them. When he had the sound he wanted, he joined in.

They went through *Ag Criost an Siol* a few times, and the three of them didn't sound half bad. Brennan pronounced himself satisfied, and Michael was keener than ever about the big night at the Pro-Cathedral.

✝

Finn Burke must have been in particularly good humour, or he may have been distracted by other concerns, if the television was permitted to quack away in the background of the pub without a hurling or football match being broadcast. Michael and Brennan had come to the pub after their rehearsal, ordered pints of Guinness, and sat themselves down at a table near the bar. Most of the patrons ignored the TV until the start of the nightly RTÉ newscast. And on this occasion, the lead story grabbed the attention of everyone in the room.

"There has been a surprising turn of events in the murder of the man thought to have been responsible for vandalizing a well-known Dublin drinking spot. The body of the man people are calling the 'Christy Burke's vandal' was found in a shallow grave near Dunsink Lane with green paint on his clothing, matching the spray paint on the walls of the venerable Northside pub. Now, another development. Garrett Logue has the latest. Garrett?"

"Quite the bombshell at Garda Headquarters today, Aideen. Unnamed sources close to the investigation say the gardaí were 'gob-smacked,' to quote one source, by lab results showing the bullets in this killing came from the same gun that was used in the shooting of two Special Branch detectives back in 1969. That shooting occurred in County Monaghan, not far from the border with Northern Ireland. The shooting of officers Philip Duggan and Owen Casey has never been solved. The Garda Síochána refuse to confirm or deny that the bullets used in that long-ago incident are the same type as in the recent murder victim. But our sources stand by their claim."

Good heavens! What in the name of God . . . Michael turned to Brennan, who looked as if he'd been hit by a shock wave. Not often you saw that; Brennan was usually such a stoic, but on this

347

occasion the eyes were nearly out of his head. His uncle, though, was standing there wiping glasses as if he hadn't heard a thing. Wouldn't you think Finn would be all ears? Perhaps he hadn't been listening. As for Brennan, what was going through his mind? Did he know more about all of this than he'd let on? Undoubtedly. And why not? Finn was his uncle; it would be only natural for him to confide in a family member, if he confided in anyone. What on earth was going on?

The news then featured a clip of the guards making inquiries at what appeared to be a car repair shop.

"That's McAvity's!" someone at the bar exclaimed. Michael watched intently as the television showed police walking past the open bays of the establishment and entering the front door, then talking to a person at a counter inside.

"That's Nurse McAvity himself behind the counter! Would you look at the face on him! You'll be needin' a drink now, Bill!"

"Oh, he's a man in need of a drop, all right! Warm milk isn't going to put you to sleep tonight, Nurse!"

The reporter's face came on, and he said, "Aideen, the gardaí are remaining tight-lipped about their investigation, but sources at McAvity Auto Service tell us the guards were taking samples of motor oil from the shop, apparently to be tested at the lab. Other sources tell RTÉ News that various substances are being collected for comparison purposes. That is, to compare them with traces of substances found on the body of the dead man. The man was believed to have been confined in the boot of a car before being wrapped in two large sheets of plastic and driven out Dunsink Lane to be buried. So, Aideen, several new avenues of investigation. Garrett Logue, RTÉ News."

An excited buzz arose around Michael in the pub. One wag said, "We thought you *were* the vandal, Nurse! Paying us back for slagging you about your drinking habits. But it seems you've done us a good turn. When we were all too sozzled to confront the vandal and cut his throat, you were out there being a man for all of us! Here's to Nurse!" The wag raised his pint, then drank it down.

Michael tuned out the banter. He was nursing thoughts of his own. There were many significant revelations in the TV news story, but one thing in particular puzzled and disturbed him: the statement that the dead man was confined to the boot of a car before being wrapped in plastic. Michael intended to follow that up next day.

He was jolted out of his ruminations by the arrival of a familiar face.

"They said He would come again. And lo and behold, here He is amongst us! If we only had palms to lay down before Him." That was Finn Burke, having a bit of fun with his guest. And perhaps trying to distract himself and others from the bombshell that had just been dropped by RTÉ News.

"If I weren't such a good-natured fellow, I'd tell you what to do with your palms, Mr. Burke. But I'm a jolly sort, so I thank you for that divinely inspired welcome."

"May I pour you a drink, Father?"

"Not this evening, good publican, thank you all the same. I am here to press this gentleman into service." Leo Killeen nodded towards Michael. "We're getting ready for the peace Mass tomorrow night at the Pro."

A murmur went through the pub in response to his words.

"Certainly, Leo. Let's go," Michael said.

"I can't promise to have him back to you this evening, Mr. Burke. I hope you will do a thriving trade nonetheless."

"We'll carry on as best we can, Fathers. Godspeed."

The two priests left the pub and walked briskly down Mountjoy Street to Dominick, across Dorset, and over to Parnell. It was past nine-thirty but still as light as day; Dublin may have palm trees but it is as far north as Labrador, and darkness falls late on summer nights. The murder investigation was very much on Michael's mind, but he knew Leo well enough to know this would not be a welcome topic of conversation. Even less welcome would be the murder of the Reverend Merle Odom, whose ghost brooded over the proceedings. Leo talked about the plans for the Mass, the procession, the music, messages to be given from the pulpit; it all sounded lovely. And, more to the point, it was the Catholics of Dublin taking a stand against the bombings and the shootings and all the other violence being perpetrated by those involved in the current Troubles, Catholic and Protestant alike. So despite all his other concerns Michael keenly anticipated the upcoming Mass for peace.

As they walked along, Michael was struck by something in Leo's demeanour; he kept glancing from side to side, and at one point he peered into the window of one of the shops as if it were a mirror.

Was he looking at something behind him? Michael started to turn. But Leo gently took his elbow and directed him forward. *Don't turn around*, was the message. What was going on? Michael made a point of catching the reflection in the next shop window, and he saw a small dark car a block behind. It didn't seem to be moving. He picked up his pace, but Leo did not, so he slowed down again. The next window check showed the car slightly ahead of where it had been. Michael thought he glimpsed two men in the front seat but he could not be sure; he was not about to linger by the glass. Had he been too quick to dismiss the notion that he was being followed that day in the rain? When they got to O'Connell Street and stopped at the cross light, he casually turned his head, but he could not see the car. Had it gone? Or was it one of the many now in view, hiding in plain sight?

There were two police cruisers across from the Pro-Cathedral when Michael and Leo arrived in Marlborough Street; otherwise, it was the usual crowd of priests, nuns, and busy-looking lay people on the steps of the church talking, carrying things, going in and out. A normal scene.

St. Mary's Pro-Cathedral looked more like a Greek temple than a church, with its six front columns and its portico. The ornate interior, with a dome, Doric columns, and side altars, was a far cry from Michael's little neo-Gothic church at home in Halifax, but he was well accustomed to the Pro after countless visits over the years. And he had given a spiel about the provisional cathedral to dozens of groups in his role as tour guide. Dublin's *real* cathedral or, more properly, its *original* Catholic cathedral, was the medieval Christ Church, which the Pope had constituted a cathedral at the behest of St. Lawrence O'Toole in the twelfth century. Christ Church was taken over by the Protestants at the time of the Reformation. Only the Pope can grant cathedral status to a church, and none of St. Lawrence's successors as Archbishop of Dublin had yet asked to revoke the status of Christ Church, so there was no official Catholic cathedral, just the Pro. Christ Church was still in Anglican — "Church of Ireland" — hands five hundred years after the Reformation. There was no getting away from history in Ireland.

Fathers Killeen and O'Flaherty genuflected deeply upon entering the building and stood for a few minutes watching a group of women place enormous bouquets of lilies and white roses on the altar. Then the two were approached by a large, burly man with a wire running from his ear to somewhere inside his shirt. He took Leo aside and spoke to him quietly. Michael strained to hear. All he could make out was "so well known, Father," and "escort you in and out afterwards," then something about "take my orders from a higher power." Leo patted the man on his powerful forearm and returned to Michael. Soon he and Leo were engulfed by a group of people discussing the liturgy, the placement of various prelates and dignitaries, and other details, and Michael threw himself into the work without any distractions. He sent up a silent prayer of thanks for being part of this event.

Brennan

It was all Brennan could do to stifle his impatience — his desperation — until closing time, when he could engineer a second nighttime confrontation with his uncle, this time about the Special Branch detectives and the gun. As soon as Finn locked the door behind the last lone reluctantly departing drinker, Brennan steered him into the dark recesses behind the bar and faced him.

"The gun, Finn. Tell me about it."

Finn, *sans* the shady glasses, regarded Brennan for a long moment with his cool grey-blue eyes, then pulled up two chairs, and they sat facing each other.

"You have to understand the effect the events of 1969 had on some of us here."

The history was well known to Brennan. Nineteen sixty-nine was the start of the new Troubles, in the North. Civil rights protesters were clubbed and beaten by the Royal Ulster Constabulary and the B Specials, a force founded by an Orangeman who once said in a speech that he "would not have a Catholic about the place." Their allies in the Loyalist paramilitaries began firebombing Catholic homes and businesses. In 1969 in Derry, the Bogsiders set up barricades to keep the RUC out and took to throwing petrol bombs at them. The Battle of the Bogside.

"Thousands on the Loyalist/Protestant side joined paramilitary groups to have a go at the Nationalists," Finn said. "That's when things got so bad the British Army was sent in. And *welcomed*, even in some Catholic quarters, as you may know, Brennan. But they've long since worn out their welcome. Meanwhile, back in Belfast, rumours were making the rounds that the *Irish* Army was coming across the border, or the Catholics were about to rise up — the massacres of 1641 all over again. Anyway, it all culminated in brutal mobs descending on the Falls Road, shooting into people's houses and setting them on fire. Nearly two thousand people lost their homes, the vast majority of them Catholics.

"Where was the IRA in all this? A handful of veterans from the old days scrounged a few weapons together and opened fire on the mob and the B Specials. If not for these old IRA hands, and a few young Volunteers, the entire Catholic community might have been destroyed. But where was the rest of the IRA? Sitting on their arses here in Dublin, dithering about the future of the movement. How far left should it go? Not only were the IRA leaders obsessed with politics, they didn't have any guns! They'd let things slide. Well, Northern Republicans were fed up with Dublin. Early the following year, the armed-struggle faction — the Provisional IRA — split from the politicos — the Officials.

"Your grandfather Christy was after us all to round up every rifle and pistol and pot and pan, and bundle them all into lorries and take them up North. Which we set out to do. But he wouldn't wait. He knew where to get his hands on a supply of guns and he did so, and he fired up one of our trucks and headed to the border in it. Seventy-six years old he was at the time, not a healthy man, but he was hard-headed and determined to do things his own way."

"Runs in the family, wouldn't you say?" Brennan remarked. There was more than a bit of that in himself; he couldn't deny it.

"Em, well, anyway the oul man is thinking he can make one last contribution to the cause. He's heading north in the dark of night in an unmarked vehicle, one that doesn't say Burke Transport anywhere on it, and he takes a roundabout route to get there because he knows people in Monaghan, and likely stops to pick up a consignment there. When he passes Emyvale he notices a car pull in behind him, and it stays on his tail until he's only about a mile from the border, and then this car whips by and veers in front of him and forces him to stop. It turns out this is Garda Special Branch, two of them in a car. One gets out and comes to Christy and demands to see what's in the back of the truck.

"'How good are you with a gun?' the garda asks oul Christy.

"'I'm brilliant.'"

In spite of himself, Brennan had to smile at that.

"'All right,' the garda says to him. 'I could lose my livelihood here. So do this right. Put a round through the shoulder of my coat. Then get on the move. On the way by, fire one at the rear wheel of the car. Our man's in the front on the radio, so make sure you go for the rear end! Don't come back through Monaghan. God go with you!'

"And the garda pulls out the shoulder of his coat away from his body, and Da fires a round through it. The man staggers back, playing out his role, and Da grinds the lorry into gear and goes forward. He fires a round into the rear tire of the garda car and another into the boot, races for the border, and gets across, then makes it to the outskirts of Belfast, where he meets his contact and unloads the weapons for the struggle. He turns around and comes back by way of Crossmaglen. And does he crow about it? He can't, except to me.

"There was an uproar about the gunrunner who shot at the guards, who were powerless to stop him; the story was, he nearly killed them. But he didn't nearly kill them and he didn't try to kill them. Nothing like that at all. Anyway, the garda who collaborated with Christy on the sly got to help the cause and keep his job, and everybody was happy. Oul Christy died with a smile on his face a few months later. Went out in a blaze of glory."

"Good man!" Brennan exclaimed, without even intending to.

"The gun Christy fired was a Russian Makarov PM, black with the communist star engraved on the butt of it. Russian bullets lodged in a garda car. Not too much trouble for the gardaí to put two and two together if they ever found that gun, so Da had it buried in the tunnel beneath the pub, and I left it there. Kept it as a souvenir."

"How did Christy get hold of a gun like that?"

"That's the sort of question you don't want to be asking, Bren, even to this day."

"Well, somebody used that gun, formerly kept on the premises of Christy Burke's pub, to kill the Christy Burke's vandal."

"You can rest assured it wasn't me."

"I believe you. But that doesn't mean the guards will, if they connect the gun to the building we're sitting in right now."

Chapter 19

Michael

The morning after the gun revelation, Michael was sitting in a taxi, barely listening to the amiable chattering of the driver. Michael was preoccupied. There was someone he had to see. Something he had to know, about a body that was transferred from one place to another and then wrapped for disposal.

He paid the driver and thanked him, then stood for a minute, getting his bearings and gathering his thoughts. He looked at a truck parked off to the side, then walked towards it. There was something slick in the open cargo area of the truck, a spill of some kind. Suddenly, there was the sound of feet hitting pavement, and Michael whirled around. A man had come up behind him. They stared at each other. Michael could see the anxiety and fear in the other man's eyes.

"Is there something you'd like to tell me?" Michael asked him.

A long moment of silence, then a barely audible, "Yes. Yes, Father, there is."

"Where?"

"In the front." The man gestured to the vehicle. "Nobody will bother us there."

When they were seated with the doors closed, the man said, "I know they're going to search here. The guards." He began to tremble. Father O'Flaherty waited for what was to come.

"He was blackmailing me. The vandal. He made an anonymous call to me on the phone and threatened to expose me unless I paid him off. Said he knew the truth about me and would make it public. And he did just that, when I told him to fuck off with himself and burn in hell. He painted a sly accusation on the wall of Christy Burke's, then called me again. I tried to suss out who he was, but I couldn't. He hung up the phone and went at Christy's wall again. A bunch from the pub stood guard but could never catch him at it. Which was fortunate for me; my secret would have been revealed. Anyway, when he telephoned me the third time, I was ready for him. I stayed on at Christy's after closing time. Went down into Finn's tunnel. I knew there was a gun there and I knew it was loaded. I took it."

Michael looked him in the eye. "Have you heard the latest news? That gun was used in the shooting of two Special Branch detectives in 1969."

"I heard." From the sudden pallor in the man's face, it looked as if he had just heard it for the first time. After a few moments, Michael prompted him to continue his story.

"I told him, the blackmailer, to meet me at Christy's at three in the morning, and I made a promise that I'd finally pay him to leave me alone. I had my vehicle parked nearby, the one we're using now as a confession box! I stayed inside Christy's, waiting, and helped myself to a couple of jars of whiskey. Then I went outside, brought the vehicle up onto the little patch of grass by the pub, retreated to the shadows with my glass, and waited. The man arrived and couldn't see me around the side of the building, so he started to spray-paint the wall again. I put my drink down, brought out the gun, forced him into the back there." He indicated the cargo area behind himself and Michael. "And I shot him twice in the back of the head. I had planned to take him out in the country and dump him, so I started to drive away from Christy's. Then I panicked and wanted to get rid of him right away. So I stopped. I knew about the old freezer that had been abandoned beside the black church. It had been there for weeks. People piled their rubbish there. I cleared the stuff off and dumped the body into the freezer. Made sure the lid was on good and tight.

I put all the sacks of rubbish back on top of it and took off. Came back here and spent an hour cleaning up the blood. Then I got into bed and got the shakes and stayed awake till it was time to get myself washed and dressed for Christy's. Took my regular seat and tried to behave in my normal way. And I guess I did. Nobody even knew the fucker had been killed. The young fellow who worked in the pub a couple of mornings a week, Kevin, he came to work and, if he saw anything out of the ordinary, he must have just put things back to normal and carried on."

Both men jumped in their seats at the sound of a car approaching. But it turned and went out of sight. The man was silent for a few minutes, then turned to face Michael.

"How can a person betray the people who love him, Michael, the people who trust and love him most in the world? I can't begin to fathom it. To me, the sun rose and set in his eyes. I killed him, Father! I launched myself at him and beat the life out of him. He didn't have a chance, from the time my fist slammed into the side of his head."

Michael stared at him. *What does he mean? What's this about a beating, and a betrayal?*

"He played our games, carried us on his shoulders, walked us to school, fought our battles for us, took a bloody nose for us. Taught us to be strong and true. But he was neither of those things, not when he became a man and —"

"You're not talking about the blackmailer now, the vandal. You're talking about —"

"My brother. Rod. I killed my own brother, Michael. God forgive me!"

Michael sat there in the cab of the truck, staring at Jimmy O'Hearn. He could hardly grasp what O'Hearn had just said.

"Our big brother, the man my sisters and I adored all our lives, betrayed us as soon as the opportunity came up to make a small fortune and keep it all for himself. A crowd of rich Yanks were looking at our family boat business. And Rod knew he could keep all the winnings if he knocked the rest of us out of play. He forged some papers that made me out to be mentally defective! He created some kind of criminal record that was meant to implicate my brother-in-law, Niall, in Donegal. All along I thought we'd been victimized by a crooked lawyer, that Rod was a broken, disappointed man living in poverty in New Zealand. But he created a whole new life for himself and a new name. Ted Hannington. We would still write to Rod O'Hearn at the post office address he kept; every once in a while, he'd send us a pathetic little note meant to show us he was living rough. Couldn't afford to fly home to Ireland. Didn't want anyone to see what he'd been reduced to. Well, I scraped up enough money to fly to New Zealand. Didn't tell the rest of the family. I wanted to scope out the situation first. I found Rod. And had my eyes opened in short order. He tried to cover his deeds with a lot of blather, but I knew. I went at him in a fury, killed him with my bare hands. I weighted his body down with stones and threw it into the sea. When they finally found it, they identified it as Ted Hannington. My sisters still think Rod's alive and unwell in New Zealand."

It took an enormous effort for Michael to hide his agitation as the confession unfolded.

"But then," O'Hearn said, "the vandal came into the picture. His name, I learned when I confronted him, was Noel Girvan. He was a low sort of person who had left Dublin and gone out to New Zealand to work, and he met some Irish people, discovered I had been there and, with one thing and another, he figured out the whole wretched business. When he lost his job and came back to Ireland, he saw the chance to make a living by bleeding me dry."

O'Hearn leaned forward, put his elbows on the steering wheel, and dropped his head into his hands. He remained motionless for nearly a minute, then sat up, looked in his rearview mirror and said, "It won't take the guards long to zero in on a man who drinks regularly at Christy Burke's and has marine engine oil in his possession. That's what their lab tests will show on the dead man's clothes. From when he was in the back of the truck. Blair McCrum was in the pub a while back, blathering on about traces of something — plant food or fertilizer — that got on a victim's clothes when he was kept in the killer's shed or his truck, whatever it was. That was a wakeup call. I'd mopped up the blood but I've got marine oil back there all the time. Now I keep cleaning it out. I even poured a bit of regular car engine oil in its place. I changed the oil, so to speak, Michael! I wonder if the guards will be fooled." He made a sound like a strangled laugh.

The guards would not be fooled, Michael reasoned, even though they had not seen what Michael had seen on his earlier visit to the

Poolbeg Marina. On that first occasion, when Michael had planned to tell Jimmy O'Hearn the truth about Rod's betrayal, he had noticed Jimmy cleaning the oil from the bed of his truck. Michael hadn't thought anything of it, until he saw last night's news report showing the guards collecting oil samples to compare with the substance found on the victim's clothing. That's when it clicked into place for Michael. It would not take the police long to determine that it was boat oil, not car oil, that they should be looking for.

O'Hearn concluded his terrible story. "The man had to die. Girvan. I could not, and cannot, bear the thought of anyone knowing that I killed my own brother, or that we as a family were betrayed from within. I confess to you, Father O'Flaherty, that I killed Roddy, but nobody will ever hear that from my lips again. They're going to get me for Noel Girvan, but not for Rod O'Hearn."

Michael waited with Jimmy until the guards came to take him away.

Chapter 20

Michael

Christy Burke's pub was in mourning over the arrest of Jimmy O'Hearn. Michael wasn't about to divulge anything he had learned from O'Hearn; he regarded their entire conversation as a confession. But he listened to the others, and murmured sympathetic replies. The sympathy was genuine despite the dreadful things Jimmy had done. Hate the sin, love the sinner.

Michael left Christy's around suppertime to get ready for Mass at the Pro and returned in the evening. There was a note tacked to Christy's door, announcing a traditional music session that night in the pub. Inside, the mood and the conversation were much as they had been earlier on. But Michael wanted to get away from that. This was a big night, the night of the peace Mass, and he wanted to enjoy it. He also intended to enjoy his last evening with Kitty Curran, who was flying back to Rome the next morning. So far he had avoided thinking of her departure, but now it was almost here. He chose a table at the back and sat by himself until Kitty, Maura, and Brennan arrived. Brennan, like Michael, was in his Roman collar, and the two women were wearing their churchgoing clothes as well.

Brennan took orders for soft drinks and went to the bar. Finn said he'd bring them over, so Brennan returned to the table. Leo Killeen arrived then, saw the group at the back, and joined them.

"Leo!" Frank Fanning called out. "I was reading about you today in the papers. They're still calling you the IRA priest. Nothin' ever goes away, does it?"

"And they're still calling this the IRA pub, so it's only fitting that I should be able to get a drink in here, and a quick one at that. The press can call me the divil's priest, for all I care. Bunch of jackals. I pay them no mind." He turned to Michael. "Congratulations are in order, I hear. Well done, Sergeant O'Flaherty!"

Maura and Kitty stared at Michael.

Brennan leaned over and said, "Word's out, Michael. You were there with O'Hearn when the guards arrived. You solved it. Good job."

"I don't exactly feel elated over it. Jimmy O'Hearn! Just shows you what we're all capable of."

"Of course," Brennan said, "we don't know why the vandal singled out O'Hearn in the first place, or what was so grievous about the accusation that Jimmy killed the man over it."

Michael avoided Brennan's eyes and, after an uncomfortable few seconds, he murmured, "It was a personal matter." He looked at Leo. "Not political, after all. I suppose that's a relief in a way."

"Your intuition was correct, Michael."

"Not much glory in being right, Leo. Poor Jimmy. And God bless and save his poor family."

"But we have other things on our minds tonight," Brennan reminded them after a moment.

"That's right," Michael replied. "A beautiful Mass. Something to hold on to when tomorrow comes." Michael's eyes rested on Kitty across the table.

Finn appeared with the drinks and announced that they were all on the house.

"Thank you, Finn," said Brennan, as he lit up a cigarette and took a puff. "But I must say I was hoping Kitty would be buying all the rounds, given that it's her last night with us here."

"Is it now, Kitty?" Finn asked. "Where are you off to?"

"I'm going back to the Vatican City, Finn, to dry out after all my drinkin' with you lot."

"Will you be back to Dublin any time soon?"

"I'll make a point of it."

Michael was emboldened then to speak of their next encounter. "Let's stay in touch so we can meet here again, Kitty. It's been lovely seeing you." That was an understatement, but what else could he say, really? Best to stick to practical matters. "Dublin's only a five-hour flight from home. For me, anyway. How long is it from Rome?"

"I can get here in three hours. Just a short hop."

"And there will always be a bed for you at the house in Stoney-batter, Michael," Leo assured him.

"There you go then. We'll meet here. Or maybe I'll be called to Rome on urgent business for the Holy Father. I've never received a call from the papal apartments in the first forty-five years of my priest-hood, but there's always hope."

"I'll have a word with him on your behalf, *acushla*," she assured him.

"Don't be listening to her, Mike!" Brennan exclaimed. "I'll bet she says that to all the fellows she hooks up with. The Pope probably doesn't even take her calls anymore."

"Ah, now, Brennan, I'm sure the Holy Father has left standing orders for Kitty's calls to go directly to his private quarters."

"If he has, it's only because she's got him bamboozled, too," Brennan replied. "Look at her."

Michael did. Her eyes sparkled at him, and his heart was filled with love for her. How he would miss her when she left for Rome. Well, there was a postal service and telephones, and there was no law, civil or canonical, against making full use of them. To maintain con-tact with a friend.

Brennan was still going on, "A woman out with three men in a bar. What does she get up to in Rome? We can only imagine. She'll leave you with a broken heart, Michael."

"What was it Daniel Patrick Moynihan said?" Maura asked. "To be Irish is to know that in the end the world will break your heart."

Brennan took in a lungful of smoke and exhaled it. "He was right. Walk away now, Michael."

"About that next visit to Dublin, Michael," Kitty said, "any chance you'll be able to get away on your own, without your little brother tagging along?" She gave Brennan the evil eye, then returned her gaze to Michael. "You and I and Father Killeen will have a much more spiritually uplifting sojourn if we don't have to put up with this unholy reprobate."

Michael laughed and looked at Leo, but it was obvious the banter had gone over his head. He appeared to be preoccupied.

"All right, lads," Kitty said, "*ad altare Dei.* Let's hope the grace of God descends on one and all, so there'll be an end to the senseless killing on this island."

The young barman, Sean Nugent, walked in then and went behind the bar with Finn.

"Does this mean you'll be joining us at the Pro, Finn?" Michael asked.

Brennan turned to look at his uncle.

"No," was all Finn said. He shared a look with Leo, but no words were spoken.

The five Mass-goers headed out into the soft misty Dublin night: Kitty and Maura, Brennan, Michael, and Leo.

As usual, O'Connell Street was thronged with people walking, talking, partying, celebrating a football or a hurling victory. But it wasn't all *ceol agus craic,* music and fun. Michael couldn't miss the stepped-up police presence. Everyone was conscious of what had happened to the Protestant minister from the U.S., and the explosion of violence in the North as a result. How many more people would fall victim to it all before it ended? The event in Dublin, the peace Mass, was meant to bring Irish people of all faiths together, but it was obviously first and foremost a Catholic ceremony. A ceremony that might not be seen in a positive light by everyone on the island.

Brennan was visibly tense as they crossed the wide thoroughfare and headed east to the church.

Michael asked quietly, "Brennan, are you expecting trouble at the Mass tonight?"

"I don't know what to expect," he answered.

Michael's mind returned to the night of the concert in Belfast, the spine-tingling high note at the end of Leontyne Price's aria, in which she prayed for peace and cursed those who profaned the sacred places. Was that high note still reverberating in Brennan's mind? What had he seen, or experienced, that night?

"Brennan, that night in Belfast, what exactly did you —"

Brennan replied in a voice that was barely audible. "If I knew, don't you think I'd tell you, Michael? Tell everyone?"

They walked along Cathedral Street to Marlborough Street, where the police presence was even more pronounced. A large crowd stood outside the church, illuminated by television lights. A stout man with thinning auburn hair and a large silver cross on his chest was speaking to a TV reporter. The man looked exhausted — perhaps he'd been putting a lot of time into this event — but he gamely answered the reporter's questions.

"Who would that be now?" Michael asked Leo.

"Bishop Clancy."

Brennan turned towards Leo, and the two exchanged a glance. Was there something significant about this bishop? The name was familiar to Michael. Then he had it. "Ah. From Meath. I've read some of his articles on scripture, and learned a great deal from them. I recognize him now, from his photograph. He's aged a bit. But haven't we all?"

"We have indeed," said Leo.

Michael heard the reporter thank Bishop Clancy for his time. Then she caught sight of Leo Killeen and his companions and headed their way with her cameraman.

"Father Killeen! Father Killeen! Some people thought you would be speaking tonight, but you're not on the list. Have you been silenced by the powers that be?"

Leo didn't bother to say "no comment." Nor did he announce that he would be addressing the congregation in song.

He and Michael and their friends waited patiently in the queue as every person entering the church was searched and scanned with a metal detector.

Finally they were in, and the Mass began. The ritual and pageantry of the occasion were heightened by the participation of the cardinal and the archbishop, dozens of sisters, priests, altar servers, and ministers of other faiths, joined by the president and prime minister of Ireland and members of the diplomatic corps. Incense rose to the heavens as a representation of prayer, and the church was ablaze with candlelight. The church's Palestrina Choir sang the Mass, the beautiful *Missa Papae Marcelli*.

And at the Offertory, the "Blessed Trinity" of Fathers O'Flaherty, Killeen, and Burke walked to the altar and turned to face the congregation for their musical contribution, *Ag Críost an Síol.* Michael noticed a number of faces that were familiar to him from his time in the city. One was a striking young woman with black curls and bright blue eyes. Someone from the pub, he recalled. He saw her do a double take when she noticed Brennan. Right, Michael remembered. There had been some confusion in her mind about just who Brennan was. And why he wasn't available to attractive young females in Dublin! Now she knew for sure; he hadn't just been putting her off. Michael saw a smile spread across her face at the sight of Father Burke. Michael had to smile himself.

Brennan gave his fellow Trinitarians their notes, and Michael and Leo backed him up as he sang of death, rebirth, paradise, and grace. Never had Michael loved the Irish language as he did that night. It meant the world to him to be singing in the Pro-Cathedral in Dublin alongside Brennan Burke, with his beautiful voice, and Leo Killeen, with his complex history as a rebel and a priest. Killeen's voice, although perfectly in tune, was rough around the edges, and it added something raw to the sound, something that made the performance all the more heartfelt. Michael tried not to commit the sin of pride by dwelling on how pleased he was to be singing in the presence of the leading lights of the Irish church and state. It only got better when Brennan invited those in the congregation familiar with the piece, and the old language, to join in a reprise of the hymn. Michael sneaked a glance at Kitty Curran and saw that she was singing along. All those voices filling the church with their ancestral language was the most moving sound Michael had ever heard.

As the Mass neared its conclusion, no one missed the significance of the *Agnus Dei qui tollis peccata mundi, dona nobis pacem.* Lamb of God, who take away the sin of the world, grant us peace.

Security was tight as the clergy and dignitaries filed from the church, followed by the people of Dublin. The cardinal and the bishops were whisked away in heavily guarded limousines. Other clerics left in squad cars. Leo Killeen was hailed by his fellow Dublin priests, and introductions were made all round. The media stayed until all but a few stragglers had left, then packed up for the night.

When they were once again among the regular Dublin crowds in O'Connell Street, Brennan's mood seemed lighter. Nobody discussed plans for the rest of the evening; like old horses plodding back to the barn, they set out in the direction of their local. Leo Killeen filled the others in on the personalities, the politics, and the foibles of the high personages they had seen at the Pro.

The city was dark, and the street lamps cast warm, bright haloes in the Dublin mist. Michael wondered if it was just him, but he was a little spooked by a car that had been travelling slowly behind the group and then stopped a block back of them in Parnell Square West. Michael glanced at Brennan but he did not show any sign of being on edge. Nor did Leo, who would be most familiar with what looked right and what looked wrong on a Dublin street at night. Michael turned and took a quick peek at the vehicle. He didn't know one model of car from another; all he knew was that this one was middling in size and silver in colour and had its low beams on. He could not make out how many people were in it. *I shouldn't be so jumpy*, he told himself, *especially if nobody else is*. He turned to Kitty and Maura, and joined their animated conversation.

"What are you two gabbing about?"

"Nothing, Father," Kitty replied in the tone of a sly schoolgirl caught talking in the classroom.

"We were just saying how lucky we are to be in the company of the Father, the Son, and the Holy Spirit," Maura said, bowing her head in the direction of Fathers Killeen, Burke, and O'Flaherty in turn. "And we have the Holy Mother with us as well." She put her arm around Kitty and pulled her close.

"Well, isn't that lovely of you, good Catholic girls that you are."

"Actually, all slagging aside, we *are* blessed to be in your company," Kitty said then, "and your singing was beautiful!" Maura nodded in assent. Michael basked in the glow of Kitty's words.

"Leo," he said, "you should be doing more of that. You sounded wonderful."

"He was brilliant," Brennan agreed. "I want to sing that piece again, and I want you with me when I do, Leo. You, too, Michael."

As they wound their way through the city to their destination, the conversation veering from the profane to the profound to the foolish, Michael noticed that the silver car stayed with them. It followed them into St. Mary's Place, the side street that met Mountjoy Street at the corner where Christy Burke's was situated. There was no room for doubt. And there they were, Michael and Brennan and Leo, wearing their Roman collars for all to see, at a time when a Roman collar would be a beacon for those bent on revenge for the killing of the Protestant minister. And of the three of them, the only one with a familiar face — a well-known *Republican* face — was Leo Killeen. Leo was in the last row of the little parade, in conversation with Brennan and, as far as Michael could tell, not worrying obsessively about every vehicle in the street.

Well, Michael had no intention of staying silent for another second. He dropped back until he was level with Killeen and said, "Leo, don't look now but there's a car following us. It's been with us —"

"Michael, pay it no mind. Don't turn around. Just keep walking. It's nothing to trouble yourself about."

"How do you know?"

"I know."

How could Leo feel so confident walking through the shadowy streets when the threat of sectarian violence seemed to be pressing in on them? Well, the answer was obvious, or so Michael hoped: Leo had recognized the vehicle or its occupants and knew they did not pose a threat. After all, this was Dublin, not Belfast. Michael felt the tension flowing out of him. He smiled at Kitty and Maura, who were intent on their conversation with one another; he passed them and caught up with Brennan.

They were in sight of home, Christy Burke's pub. Warm golden light shone through the windows, and Michael could hear music. That's right, he remembered, there was a session scheduled for tonight. He could hear a lovely version of "Macushla." Wouldn't a pint go down nicely right now, all of them sitting around a table, basking in the glow of friendship, and love, and the grace of God still with them after the Mass for peace.

Still, Michael was going to put his foot down. He intended to escort Kitty to her convent on this, her last night in town, to say his goodbyes and make sure he had her address and phone number in Rome. So he would not be going to the house in Stoneybatter with Leo Killeen. Therefore, Michael had orders for Leo.

He turned to Brennan. "I've heard enough about you and your family to know that your oul da, Declan Burke, is a forceful personality."

"You said a mouthful there, Michael. A tough old skin is Declan."

"And yet he takes orders from that mild-looking gentleman right there." Michael nodded in the direction of Leo, who had stopped and was peering down the street behind them. "Is that not a fact?"

"It was. Maybe it still is! How much do we really know about what these old warriors are up to?"

"Exactly. Well, you can tell Declan next time you see him that there's been a change of command. Leo Killeen is taking orders now, and he's taking them from Michael O'Flaherty."

"Is that so? What orders would these be?"

Michael and Brennan arrived at the pub and waited by the door for the others to catch up. Michael raised his voice so all could hear, as he laid down the law.

"Tonight, when we finish up here, Father Killeen will not be walking home but will be tucked safely into a taxi. If he puts up an argument, I'll dig down into my pocket and pay the fare myself. And I shall see to it —"

The scream of tires cut off Michael's words. Everyone looked to the sound in Mountjoy Street. A small dark car came rocketing towards them. It screeched to a halt at the corner, and the back window was rolled down. It happened so fast the group on the pavement just stood and gaped.

Leo was the first to react. He turned to the others and shouted, "Get inside!"

As so often happens to people in moments of extreme danger, time slowed down for Michael. He saw a face in the car window — two faces. He recognized them. From where? A car. He had seen them in a car before. And now Michael saw the barrel of a gun.

Michael shouted, "Leo, no!"

Leo turned to the women and cried out again, "Get inside!"

Brennan made a dive in Leo's direction, but he was too far away to reach him.

Michael couldn't move his legs. He was rooted to the ground in shock and fear. He saw the muzzle of the gun pointing directly at Leo. *Oh, no, please God, don't let this happen.* Michael saw the gun move and he heard a voice from inside the car. It seemed to say, "It's that one! Now!" A northern accent. Michael heard gunfire. Two shots. He felt something hit his forehead. The car took off.

Another vehicle roared up behind them in the side street. It was the silver car that had been tailing them. There was a squeal of brakes and a man leapt out of the passenger side. Then — another shock Michael couldn't absorb — the man straightened up and opened fire with a machine gun. As the strains of "Macushla" wafted out into the night, the man stood in the road and kept on firing at the dark-coloured car as it vanished into the darkness in Mountjoy Street. The escaping vehicle was hit several times, but it kept on going. The man with the machine gun got back into the silver car, and it sped away in pursuit.

Something trickled into Michael's right eye, and he wiped it away. He looked at his hand. Blood.

And then reality hit him like a shot to the heart. Kitty was on the ground, blood seeping onto the pavement from a wound in her head and another in her chest. Maura was lying on the ground with her arms around Kitty. Brennan was bending over them. People came pouring out of Christy Burke's even as the song went on inside. Someone said the guards were on their way. Michael stood there, his world blasted to pieces. How could Brennan and Maura both be at Kitty's side while Michael was still standing there, useless?

Leo Killeen was alone in the road, his face white as a shroud. "God forgive me, it should have been me. They went for her. They had me, and they went for her." He moved towards Kitty. "Let me see her, Brennan. Move out of the way."

Michael saw that Maura had opened Kitty's blouse and was applying a garment of some kind to try to staunch the bleeding. Leo looked at the head wound and then gently pulled Maura away. It was no use.

Leo turned to Michael, who was still standing there, catatonic.

"Michael, I heard them say 'it's that one.' I'm thinking they recognized her from the Mass with the tanks in South Armagh. The television or the newspaper photos. They must have made a split-second calculation, that this, gunning down a woman, would cause more pain than the loss of a Republican priest. And the Republican priest would have to live with it for the rest of his days. It should have been me."

Michael heard sirens wailing, coming closer.

Then Finn Burke was on the scene. He shouted to Leo, "The car's abandoned up the road. They had another car waiting. They got away. For now."

Only then did Michael realize it had been Finn Burke following them from the Pro in the silver car, watching their backs. It had been Finn Burke standing in the street in front of his pub firing a machine gun at the killers as they fled.

Michael stared at Kitty on the pavement. One hand looked as if it was reaching. Reaching for Michael? But he knew better; she had been shot in the head. All thought, all personality, all the earthly life of Kitty Curran had been extinguished by the time she hit the ground. It was unbearable to contemplate. It broke his heart.

Brennan Burke had warned him, Leo Killeen had warned him. Both men knew how misplaced was Michael's determined optimism. They knew all too well how the unfinished history of their beloved country could erupt any minute, bringing devastation in its wake. Leo's words came back to him, about the Civil War, "Someone fundamental to your world was gone from the world in an instant." Michael thought he had understood. But he had understood nothing, until this moment. This is what it was like: the Troubles, then and now.

He saw Brennan comforting Maura. Or was it the other way around? Was she comforting him? He looked at Michael, then gave Maura a little nudge. *Go to Michael, a man even more in need of a woman's consolation.* She came towards him, her face streaked with tears, her clothing soaked with Kitty's blood. She, too, needed consoling. They all did. But there was no consolation.

There was only loss and pain and grief, of a ferocity Michael would not have thought possible. For the first time in his life, he felt utterly forsaken. How could a loving God allow this to happen, allow a woman who had served Him all her life to be annihilated by people who were unworthy to speak her name? But even in extremis, Michael counselled himself against such thoughts: every life was precious, every killing was unjustified, every murder was committed by man, not God. That's what Michael told himself. But God seemed very remote to him as he stood in the blood-stained Dublin street and saw what was left of the woman he loved.

Michael's life would resume, he knew. But he could not imagine how: he had no desire to take another breath, to take another step, to hear another song.

Macushla! Macushla! Your red lips are saying
That death is a dream and love is for aye
Then awaken Macushla, awake from your dreaming
My blue-eyed Macushla, awaken to stay.

Acknowledgements

I would like to thank the following people for their kind assistance: Rhea McGarva, Joan Butcher, Joe A. Cameron, Barbara Fradkin, Edna Barker, and, as always, PJEC.

In addition to my own personal research in the pubs of Dublin, Derry, and Ballybofey, I am indebted to Kevin C. Kearns for his comprehensive and fascinating examination of the history of Dublin pubs, in *Dublin Pub Life & Lore: An Oral History* (Niwot: Roberts Rinehart, 1997), first published in Ireland by Gill & Macmillan Ltd.

All characters and plots in the story are fictional, with the exception of some historical references. Endastown is a made-up town. Christy Burke's is a fictional pub, as is the unfriendly pub Michael enters in the North. All other pubs are real. Any liberties taken in the interests of fiction, or any errors committed, are mine alone.

*Here's a sneak peek at Anne Emery's
next Collins-Burke mystery*

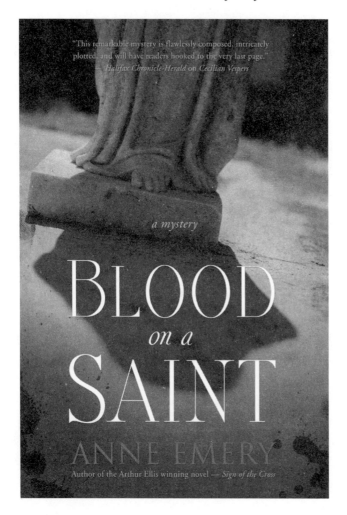

"This remarkable mystery is flawlessly composed, intricately
plotted, and will have readers hooked to the very last page."
— *Halifax Chronicle-Herald* on *Cecilian Vespers*

a mystery

BLOOD
on a
SAINT

ANNE EMERY

Author of the Arthur Ellis winning novel — *Sign of the Cross*

Chapter 1

Monty

"Burke fired her."

"Eh?"

"The wrongful dismissal file. She was hired as a secretary at the church. Turned out she couldn't spell, and she kept taking bogus sick days. So Burke sent her packing. Now she's suing for damages."

Monty Collins's law partner, Ronald MacLeod, pointed to one of the files on the desk, files that had piled up while Monty was out of town for the first week of a two-week trial.

"Oh." Monty picked up the folder. Befanee Tate. "*Befanee?* When did they hire her? I remember seeing a new face over there. I said hello on the occasions I was in, but I never actually met her."

"She wasn't all that new. Four months ago."

"How much did they offer her as severance pay?"

"Month's salary."

"So what's she complaining about? That's more than a judge would give her if it went to court."

"She wants it all. Compensation for mental anguish, loss of reputation, punitive damages, you name it."

"Burke won't be too happy about that." Monty knew Father Burke well. The priest had a limited tolerance for this sort of aggravation.

"You got that right. He asked for you, and I told him I'd bring it to your attention as soon as you got back. I'll leave you to it."

"Thanks, Ron." This was the Saturday of the Labour Day weekend. A lost weekend, but not the kind Monty had enjoyed before becoming a partner at Stratton Sommers. He was in the office, and he would be flying back to Toronto Sunday night for the second week of the products liability trial. "I'll have a word with him next week."

"I'm sure he'll be fine with that," Ron said.

"Right," Monty answered. He was distracted by all the work in front of him. "Can't say this Befanee Tate matter is the most urgent case on my docket!"

"I hear you." MacLeod headed for the door, then turned back. "Oh, and she claims the Virgin Mary appeared to her in the churchyard."

Monty rolled his eyes and tossed the file aside. He would see Burke at some point and reassure him that he had offered Befanee Tate more than enough in compensation, Virgin or no Virgin, and he could put it out of his mind. End of story.

✝

The following Friday night Monty boarded the plane in Toronto and flopped into his seat for the flight home to Halifax, exhausted but relieved. The trial had come to a successful conclusion, the fourteen-hour work days were over, and he was on his way back to a saner, kinder, gentler way of life. He fastened his seat belt and nodded yes to the flight attendant when she came by with the day's newspapers. He took the Halifax *Chronicle Herald* and proceeded to catch up on the news in his hometown. On the front page, below the fold, was a photo of a crowd of people taking part in some kind of protest or gathering in a parking lot. He looked closer and saw some people kneeling, others carrying what appeared to be religious icons. One person was lying on a stretcher, with attendants at both ends. A bearded man in a long, belted robe appeared to be making a speech. A young girl with a round, pretty face and thin hair pulled back in a ponytail stood gazing at a statue. Monty recognized it as the figure of St. Bernadette in the churchyard on Byrne Street. There was often a group of people around the statue, devotees of the saint. But now there were tents on the site. And what was that? A cart — no, three carts — piled with goods of some kind.

Looking over all this was . . . he was shown from the back, but Monty would have known him anywhere. The caption read, "Father Brennan Burke looks out at the crowd gathered in his Halifax church-yard in response to the claimed sighting of the Virgin Mary." Neutral the prose may have been, but Burke's posture spoke volumes to Monty. He could tell that the priest's arms were folded across his chest; Monty could picture the profile, the hawkish nose, the lips clamped shut, the black eyes scourging the scene, the animosity emanating from him in waves. Monty let out a bark of laughter, which caused heads to turn in his direction. Then he read the piece.

VIRGIN MARY APPEARED IN HALIFAX, WOMAN CLAIMS

A carnival atmosphere pervades the once-staid grounds of St. Bernadette's church, in the wake of a claim by a Halifax County woman that the Virgin Mary appeared to her above a statue of St. Bernadette. Pilgrims from as far away as Montreal and the eastern United States have travelled to the city, some of them sleeping in tents on the church grounds. There was a clash yesterday as two self-styled prophets strained to outdo each other in proclaiming the Word, and police were called when one tugged at the beard of the other and smote him with a homemade wooden sword. Souvenir vendors jostled for space in the parking lot and offered such wares as plastic rosaries, vials of "Lourdes water," and even "Bernie Bears," teddy bears garbed in the religious habit worn by St. Bernadette, the young French girl who, in 1858, reported receiving visions of the Virgin and then dis-covered a miraculous spring. Thousands claim to have been cured at Lourdes ever since.

Befanee Tate says her attention was drawn to the statue initially when she saw a homeless man staring intently at it. Befanee had seen him frequently during the four months she worked as a secretary at the parish office. One day, she decided to approach the statue herself and, after a few minutes of silent reflection, she saw a form materialize and hover above the figure of Bernadette. At first, she said, she refused to believe it was the Virgin Mary, but later she could no longer deny the presence of the Mother of God. Asked whether the apparition had spoken to her, Befanee said she would be making a statement at a later time. Another woman, interviewed after a spell of kneeling before the statue, said she could "feel the presence of the heavenly mother" and felt at peace for the first time in her life.

Father Brennan Burke, parish priest at St. Bernadette's, tersely refused comment on the situation. But the church's pastor, Monsignor Michael O'Flaherty, reached while on a retreat at Monastery in the eastern part of the province, said he would take a wait-and-see attitude to the hubbub surrounding his parish. "I hope and trust that people will comport themselves in a respectful manner until we see what is happening, and I will keep the pilgrims in my prayers until I return."

"Look at them!" Burke stood at the window of his choir school, the Schola Cantorum Sancta Bernadetta, glaring down at the motley crowd of pilgrims, seekers, gawkers, and hawkers. "Where did all these people come from?"

It was the Monday after Monty's return to Halifax, and Monty was waiting for Father Burke to wrap up his workday at the schola, where he taught traditional sacred music to church musicians from around the world. He and Monty were heading out for a draft or two at their local drinking spot, the Midtown Tavern. Monty's wife, Maura, would be joining them later.

"Many of them are well-known characters in the city, Brennan. Habitués of the courts and the wall in front of the library. And the mental health wards. You've given them a new home, Father."

"I've not given them any such thing. It wasn't my image that appeared above the statue, for the love of Christ."

"Is that a backhanded confirmation of the claims, Father, an acknowledgement that there was an image? Should I alert the press?"

4

"Oh, your bollocks, Montague. This is highly amusing to you, but highly aggravating to me. I can't walk from home to my church or my choir school without becoming part of this carnival of charlatans."

They left the choir school and headed out for the brisk ten-minute walk from the corner of Byrne and Morris streets to the Midtown on Grafton. It was ten minutes mostly uphill on the way there; sometimes it took longer on the way back, even with the downhill advantage.

"An Irishman walks into a bar," Monty said when they arrived at the door.

"And?" Burke prompted him.

"Just stating a fact."

"Two Irishmen walk into a bar. You're an Irishman yourself, yeh gobshite."

"Half."

"All right, a half-arsed Irishman walks into a bar. We're here. Anything else you have to say? No?" Catching the eye of the waiter, Brennan said, "Two draft, Dave, if you please."

"They're already on the table, boys. Saw you coming."

"They say the universe is fine-tuned to support life. Here's the proof," Burke said with a sigh of contentment. "Thank you, David."

They talked sports with the waiter for a few minutes and consumed their first draft with pleasure. But the mood did not last.

"I can't take much more of this bedlam," Burke remarked as he lifted his second glass to his lips. "The self-styled preachers in the churchyard, the hawking of the tawdry souvenirs, the transparently phoney claims of *Befanee* Tate that she's been unjustly dismissed and visited by the Blessed Virgin, the cacophony of noisy gongs and clanging cymbals. What the hell is wrong with people?" He sank half his draft in one go.

Monty had to feel sorry for the beleaguered priest — a man whose approach to religion was a melding of faith and reason, emphasis on the reason; a man who revelled in the complex intellectual gymnastics of the great philosophers; an intellectual who took the rational pathway to the irrational; a man who revered those who had reached the summit of human achievement: Plato, Aristotle, Mozart, Bach, Newton, Einstein. Now, all he was seeing around him was the irrational, the absurd, the loud, and the loony.

"This too shall pass, Father."

"Not soon enough." He signalled Dave for another round and thanked him when it arrived. He picked up his glass and took a mouthful. "I don't want to be associated with this, particularly if . . ."

"If what?"

"Well, nothing's cast in stone yet."

"What are you talking about?"

"There may be a well-known . . . musician coming to visit the choir school, if the fates allow."

"Who?"

"No point in telling you in case it doesn't work out. And this sideshow in our churchyard does nothing to enhance our reputation and our chances of being included on the tour. I'm thinking of disappearing until this blows over." He drained his glass and brought it down hard on the table. "I'm thinking of heading to Antigonish County for a spell in the monastery."

"What?" Monty halted the mouthward motion of his glass and stared at his friend. "You? A monk?"

Then someone else chimed in. "Did I hear you correctly, Father, or am I having a psychotic episode?"

Burke's head jerked up at the sound of the familiar voice. "Ah. The MacNeil."

Maura MacNeil took her place at the table and stared at Burke. Her mild appearance — a sweet face, soft shoulder-length brown hair with a bit of grey, and matching grey eyes — sheathed a sharpness of mind and of tongue.

Dave came by with a tray of draft, took a glass, and raised his eyebrows in inquiry.

"Normally I would," she said, "but I'm wondering what's in the stuff tonight. I'm hearing some crazy talk at this table. But sure, I'll have one. This pair of reprobates will ensure that I'm not drinking alone, so you might as well give us three."

Dave put three down and moved off.

"What did I hear you saying, Father? Please repeat it and I'll try to comprehend it as best I can."

"I'm going to enter the monastery."

"And thereby become the least likely monk in the history of the world."

The idea of the worldly, hard-drinking, sexually-been-there-done-

6

that Burke removing himself from the world and living the life of a monk was inconceivable.

"Time to take Father to the detox," she said. "I wonder how many times that sentence has been uttered in this province, eh? Dad's off to the detox."

"I'll give you another sentence that's been uttered frequently in this province and elsewhere in the world," Burke replied, "and it's a lot shorter and to the point."

"Now, Father, don't be bitter. And don't worry. The monks have done wonders with hard cases before you. You may come back to us boasting of a miraculous cure!"

They did have a rehabilitation centre there, but that was not on Burke's agenda. Monty knew his drinking history well. Burke had a considerable tolerance for booze but could give it up for extended periods without any adverse effects. He liked a drink, certainly. But he was not addicted.

"Whatever it's like in there, it can hardly be worse than what is happening on the grounds of my church these days."

"Now, Brennan," she replied, "life should have taught you this much by now: there is always something worse." And there was. Duty called upon Father Burke before he could flee to the cloistered life.

He and Monty were walking across the churchyard two days after the session at the Midtown.

"Brennan, watch where you're — "

"Christ!" Burke stumbled and landed on his knees, hands flat on the ground. Monty could see his lips moving. A colourful string of curses, without question. He had tripped over a pair of crutches lying in the grass. He batted at the knees of his pants when he got up.

"Leave them, Father. Dirty knees will send the right message to your public; you've been kneeling in prayer at the shrine."

"Feck off."

"Isn't that a fine way for one of my priests to be talking!"

No! His Grace, the Most Reverend Dennis Cronin, Archbishop of Halifax. But there wasn't a trace of embarrassment on the face of his priest.

"My apologies, Dennis. I allowed myself to be baited by one of my parishioners here, and failed to control my tongue. If you knew him, you'd understand. Your Grace, may I present Monty Collins. Not a bad fellow really, when all is said and done."

"Your Grace, it's an honour to meet you."

"Likewise, Mr. Collins. I have seen you and I know of your legal work, but this is the first time I've had the opportunity to be introduced. What do you think of all this go-ahead?" He made a sweeping gesture with his left arm, indicating the circus that had grown up around the church.

Monty just shook his head.

The archbishop was in his late fifties, tall, broad-shouldered, and handsome, with thick, fair hair going white and shrewd blue eyes behind a pair of stylish glasses. He wore a Roman collar and black shirt under a sports jacket.

"Are you here to take in the festivities, Bishop?" Burke asked him.

"No, I'm here to see you."

"Ah."

"How fortuitous that you should stumble into my path."

"Yes. I am here to serve in any way I can, on my knees or otherwise."

"Good man. Let me ask you this: have you ever heard of Pike Podgis?"

"Say that again?"

"Pike Podgis. Familiar to you at all?"

"No. What is it?"

"You don't know?"

Monty knew, but he was not going to help Burke out. More fun to see him floundering for a connection.

"I know what a pike is," Burke replied, "a long pole with a spearhead on it. You see them on monuments to the Rebellion of '98 in Ireland. That's 1798, Collins. Is that what you're talking about, Bishop? If so, why — "

"No," the bishop said, "it's not a *that*. It's a *he*."

"That's someone's name? Poor soul."

"You may want to reserve your sympathy. He's a talk show host."

"Ah. One of those blathering individuals who gets people all excited on the radio?"

"He used to be on radio. Now he has his own show on CTV. Nationally televised."

"Well, isn't that grand. I don't watch television, except for the odd football game or the World Cup. Or Midnight Mass from St. Peter's of course, Your Grace. So I've never seen this fellow's program."

"That's about to change."

"How's that, now?"

"The *Pike Podgis Show* is coming to town and I want you on it."

"Are you *well*, Dennis?"

"This man intends to run a show about religion and miracles."

"God help us."

"Exactly. Michael O'Flaherty is dying to take part, though he won't admit it. But I don't want him on there. Mike knows his stuff, but this Podgis creature will eat him alive. Do you know Rob Thornhill at Dal?"

"Yes, I've met him. Teaches in the sociology department."

"Well, he's your opponent. He's taking the atheistic position, and you're on for Holy Mother Church."

"This debate, will it be a reasoned, thoughtful — "

"I won't lie to you, Brennan; it will be the verbal equivalent of mud wrestling."

"Then why on earth would we have anything to do with it?"

"Because if we don't, it will look as if we are not willing to defend the faith."

"We defend the faith every day, in our liturgy, our sermons, our service to the poor . . ."

"A week from tonight, nine o'clock, ATV studio on Robie Street."

Burke bowed his head. "As you wish, Your Grace."

"Offer it up, Brennan. Sorry to stick you with this, but it has to be done. You should watch the show tonight to get some idea of what it will be like."

"Life is short. I don't want to waste any more time on this than I have to."

"Suit yourself, my lad."

†

At ECW Press, we want you to enjoy this book in whatever format you like, whenever you like. Leave your print book at home and take the eBook to go! Purchase the print edition and receive the eBook free. Just send an email to **ebook@ecwpress.com** and include:

- the book title
- the name of the store where you purchased it
- your receipt number
- your preference of file type: PDF or ePub?

A real person will respond to your email with your eBook attached. And thanks for supporting an independently owned Canadian publisher with your purchase!